CITY OF RANCHO MIRAGE ©

PUBLIC LIBRARY

Presented By:

**Friends of the Library
Endowment Fund**

FORM 4(6/95)

# THE DARK WATER

# THE DARK WATER

*The Strange Beginnings of Sherlock Holmes*

## David Pirie

PEGASUS BOOKS

NEW YORK

THE DARK WATER
*The Strange Beginnings of Sherlock Holmes*

Pegasus Books LLC
45 Wall Street, Suite 1021
New York, NY 10005

Library of Congress Cataloging-in-Publication Data is available.

ISBN: 1-933648-11-2

Printed in the United States of America
Distributed by Consortium

*For Burton Pirie*

# PART ONE:
# THE PURGATORY

# The Wakening

The room was in darkness. I felt that even without opening my eyes. Sometimes there were sounds, though none that meant anything. I had no sense of physical space. When proper memory threatened to drift into my consciousness, I resisted it at once, knowing how unwelcome it might prove. For the moment, I wanted only the dark.

So I slept again, I have no idea how long. Until at last, reluctantly, I opened my eyes. The room was black as I had anticipated and now I was forced to wonder where I was. As some sense of identity started to return, I guessed I had been taken ill with a fever, for the bedclothes smelt rank. But I could not be in the familiar bedroom of my house in Southsea: for one thing this place was too dark. And then I recalled the lodgings in London and my short-term position as a locum at a riverside practice.

Yet I was sure I could not be lying in the tiny bedroom I had rented from the Morland family. It was too quiet here and the bed was strange. After a time, I forced myself away from its lumpy pillow but was quite unprepared for what followed. My head throbbed with a violent pain. This was bad enough but what was worse, I suddenly recalled my last few minutes of consciousness.

Their climax was a face, the face of the only man I have ever met who deserves worse than the description 'evil'. I first knew Thomas Neill Cream in Edinburgh, indeed we had been friends until I discovered that he was a murderer. And then he murdered the woman I loved.

I swore to avenge her while my teacher at Edinburgh, Dr Joseph Bell – who had recruited me as his clerk and allowed me to help in his criminal investigations – declared a fight against the future of such crimes without motive. But in 1878, Cream disappeared into the American continent, sending only tormenting notes and, on one occasion, a lethal instrument that was designed to kill me.

Despite this, neither Bell nor I had forgotten our quest and chance had brought us together recently during a London case, when I became convinced Cream had returned to England. The Doctor disagreed. He was sure the strings were being pulled from far away and finally persuaded me he was right before he said his farewells.

I walked back to my lodgings at the Morland house, a safe haven where Sally Morland, whom I loved as a friend and greatly admired, greeted me with the news that an American uncle, whom she sometimes mentioned, had made a surprise visit.

I thought nothing of this at the time but now, as I recalled it, I felt the hair stand on the back of my neck. Once again I saw Sally's flushed excitement, her eyes laughing in the light that flooded the hall from the candles that celebrated the uncle's visit. She had, I remembered, given me a cordial, a green drink he had prepared, which she said was part of the surprise and which tasted refreshing and bitter.

Then I had entered the living room and her children were there, laughing, with their oranges and nuts, and a figure in the rocking chair had turned around, smiling to see me. It was Cream.

Just before unconsciousness, I grasped some of it. How months earlier he must have set in train the events that led up to this moment; how he had befriended the Morlands (for the 'uncle' was only a family friend) and discreetly provided my name to a nearby practice.

All of this I saw with a kind of passive awe before losing my senses. Now, lying here in the darkness, I felt terror. Cream was an expert poisoner, indeed it was his preferred instrument of murder. If he had intended me to die, he could certainly have done it with his green cordial. Which could only mean his plans were more extensive. Was he somewhere beside me now in this black space?

The prospect was so awful I tried to gather my strength, forcing my head higher, opening my eyes as wide as I could. Still I could see nothing, only vague insubstantial shapes. There was a low noise from somewhere outside, perhaps a wind.

'Are you there?' The words came out as a whisper. My throat was parched and I began to sense body pains, no doubt masked by the poison. It occurred to me he could have done anything, even severed a limb. I tried to move my legs. They seemed to function, but then a man feels his legs long after they are amputated, so I touched them quickly. Thank God they were whole but my legs and arms were feeble. I noticed too that I was drenched in perspiration. 'Are you there?' I tried to shout. There was nothing. Absolute silence.

I knew I must try to move though I felt so weak, even the simplest movement was horrible. I forced myself up further. And for the first time I realised that I was still wearing clothes, a shirt and undergarment, and the blankets on me were heavy.

Shutting my mind to the stench of this bed, I forced myself into a sitting position. It was still dark but there was a slight movement in the shadows before me and I expected him to step forward. Again something moved, this time accompanied by a low sound. I decided it must be some kind of reflection, and when it came again I was sure. The sound was wind, the shadows were of branches. That meant somewhere behind me was a window. Perhaps I could reach it.

I summoned all my strength and pushed my left leg out from

under the blankets. It found support below me but I knew it would give way if I put any weight on it. I paused, not sure how to proceed, and suddenly had to endure a violent bout of shivering. This made me swing the other leg down. But, even with both feet on the ground, it was obvious there was no way I could stand and I sank quickly to a kneeling position, clutching the bedclothes.

My head was facing the bed, so if I crawled to my right I should come to the window that cast the reflection. I turned my body, registering the floor was stone and cold to the touch. If Cream were here, how he would be enjoying this humiliation. In London I had felt such an overwhelming presence of the man, now I could not sense him.

I began to crawl but it was painfully slow. As a distraction, I made myself think more about that last evening. My main dread was that Sally Morland and her children had been given the poison. I was sure my glass of cordial had been poured before I got there. Obviously he wanted everything to be normal, so no harm could have come to the Morlands up to that point. This gave me hope but I had also to face the plain truth, which was that Cream would think nothing of slaughtering them all.

Here was the worst possibility for me, far worse than the fact he might be watching me now. There had been nothing improper in my friendship with Sally Morland, whose world was built around her two young children and her husband. But she was so full of transparent joy and mischievousness, and reminded me so much of my first love, that when I began to suspect Cream had returned to the capital, I made a private pledge. Namely that if Sally Morland or her family came to harm because of me, then I must be better off embracing solitude, anonymity or even death. How could I do otherwise if all I brought was misery to those I cared for?

My movement forward was still agonisingly slow. As yet I had come to no furniture but sensed a shape ahead. Meanwhile, I took some small consolation from the knowledge that even Cream could

not have the slightest suspicion of my private thoughts about Sally
Morland. Therefore, why should he bother with her? It was true he
often killed for little reason but the wholesale slaughter of a
respectable London family is not a common event. It would cause
a full-scale alarm; and both of us would be key suspects. Would
even Cream risk a manhunt on this scale when he merely needed
to tell the Morlands I was in need of treatment and carry me
anywhere he wished?

Of course I knew the answer. Yes he would happily take such a
risk if he thought it would hurt me. It came down to that alone.
And it was just at this point in my reflections that my hands felt
cold stone blocking my way. I had reached a wall.

From above my head came the sound of wind. I succeeded in
walking my hands up the wall till I was kneeling and finally, using
this support, I pulled myself to my feet. At first I swayed and nearly
fell but I had the wall to steady me and I leant against it, breathing
heavily. There was cold air here, which cleared my head. I reached
out and touched a curtain and then the ledge of a window. The
material was rough and quite thick but I pushed it back. Outside
there was just enough moonlight to show me I was at ground level
and a dank overgrown wilderness lay beyond the window. A slight
wind shook the branches of a small sycamore tree, the source of the
moving shadow.

My last conscious memory had been of night-time, but I was sure
this could not possibly be the same night. It was not just my pain
and hunger. The air here was only mildly cold, yet the night at the
Morlands' had been frosty, indeed there was snow on the streets.
How long had I been unconscious and where was I?

As I stared, it did not even seem to me that I could be sure this
was London. There was no gaslight, indeed not a flicker of artificial
light anywhere. Of course I might be looking out on some large
garden or park, but it hardly seemed cultivated and there were no
lights of any kind from other buildings.

I tried to open the window but it was nailed shut so I turned back to the room. The opposite wall looked to be bare and without openings of any kind. In fact, as I discovered later, there was a small high window on that side but nothing else. Beside the bed, I could make out an armchair and, beyond that, a table. I staggered forward and rested myself on the back of the chair, which was ancient and badly in need of upholstering. This was no smart establishment, it was a hovel and how many hovels in the heart of London could boast a large garden out of sight of any houses?

To my right, I saw an old screen of some kind. Past that I thought I could make out the outline of a door. Knowing I had to reach it, I took a pace and nearly fell but managed to keep upright. I staggered three more paces until I was there and the handle supported me. But the thing was solid oak with two huge locks and, of course, no keys. I tried a feeble tug, but I might as well have been tugging at brickwork. In my present condition there was no hope here.

From somewhere beyond the door came an evil smell and I staggered back to the armchair where it was less pronounced. As I sat, knowing my strength was nearly exhausted, a new sensation assailed me. For suddenly I smelt and then spied food on the table beside the chair. Here was a bowl of milk, a half loaf of bread, even a slice of bacon. It was not very fresh but I was ravenous and did not care. I lifted the milk with trembling hands and drank it down. Then I clawed at the bread, which was hard but otherwise good, before gnawing the bacon. I swallowed as much as I could, wondering if, now that I had some relief from my hunger, I could smash the window.

But I knew in my heart I was far too weak. Even lifting that bowl of milk had been an effort. Already, despite the food, I could feel consciousness ebbing away, and I stumbled back to my bed. A little more rest, I told myself, allowing a chance for the nourishment to do its work, and surely I could get up enough strength to break that window and get out before he returned.

But now, once again, the darkness descended upon me. It was

many hours before I regained consciousness and heard what I took to be the noise of rain. Outside it seemed night but not, I was sure, the same night. My head was heavy and I felt a curious lassitude. What did it matter in the end if he came back here to torture and kill me? Ultimately, whatever happened, I would die and sink into this. What reason on earth was there then to fight the sensation of numbness in my limbs?

It was only when I thought of my enemy that I began to distrust this feeling. Slowly I became aware there was a flickering in the room behind me. With some difficulty I turned my throbbing head around and found that someone had lit a candle, now almost extinguished.

A fear ran through me, which at least dispelled some of that hideous complacency. Yet I could see nobody. Using all my strength, I raised myself up. There was the armchair I had inspected previously, the table with the bread and milk, now replenished. And the screen. But nothing else. Was he hiding? There was no reason why he should bother and the candle had burnt a good way down.

Of course I wanted to slump back into the darkness, but the shock of knowing he had been here sharpened my senses. I had to eat and drink. So again I got my feet to the ground and now, with the benefit of light, I dragged myself to the table and slumped into the chair. Suddenly from somewhere came a sound, a soft rumbling clattering sound. I tensed, waiting for footsteps, and the turn of a key in the lock, but the noise receded. I decided it had been a cart on the road outside.

Turning back to the table, I got the milk to my lips and drank some of it down. It had been heavily sugared and I was glad of it. Then I put out a hand and pawed the bread into my mouth.

Suddenly I stopped. The bread was rough-grained and wholesome, but I had begun to recognise a taste. It was a chalky bitter undertaste I knew only too well. With fury, I spat what was left of my mouthful on to the table and lashed out with my hand in an attempt to knock the milk jug to the ground. But – fortunately as it happened – the effort only made me lose my balance and I missed the jug altogether, falling hard to the floor.

How could I have been such a fool? Only my own ravenous hunger and the weakness of my mind could possibly have blinded me to what was obvious. Here I was, meekly accepting day after day the sustenance of an accomplished poisoner. The bread was certainly saturated in laudanum and the sugared milk would have contained even more. Little wonder every time I got up, I seemed to be slipping further into the darkness. As long as I survived on this fare, I was his prisoner and he could visit me whenever he wished and do whatever he wished. The diet would only make me weaker and weaker until I was a passive craving thing, entirely in his hands. No doubt he was looking forward to that, and would arrive soon enough to enjoy it.

In a feverish burst of activity, I determined now I must get out at all costs, even if I collapsed in the rain. I forced myself to my feet.

What I needed was an implement of some kind but there was nothing that I could see. The door was hopeless. The window must be the best opportunity and I turned back in that direction. But to my dawning horror I could already feel the effects of my meal. The black waters were rising in my brain and my feet felt like blocks of wood. There was no chance of fighting this. As it stole over me, I began to wonder if even my own memories were at fault. Perhaps this nightmare of Cream's return was some phantom conjured up by the laudanum. Had I merely, as Bell once feared, succumbed to addiction?

But then my eye fell on the milk and the bread. What addict ever went to the trouble of lacing his food with the stuff or of hiding the precious bottles? No, this was his work and at all costs I must hold on to my reason.

The only point in my favour had to be the realisation of what he was doing to me. With the last of my strength I disposed of the bread under the bed and spilt some of the milk there too. Let him suppose I had consumed most of my meal, while in truth I had taken much less. This was my final desperate thought as I collapsed.

When I woke up, he was by my bed. And he was singing.

# The Visit

And one could whistle
And one could sing
And one could play on the violin
Such joy there was at my wedding
On Christmas day in the morning

It was the cruellest thing he could have sung. Of course he knew it was a song Elsbeth and I had shared in Edinburgh. He had killed her savagely for no reason. And now he was above me as I lay there, carolling it in his soft voice. The features I saw as I opened my eyes were as handsome as ever, the thick black hair swept back from his face. I had always imagined by now that face would reflect all the cruelty and insanity of his acts but it did not. In fact, as I watched, his features shone with an almost innocent merriment.

'Doyle,' he broke off from his singing. 'You recall the melody, I am sure.' With some effort, because I could not bear to lie prostrate in front of him, I forced myself up.

He reached back for something behind him and I braced myself. At this point I was still so weak he could inflict any wounds he liked on me. But, when he turned back, there was only a cup in his hand.

'I trust you are not too tired,' he said. 'You have had a strenuous time.'

'Perhaps,' I said at last, and the words came more firmly than I expected, 'you could tell me why.' It was daylight I now registered, the sun was shining into the room, making his hair gleam.

He laughed. 'Why?' he said. He got up from the chair full of energy, the cup still in his hand, and took a few paces away and then back again. 'Because it was necessary to bring you here in the first place. That in itself took some trouble, though hardly yours. I had a good coachman but I had to carry you inside here myself, for, as you will recall, you were not well. In fact, you are still out of sorts. You must drink. I will have some too, the morning train here is tiresomely early.'

My head was clearer now but I knew it was important he did not see this; he must think me still under the influence. It was the tiniest of things, but it gave me a hope of deceiving him. As he sat down again on a chair he must have placed by the bed, I took the cup with a shaking hand. That shaking was real enough. Then I tilted it and pretended to drink the milk deeply, making sure some dribbled from the corner of my mouth. In fact, I took little but as I returned it, his eyes were not on the cup but on me. The hand was still shaking and I managed to slop a quantity on the floor, which was not difficult for I was so weak I barely needed to act it. Still he stared at me with concentration, as if I were a difficult case in his surgery.

'Again I ask why?' I said with a deliberate slur. I was happy to let him think I was weaker than I was.

'I think you must agree,' he said, 'it was the greatest joke in all the world. I wanted to renew our acquaintance. But I had no wish to be caught. So I befriended the Morlands. And it was a trifling matter to circulate your name to the practice.'

The mention of the Morlands sent a chill through me but the last thing I wanted was for him to see this. I lolled my head as if fighting sleep. 'What do you want?' I said.

He sprang up again and he laughed now. 'You have soiled your clothes, Doyle, do you know that? You are truly a wretched man. Nobody cares for you, you have no loved ones at home waiting, nobody misses you. You could rot here for years and nobody would care.' He turned back, put his head close to me. 'No, not even your mother.'

My heart leapt; this was a new tone. I cursed myself, for he saw my reaction at once.

'Oh, she is at Masongill where Dr Waller keeps her very happy. They would hardly miss you.'

This was painful. Of course I knew Cream had heard of our family 'lodger', Dr Waller, but I never dreamt he would know Waller had entered into an affectionate relationship with my mother, a relationship even I did not understand or like to contemplate. I turned my head away, for I could not bear to see Cream's eyes burning with laughter.

'Oh yes,' he went on, 'I know. And as I say it leaves you with nobody, Doyle. Nobody except me.'

'I want no part of you.' The emotion in my words was genuine, for I saw I had been right about the drug. Breaking my body was too easy for this man, he wanted to break my spirit first and utterly reduce me. I tried desperately to take my mind off his words by analysing his motive. Something about me must have goaded him so deeply. Why otherwise should he have gone to such lengths to hurt me? There was a key here if I could find it.

His expression had become serious. 'That is a lie. You and your precious Dr Bell have tried to find me for years, you can hardly deny it, though I have to say it has occasioned me little inconvenience. Even in Edinburgh I was ahead of you both.'

'We rid the city of you.' It was feeble but to my amazement his mouth tightened a little.

'I do not understand how. Of course the man thinks he is so clever with his chemistry and his clues and his endless reasoning, yet how could he possibly understand me? How could you?' It was

14

only a flash but it gave me something. He evidently felt he had been defeated by Bell and myself in Edinburgh, for we nearly caught him and he had to flee. This explained some of his desire to hurt me, as did the fact we had once been close friends with a shared passion for the stories of Poe. Only, as I later realised, we came at them from opposite perspectives. He actually admired their cruelties and hoped I would join him in imitating them.

As I reflected on this, he was pointing out he could do what he wished with me. 'I can end your life now. Perhaps it is better I should.'

The sun gleamed on the bed and I noticed the angle of light was higher so it was rising, which meant that the window I had looked out of must face east. I was trying at all costs to find some distraction. I hated to give this man the satisfaction of observing my fear.

From his pocket he had drawn a surgical blade almost seven inches long with a short handle. He placed it against my neck and there was a stab of pain as he cut the surface skin. I had no time to defend myself even if I had the strength. But the blade stopped just at the edge of my windpipe.

'I believe I prefer another place to cut than the obvious,' he said, pulling down the covers. And, with a sweeping movement, he stabbed both my breast and stomach and then the top of my left leg. I cried out, for here he slanted the knife a little and went deeper, opening a real wound and causing a burning pain that made me writhe. Then suddenly he seemed to tire of it and pulled the knife out. For a while he watched me twisting in agony before he wiped the knife with a white handkerchief and returned it to his pocket.

'No,' he said, 'it will be far more fun to keep you a little while yet. After all, we have so much to talk about. Do you think I am mad?'

I was gasping for breath, but would not in any case have deigned him with a reply. I had no intention of satisfying his vanity or his need for debate. 'I can justify everything I do,' he went on, 'and in a way neither you nor Bell can refute. Your country here is rotten, it is eroding before your eyes, eaten by the sea. Why, there are places literally collapsing into the water. A fine symbol of the corruption of England's soul. But there is far more to it than that. I am the future, you are the past. I am a child of the next century. I celebrate its freedom, you are imprisoned in the ludicrous codes and restrictions and superstitions of this one. When you are dead there will be many more like me; fifty years after your death ten times more than that. And their code is mine. I will tell you what it is: Do not dream it, live it.'

'We will fight it,' I said.

'Ah,' he replied. 'Yes there was some reference to that in a letter Bell wrote that I once saw. "The fight against the future." It sounds very grand. But you might as well stand on the seashore and fight the tides. Or howl at the moon.'

I was losing consciousness now and he smiled at me almost tenderly. 'I have enjoyed our little talk, though your life has been so wretched, you are less fun than you were at university. You must sleep now. I will see you soon enough. One more talk, perhaps two, before I kill you. Not with my knife. I was intending to take a limb today but I think instead I will roast you alive in the morning for your heresies. Then I might take the dish cold to your mad father and get him to eat you. The regime in such asylums is foul; I am sure he would eat anything so he might as well eat his son.'

Thankfully I lost him here, the drug and the shock of the pain had done their work and I went into the darkness. When I awoke, my leg was still throbbing but I reached down to find it had been neatly bandaged, and my other wounds, though more superficial, were tended too. Evidently he did not want me to die from loss of blood while he was absent. After a time, I decided from the evidence of the bed and from my own senses that I had not lost very much blood. The bandage of the deeper cut in my leg had staunched the flow, while the other wounds would leave scars but were less deep.

My head felt clearer and I forced my legs out of the bed to the floor. I dreaded the wounded leg would give way. It nearly did and I had to put my hands on the chair to support myself. But after a time I was able to shuffle forward. There was still pain, but I thought I would be able to walk and, for the first time in my life, gave thanks for the expansiveness of my enemy's imagination. There would have been little hope if he had stuck with his original plan of taking a limb.

Outside it was dark, but the night was clear and the room, which I now felt sure was a cottage, was illuminated by moonlight. My first task was to conduct a proper search, above all I must try to analyse his movements to see if there was some pattern. From what I could understand, he always came in the morning, he had spoken of the tiresome morning train. That could only mean there were few other trains, for he would do nothing tiresome if he could avoid it.

I must hope, therefore, I had until morning and I moved quickly. The food had been left out for me again. I took the precaution of emptying the milk into a coal scuttle that was full of coal, for nobody had made a fire. I hid the bread at the bottom of it.

I was already sure there was nothing of consequence near where I slept and I had come to hate those stinking sheets, but I was uncertain about what lay beyond the screen. As I passed it, the same sickening smell returned to me, making me almost retch, but I could see nothing to tell me what was causing it for this side of the room was almost bare. I pushed my hands along part of the floor and found only a carpet nail from which I assumed someone had recently pulled up a carpet and removed it.

The door again proved hopeless as I already knew, which left the window behind my bed. Surely there must be something in here to smash its panes. I returned to the coal scuttle, pleased my leg was becoming more malleable though I was still very weak. The lumps of coal in it were small but they could surely break a window. I got one in my hand and found I could lift it. At last, I thought, I could do something.

But, just as I got to my feet, there came a sudden noise, the last noise in the world I wanted to hear. The key had turned in the lock and now the door opened.

# The Vigil

My first instinct was to face him with what little strength I had. At least I could fling the coal at his head. That was my thought as, for a moment, his view was blocked by the door which opened inside. But in that moment, I knew I would have no chance at all. I could not even surprise him, for he would see me long before I reached the door or even the screen. And, since he was fit, healthy and armed the only result would surely be that he would kill me at once. Though I hated it, my only hope must lie in deception. I dropped the coal and lunged into the bed.

I had only a few seconds but I was quiet and, because of the angle of the door and the depth of the shadows, I was sure he had not seen me. I lay under the covers, eyes shut, as he closed the door carefully behind him and walked over to inspect me. Then he lit a candle, put it on the table and examined the remains of the food. This seemed to satisfy him, it would certainly explain my immobile shape in the bed. I felt the light of the candle full on me and sensed him inches away, staring at my face. Perhaps, if I remained too rigid, he would see through me so I pretended to stir slightly. This was a mistake.

'I hope you have had enough milk and bread,' he said. 'I am glad to see it is finished. Even so, you are not sleeping as deeply as I would prefer.'

I heard him opening something. And then I felt a bottle pressed against my lips. 'I am sure you can hear me, Doyle. Swallow this down, swallow it now.'

Of course it could have been strychnine, but I soon recognised the sticky bitter undertaste of the laudanum mixed in with the alcohol. There was a greater concentration of the stuff here than in the milk and I knew I must not drink it, yet to show any resistance would be to give away the sole chance I had.

In the agony of this moment I pressed my fist together and felt a sharp stab of pain, it was the carpet nail I held. The pain cleared my mind. I took several apparent gulps of the liquid, allowed some to go down but kept most in my mouth as I slumped back in what I tried to pretend was total unconsciousness, my head lolled away from him, half off the pillow. I heard him put the bottle down, and the candlelight was no longer on me as I slowly spat that noxious mixture out into my pillow and the blanket. I knew the smell would never alert him, for it was just another foul odour in that bed and the pillow was in shadow.

After a time, I heard him walking about and noted – rather to my surprise – he was tapping the walls and moving back and forth around the space beyond the screen. He seemed a little out of sorts too. More than once I heard a muffled curse.

At last he came back to me. 'You are a poor sort of opponent, Doyle. I can smell the blankets are soiled again, I had hoped for something better. In the morning, when I have time to make a fire, I will come back and kill you, for I have had quite enough of this place, which has yielded only the pleasure of torturing you. I believe it will be exquisite and I meant what I said about your father. He will have his son for dinner. I am sure he will relish it. And of course after he dines he will discover the nature of the meat he so richly enjoyed.'

There was a lull then, for he moved away and I heard no more of him. The laudanum I had swallowed caused me to sleep though, because of my evasions, not I think for very long. When I awoke it was still dark but my memory was clear. I waited, but no sound came. Soon I was convinced he had left.

Slowly I raised myself up and found I was able to get to my feet and that I felt stronger. Partly no doubt this was because the effects of the drug were lifting but also because I was spurred by the knowledge that here was my last chance. I was ravenously hungry and my throat burnt, but I had taken only a few sips of laudanum in two days and I had a sense of myself again.

For the first time, I told myself that so far as hunger was concerned I had known this kind of want before and had got through it before. There was a time in my practice when there had been simply no money for food and I had gone for days without it. That had been hard but I had coped. Admittedly, I had wounds to contend with now but, thanks to his games, they were not crippling. My wounded leg was sore but it worked. I would just have to summon up all my courage in the battle to live. This notion reminded me of all the stories I was told as a child about my great-uncle who led the Scottish brigade at Waterloo and I rejoiced that, despite the pain, the hunger and even the thirst, at least I had been strong enough to throw off that awful weakness and passivity.

Not wishing to linger any longer by that disgusting bed, I found and lit the candle with matches that lay beside it. The bread and milk were there as ever but I did not even bother to pretend I had touched them. Taking up the candle, I made a quick tour but all was exactly as before, though the smell by the door had become so indescribably putrid that I began to wonder if Cream had slaughtered an animal and left it there as an additional taunt.

There was nothing here beyond what I already knew and I did not intend to wait. Going back to the bed, I stared down at the clothes and blankets heaped upon it and found to my joy some garments had been cast aside at the bottom. No doubt he had thrown my shoes away on the journey but here was a pair of trousers and an ancient coat.

Once I had them on I felt far better but, for the moment, I

would have to proceed barefoot even though my feet were becoming cold.

I turned back to the coal scuttle, seizing the largest lump I could find, and advanced to the window. Suddenly, a rattling sound came from outside. I felt a stab of terror. Was I again to be frustrated? I stood there, coal in hand, certain only that whatever happened now I was not getting back into that bed. But the sound receded. It had been a cart on the road outside.

This meant it could be later than I thought, perhaps nearly dawn, and I turned back to the window. Without any further delay, I raised my hand with the lump of coal, brought it back and hit the pane with as much force as I could muster. My arm jarred at the collision but the result was hopeless. No glass splintered. I pulled back and struck another blow. This time, to my great relief, it gave and I heard glass falling on the other side and felt the breath of cold air on my face. I waited but outside remained quiet. As I expected, there was nobody to hear the noise.

That gave me courage and I struck again more than once. When the pane had completely shattered I turned to the one beside it. I had to take another lump of coal for the original had crumbled away but soon the second pane too was gone and I went for the one above.

Finally, four were gone and I stood there, panting, listening again to see if my exertions had alerted anyone. The only sound was the wind.

All this activity had taken its toll but I knew the biggest tasks were still ahead of me. Somehow I had to use my weapon to break the middle of the frame and this would require much greater force than the glass. I put my hand on the wooden frame and to my great joy found it was old and not well cared for.

I summoned up all my strength, gripping the coal tightly, swung my arm back and hit the wood hard where it crossed. There was a horrible jolting sensation in my arm as the coal broke in tiny pieces, but the frame stayed quite intact.

I returned to the coal scuttle to see if there was a better lump of the stuff, only to find the other pieces were so small as to be useless. And then, for the first time, I began to think about the scuttle itself. It was made of some cheap metal, but it was still metal. I got it up and emptied the coal out without too much difficulty. Soon I was swinging it by its handle, marvelling to think how much better this was as a weapon than my feeble lump of coal and imagining the crack it would make if I smashed it into my enemy's skull. That cheered me and I was soon back at the window. I took a breath, gritted my teeth and swung the scuttle with all my might against the frame, loosening my grip at the point of impact.

I know I imagined Cream's head was in its way and the results could hardly have been more pleasing. The wood splintered and gave way while the coal scuttle itself hurtled out through the window on to the grass outside. Examining the damage closely, I was sure that, with a bit of effort, I could now clamber through the space I had opened, though I still had to contend with the remaining glass.

Uneasily aware that outside it was becoming lighter, I pushed every large piece of glass out of the window, but there was no hope of removing all the smaller splinters. I went back to the bed and got one of the heavy blankets, throwing it out of the window, making sure that its thick wool covered the base of the frame.

What followed was, as it turned out, the most difficult task of the night, for I had to hoist myself up and work my way headfirst through the window in one reckless move. The blanket and my clothes offered some protection but, despite this, the window was so narrow that, as I thrust myself forward, I felt tiny slivers of glass raking my shoulders and arms. One long piece that I must have missed pierced my coat and I was forced to push myself on recklessly without even calculating my fall. And then I was past the point of balance, plunging forward.

As I fell, the blanket moved aside and my naked feet raked

excruciatingly against the splinters. Then I was tumbling forward on to wet ground and my right leg hit something hard with an agonising impact. It was the edge of the coal scuttle and I had to roll away from it, cursing my stupidity for letting the thing land here in the first place.

I lay there, feeling blood on my feet and shoulder, finally concluding that, though my leg was badly bruised, no bones were broken. And at last I was out of that foul place. In fact, as I sat up to look at my wounds, I knew I had been lucky. If my head, rather than my leg, had connected with the edge of the coal scuttle, my opponent could well have returned to find my corpse on the grass.

That thought drove me to my feet and, as my eyes grew accustomed to the light, I took stock of my surroundings. I was, as I had long suspected, standing beside a small cottage in open country in early dawn. The garden around me was unkempt and overgrown with some larger trees at the bottom by a dilapidated stone wall. Past the garden there seemed, from what I could make out, to be a field and, beside it, a track led away through a wood. Turning to one side, I saw this track ran on round the front of the house. Heaven alone knew what county I was in, the land looked far from rich and I could see no other houses, though of course much was masked by trees and it was not yet full light.

Something had already caught my eye beyond the nearest corner of the field and I clambered down though the thickets and out of the garden. There, descending a bank, I was soon, as I had suspected, on the edge of a stream. It was muddy but otherwise quite clean and, caring nothing for the cold, I lay down on the lowest bank and lapped the water. Then I poured it over my head and neck, wanting only to rid myself of the stench of that cottage.

Once my thirst was quenched and I felt clean in myself, I turned my attention to my wounds. I was cold and shivering now but it was not frosty and – removing my coat and trousers – I washed the blood away, though I took great care not to get the clothes wet. Last of all I cleaned myself up and examined the bandage on my left leg. It was still tightly applied and though acutely painful, the wound had been too high to affect my movement. What an irony it was, I thought, that I owed my life to the ambition of Cream's cruelty. A less evil man would merely have tortured and killed me in a conventional way, but he wanted to go further.

By now my feet were ice cold and I put my coat on, thanking God for it as I moved back from the field into the garden. There was still no sign of anyone or anything as I came back to the window but I had thought of a use for that blanket and also made a decision. I tugged the blanket away from the frame, making quite sure all the glass was gone from it. Then I got down on my knees to study the ground and picked out the most lethal dagger of glass I could find. Finally I moved through the trees at the bottom of the garden till I was quite invisible from the house. Here, I wrapped the cloth around my feet as some protection from the cold.

It would have to be taken off when I walked. But I had no intention of walking. Until this moment, all my energy had been expended on my escape from the cottage and his power. Now that was partially achieved, I recognised for the first time what was truly motivating me: and that was to kill him. I have to own that no thoughts of courts or justice or authority even entered my mind. I wanted only to strike out against the depraved criminal who had humiliated me and who had already, for sport, destroyed the one person in this world that might have made me whole. I had not, and still have not, the slightest moral compunction about the feelings I had in that garden as I watched the dawn. No doubt if men take the law into their own hands it is an evil. But, after all that had happened, I felt that I was acting in defence of my whole being. And even if Dr Bell had been there to caution me, I would have asked him how it could ever be moral for me to let such a man live when we had absolute proof of his deeds and an opportunity to prevent further deaths by ridding the world of him for good.

It seemed certain my enemy would be here within a few hours, and would come by the road I had seen. There was no reason for

thoughts. Of course I thought of my lost love Elsbeth and of how much I wanted to avenge her for his imbecilic crime. I thought of the torture I had just endured, and how I must never put myself in such a position again. For some reason, my mind went to my father who was still incarcerated in a bleak mental institution in Scotland. And then I found myself reflecting on the Morlands and hoping, with every ounce of my will, Cream had not harmed them. But always, throughout these reveries, I kept returning to what it would be like to plunge my weapon into the evil thing who brought me here. For now I could hardly think of Cream as a man. The days when we discoursed and drank merrily together seemed like something out of a different life. It was my history and I remembered it, yet it was as if it had happened to someone else I once knew.

And then I heard the cart. Of course I could not see it but it was coming from the direction I expected, that is from the other side of the cottage downhill through the wood, which seemed the most likely route to civilisation. The creaking of its wheels got closer, and I could hear the horses' hoofs on the ground. Their clatter was louder and louder. Finally I could tell it was here by the cottage and then, I was sure, only a few feet away from me on the road. Would it pass? No, it stopped, and someone got down. I braced myself, every nerve stretched, waiting for him.

# BEHIND THE DOOR

For a time nothing happened. My nerves were so taut I could hardly breathe.

Then someone was walking along the path, I saw a shadow, then boots. They stopped. Just out of reach. A blow now would only wound. Had he somehow guessed? I braced myself.

A voice came. 'Well, I can't see nobody. Yes, old Lucas always keeps himself to himself but it's odd. No sign of him.' It was not his voice.

Another voice from further away. 'Well, you've no call to go poking your nose in or he'll cut it off for you. They say he's a bag of gold or two.'

The feet now turned and walked away back to the road. 'Aye, well he'd do anything for money,' their owner replied. 'But it's strange, for though he don't like company you usually see him peering from his path here. But it's weeks now. Well, let's be gettin'.'

At this I heard the noise of someone climbing back into the cart. Then there was a crack of a whip and the vehicle moved on. Could he still be lurking somewhere? In order to deceive me, had Cream perhaps instructed them to say nothing of him? But then, I reflected, he would never use the service of such gossips as these and the conversation seemed quite genuine. This could only mean it was a false alarm: two curious local men passing by.

My palms were sweating so much that I had to lay my weapon down and wipe them on the bushes. The man, Lucas, they talked of would be the tenant of the cottage and Cream was his visitor. Doubtless if the man would do anything for money he had been given money to keep away, which is why his neighbours pondered his absence.

I felt a great sense of disappointment but I geared myself to wait. And wait I did. The hours went by, the light softened. I listened to the birds and once I was sure I saw a mouse scurrying into some hole in the side of the house but otherwise there was nothing at all. Not a single other vehicle even passed. And at last I saw that the shadows were lengthening and knew, in my heart, he had eluded me again. For now, at least, he was not coming back here.

I felt very stiff and was more than ever conscious of my pain and my hunger. Was it possible, I was thinking, as I started to crawl back away from the path, that he had known? That he had seen through me and was playing another of his games? Perhaps he was even watching me now and would suddenly tire of my antics and pounce.

I stared round but soon some sense returned and I realised none of that could be true. There was no way he would ever have risked my escape or allowed me a weapon, for I still clutched my glass dagger. And, even if he were here, he would hardly have waited all day to attack me from behind.

No, his absence must be to do with something else. Perhaps he had become wary of appearing here, because of the kind of gossip I had overheard? Or he had been detained by some other business? Whatever the reason, I felt utter dejection. It seemed as if fate itself would never let me close with him. Here, for once in five long years, I had had the advantage and the opportunity, only to see it melt away.

There could be no sense in lingering here further and, as I emerged from my shelter, I registered that the temperature was dropping. From the sun there was still an hour of daylight but despite the blanket my feet were already cold, and it seemed I had a desperate journey to make, most of which would be at night. Thanks to my blood lust, I had thrown away the chance of undertaking it in less challenging conditions.

I came round to the back of the cottage again, wondering what Cream had done with Lucas's things, for surely the man had not removed all his clothes. As I was passing the porch, it occurred to me to wonder if they might be in the space between the two doors. I put my weight against the outer one. To my amazement, it swung open.

Now I cursed my stupidity for not doing so before. I had been so preoccupied by my plan I had just allowed myself to assume it was locked. But as I stepped into the shadows, the stench was indescribable, making me recoil in disgust. It was the smell of rotting flesh and its source was obvious as soon as I looked down.

The body of the man was already putrescent, with dark patches of peeling skin. There was a great hole in his skull which was almost certainly the blow that killed him, and he lay in a little pool of dried blood. On a quick reckoning the body must have been dead for a week at least and I felt certain his murder preceded my arrival.

I was ashamed now by the feebleness of my deductions about the missing Lucas. Cream had evidently selected this place for its isolation, but of course he would never have bothered to come to an arrangement with the tenant even in the event that such an arrangement were possible. He had simply disposed of him.

Yet there was more to it than that, for as I stared at the wretched underfed corpse below me, I thought of the gossip I had overheard from the roadside. Lucas 'kept himself to himself', they had said. So the man must have a reputation as a recluse, which would have suited Cream admirably. It gave him the opportunity to do away with the tenant and use the cottage for his own purposes. And had not one of the voices mentioned 'a bag of gold or two'? Little wonder there were two stout oak doors. Cream must surely have heard of this miser and his hoard. Perhaps he had seen the chance of procuring some assets while he was torturing me.

That must be what lay behind the tapping of the walls I had overheard as he moved around. But from his remarks he had found nothing. And I was sure I knew why. Cream might know many things but he could have little awareness of the eccentricities of English village life. The gold that was the talk of this community might possibly exist but it seemed much more probable it did not. A strange reclusive man who fears and dislikes his neighbours, and who jealously guards his privacy while living in miserable squalor, is often presumed to be sitting on a hoard. But it is much more likely he is suffering from some mental sickness. Little wonder Cream's harvest had been poor.

I took some grim satisfaction from this, as I knelt down, blocking my nose with my sleeve to examine the body more closely. Then I heard the clatter of a vehicle on the road.

My heart raced, could it be him? Had I lost my advantage? My first instinct was to dart back out but I now saw the feet of the body below me were clad in brown boots of a size that looked close to my own. I had no idea whether Cream was in that carriage, I had been wrong enough times, but if I needed to get away, here was my one chance.

I bent down and pulled at the boots but the feet were stiff as planks so I was reduced to fumbling with their laces. The sound of the conveyance was louder now. Finally I got one boot off and then another. I took the socks with them and at that moment I noticed something lying by Lucas's feet and snatched it up. It was my wallet, and sure enough inside were several of my visiting cards though no money.

Could this be the true reason why Cream had not returned? Perhaps he had decided from the beginning it would be amusing to see me hanged for murder? The laudanum would help the case against me and even the locked inner door would prove no legal defence if he had left a key concealed inside. But there was no time to search further, for to my horror the sound of the cart had stopped. It was at the other side of the house.

Quickly, carrying the boots and wallet, I moved back out and through the rough grass, dreading I would lose the advantage. It was still lighter than I would have liked and I could hear voices. However, I reached the thicker vegetation at the bottom of the garden and turned to take stock.

Three men moved slowly along the side of the house. Cream was not among them. The man in the lead was not in uniform but he had an official bearing, making me sure this was a party from the local constabulary. 'Lucas,' he called out as they came round the back. 'Are you there? We do not wish to disturb you but we have had word all may not be well.'

I thought now only of flight. Thankfully there was no need to move through the field beside the cottage where I would have been observed at once. A line of scrub oaks stretched away before me, and I could go that way so – still carrying the boots – I ran off quickly, keeping low.

Almost as soon as I left that overgrown garden, I had to ford the stream, though at a lower point than where I had bathed earlier. After that I hurried on barefoot, wishing only to put some distance between me and them. Even so I heard a cry. Someone must have found the body. Of course they would not be sure whether the felon was in the house and soon there was loud banging. They were trying to force that inner door.

No doubt the broken window would make them even more eager to get inside. It was true all the broken glass was outside rather than in, which should have made it obvious to any competent detective this was a violent exit rather than a break-in. But, as Dr Bell had pointed out to me more than once, in the earliest stages of an investigation, people generally see what they want to see. These men would certainly suspect Lucas had died protecting his hoard and would be looking for a point of entry to the cottage. As soon as they found the window they would feel sure they had discovered it.

Dusk was now advancing and I took advantage of an oak tree to sit down and try the boots, discovering to my joy that, though a little large, they were a rough fit and the socks would help me avoid too much abrasion. I donned them quickly and found that I could walk perfectly well.

It was obvious all my energy must now be concentrated in putting as much distance as I could between the cottage and myself. I moved through the trees, taking care to keep low. My wounded leg was hurting but I had to force myself on.

From somewhere behind I could hear cries and soon, as I turned, I noted the glimmer of a lantern. My guess was that one would have climbed into the house to search while the other two explored the garden. I was glad to have my wallet but still cursed myself for my carelessness as a detective. If I had properly investigated the door as soon as I escaped, I would have had ample time to search the body and the garden, for Cream could easily have planted further incriminating evidence. This unpleasant thought spurred me on, though my leg was becoming very painful.

Suddenly there was a noise ahead of me. I crouched down as a horse-drawn vehicle with a lamp went past at speed. Its lone driver was one of the men I had just seen and he had evidently been dispatched to summon help.

I crossed the road and tried to keep on but, now the immediate fear had passed, I found I had used up all my strength. Looking back on it from a medical perspective, I am sure I must have been deeply dehydrated during that awful time in the cottage where all I drank was the milk laced with laudanum. Drinking copiously from that stream had helped to revive me, as had the mad scramble of my escape, but now the lassitude of hunger really set in. If it had been summer, perhaps I would have found some berries to help me on, but there was nothing edible in these woods.

Because of this and the darkness and my ignorance of the terrain,

I now failed to keep a clear line. After a time as I continued, I was aware a moon had got up and then I found myself looking down into a dip. There was a sudden shout and like a cursed fool I realised the moonlight was full on me and below I could make out men with lanterns. It was then I realised to my horror I had doubled back on myself and these were my pursuers.

I turned away and struck out across country uphill in the opposite direction. The fear gave me some new energy and I desperately tried to keep the line, splashing through streams to do so, but it was very hard going and mostly uphill. I have no idea how long I kept on or whether it was safe but eventually it was plain I could go no further until I had rested. Fortunately the night was not cold. I found a sheltered thicket deep in the wood, pulled my coat around me and lay down. Sleep must have followed almost immediately.

When I awoke it was dawn and I felt stiff, cold, weak and ill. Looking round, I had no idea where I was but strongly suspected it was not nearly far enough from where I had started. Yet I knew I had no stamina to go much further without food, and no money to buy food even if it was offered.

For the first time it occurred to me it might be better if I gave myself up. And then I reflected on the enormous pleasure it would give my enemy. I would certainly be arrested, much would be made of my consumption of laudanum and, judging by that wallet, there might well be other incriminating evidence against me. Even if somehow I got an acquittal, my father's mental condition would certainly be paraded in court as proof of my degeneracy. The scandal would probably kill my mother. It was unthinkable. I had to get away.

From what I could observe I was about three-quarters of the way up a wooded slope with a wind blowing down into me and I only hoped the top of the hill would take me out of these trees. I moved slowly up towards the top, noting my leg was worse than yesterday and I was finding the going far harder. Any obstruction was agony.

Worse, I became sure that some way behind I could hear shouting. It was distant but it seemed to me very likely it was my pursuers. My only hope was to get out of this wood unobstructed and unseen. I plunged on as fast as I could. And then stopped.

Someone was waiting ahead of me.

# The Flight and the Wildfowler

He was crouched in a nook about twenty yards away. There seemed
little point in turning back so I went on a few paces. Then I saw the
gun in his hands and his old green jacket and realised this could not
be one of my pursuers. From his stillness and the angle of his vision,
all this man's energies were concentrated on the sky.

He had not observed my approach because I was behind him, but
there was no way on earth I could pass him without being seen so I
took cover behind a tree while I considered my options. The
sounds of pursuit, for I felt quite sure now that was what I heard,
were no louder. They were making slow progress which meant they
were being thorough and there seemed little hope of moving back
through them. But the man before me would surely give the alarm?
As I watched, he began to disentangle himself from the nook,
turning a weather-beaten face in my direction. To my amazement
he was smiling.

At first I thought he had seen me. But it seemed he had not and
soon I found myself reflecting there was something oddly familiar
about this smile. I was brought up in a town, but sometimes as a
child I had been carted out to the great shooting estates on the
edge of Edinburgh to make a few pence as a beater. Afterwards we
were given tea and I observed the 'guns' (that term used to

describe members of a shooting party) with interest. Many of them were, as might be expected, ignorant and unsympathetic bullies who cared only for their social standing, dwelling on their achievements in the field and the size of their bag.

But there was another type of 'gun' that could hardly be more different. These men had a keen appreciation of the countryside and an almost mystical regard for every aspect of it, even its foul weather. They took their shooting seriously but the actual kill was in many ways the thing they liked least. Indeed they showed such an appreciation of their prey that they often refused to take a shot at all, claiming that some circumstance or other was 'unsporting'.

The smile on the face of this man who had clambered out from behind the trees made me sure he must be of the second kind. Few men will squat for a long period in damp and discomfort at dawn and come out smiling. But I was also aware that one of the great delights of such wildfowlers is to catch the first flight of duck at the earliest hour. This meant getting into position while it was still dark, and it gave me some confidence the man in front of me had heard nothing of my pursuit, indeed he could well be my only hope.

And so on an impulse I walked up out of my cover towards him.

He looked at me, showing absolutely no anxiety, only cocking his head slightly as he considered my appearance. It must certainly have seemed far from promising. My face sported a growth of unkempt beard, my overcoat was torn and covered with dirt, my boots clogged with mud. But I decided from the start it was best not to apologise for it.

'I hope I have not disturbed the flight for you,' I said in as cheerful and steady a voice as I could.

'Oh they were too high,' he said, his voice cultivated but kindly. 'It is so often the way. 'Nine times out of ten they come out ahead but I would not have missed them for the world. A flock of six and then a great one of more than thirty. Did you see?' he asked, even my appearance forgotten in his enthusiasm.

'I regret to say no,' I replied. 'I have had quite a walk tonight. I am a doctor. And I have lost my way.'

'A doctor,' he said with wonder but not with malice. Now I was sure I had guessed correctly that he had heard nothing of the recent alarm.

'One who was vain enough to accept a challenge from a friend who wished me to see if I could live in this valley in the open for a week without proper supplies. It has not been a pleasant experience.'

'I should think not,' he answered, still with his eyes bright and friendly though the smile had left him. 'But which valley do you mean?'

Of course now I cursed myself for underestimating so formidable a countryman. 'To tell the truth,' I said quietly, throwing myself on his mercy, 'I was the victim of a crime, an attack. I am a doctor and can prove it but if I encounter the police here, they will certainly suspect me. I am prepared to answer any charge but I have a great friend, Professor Joseph Bell of Edinburgh University, who knows the truth about what I have suffered and I want to try to make my way to him.'

'Joseph Bell,' he repeated slowly. He stared at me further. 'I cannot say I know the name. Can you tell me what is the flat triangular bone that forms the posterior part of the upper joint of the arm?'

'The scapula,' I said, for it happened the shoulder had been a key aspect of my final anatomy exam. 'This was lucky, for I am certain plenty of questions would have stumped me.'

He relaxed now and started to unload his gun. 'I only know it because I dislocated my shoulder last year. I suppose you trained at Edinburgh.' And I confirmed this.

'Well I read law at Pembridge College,' he said. 'And now we have spent quite enough time here. The birds are on their way to their feeding ground and so should we, for you look all in. My place is only about twenty minutes on foot.'

To hear these words was the biggest relief I had enjoyed since the ordeal began. I have little memory of the walk that followed but I know it was short and my companion talked carefully yet happily of his country pursuits. Indeed, when I look back on this whole strange episode I see it framed by two bright interiors, the first of horror as I faced Cream in the Morland house, the next of sheer relief in that wildfowler's little one-storey home as I entered his hallway and caught a glimpse of a bright sitting room with a fire.

On the first occasion I passed out altogether, on the second I very nearly did. But my companion took my arm to steady me and led me away to a small guest bedroom. There was no fire here but it was warm enough and he indicated a basin of water, some toiletries and a bed. 'You are exhausted,' he said. 'We will put some food out but rest for now.'

I slept a little but it was not so much sleep I needed and soon I opened my eyes to find someone had placed some food on the table. I got up and though my legs were like jelly, I was soon looking down at warm milk, oatcakes and marmalade. I ate it all greedily and in as uncivilised a fashion as you could imagine, using my hands more than the cutlery.

There was water too and after my feast I did sleep, though only for an hour or so until I was awoken by a great knocking on the outside door. The noise filled me with horror for I could hear barking only a little way off. I waited, dreading the prospect of the door being flung open and policemen standing there. Once my lawyer had heard the facts, might he not relent on his charity?

After a time I heard footsteps coming to my room and the door opened, but it was only my host. 'I am sorry if you were awoken,' he said. 'The police have been here and they are looking hard for a stranger, but I made no mention of you, for they were hunting a murderous thief with stolen gold, not an impecunious doctor from Edinburgh. But there is always the chance they might bother you if you set off today. Tomorrow would be better.'

I thanked him seriously. He then offered me his razor and the use of his mirror and some of his old sporting clothes, so that an hour later I was sitting opposite my host by the fire in the sitting room, looking perhaps a little shabby but not, at least, like a wild man of the woods. And when Mrs Herne, his kindly housekeeper, came in, she greeted me with a smiling politeness that could hardly have been possible a few hours earlier.

The ham kedgeree she had made was delicious, all the more so because the lawyer, whose name was Stephen Middleton, insisted we should not spoil it by discussing pressing matters. Instead he talked of everything under the sun, not least of his collection of local natural history books, and I gathered I was somewhere in Wiltshire.

The afternoon was spent uneventfully as Middleton had some clients to see. But, as the day wore on, I found, to my distress that I was starting to imagine what Cream would make of this little household. I knew he would want to destroy it at once, just because of its unreflecting kindness. I imagined his long white hand knocking on the door and his knife cutting down my host as soon as it was opened and then smashing and defiling every little object he could find in order to express his hatred of the place. Such thoughts only reinforced my wish to keep him away from these people's lives.

So that night, over dinner I avoided the most sensational aspects of my story. I merely told my host that at Edinburgh I had assisted Professor Joseph Bell in the pursuit of a criminal who had later sworn to avenge himself on me. That the grudge had grown over the years and, in the last few weeks, he had imprisoned me near by until I had escaped. Any crimes the police had discovered would have been committed by this man who was now likely to be far away.

After that we turned to other topics. I gathered Middleton's wife was on a visit to her sister in Ireland. But he assured me it would have made no difference if she had been here, for she was a champion of all waifs and strays. His library, as I might have expected, was largely composed of wildfowling, rural and ornithological works, and as the evening wore on he showed me some of his favourites with such delight that it helped to stem some of my own anxiety. Then, before we retired, he outlined his proposal for the morning.

'My housekeeper's son has a trap which we use to collect provisions and I have arranged for him to take you to the railway station at Salisbury. You will have a mixed-up journey in the cheapest seats, for I can spare no more, but I dare say you will get to Edinburgh via a great many other places in due course.'

I could tell from the whole bearing of the man the last thing he would want was fulsome thanks. I therefore told him I was grateful for all his trust and hospitality, that I would never see a morning flight of duck again without thinking of him (something that remains true) and that he could be confident I would repay the debt within a few weeks. He waved this away and I returned to my bedroom.

I was ready next morning as Mrs Herne arrived in the trap with her son and I got on to it, thanking her all the more profusely since she had returned with my coat, now miraculously cleaned.

The start of the journey was uneventful. Nobody challenged us, the search having moved elsewhere. John Herne was a quiet, reliable boy of nineteen who was dutifully polite, obviously not having any idea, or indeed any interest, who I might be. After about twenty minutes, slightly to my alarm, we stopped at a large coaching inn called the Quarter Moon where he had an arrangement with the landlord to change the horse.

'My apologies, Dr Doyle,' he said, for his mother must have told him my name. 'I had no chance to do it earlier. Do you wish to get down and take something? I will only be a few minutes.'

I declined and in truth I felt a little nervous to be there at all and looked around me warily as Herne uncoupled the horse and disappeared into the stable. It was a large and comfortable-looking place but fortunately nobody in the main building was up, all the windows were dark and I sat there alone, listening to Herne jesting with the stable boy, though I could not hear what was said. He was true to his word, for once his horse was settled he appeared with a new one and hitched it up. I was relieved the stable boy never ventured out to look me over and then we were on our way.

We were about an hour to Salisbury, where he left me, wishing me a safe journey. And Middleton had been true to his word. I travelled third class and it was a long uncomfortable journey with many changes but eventually I was sitting in a freezing waiting room in York in the early hours of the morning, almost on the last leg.

There I dreamt I was back in that infernal cottage and Cream was standing over me, his hand gripping me like a vice, that ghastly handsome face glaring down into mine.

I woke to find an arm was shaking me firmly. But it was a porter telling me the train was in and almost leaving.

I needed no encouragement, but got myself up and ran out to see the London express and its doors being finally slammed shut. Fortunately the platform was directly by the waiting room and I managed to pull one of them open and clamber in. A mother and child were the only occupants, sleeping peacefully in the far corner.

Feeling churlish if pleased with myself, I tried to wave my thanks to the porter but he was moving off in the other direction. At last, I thought, I could sit here until Waverley Station. I would soon be with allies I knew. I had escaped him. It was as well I had no idea then, not the slightest inkling, of the cost of the escape.

# An Old Enemy

We arrived at Edinburgh in late morning. I had not slept much, but as I stared around me at a frosty Waverley Station with its bustling crowds and porters I could hardly believe how sane and normal it looked. I felt greatly lifted and, after some reviving tea, I decided I would walk though the frost to the university, which was not after all so far up the hill in the old town.

I strode out briskly, turning up the collar of my coat against the cold and once again uttering a silent prayer of thanks to Stephen Middleton. There was a spring in my step, for I longed to enlist Bell in a counter-attack on my enemy. At the university I encountered a porter who had been there since the old days and gave him a friendly wave. He did not recognise me at first but then smiled broadly and came over.

'Why, Dr Doyle,' he said, 'are you back in the town, sir?'

'Only on a visit,' I replied. 'I intended to catch Dr Bell. I know my way.'

'I am sure you do,' he said. He was staring at me now, no doubt thinking I must have fallen on hard times, for though I had done my best with my appearance it was hardly that of a prosperous traveller. 'But you will not find him, sir. He is in Berwick at a funeral. Professor Fleming died earlier this week.'

Professor Fleming had been an elderly anatomy teacher of some repute. I had never met the man and at that moment dwelt only on how inconvenient his death was to me. 'When is he expected?' I asked, trying to disguise my disappointment.

'Why, he only just left, Dr Doyle. He will be away three days.'

I thanked him and turned away, thinking furiously. There was nobody else at the university I could turn to. My friends were all long departed and I had no real rapport with any other teacher besides Bell. Of course in the past, I would have gone home but that was now impossible too, for there was no home for me here – not since my mother had decamped to Masongill in Yorkshire where Waller had his estate.

As I walked those frosty streets, trying to keep up my spirits, I considered the position. Obviously I must await the Doctor's return. But what could I do in the meantime? I had been sent away to school so I had no old school friends here. I suppose I could have approached some of my family's older acquaintances; my mother still had friends here. But I had not heard from them in years and what exactly was I supposed to say? The idea of turning up in this condition, effectively begging for board and lodging, was simply not to be countenanced. Almost the first thing they would do is to contact my mother. I would rather freeze on the castle mound than that.

Eventually I turned back down the hill towards Princes Street. Looking at it and the new town beyond, it suddenly occurred to me that there *was* one other person in the world who knew something of what I had endured from Cream. Sarah Carlisle was the sister of Elsbeth, the woman Cream had killed purely to spite me.

I had not, it is true, told Sarah, whose husband was a knight and a member of parliament, everything that happened. But she knew from me that her sister had died at the hands of a man who was still at large, even if the authorities refused to accept this. Other than Bell, she was the only person in the world who might believe and understand the significance of what had happened to me. The house was down in the new town and I resolved to walk to it.

Trudging back down the hill, I started to feel the cold and also my own hunger. A little of my strength had returned, but it would not last long unless I found some food and shelter. The money Middleton had given me was already exhausted.

After about half an hour, I reached the Carlisle house, which lay in an imposing street, and stood before its magnificent doorway. Of course I had no knowledge Lady Sarah would be here and I was doing my best not to think about her husband, a raffish, self-important man who had made a packet in the colonies. Ever since I first set eyes on the man at the university, playing up to an adoring band of students, I had disliked him and did so even more after the night I saw him swaggering lecherously into one of the brothels of the old town. Indeed for a time, I had been quite convinced he was the murderer we sought.

In the end he was proved innocent, and Bell told me shortly afterwards that Sir Henry seemed genuinely chastened. But that was years ago and I had no idea whether he had returned to his old habits. Nor, I thought as I stood on that doorstep raising my hand to the knocker, did I have any great wish to find out.

It was after all a weekday morning, which gave me every hope I would find Lady Sarah at home. The knock rang out and I waited a little while for a servant to come. On the last occasion it had been a friendly housemaid, though when Sir Henry had been at his most imperious, an odious manservant had done his bidding.

Still I waited. It seemed hard to believe the house was empty. It looked quite as prosperous as ever and I knocked again. Finally I heard footsteps and the door did open, but it opened slowly. At first I could see nobody, for a figure had stepped back a little into the shadows. And then I saw his face.

Sir Henry had not aged badly. He had always been a good-looking man, if a trifle ruddy in complexion. Now his face was more lined but had lost none of its sensuality. I was startled, all the more so because he was staring at me, not in surprise but fascination. Why had a servant not come? I had never known Sir Henry to open the door in his life and where was Sarah?

He must have seen my expression. 'A thousand pardons, Doyle,' he said, 'for it is you and you have not changed so much. You will wonder why I open the door and show so little surprise. I saw you coming from my study and was curious. So I said I would greet you myself. Come in now.'

He beckoned me to step inside and I did so, grateful at least for the warmth. The interior was pleasant enough. A lamp burnt brightly against the winter gloom, there were flowers and a smell of polished furniture. All of this showed Lady Sarah's touch, but there was something about Sir Henry's tone I did not like any more than the fact he had been observing me. Indeed I almost preferred his old hauteur to this curiosity, which made me feel like some strange and not particularly wholesome specimen on a slab.

A housemaid came into the hall now and bobbed. 'Ah, Rose, you may remember Mr Doyle – I beg your pardon, *Dr* Doyle. Please bring some refreshment to my room, I am sure he is tired.'

We entered his drawing room, which was much as I remembered it with rich hangings and a blazing fire. 'Ah,' said Sir Henry, rubbing his hands, 'I forgot to say, I am sorry that Lady Sarah is not here. She visits with an aunt in Harrogate, and will be away for a week more. She is back for Christmas, of course.'

So all my hopes were dashed again and I felt suddenly overcome by despair. There was nobody else in this town to turn to and I could hardly trespass for long on the hospitality of a man who was once my sworn enemy. Still, I thought, I might as well take advantage of his refreshments. They were sorely needed. And so I sank down miserably into the comfortable armchair he indicated.

The chair was by the fire and was one of the most luxurious I had ever encountered. For a moment, as I enjoyed the warmth of the blaze on my legs and the softness of the cushions below me which contrasted sharply with the train's hard boards, I almost lost track of the fact Sir Henry had been speaking to me.

'. . . of service?' he was saying. It was obviously a question but I had no idea of the rest. Presumably he was asking in polite terms what in heaven's name I was doing there.

'I merely wished to pay my respects to Lady Carlisle,' I said. 'I have absolutely no wish to intrude.'

'No no,' he said. 'You misunderstand me. I said I wish to be of service to you. I wish to offer that to you.'

I was a little confounded by these words. Admittedly, I had missed their beginning but what exactly was he talking about? I had walked off the street to his house for the first time in several years, and he spoke as if he were waiting here only to oblige me.

'Of course I am very grateful for your kindness but I have no intention of disturbing your work, Sir Henry.'

At this he smiled as if I still misunderstood him but before he could say anything further there was knock and the maid entered with a tray. I had expected some tea with perhaps a few biscuits. Instead, to my joy but also to my perplexity, there was a feast on the tray: bacon, oatcakes, some sausages, toast, porridge, scones, butter and poached eggs, not to mention coffee and milk. My eyes fairly bulged.

'I was quite sure you would want some real sustenance,' said Sir Henry. 'There was plenty left over from breakfast. Now I suggest I leave you to it for a short time while you do the best you can with this and then I will return and we can talk.' And, once the food was laid out, he smiled and went out, closing the door.

I really did not know what to make of this but I was in no mood to hesitate. I ate as much as I could. Then I drank two cups of coffee. After that, feeling far more robust, I returned to the problem at hand.

I decided there could only be one rational explanation. Sir Henry had indeed been chastened by the experiences some years earlier. Perhaps he spent more time at home now and had become lonelier and altogether more charitable. No doubt he saw me as an opportunity to practise his charity, possibly because he felt guilty about his past dealings with me. Here was the only possible conclusion, yet it squared so little with the man I had once known that I did not come to it easily.

The maid appeared to clear away the things and I sat on there, feeling pleasantly sleepy and wondering where Sir Henry had gone. No doubt it was the warmth of the fire and the copiousness of the meal but soon I was falling asleep.

I heard the door open and Sir Henry was back with me. I opened my eyes with difficulty.

'So,' he said. 'You have dined well, I hope?'

'I am most grateful,' I said, forcing myself to be more alert. 'And now I am sure I should not trespass on your kindness any longer.'

'My dear fellow,' said Sir Henry, 'I would hope you are going to stay here for a few nights. I would take it as a means of repaying past wrongs I may have done you. It is a long time ago but not forgotten.'

That certainly was true. For in this very room I had once denounced Sir Henry before his wife and been ejected from his house. Of course, given my predicament, his offer could only be extraordinarily welcome, and yet it also made me feel uneasy. Even if he was consumed with the need to make amends, it still seemed odd and why did he not ask me more about myself? For all he knew I was already staying somewhere else in the town.

'You are very good,' I said. 'I would like to explain something of what has brought me to Edinburgh . . .' At once I started to relate some utter fiction about a misunderstanding with Dr Bell over dates but, to my astonishment, Sir Henry stopped me.

'Much better,' he said, 'not to go into it now. There will be plenty of time for such things and I have a visit to make, in any case. Can I just say that the house here will be at your disposal? The maid is a good enough girl as you saw and you can summon her by the bell on the wall. There is a tolerably comfortable room on the second floor, and you may come and go as you please.'

I was so taken aback by all this that I found myself almost wondering if he had some design against me. But how could that be so? It is true Sir Henry's fall had been harsh, but Bell thought he was a chastened man. And, if he wished to take revenge, he could surely have accomplished it years earlier while I was still at university. It seemed only sensible, therefore, even though I sensed something behind his manner, to accept this gift from the gods. I had nowhere else to go and did not much welcome the chance of dying of cold in the streets. So I thanked him, telling him it would indeed be convenient for me to stay a few nights, since I was awaiting the Doctor.

I was testing the ground, expecting his face would fall at the prospect of having me under his roof for that length of time. On the contrary he became positively effusive. 'Of course, of course,' he said. 'Now I will get Rose to show you your room. And from there you may do as you please. I will look forward to talking to you over dinner.' And he rang the bell.

The room I was shown was a large and comfortable bed chamber high up on the second floor with its own dressing room and water closet, containing all necessary toiletries.

There was also a desk at the window and Rose informed me that I could ring for whatever I liked from there or come down to the sitting room and ring its bell if I preferred. The master would not be returning until we both dined at eight.

After she left, I looked down from the window and saw Carlisle enter his carriage. Once it had driven off, I stared round at my handsome quarters with surprise but a sense of foreboding. Once I had been treated as an enemy of this house and now, for reasons I could not fully grasp, I was being given the run of it.

# The Unlocked Door

Despite my apprehensive feelings, I was determined to put the opportunity to good use. I began by restoring a little dignity to my personal appearance. I bathed and washed and shaved. Then I sat at the desk and started to write some notes of my experience, making sure, of course, they would mean nothing to anyone else who should read them, but concentrating largely on trying to establish dates and places.

Hours later, when I came down to dinner and a roaring fire, Sir Henry informed me with satisfaction that it was bitterly cold outside. I had already observed the frost on the windows and was happy to express my gratitude. But he waved it away. An excellent dinner followed, though I was too weak to do it justice and, under the eye of Sir Henry, I was all too aware how my hands shook. On my own I was less conscious of my condition, but in company it was obvious I was still far from fully recovered. Sir Henry clearly wanted to put me at my ease and did his best to talk about innocent subjects we might have in common. After he had finished outlining some of the more recent events in the medical school, we turned to politics and the failed attempt of Irish-American terrorists to blow up the office of *The Times* in London. I knew far less about this than he did and after that we moved on to the new commercial railway venture which had made its inaugural journey between Paris and Istanbul seven weeks earlier. It was strange to me to think I had read with interest about the *Orient Express* only a short time ago, for it seemed like another world.

At last we repaired to the sitting room and he offered me a liqueur, which I declined. Then he helped himself to brandy and leant back in his chair for a time, regarding me ruminatively. 'You are probably wise,' he said at last. 'It is something on which a man can become reliant, something that can in certain circumstances sap his strength. I am sure both of us can think of other things like that.'

I supposed I knew what he meant, but the last thing I wished to discuss was his lecherous activities in the old days so I said nothing at all and then changed the subject, proposing that I would have an early night.

His eyes gleamed a little. 'Yes,' he said. 'I have found mental and physical rest a great solace. Sometimes to be honest with you I will admit that I have weakened, but my wife has not often had any reason to complain. That is why I am happy to provide any help I can offer to a fellow sufferer.'

This was too much. There *was* some other agenda in his charity, even if it was an unaccountable one. And why did he include me in his miserable self-reproach?

'I fear I do not quite understand what you mean, sir,' I said quietly.

'Ah yes,' he said. 'It is a painful thing to admit even to oneself, let alone to a fellow. I have no wish to hear the details unless you wish to tell me them. But you might be interested in the experiences of an old campaigner in that regard. A fellow who has been in the same boat.'

His eyes were glittering again and, as he lingered over the phrase 'an old campaigner', there could be no mistaking the 'campaign' he meant. He was talking about women or more precisely the pursuit of them. Even if he was now reformed – a question I had absolutely no wish to explore – for some reason this man had got it into his head that I had had similar experiences and tastes to him. Perhaps some student gossip was the cause. After all, during that investigation, Bell and I had frequented some of the old town's more notorious streets and brothels. It was perfectly possible that Sir Henry recalled or mis-remembered some idle malice he had heard at the time. Was this why he had been so welcoming? Did he anticipate exchanging some lustful memories of past temptations and conquests?

I forced myself to control a deep sense of revulsion. It was not so much his lust that I found despicable, as all the hypocrisy I associated with it from the old days. My contempt for this man had once been intense, nor had he been any friend at all to his wife's sister Elsbeth, the woman I loved. In fact, she hated him. At that time, faced with such provocation, I would certainly have got to my feet and quit his house. But now I was less headstrong and had just escaped death at the hands of my true enemy, so the stakes were far higher. I told myself Elsbeth herself would have cautioned me to hold back my rage rather than risk freezing to death before I could even describe to the Doctor all that had happened.

Even so, I was not prepared to be humiliated. 'I think you are making some mistake,' I said with more gentleness than I felt. 'I am not aware we have been in the same boat, as you put it, except of course in the awful crimes we once saw perpetrated in this city.'

He showed not the slightest offence. 'Indeed,' he said and he became a little more solemn, 'that was something we shared, but I was not referring to that time. I was merely alluding to – how shall I put it? – a similar propensity. But please, I am not at all surprised you do not wish to take me into your confidence. I hardly expected you would. I am happy for you to rest and recuperate here as long as you wish. I only meant to let you know I understand the nature of the struggle we men sometimes have to endure in our hearts, that is all. Now let us move on to other matters.'

And with that he returned to the topic of Watkin's proposal for a tunnel under the Channel. Sir Henry thought the project was a risk to the security of our islands, but I was barely listening, for now I was truly baffled. This could not be some rumour from long ago. He had specifically excluded 'that time' and in any case, if it were, he would be far less certain of what he was saying. What was he referring to? The more I thought about it, the less I liked his tone. But for the moment I had no real wish to raise the subject again.

Somewhat to my relief, Sir Henry was out again most of the next day and did not dine with me that night. He had some dinner to attend at which he was speaking and slept in late the following morning. I took the opportunity to return to the university and was pleased to discover Bell was expected quite soon, possibly the next morning.

Then I made a solitary pilgrimage along Leith Walk to the Rosebank cemetery, which I had last seen when there were leaves on its trees. The grave lies beside a low wall right at the back and not far from a large ash tree. Its wording is very simple.

Elsbeth Scott
Beloved daughter of Clive and Judith
1859–1878

We had kept the unusual spelling of Elsbeth, which she always thought might have been only a slip of her mother's hand. I looked at the grave for a while. Here was all that remained of my love, a love that I still felt with all the strength of my body, so intensely indeed that I would have given anything I had in the world just to see her again in the flesh.

Did I think she was here somewhere, a lingering spirit? No. In my heart I felt this place had only a tenuous connection to her. Yet it was a connection. And though I had lost the Roman Catholic faith of my forefathers, I did believe she was somewhere. In fact, I refused to give up the notion.

And now, as I allowed myself the luxury, I saw her again. I saw her bright laughing eyes and the curls tumbling down her face and the way she threw her head back like a child when something amused her. I saw her seriousness, which was sweet and rather tentative. And yes I allowed myself to feel her love for me, something that on occasions gave me strength and at other times caused such a feeling of loss and sadness that it was unbearable. But as ever this took me back to that awful moment when we had found her splayed out and lifeless on a beach and I promised to hunt down the man who had done this without reason, calling it his 'message to the future'.

Within the last month I had been nearer to him than at any time since Elsbeth's death. As I stood there, I found myself yet again wishing fervently he had returned to the cottage while I waited. If I had succeeded in cutting him down I would have welcomed the police with open arms and shown them my dead victim with pride and a full confession. Of course Elsbeth might not have approved the idea of revenge, but she would surely have supported me in order to save the lives of future victims. For this man was, as Bell once observed, less a mere murderer than a killing machine. In a busy week on the terrain he preferred – that is the poorer streets where his victims were almost always prostitutes – he was perfectly capable of killing into double figures.

I must have stood by the grave for an hour or more. Towards the end, I tried to rid myself of all thoughts of him and think only of her. Then I turned away.

That evening I entered Carlisle's drawing room to find my host ebullient. He was already charging his second glass of brandy because, as he said, he had been necessarily abstemious the night before. And it was not long before the old gleam came into his eye.

The lights in the drawing room were dim, perhaps because he preferred them that way. Shadows from the flames of the fire flickered across his face as he eased back into his chair. No doubt because of the brandy, his words were a little pompous. 'I wonder', he said, 'if you have had occasion to think again of what I mentioned the other night. I feel sure any confidence you will bestow on a fellow is entirely between us. I would not break a gentleman's trust, you need have no fear my wife would hear of it.'

This might have repelled me but I was forewarned by the previous conversation and knew exactly what I wanted to say. 'Sir Henry, I would like to take you into my confidence, but need to know exactly the matter you refer to. I am not quite clear if we are discussing the same subject.'

This seemed to please him, for his smile broadened. 'Of course, of course.' He winked. 'I talked of a "similar propensity". Let us just say I understand something of your difficulties.' The pleasure these insinuations were giving him seemed quite palpable. His face was a little flushed and I am sure his palms were sweating. 'Namely,' he went on, 'that you conceived a passion of some kind for one of the denizens of the street, an unfortunate who can prey upon a man's nerve so.'

For a moment I lost my breath. I knew something was terribly wrong. All the oddity of his manner since my arrival was explained. But I also knew I must contain myself. 'Ah,' I said, 'but I am still not quite clear how you were alerted to this conclusion.'

'As to who it was,' he said, almost whispering, 'I am no less ignorant than you. The letter said a mutual friend wished to inform me of this unhappy development with Arthur Doyle. Naturally I told nobody.'

A mutual friend! My hand tightened on the arm of my chair, and it was all I could do to keep myself from jumping to my feet for I half expected Cream to walk in the door.

'When did you receive the letter?'

'About twelve months ago,' he replied, staring at me fixedly. This came as a relief, for it showed me Cream was not all-seeing. The letter was obviously just one early, if vicious, dart in his current campaign. Of course he would do anything to blacken my name and had tried twice to compromise me in London. Had he written to others? If so, I knew nothing of it. But then most people, unlike Sir Henry, would hardly take such a letter seriously. No doubt Cream hoped Lady Sarah would be told and rumours would spread, but he had no way of knowing Sir Henry was not the man he once was. The letter had preyed on a weakness but otherwise its only result had been to save me from the Edinburgh cold.

'Have you the letter?' I said lightly.

'Of course not,' said Carlisle with a little smile. 'I destroyed it. I would never leave such a thing for prying eyes. Now tell me, is she one of the lower kind who get under a man's skin? You see I am quite familiar with the type. I saw some rare beauties on the street in the old days.'

His tone played on my nerves. On balance, I supposed he was telling the truth about the letter and I was not unmindful of his hospitality but it was also hard to forget how he had behaved in the time leading up to Elsbeth's death. Once again I nearly got to my feet, but controlled myself. Outrage would in any case be instantly interpreted as guilt. So I paused.

'Sir Henry,' I said at last, 'you may not believe this, perhaps in one way it does not matter, but your letter was entirely false.'

He looked at me, taking this in. The brandy was making him slow. 'Then who sent it?'

Of course I could have told him. Bell had certainly informed Carlisle of our suspicions and he had even met Cream at some of his haunts. But the last thing I now wanted was to bring this man any further into the case than he already was. His proximity to it had harmed and delayed us before. The idea of entrusting him with any more confidences was not to be countenanced. I would almost prefer that he disbelieved me.

'I am afraid there are several people who like to spread wicked gossip about me. You may remember James Cullingworth who studied medicine here and ran a quack practice I joined for a time. He is one. What you are saying is not true, I fear, but it is up to you whether you believe me.'

He considered this for a time. I think he was genuinely

undecided whether I was speaking the truth or merely being reticent. Possibly it was lucky he had already drunk so much, for otherwise he might have become more spiteful at my refusal to indulge him.

'Well,' he said, 'that is that. I suppose a man must keep his own counsel if it is what he wishes.'

He looked across at me and perhaps it was just the flickering light from the fire but at that moment there seemed something monstrous in his face, a spasm of frustration, as the muscles around the mouth quivered. A log on the fire gave way with a little crunch and suddenly it felt so strongly to me as if the spirit of someone else was in the room, as if one of those wronged women (for often their lives were short) had returned to spit out their hatred at this man. It was a huge relief when the maid entered shortly afterwards to ask if we required anything else before we retired.

I did not sleep well that night and was glad next day to quit that comfortable house for good. There was no longer such a hard frost on the ground, so even if Bell did not return I would take my chances elsewhere rather than face the leering suspicions of Henry Carlisle. If his wife had been present, I might have felt differently, but she was not expected for days yet.

With these reflections, I made my way down the dark stone corridor to Bell's old vault-like room at the university. In front of me, as ever when I stepped through the door, was a kind of tunnel between huge shelves of various compounds and chemicals leading to the enormous tank that ran halfway to the ceiling. It was a wonder more people did not wander in here, for the door to his rooms was constantly open, but I suppose they were repelled by the Doctor's fierce reputation.

I lingered by the tank where the water was a dark ugly red. The bottom of it seemed to contain a pale grey material like parchment. It was, as I later discovered, human skin.

Beyond it a huge book case towered and I came round it to find his empty desk. There was no coat or silver-topped cane, no sign whatsoever of his return. I was deeply disappointed. And then my eye fell on the door that led to a secret staircase and beyond it to the inner sanctum where Bell kept a number of ghoulish mementoes and memories relating to crime. The door was wide open.

This was remarkable. Bell was always meticulous in locking it. Indeed, I had never known him to fail in this respect whatever the occasion. At once, considerably alarmed, I passed through it and moved quickly up the stairs, dreading what I might find at the top.

It was obvious Bell had not returned, but Cream must know of this place's existence. And I could just imagine the pleasure he would take in destroying it. I could see in my mind the artefacts smashed and vandalised, the books and papers – including the vital records of our attempts to track him down – torn and burnt. He would only need a few minutes to achieve this. Now he was back in the country, what was to stop him? I turned the corner and halted.

The room was exactly as it always had been. Not a book or item was out of place. I felt huge relief. And then I heard the sound. Someone was crouched in a chair beyond the shelves, holding something high up in his hand.

I moved forward and stopped dead. For, raised above the chair before me was a human head. Not a skull, but the severed head of a man, its eyes open and staring, with medical dressings around the stump of the bloody neck.

# Return of the Doctor

A voice rang out with excitement. 'The dead eyes still reflect you, Doyle. Even though the pupils do not dilate in the light. I can see your image in them quite clearly.' The figure jumped to its feet and Dr Bell deposited his grisly relic on a nearby table. Then he grasped me by the hand. 'Well,' he said more politely than accurately, 'you catch me quite unawares.'

And then he stopped, for he had noted at once the change in my appearance since we last met some weeks earlier. 'Yes,' he spoke more slowly, surveying me. 'But the image in the dead eyes is certainly a poor one, I was unable to see detail.' It was only too clear what he saw now worried him. His eyes flicked over the scar on my neck, the incongruity of my clothes (for I was still wearing what Middleton had given me) and not least my near-skeletal appearance.

The Doctor insisted we should go downstairs at once. 'It is, you will admit, unusual, Doyle, for me to leave the door unlocked. The truth is I decided after our London adventures that I needed to be more secure and a locksmith is arriving any minute. He has instructions to go no further than the door for I was anxious to inspect my new acquisition. As soon as his plans are laid, we will talk.'

The locksmith in question, a sandy-haired man with a very serious manner, appeared shortly after we came downstairs and, in view of my anxiety, I was relieved to hear Bell ordering a range of devices for his door including a metal plate for one side of it and a Rutherford lock which would effectively prevent any unauthorised entrance while he was away. I knew from past experience there must be another entrance somewhere but Bell was obviously content with the security of that, for he made no mention of it. Since even I had no idea where it was, I decided it was unlikely Cream would be any better informed.

As soon as the man had gone. Bell suggested we repair for some lunch. 'We must talk in confidence,' he said, 'but if we go now the place will be empty and it seems to me you need all the sustenance you can be given.'

And so it was that we found ourselves in the private dining room of one of the city's travelling hotels. The place was brightly furnished with a large fireplace and, since Bell was known to its proprietor, we were treated handsomely enough. Even so, that room aroused very sad memories. Long ago Bell had arranged for us to meet my beloved Elsbeth here for some private discussion during the investigation that culminated in her death. The Doctor was not a man to forget such things and I am quite sure he was aware the place might stir associations, but he had always been utterly practical about such matters. It was his firm belief, ever since the loss of his wife, that only by living on in the same places and things could you honour the dead. 'There is no sense,' he said to me once, 'in running away from memories, for it is to run from the love of those we have lost. And they would not wish that.'

So I tried to put such thoughts to one side, though I hardly did the food justice and I noticed my hand was trembling more than ever as I lifted my glass. However, once the waiters had retired and we were alone, I told him everything. At first he was utterly astonished. He found it hard to credit I could be describing events that had commenced only a few minutes after he last saw me when we parted on the streets of London. It troubled him that he had taken his train north with no notion whatsoever of all that was happening to me.'

'But why did the Morlands not send word to my hotel?' he said. 'Even if they assumed you were ill, they should have.'

'I doubt they would even know where you were staying,' I said. 'I had never mentioned it to them.'

He nodded and waved a hand for me to proceed. After that his astonishment seemed to subside a little and he paid the utmost attention to my words, interrupting merely to clarify this or that detail. Sometimes he frowned, though whether this was a frown of worry or of doubt that I was telling the truth, it was impossible to say.

At last I was finished. I suppose I had expected some reaction to the enormity of it all. But he was silent and, as was typical, he sat there, drumming his fingers on the table, looking at me closely.

Then he seemed to remember himself. 'I apologise,' he said slowly and uncharacteristically, for in matters of criminal investigation he always did as he pleased without any reference to anyone. 'Whatever the truth of all this, you have obviously suffered a good deal. I suggest we return to the university now.'

I did not quite know how to take this. But I said nothing and we spoke not at all on the journey back to his rooms. They were as we had left them, the locksmith would not commence his work until the following week. The Doctor unlocked the door leading to his secret room and locked it carefully behind us as we climbed the short staircase.

We walked past the shelves, which contained such a strange assortment of objects connected to murder – as well as photographs, pamphlets and books – until we reached the chairs and fireplace by the window. A fire now burnt here cheerfully and, in normal circumstances, I would have pressed the Doctor to reveal the identity of the mysterious person who tended this room, for it was one secret I had never discovered. But I was in no mood to do so now.

Bell himself looked grim as we took chairs on opposite sides of the fireplace just as we had done so often before in happier circumstances. He stared at the fire for a moment and then back at me.

'You must understand, Doyle, when you hear what I am about to say that, even during the last case, I became very worried about your self-prescribing habits.' I opened my mouth to protest but he raised a hand to stop me. 'I was, as you know, extremely concerned about the effect laudanum might be placing upon your constitution. Now you appear before me with every appearance of addiction and tell a story which you admit yourself has certain aspects of a dream. None of its details have any corroboration. I have heard nothing from any of your friends or relatives as to an absence, there is no news of a murder in Wiltshire in the press, let alone a manhunt. Also . . .'

But he never finished for this was too much. In my agitation I jumped to my feet. 'You do me a great disservice, Doctor.' I took a pace away and then back. 'He wanted to make me an addict and, if he had only kept in the background, I am sure he would have succeeded. But my contempt for him was strong enough to over-come even the spell of drugs. Of course there are no letters to you, for I was in London where nobody at the practice knew of our association. Even if they did, why would they write when they have simply been told I am recuperating from illness? As to the press, I have no idea what the Wiltshire police wish to give out. But a weekend has intervened and I expect you will find something tomorrow. I have to say that I had hoped for a more sympathetic response from the one man in the world who knows what he is.'

And with this I pulled open my shirt to show him the scars on my chest and stomach, loosening my collar to reveal the full extent of the cut on my neck. 'Do you really think,' I said, 'I would have stabbed myself?'

The Doctor got to his feet and studied the wounds with excitement, the physical evidence acting upon him as my words had not. 'I accept,' he said, looking troubled. 'I accept it is unlikely but you will have to be patient with me, Doyle. I will always test the veracity even of a friend in order to be sure of my facts. And these facts are, as I know you will agree, unexpected.'

'So what are you proposing?' I said.

'To lend you some money.' He moved over to the drawer which he unlocked. 'You must buy some clothes and whatever else you need. The hotel where we dined can put you up for the night, I have already spoken to them and I doubt it need be any longer than that. I will see you there later and offer you my conclusions.'

I had been so angered by his disbelief that I was in no mood to turn down his offer, indeed I felt it was the least he could do. We parted shortly afterwards and I trudged around some shops buying a coat and jacket of Edinburgh tweed, some shirts and trousers and undergarments as well as shaving tackle. The hotel was, as he said, ready to receive me with every courtesy. I remembered now that Bell had once operated successfully on the proprietor's mother and I was shown to a suite of rooms that in normal circumstances I would have considered palatial.

Here I fretted and paced, wondering what would occur. He was not there by six, nor by seven, and I was struggling to find some distraction in the morning paper and an article about the situation in Egypt and the fate of poor Captain Moncrieff at the hands of hostile Bedouins in Souakim when there was a sharp knock on the door.

I sprang up to open it. Bell stood there on the threshold and his demeanour was entirely changed. He had a fistful of telegrams and an evening newspaper in his hand, as he strode forward into the room, flushed with excitement.

Scattering the telegrams on the table beside the newspaper, he turned to face me. 'I will not apologise again, Doyle, I did only what I had to and now we must move on. It is fortunate the student term here is all but over and I will explain I am having to go south to sort out some odd bequests of property Professor Fleming made to the faculty. So he did but it need not take up very much time.'

I seized the first telegram which was from Sally Morland. 'Yes,' said Bell, 'Mrs Sally Morland confirms your account in detail. You were taken away for urgent attention. They were assured you were making a good recovery but are now becoming concerned they have heard nothing of you or, you will note, of their friendly uncle, apart from a cable saying you were all right and convalescing.'

So they were unharmed. It was a massive relief. Silently, too, I blessed Sally for her promptness in the reply. Bell must have read my thoughts. 'Do not worry,' he said, 'I have already replied saying you are safe and we intend to visit them.'

'Do we?' I said, for, as so often before, the Doctor had switched from passivity to action at a pace that was dizzying to behold.

'My dear Doyle,' said Bell, 'we have waited five years. I wished to test the ground but now I know it is firm, I have no intention of delay. He has chosen to return to the field. It is the opportunity we sought and we must take it at once.'

# Part Two:

# The Quest

## The Valley of Death

I have written that my cases with the Doctor were conducted in the greatest confidence, a confidence I only break now because of certain events. Yet inevitably there were echoes in the fiction, written so many years later. Some of these were distant, all (as I have shown with *The Speckled Band* and the matter of Heather Grace) were expurgated. And the harrowing affair in southern England that began on our long and complicated train journey out of Edinburgh in December 1883 was to find its most obvious, if not its only, echo in what would prove to be my most notorious story, *The Final Problem*.

That tale, in its truncated and softened way, was almost more of a parable of some aspects of the following events than anything truly resembling them. Yet in one respect at least I do see a direct match, namely the urgency and excitement with which Bell and I embarked on our journey from Edinburgh the following morning, just as my heroes embarked on the continental express from Victoria to escape the hand of Moriarty. The major difference being that in our case there was to be no peaceful Swiss wandering, in fact the urgency only seemed to increase with each new development.

As we sped through the outskirts of Edinburgh in an otherwise empty carriage on the first leg of our journey, I had rarely seen the

Doctor so energised and at once he started to explore the newspapers. It turned out there had been a small item the previous evening, in the *Edinburgh Evening News*, a newspaper that had begun publishing shortly before I became a student and tended to feature slightly more *outré* items than its morning stable-mate *The Scotsman*. Even so, the paragraph was small and rather cryptic.

## Mystery of Body in Cottage

Police in Salisbury have reported the discovery of the body of a man in an isolated country cottage near the Meldreth valley. His small home was utterly disordered and he had clearly been cudgelled to death though it was several days before the authorities were alerted and he was found. A full investigation is being undertaken and further details are awaited.

Dr Bell had searched the morning papers eagerly but found only one item which added little more. 'It can only mean,' he said, 'that the police are not anxious to stir up interest in the matter. They have probably decided their fugitive has gone to ground locally and the last thing they wish to do is alert him with headlines.' He pushed the newspapers away. 'You did very well, Doyle, to escape their net, but in any case what need have we for newspapers when the primary witness is here with us? I would like you to go through it with me again in every detail.'

The Doctor was back in the hunt he loved and it made his questions exhaustive to a point, I will admit, that was not altogether pleasant. Especially when he bade me to close my eyes and see that cottage again in all its grisly detail. He asked about every aspect of the interior and also of the terrain round about. Finally, after he had heard all my adventures at the greatest length, he was satisfied and he leant back and closed his eyes.

For my part I was quite happy to think of other things and I read the newspapers from cover to cover. After Darlington, the Doctor broke his silence but only to discuss mundane matters like our strategies at the various stations ahead and our best hopes for refreshment when we stopped.

That night was spent in Northampton in a small hotel adjoining the station. The Doctor had paid for our rooms and I raised this matter with him the next morning while we were enjoying a large breakfast, for, as he pointed out, we could not be sure when we would be eating again. It did not, I told him, seem right that he was personally funding our whole excursion and I intended to repay him on my return.

'My dear Doyle,' he said as he attacked his ham and eggs with some gusto, 'that is an absurd suggestion. You are only starting out and have little enough, I have enough and a little more. But more importantly what you cannot know is that I have been preparing a long time for this eventuality. It was obvious to me we would encounter him again and that, quite apart from everything else, it might prove costly to our purse. Fortunately in the years since you left Edinburgh I have on occasions been able to help private citizens requiring a solution to their problems. Few would fall into the category of major cases but quite a number involved wealthy people who insisted on reimbursing me handsomely. I decided from the first that any money I earnt in this way should be repaid to society and I was sure I knew the best way to achieve this. I therefore placed it in a war-chest to be used against him as and when required and I can assure you this has nothing whatsoever to do with charity. You are no use to me unless you are fed and rested and watered. The money will be employed as long as it is required. It is certainly required now so I will hear no more about expenses. There is much more pressing business at hand.'

I had often chided Bell for not doing enough about Cream while he was counselling patience so I could hardly fault him now. It was, as I reflected at the time, the Doctor at his best and, after gratefully agreeing, I never raised the matter again.

By late morning our train was past the dull clay vales of Oxford and into the rolling hills and green water meadows of Wiltshire. The Doctor pored over his maps and started to make many notes, for he already used my description, and what I had learnt about the locality from Middleton, to identify the likely whereabouts of the cottage. We arrived at Salisbury in the early afternoon and at once he commandeered a cab. Naturally I expected him to head for a local inn where we could make ourselves comfortable and begin our enquiries, but to my amazement he handed the cabby, a small and rather thickset man, what appeared to be detailed directions to the cottage itself.

Our cabby showed no particular surprise beyond pointing out the fare would be considerable as it was more than two hours' journey, but Bell seemed perfectly happy and settled himself back in his seat.

I, however, felt a good deal less sanguine. 'You think it is prudent?' I said. 'Will not the police be there?'

He hardly seemed to consider my words. 'What?' he said. 'Oh well we will no doubt have to encounter them at some point,' and went back to his map. I did not find this particularly reassuring. I was all too aware that once the Doctor had the scent of a case he was often so absorbed that he became entirely reckless about personal risk. The fact that I might be under grave suspicion of murder was simply of no interest to him, indeed he would regard it as irrelevant.

It was, therefore, with a sinking heart that I saw the terrain around us change. The pleasant hills gave way to more dramatic scenery, and within the hour we were approaching woods that I knew would take us into the heart of the valley I felt no wish to see again.

The day was damp and cheerless, though not particularly cold, and, as we drove under the trees, I began to experience a grim sense of recognition. But my companion was, in contrast, increasingly animated, lecturing me on various standing stones we passed and the pattern of a Roman road we crossed, as if we were embarking on some topographical outing.

The cab found it rougher going as we began to climb back out of the wood and the road made a series of bends. Above us now were green and sodden fields, and I knew exactly where I was. Within a few minutes the cottage itself was in sight, an ugly sentinel of grey stone.

Bell gave me one glance to ascertain we had indeed found our destination and soon he was calling the cab to stop and jumped out. I got up to follow, despite a distinct reluctance to renew my acquaintance with the place, and after just a few paces I was standing close to the spot where I had waited for Cream. It was a little brighter now but the walls of the cottage still looked blank and foreboding and I felt a terrible sense of impotence. Strangely perhaps my feeling of humiliation was almost more intense now than it had been when I was a prisoner here, facing death. Then I had been drugged and was subject to the fierce animal instincts of pain, dread and revenge. Now, more my old self, my mind was consumed only with the enormity of what my enemy had done and could do. Behind me, the cab clipped away down the hill, leaving us utterly alone. Bell had made arrangements with the man to return in two hours. He had been given money for his lunch as well as the fare thus far. Yet a part of me wondered whether he would bother to return. Would it not be easier for him to travel back to Salisbury and find some other custom?

The Doctor was wasting no time and I followed him round to the back, only to find the door had been fitted with a new stout padlock. We went to the window which had been boarded up and nailed. With the help of a stone which we rolled into place, we took it in turns to peer into the room through a gap in the wood but there was little to see for it had been largely emptied.

Next, the Doctor made what I strongly suspect was a fruitless examination of the grounds. I have no idea what he had expected, for several days had after all elapsed since the discovery of the crime. But of course he was used to being given unlimited and immediate access to any criminal scene he investigated and no doubt he felt as if he were being deprived of his most essential tools. At one point he returned to the door and I could not help noticing how he eyed the heavy stone we had used to stand on, and its proximity to the padlock.

'I do not think it would be wise,' I said, 'to enter by force. We have no authority here and indeed I was once the chief suspect. The police would certainly be highly suspicious.'

He cocked an eyebrow at me. 'I suppose you are right,' he said, 'though it is tantalising.'

At that moment both of us heard the noise. Occasionally vehicles had passed during the afternoon but this was closer and I was sure too I saw some movement in the vegetation at the bottom of the garden. We had no time to move away from the door as footsteps came rapidly round the house and two figures appeared: a uniformed policeman and a tall man, evidently a detective whom I was sure I recognised from the last time I was in this garden.

'So our surveillance has proved successful,' the detective said. 'I believe you have been here before. You are under arrest.'

# The Face at the Quarter Moon

Before he could reach us, however, Bell himself strode forward to meet them, his silver-topped cane in hand. 'I apologise, Detective,' he said in his most affable manner, 'if I have startled your men and I am glad you had the cottage watched. But my business is the same as yours. I am Professor Bell of Edinburgh University, this is my colleague, a medical graduate of the same university, and we have an interest in this terrible case.'

I noticed Bell did not offer my name. No doubt he was being careful, for he had shown concern when I told him it was known to those who had helped me escape.

As it was, the detective looked little reassured, and I reflected how fortunate it was that they had not arrived to find us breaking down the door. 'What interest could that possibly be, sir?' he said in an accent with a slight West Country lilt, as another uniformed policeman appeared from the garden. 'It is a long way to come from Edinburgh and what in the world has this crime to do with Scotland?'

'Nothing whatsoever,' said Bell, 'but you can verify with Inspector Miller at Scotland Yard that it may well have a connection to a case that my colleague here and myself resolved in London with Miller's help only a few weeks ago. That is what brings us here and Inspector Miller himself or his superior will be able to answer for our bona fides.'

Spoken, as this was, in Bell's confident tones, it had an altogether different effect. The policeman did not smile or offer his hand, but he looked the Doctor up and down, no doubt reflecting that Bell's story, while unexpected, was perhaps more likely than the idea of two reckless criminals returning for no apparent reason to a savage crime scene.

'Well, I am Inspector Randall,' he said. 'I am in charge of this matter and if there is any truth in what you say, you should have informed me. How long have you been in the area?'

'Only two hours,' said Dr Bell. 'We arrived by train this afternoon and I would take it as a great favour if you would let me examine the inside of the house.'

Randall paused, considering. 'Well, I can establish the truth of your claim very easily. I was going to enter anyway to see all was as it should be. You can come in but we are not leaving you here alone.'

'That suits us perfectly,' said the Doctor, smiling. 'I am sorry to have created a false alarm but it is extremely fortunate you arrived when you did.'

The policeman now turned his attention to me. 'And you are a doctor too, sir?' he asked, but I could see he was looking at the scar on my neck that had been left by Cream's knife.

'I am,' I said. 'I qualified under Bell here and now practise in Southsea.'

'And your name?'

I had been avoiding this of course. 'It is Arthur Conan Doyle.' I put the emphasis on my middle name, which I would not normally have used.

He did look at me with more interest than I liked, but in the end it cannot have meant anything to him for he turned back to the padlock.

At once the first uniformed man stepped forward with two keys and the doors were opened. Of course there was no trace at all of the body that had once lain in this space and even the smell was gone, leaving only a faint musty odour.

The policeman went in first but Inspector Randall and the other policeman waited behind for us to enter. And so it was that Bell and I found ourselves walking into the room where I had been kept captive.

It was still a horrible place, dull and cold, but now there was enough light from the open door and the unboarded parts of the window to see the interior. That screen was still there and I moved past it quickly to find my bed had been stripped and was now little more than a bare wooden frame. But, as we had seen from the window, everything else had gone. It was not merely the furniture which had been removed. I could find nothing else at all, not even the breadcrumbs I had swept to the ground when I resisted the food. Even the fireplace was clean.

The Doctor was scrutinising the floor and the walls but I cannot imagine what he hoped to find. Meanwhile Inspector Randall looked round with satisfaction, though why he thought anyone would have had the slightest interest in breaking into this empty space was a little baffling. Perhaps his feelings in this respect were almost proprietorial. He had found serious disorder here, a putrefied body, a filthy bed, a dirty room with rotting food. He had transformed this into the sterile space we found before us, and now merely wished – with a policeman's love of order – to reassure himself the chaos had not returned.

This was hardly an attitude designed to appeal to Bell, who looked more and more irritated as his examination progressed. 'As you can see, gentlemen,' said Randall smugly, 'we put the place back in order. There is not a great deal to interest you here.'

'Indeed there is not,' said Bell, coming back from the far corner. 'You have cleaned it out so well it can only mean you have solved every aspect of the case and have no need of further clues. My congratulations. What happened here and where is the arrested man?'

Not knowing Bell and being, from what I could see, a somewhat unimaginative man, Randall had no idea he was being insulted. At the same time the words did make him a little uneasy. 'Well,' he said, 'you are aware we found the proprietor of this cottage bludgeoned to death between the two doors. Lucas Weltham was a strange man who kept himself to himself. There were rumours he had a miser's hoard, though I am very doubtful it was true. In any case, he had been dead for around two weeks when the body was found and there was certain evidence his attacker had been living here for several days after his death. No doubt the man wanted to make as thorough a search of the place as possible in the hope of finding more than he did. There was food, and we also discovered laudanum. The criminal was clearly a degenerate individual, for not only was the place rank and filthy, but he engaged in quite pointless destruction.'

'Of what kind?' said Bell. And I marvelled, not for the first time, at the Doctor's ability to assume authority even in the most unpropitious circumstances. A few moments ago he had been considered a possible felon, now it was as if he were interrogating a junior officer and the other policemen hung on his words with respect.

'Well, the window was needlessly smashed,' said Inspector Randall, indicating the boards. 'We know he was not breaking in for the glass was on the outside, so what conceivable reason could he have for the destruction?'

'Tell me,' said Bell mischievously, since of course he knew the answer, 'were both doors open when you got here?'

'No,' said Randall. 'The outer had been broken but the inner was firmly secured. We also found a key to the inner hidden inside, so our man must have had a duplicate and come out and locked it behind him.'

'Why?' said Bell.

'I can only suppose he felt it might delay the discovery of his crime.' Not surprisingly Randall's tone was uncertain.

'But there was a body,' said Bell, 'lying in almost open view through the unlocked outer door. What possible good could it do for the criminal to lock the inner door but not the outer one, which was the only way of concealing his crime?'

'This had occurred to me and it is not easy to say,' admitted Randall.

'Not,' said Bell, 'as long as you persist in describing the broken window as an act of pointless destruction. If, however, you consider the strong possibility that someone was breaking out of the place, all becomes clear. The inner door afforded the prisoner no possible passage, the key was hidden. The only means of escape was the low window on the back. At once both the locked door and the window fit a perfectly reasonable pattern.'

'But it is a strange kind of idea,' said Inspector Randall, who had clearly never thought of it. 'Who could such a prisoner be?' Everyone's attention was now on Bell and he looked at me with a half-smile on his face, which fortunately they could not interpret. 'I think you must tell us everything you know, sir,' Randall added more sternly. He was becoming increasingly uncomfortable as he saw the looks of admiration for Bell on the faces of his men. For once, of course, these were utterly undeserved since the Doctor had the inside story, but I had been with him enough on such missions to know he would have reached the same conclusion without any help. Quite inadvertently I had created exactly the kind of puzzle he had solved so many times.

And now he became effusive. 'Then I will,' he said. 'In London we were hunting a murderer, a man who to our certain knowledge has killed many times. His name was Cream and he was using a seaman called Hanbury to further his own ends. The seaman made mention of a cottage such as this where Cream intended to mount a murderous assault on a man who was thought to have money. However it was only part of his plan. He also intended to use this isolated place to imprison another. Unfortunately we knew nothing of the other man's identity but, as soon as we saw this case in the newspaper, it seemed very likely there was a strong connection and we made our way here.'

'That is remarkable,' said Inspector Randall eagerly, 'and I must talk at once to this Hanbury.'

'Alas it is impossible,' said Bell. 'He was drowned some weeks ago. And as yet we can find nobody who can tell us more of Cream's intention.' The essentials of this story were true but I am afraid its detail was not. Hanbury had indeed been Cream's henchman and he had drowned. Randall could verify that and no doubt would. But the rest was invented. Even so, where Cream was concerned, the Doctor was always prepared to dissemble and his words had a very good effect.

Inspector Randall looked extremely impressed, for he must have known it would be relatively easy for him to establish that Hanbury had featured in a Scotland Yard investigation. His own case, too, had now been elevated in importance and all his suspicions seemed to evaporate on the spot. 'Well, sir,' he said, 'this is all most interesting. You may examine what you will here and outside and then I would be very grateful if you would tell me everything you know about this Cream while we will tell all we know of what happened here. I believe it is true to say we were extremely close to him at one point but the devil lost us.'

Bell spent another hour or so examining the ground. Meanwhile, contrary to my fears, our cab dutifully returned and was discharged with suitable recompense, for the police had already indicated they would transport us to the nearest inn. It is my suspicion Bell discovered almost nothing that interested him at the site, other than a first-hand glimpse of the actual terrain. The place had been cleaned out too thoroughly and so, as the light began to fade, we found ourselves in a police cab trundling back down that road while Randall recounted his side of the story.

'As I said, sir, we nearly had him. The man must have doubled back, for a while after we first chased him he was seen on the hill about half a mile from the cottage. He left a very obvious trail.

And we followed it too next morning. We were not far behind.'

Bell's smile was a little too broad for my liking, but they took it as a smile of congratulation. For my part I was shocked they had been so close. 'What happened then?' he asked.

'What happened then!' said Randall in a disgruntled tone. 'Why, he seemed to disappear off the face of the earth. To this day we are unable to understand it. Perhaps he outran us but it is unlikely, for we had other police looking further ahead. The man is the very devil. I was sure we would have him.'

The Doctor gave a murmur of sympathy and now they asked him to tell his whole story. He did this well, leaving out, it is true, far more than he put in but still amply providing what was needed by the police. He never once touched on our personal involvement, merely suggesting we had come upon this man in the course of an Edinburgh investigation. He dwelt on Cream's recklessness and his cunning, his ability to do the utterly unexpected, yet he also gently raised the possibility that Randall's men might have been chasing not Cream himself, but the man he had abducted. Of course the policeman stoutly rejected this theory and the Doctor did not pursue it, but I think he was trying to be fair with the detective, not wishing to deny him anything that might help.

As we came into a village, and turned at a crossroads by a green, the surroundings started to seem familiar to me and soon we were turning into the Quarter Moon, the very establishment where we had changed horses while I was huddled in the back of Mrs Herne's fly, only days earlier. I felt extremely fortunate now that I had been seen by nobody on that occasion, not even the stable boy.

Inspector Randall agreed he would contact Scotland Yard about the Hanbury case the next day, but he recalled something as we got down in front of the inn.

'Oh, before you go for some refreshment, there is one thing,' he said. 'We do have an inspector – his name is Ian Yates – who got quite a good look at your fellow. It so happened he saw him in the moonlight that night on the hill after he doubled back. It was Ian who gave the alarm. He had a clear view of his face and claims he would recognise him again, even when he was not unshaven. I believe him too for Ian has a sketch-artist's memory. We will send him over to the inn later and you can talk to him.'

This was appalling luck. Just as we seemed effortlessly to have cleared the serious hurdles, a major new one had appeared. 'Thank you,' said the Doctor smartly. 'If you would ask him to meet me downstairs at eight o'clock, for I have much to do.' And, after saying our farewells, we entered the inn.

The interior of the place was comfortable and sprawling. The police had already sent word of our arrival and we were greeted by a cheerful if somewhat garrulous landlord who introduced himself as Mr Hodder and showed us to pleasant bed chambers on the third floor, arranging for some food to be brought to us shortly in the downstairs sitting room. Bell's room was near the stairs while mine was right at the end of a long corridor and, as I soon saw, overlooked an enclosed graveyard of the adjoining church. There had been little frost here in recent days but the damp weather had made the place into a sea of rotting vegetation and dank grass, while the graves themselves were ancient and covered in lichen. I stared at it for a while before I turned to wash in the basin that had been provided.

Later, the Doctor and I sat in armchairs before a roaring fire in the inn's large sitting room, enjoying tea and sardine and cucumber sandwiches while we reconsidered our position.

'The first thing I ask myself,' said the Doctor, closing his eyes and swallowing a last mouthful of sandwich, 'is how Cream came to that place at all.' The room behind us was entirely empty so we could talk quite freely. 'Of course I can see the cottage represented a useful opportunity. The owner was easily dispatched, it is isolated and he knew there was every chance he could use it undetected for weeks. He thought there would be money and that may have saved your life, Doyle, for he meant to keep you alive and torture you while he searched. But the point remains there are isolated cottages all over England, so why here? It must be extremely doubtful he had heard of this place in London. The chances are all against it. I assume, therefore, he was travelling around in an opportunistic way, talking to local people. He would need somewhere to stay, which could well mean—'

'That he came to this inn,' I said with excitement.

'It is more than possible.'

'But how can we discover?' I looked around me, considering.

The Doctor was very still, thinking. 'I will come to that,' he said. 'But first we must try to establish exactly the point our enemy has reached now. We seem to have one vital piece of information out of all this, other than the fact he is truly here in England. Namely that he desires money.'

'He seemed always to have means,' I said.

'Then he risks exhausting them. Which is hardly surprising,' the Doctor leant forward, his face eager in the firelight, 'given his preferred activities and constant travel.'

'Also,' I added, 'I cannot imagine him eschewing any comfort. It was obvious he found even spending time in that cottage an irritation.'

'Therefore he must spend considerable sums,' said Bell, getting to his feet. 'If you wait here I will see what we can find out about recent visitors.'

I waited as he left the room. The effect of the food and warmth was already making me lazy. I was also quite tired from the journey. I had, therefore, almost dozed off when I heard the voice.

'Excuse me, sir, I am looking for Dr Bell and his colleague, though I am an hour or two early. I am Inspector Yates.'

The figure was at the door of the room and I was just moving round to face him as I heard the last words and instantly turned back to the fire. I stared into it so he could only see my back.

'You will find Dr Bell with the landlord, I believe,' I said.

Heaven knows what he made of this rudeness. There was a

pause. 'Ah, with the landlord, you say?' To my alarm this reply came from far closer.

It was blazingly hot but I got down on my knees and started to stoke the fire with the poker, so he could only see my back, anything rather than look straight at him. Perhaps he might not recognise me but I was hardly prepared to take the risk. If this man had the abilities Randall claimed, and proceeded to swear I was the one he had seen in the woods, our position here could very quickly become desperate. There was no way I could account for my movements and the Doctor would have to change his story or perjure himself, which he would never do. In the end we might, I suppose, have convinced the police of the truth but it would be a battle, during which I might well spend time in prison and our chances of finding Cream would vanish.

Therefore, although the flames were burning my face, I continued to poke the fire as if it were going out. I told myself it did not matter how peculiar my behaviour seemed, the man would never guess its reason as long as I did not face him.

'Well then I must find them,' he said in a faintly irritated voice. And I heard some movement and the sound of the door closing.

My face was red and sore as I turned away from the fire. The room was empty but now I had to think very hard. The inn was a veritable labyrinth of corridors and rooms and I was quite sure I could evade this man once I was upstairs. But here was the problem: there was no other door to this sitting room except the one he had taken. It led to a corridor. Turning left, which I assumed Yates had done, would lead him to the landlord's office and then to an open hall which gave access to the front bar and dining room as well as the stairs.

I could not risk encountering Yates with Bell in the landlord's office, so I was forced to turn down the corridor to my right. This ended in an outside door with a glass panel. I started to open it, thinking I would stay outside until Yates was gone, when suddenly through the panel I saw that, only a few feet away, two uniformed men stood by a police cab. I recognised both of them at once, they had been with us all afternoon and had now evidently escorted Yates to the inn. There could be no avoiding them if I went out there and they would be almost certain to inform me Inspector Yates had arrived and expect me to go back inside to meet him. Meanwhile, the Doctor might well dispatch Yates promptly on the assumption he was helping me and in that case I would meet the inspector outside.

On balance, I decided this option seemed even worse than the inn itself and I turned around. There was still nobody in the corridor. I moved stealthily back along it, thinking if I could just get past the landlord's office I would be safe. As I drew closer to it, I heard voices and realised to my irritation the door to the room was wide open. 'I think,' this was Bell's voice, 'you have given me a clear idea, sir.'

'And it is the man you seek?' This was Yates's voice.

I was close enough to see how dangerous it would be to slip past. The Doctor would try to ignore me but the landlord had made a great fuss of me on our arrival, asking about Edinburgh and other matters. What if he called out to me? There was a limit to the amount of odd behaviour we could expect Yates to tolerate.

A pretty servant girl entered the corridor, smiling at me, but as she passed the door a cry went up from the landlord, calling her in, proving at once I had been wise not to try to pass it myself. 'Ah, Peggy,' said the landlord, 'I think we should offer our policeman friend some tea in the sitting room. Inspector, you will have some with Dr Bell, will you not? And where is Dr Doyle? Surely he wants to hear the policeman's story?'

As if in a nightmare, I moved back towards the sitting-room door. Meanwhile they were all coming out of the office into the corridor and I made out Yates's voice talking. 'Yes, as I say, I pride myself on it and I am absolutely convinced I would know the man's face anywhere but I have two men waiting and cannot be much longer, Mr Hodder.'

This was maddeningly ambiguous. Was he leaving now or accepting tea? He had probably nodded or shaken his head to Hodder's offer and I had no possible way of knowing which it was or where he would go. Even if he were leaving, he might well drop into the sitting room on his way to look for me. But outside would be an even worse option for me if he exited the inn.

In the hope he was leaving I darted back into the sitting room but the voices grew louder. I moved to the window but it was stoutly locked with no sign of any key. There was indeed no place to hide in here and any attempt to do so would only draw attention to myself. So, for want of anything else, I went back to my position in the fireplace, bent down with my back to them. For a moment nothing happened and I thought I was safe. But then, with a sinking heart, I heard them all enter the room.

# The Green Night

A voice came. 'Dr Doyle.' It was Hodder's voice. At all costs I pretended not to hear. But now it was louder and he was coming towards me. 'Dr Doyle!'

There was no more to do. And so I turned. Hodder was staring at me. The Doctor was in the doorway, his back turned, evidently talking to Yates but fortunately blocking his view.

As I watched, Bell said something about how much he wished to talk to the constables, before sweeping Yates out. It was rude enough but it achieved its purpose.

'Dr Doyle,' Hodder was saying, 'you have just missed Inspector Yates. Shall I call him?' He was moving to do so.

'No,' I said quickly. 'It is absolutely not necessary.' He stopped, looking doubtful. 'The truth is the Doctor prefers to settle all of that himself.'

'Oh.' He nodded, not quite understanding but assuming this was something to do with some arcane police and medical procedure. 'Well, you must be cold,' he added with evident bemusement, for the hearth was baking. 'Shall I tell Peggy to build the fire?'

'No,' I said, 'it is perfect now.'

'Inspector Yates had people waiting for him,' he added apologetically. 'Even so, I think he would have liked to see you.'

87

'A great pity,' I said with what I hope was some semblance of conviction. Hodder departed with the offer of more tea, which was declined, for we still had some in the pot warming on the hearth.

Within a few minutes Bell appeared in the doorway, closing the door with a broad smile on his face and a large book in both hands.

'Too close even for my tastes, Doyle!' he said. 'From his description, I feel fairly certain that man would have known you. His powers of observation are remarkable and I had to intervene or he would certainly have come back in here for a few minutes. No doubt he thinks I am a pompous snob who likes to spend as little time as possible with an ordinary policeman. That is a shame, for he would have made a first-rate pupil in my method. But it is a small price to pay in the circumstances. You were the impolite guest who gave him directions, I take it?'

'I am still half burnt,' I said, nodding.

'I thought so,' said Bell, throwing himself down in his chair, still smiling. 'He said the guest had been extremely offhand. The landlord was sure it must be a military man who lodges here and is very deaf. I knew better.' He opened the large book on his knee. 'Now the tea has been kept tolerably warm by the fire, has it not? Good, pour me a cup if you will while I make my study. Hodder has been so kind as to provide us with his ledger of the last year. Let us see if it is any help to us in our present need.'

Bell pored over the book, his teacup in one hand, turning the pages with the other.

'A boring assembly in general,' he observed. 'Mainly travellers *en route* to Salisbury and Bath. Some, I would say, were here for the fishing and—' He broke off. His hand, which had been tapping the book as he searched, froze. His head darted forward a few inches after a fashion I knew so well.

He was silent for a time and his right hand made one slow beat upon the page as he sat there. At last he looked up at me, putting down his cup and handing me the book.

I knew he had been looking near the beginning of the page and it did not take long to see what he meant. There were two names that meant nothing and then another that seemed to stand alone. The two at the top were in differentiating but neat copperplate, the third quite different.

John Hargreaves and daughter, 45 Montague Road, Reigate, Surrey

Daniel Semple, C/o Westhouse & Marjoribanks, Fenchurch St, London

*Dr Mere, C/o Poste Restante, Albermarle St, London*

It was not that I recognised the hand exactly, for I knew quite well he could disguise his writing, but there was something in the name and in the style of those small letters – their slanted confidence – that caused my heart to beat faster.

The Doctor had his eyes fixed on me. 'Yes,' he said, 'I see we are of the same mind. And note the name is a local one. He might well have passed through Mere on his way here. Did he adopt it for that reason? Of course it may be perfectly innocent, some local medical man who has moved away and returned to visit his relatives. But like you I suspect otherwise. Now I started well back in the book, so this entry is some months ago. Let us see if the man made a further visit while you were here.'

He turned the pages quickly to scan the last two weeks and gave a cry of excitement. I looked over his shoulder and saw at once the same name was there around eleven days earlier.

Bell was studying the departure date which had been noted beside the name. 'Yes, it seems Dr Mere quit this place on the day before you broke from the cottage. I think we can almost call that conclusive, but let us see what Hodder has to say.'

The landlord was in his office and, as so often when the stakes were rising, the Doctor's manner was highly deceptive. In response to Hodder's eager enquiry as to whether our search had yielded anything, he shook his head.

'Alas no,' said Bell, and proceeded to ask a few desultory questions about names in which I was quite sure he had absolutely no interest. All were cleared of the slightest suspicion. Having discussed these, he was on the point of leaving when he seemed to remember something. 'Oh, I did wonder if you had a colleague of mine here a week or so back. It is nothing at all to do with the case but I would be interested to see him again.' And now he pointed to the neat entry for Dr Mere.

I could only admire the studied casualness of this approach but what followed was an intense disappointment. Hodder frowned at the name. 'Yes I believe there was a doctor here,' he said, 'but unfortunately I was not. All of that week I was away, for my sister was ill in Bristol. She is much better now, I am glad to say, but I would have missed your friend.' Naturally Bell pointed out the earlier entry. And the landlord seemed slightly surprised, shaking his head. 'Ah, so it was the same gentleman, but then I barely recall him,' he said. 'Let me see now, did he arrive on a Thursday? Ah yes, the day of the monthly market at Wilton. It is quite possible I hardly saw him. My cousin often helps here on a day as busy as that, it is more than likely he signed the gentleman in. I would barely have had time to talk, for the inn is always so full on that last Thursday of the month. I am glad you gentlemen missed it, for it is hard to keep up the level of comfort and service. But shall I mention you if your friend returns?'

The Doctor said he would be pleased and wondered if he could talk to Hodder's cousin but even here we were to be thwarted, for he was away trading some horses and would not be back before the weekend. After that we left the landlord and walked to the inn's outer door. 'Could he be lying?' I said as soon as we were out of his hearing.

'It is possible,' said Bell, peering through the door to make sure the police had gone before he opened it. 'But, to be fair, this is a large inn with many customers. And he seems genuine.'

We were outside now, for Bell wanted to see the lie of the land and, as if to prove his words, the courtyard of the inn provided an extremely busy spectacle. Two coaches were about to move off and another was unloading some baggage. It was already getting dark and the carriage lanterns had been lit, casting flickering shadows on to the grey stones as the horses pawed the ground, impatient to be back on their way. This place was a crossroads of activity, which was probably why my enemy had chosen it.

We had walked a few paces into the yard and now Bell paused, ruminating over the spectacle before us, tapping his silver-topped cane. 'He may well have used other inns too. No, it is more likely we were just unlucky. But then . . .' he turned to me. 'So was he, Doyle, so was he.'

'Unlucky?' I said. 'In what sense?'

'You must recall that your humiliation and death were not his only object in this place. It is perfectly plain he was attracted by the notion of a hoard of money. Unfortunately for him, the so-called local "miser" proved to be nothing but a sad eccentric. We can have every hope Cream returned to London empty-handed.'

The Doctor's eyes gleamed in the flicker of the lanterns. Without a coat, I was starting to feel the cold. 'But,' he continued as he turned back to the inn, 'although the landlord held no interest for our man, we should not despair. He must have talked to somebody. I suggest we both make discreet enquiries. And do not forget our enemy's instincts, Doyle.'

Of course I knew what the Doctor meant. As soon as I was back in my room I rang a bell for service and by good fortune the pretty housemaid I had seen earlier arrived at my door. She had an elfin face and long dark hair, meticulously tied back.

I requested some early supper downstairs and after that had been arranged and the lamps were lit I asked her how long she had been in service. It turned out she had been working at the inn for a full year and seemed to enjoy it well enough. Although, as she said, she was rather frightened of the horses and liked to be well indoors when they clattered across the courtyard. We laughed about that and I dismissed her and then, taking my cue from Bell earlier, I called her back as if suddenly remembering something. 'Oh Peggy,' I said, 'it seems a friend of mine was here a week or so ago. I wondered if you remembered him. He is a Dr Mere.'

At once her face brightened. 'Oh yes, sir. A real gentleman, sir. From the colonies, am I right? All the way from Canada?'

I turned quickly away to lower one of the lamps so she did not see my reaction.

'That is the man,' I said. 'Did you talk to him?'

'Oh yes, sir, he was very friendly. I had seen him here before but hardly talked to him then, it was so busy. But when he was here just the other week, we were quiet and he was good to me. Told me of his medicine and all the patients he had back in Canada as well as his estate there.'

'Did he say where he was going?' I asked, for, though Bell would undoubtedly wish to hear everything, I was not so very interested in Cream's lies.

'Why back to London, sir, I am sure,' she replied. 'There was little to bring him here.'

'So why was he here?' I ventured.

'Oh a very wealthy patient, he said. But that was all he said.' So one had only to substitute 'victim' for 'patient'. How glad I was his avarice had been thwarted.

'Mind you, sir,' she added plaintively, 'I wish I could have had one of his cordials. I am sure it would have made me feel very much better.'

I nearly exclaimed aloud. 'Ah, he offered you one?'

'Why yes, sir. On the last evening I was turning down the bed. It was quite late, sir, and he was packing for the morning. He said he thought I looked a bit low and got out one of his medicines. He even poured it for me. I had it in my hand, sir. But then he seemed to change his mind. He said it was the wrong draught and tipped it back in the bottle. He claimed it would have done me no good. But you know what I think, sir? I think he did not want to waste it on a poor servant girl. And we are perhaps the class that could really do with such a thing, sir, for we work hard for our years. I had hoped he would change his mind when I served him breakfast. But I did not see him again.'

There was something so plaintive and affecting in the girl's expression at that moment, all the more so when you reflected how near to death she must have come without knowing it. Cream loved to poison women simply for the sake of the act. Indeed, he once sent me a gruesome account of the slow poisoning of a woman of the streets in North America, which delighted in every small detail, not least the way her eyes looked at him when she knew it was the end. It seemed to me certain he would have taken this girl's life with impunity, but finally perhaps feared discovery.

Peggy said she had told me everything she knew and then asked slightly unexpectedly if I would be here the next night for she would try to recall more. But I told her I could not be sure for I had no idea of our plans.

Half an hour later, I was in Bell's small chamber which was full of shadows, for the lamps were turned down very low as he sometimes preferred when he was thinking. My report interested him greatly. Indeed, he insisted on my recounting every word she said, even those that seemed trivial.

'I agree with you, Doyle,' he said quietly at the end. 'It is sobering to think how near, how very near, the girl was to death. But there also lies our opportunity. For as you see, he is still a creature of instinct. Even in this place, where it could only impede his whole strategy and cause real risk to his person, he could not resist dallying with his sport.'

'But he stopped himself.'

'Yes,' agreed Bell. 'She was not one of his usual kind. Such a death would be investigated. No doubt he might have got away but he would have had to leave at once and it would hardly have helped his plans. He saw this and changed his mind. Yet . . .'

I waited. I could see he was frowning, otherwise he sat perfectly motionless. It seemed something troubled him.

Finally he broke the silence. 'She says she did not see him again, but this took place late on the last night. He was packing. Had he already decided then not to go back to you? If so, he could easily have done the deed, and left.'

'Perhaps he did not make the decision to leave for London till the next morning? He heard then the police were going to investigate Lucas Weltham's cottage and decided to return to London at once with every hope I would be arrested for murder,' I said.

'And yet he would only be likely to hear such gossip at breakfast in the inn parlour, but, as she herself told you, he was not there. It seems he left before.' With this, Bell got up from his seat and took two paces, bent in thought. Then he turned. 'Well no matter, we should have an early nigh,t for we have come far. I will arrange to have my supper here and see you in the morning.'

I was a little surprised by this but I merely assumed the Doctor wished to have some time for reflection. I ate a plain but welcome dinner of cold roast pork and bread and cheese downstairs and then I retired to my room.

Before I went to bed I looked out of my window. The strong winter moon sent a watery light over the whole graveyard, an effect enhanced by the ground mist. The starkness of the spectacle gave me a sudden pang. No doubt some of these stones marked the bodies of men and women who had been sorely missed by their loved ones and I thought of the visits they would have made here, just as I had visited Elsbeth's grave in Edinburgh three days before. There was about the whole place such an air of melancholy that I quickly turned away, rearranging the curtains.

# THE IMPLICATIONS OF MOONLIGHT

Unfortunately the curtains were thin and some moonlight still shone into the room as I lay there. I was tired but sleep did not come. I was trying not to dwell on the feeling of sadness the sight of the little graveyard had suddenly aroused in me and the terrible sense that all my life since Elsbeth's death – my work as a doctor, my investigations with Bell – had been utterly pointless. How I wished now I had been given a room at the centre and front of the inn, like Bell's, which looked out on the street.

To make matters worse, the weather was turning and a wind got up, rattling the window. Soon there was rain too. After a time I slept fitfully, but then came awake, sure that I had heard something in the room. But all I could make out was the rain on the window and eventually fell asleep again.

Now I began to dream. It was a vivid dream that the inn was surrounded entirely by water. Slowly the little graveyard was utterly submerged, the graves lost in the rising pool. And at last the floods entered the ground floor. But, what was worse, something was coming up out of the water, a strange shapeless thing. It had emerged from the depths and was crawling along the corridor, slithering its way forward towards my door.

It came closer and closer until it was directly outside and I could hear it pushing its loathsome form against the wood.

I awoke with a start yet I could still hear the sound. There was a great rustling outside my room and something was pushing at my door.

The door swung open. There was just enough light to make out a crouched shape. Then it rose up.

And I recognised the figure, it was Peggy, the servant girl. Her eyes looked frightened and she wore a nightdress. 'Please, sir,' she said. 'Oh please, I have had a dream.' I was still a little amazed but I was about to offer some reassuring words, for I supposed her room was near by and she had opened the closest door.

'Someone came to me tonight, sir, in a dream. She said her name was Elsbeth,' she went on, coming closer to me. 'She was a lovely thing and she said you once loved her, sir.' She trembled with agitation.

I was stunned, still half asleep. She was near me now, her hair swept down to her shoulders, making her look more beautiful.

'I have never had a dream like it, sir. And it made me feel I must do what she wished. As I say, she spoke of how you once loved her as she loves you. And that you are tired now. And she asked something of me, sir. Because she cannot be with you, she asks that I take her place, she wanted me to show you her love.'

And she bent down and kissed me sweetly on the lips. Her skin was warm, her lips soft, and I responded. Could this be true? My mind was still fogged with sleep or perhaps I would have resisted more but as she put her arms around me I held her close, in spite of all my questions.

Why, after all, should I not believe what I was hearing? This girl knew nothing of Elsbeth. Could she not be a vessel for all the love I had lost?

But even as I kissed her and felt her hands clasp me tightly, I sensed something was wrong and became aware that elsewhere in the room there was movement. By the window a figure was drawing itself up to its full height.

The girl saw it too and screamed. But, as it stepped forward, some shafts of moonlight picked out familiar features. The Doctor stood there, his voice soft. 'It is only a trick, Doyle, a foul despicable trick.'

At once the girl let go of me and turned and no doubt she would have run but Bell grabbed her by the arm.

'You must tell the truth,' he said. 'We will not hurt you but you must tell us everything.'

The girl offered some token resistance but then her face crumpled and she started to cry. At once the Doctor released his grip and offered her a handkerchief, allowing her to sit down in a chair as he lit a candle. I was still trying to understand though slowly, as sleep left me, some light began to dawn.

'Now if you would just tell me all,' said Bell to her, 'we will forget about this intrusion. But you must leave nothing out. It is Dr Mere I wish to hear of.'

'Yes, sir,' she said, overcoming her sobs.

'Everything,' emphasised the Doctor.

She nodded. 'Well, what I told the gentleman of him before, sir, was the truth but it was not all. Dr Mere did offer me a cordial and he took it back. He was a marvellous man, sir, a real gentleman. He gave me some money to make up for it.'

'Go on,' said the Doctor grimly, standing over her.

'He says to me, "Peggy, you are a good friend," and I was a good friend to him, sir, I had enjoyed his company and he said he had not been able to finish his business here, sir. That he was interrupted and he must go. For he had heard two gentlemen talking in the yard, sir, about some action to be taken, and he said it was no longer safe for him. But he promised he would write to me and might ask for favours for the money he had given me.'

'Have you his letter?' said Bell.

She hesitated, but one look at the intensity of his expression convinced her. 'Yes, sir. He told me to destroy it, but I wanted a memory of him.'

Bell sighed. 'I must have it, Peggy.'

She nodded. 'Has he done wrong, sir? I cannot believe it.'

'I will tell you after you have fetched it. But I warn you, if you do not return within a very short time I will awaken Mr Hodder and tell him everything. You do not want to lose your place?'

She shuddered, shook her head.

'Then bring it,' ordered Bell, 'and I promise you he will hear nothing about any of this, indeed we will say how well you have served us here.'

This seemed to encourage her and she left. Bell looked over to me. 'I am sorry to have trespassed on your sleep earlier, Doyle. You woke up and nearly saw me when I took up my position in the corner there. But fortunately it was dark enough. The truth is, the more I considered it, the more sceptical I became of the girl's story. For one thing Cream appeared too much of a gentleman. For another it made no sense for him to resist his usual temptation unless he had some other use for her in mind. There was also that odd detail you yourself noticed when she asked – in the midst of your questions – if you were staying a second night. On reflection it made sense only if she wished to discover whether she could delay some undertaking involving you. Your answer told her she must act tonight making it worth while for me to watch and see if my suspicions were borne out.'

I was already feeling ashamed for having almost believed a story so crudely yet effectively designed by my enemy. No doubt he thought it would appeal to my romantic credulity, and what would have been the sequel? Would she have mocked me afterwards? I did not want to know and was glad when Peggy returned, carrying a letter.

The wind and rain was still beating on my window but Bell had turned up the lamps and now, as the girl stood before us with a frightened expression, he took the letter from her, eagerly scanning the return address. 'A different post-office box, Doyle, near Charing Cross,' he whispered, 'and I suspect a truer one.'

After a time he handed me the letter. In fact, it lies on my desk before me, a little faded, the writing being cramped and slanted like the writing in the inn's book.

Dear Peggy,

I hope you have been a good girl. I may not be back for a long time but have a fondness for you in my heart. As I told you, I have a commission I wish you to perform and it will repay me for the sum I left you. I want you to tell me if a man called Doyle should ever come and stay in your inn. It is a possibility only, most likely a few weeks from now, but an opportunity for me to pay him back for several unkindnesses.

I wish you to play the kind of trick on him you and I once discussed. Make yourself pretty and go into his room late at night while he sleeps, pretending you are startled to have had a dream of a woman called Elsbeth, a lovely woman with reddish curly hair who came to you and told you how Doyle once loved her as she still loves him. Say she has asked that you will take her place and show him her love. He will probably believe you, for he is very gullible on such things and you can seduce him, a task I know you need not find difficult.

In the morning you may admit he has been deceived by his old friend Neill. And be sure to mock the memory of the woman. He will be too ashamed and compromised to do anything to punish you but I want you to report on all he says and does and whether he has a travelling companion.

Once you have written to me on this I will write again and I may even send more money when your task is completed if the opportunity comes.

Your loving friend,
Neill

There was something horrible in the candour of that signature, no pretence of a Dr Mere here. And I found it particularly hateful to hear Elsbeth's memory defiled in this way. I would probably have burst out with something but the Doctor made it quite clear he wanted to speak first.

'What you were going to do, Peggy, was extremely wicked,' said the Doctor, though his words were harsher than his tone, which held a hint of kindness. Even so the tears sprang into her eyes again. 'But, because you were led by this man, we will say nothing of this to anyone provided you do exactly what I say. You will write to him, saying you have seen nothing of Mr Doyle, I wish you to do that now at this desk. Your letter can be perfectly polite and affectionate and I will post it myself tomorrow. I think it is highly unlikely Dr Mere, or Neill as he writes, will return and you must try to forget him and say nothing about any of this to a soul. You have asked me if this man has done wrong. I am sorry to tell you he has done more wrong than any man I have ever known and I have known plenty of murderers.'

The girl flinched at this. 'Oh yes he has killed,' added Bell, 'and he would certainly have killed you. In that way you are very lucky. Now, do you think you can do as I say and go back to the way you were?'

She nodded. 'I have never done anything like this before, sir, I swear it.' And as I looked at the flash of hope alongside the fear in her eyes I realised this girl was not some kind of harlot at all. She had simply been corrupted. Once his influence was removed, she could probably go back to what she had been.

Bell made her write and address the letter on the inn's stationery. Then, before dismissing her, he asked if she would go through every meeting she had had with Neill. She did so and it was all much as we now assumed. He had seduced her on his first visit, beguiling her with his lies. On the second there had been even more time for them to spend together. Most of what he told her of himself held little interest, it was more of the same lies and boasting she had repeated to me earlier. But it seemed obvious to me he had intended to kill her on the second visit and her life had been saved only when he saw a further use for her.

After she had gone back to her room, Bell moved quickly to pick up the letter. 'I apologise if I did not spare your feelings, Doyle. What he planned was very cruel but his cruelty is a weakness and it has offered us the best opportunity we have had in all the years since our quest began. For once, we are ahead of him. You must sleep now, for we leave early. He is clearly in London and will not be returning here.'

The landlord was up early and perfectly willing to co-operate with our plans. A cab was summoned to take us to Salisbury station where the train to London could be easily secured. We ate a hasty breakfast in the parlour as the sun's early rays beautifully illuminated the fields beyond the inn. But I could not help noticing that Bell was uncharacteristically gloomy for a man who had, to quote his words, 'the best opportunity' since our quest began. I could only assume he must be reflecting on the difficulties of tracking our quarry down in London. He said nothing as we saw our luggage aboard the cab, only whispering a few words to the cabman.

Once we had started, he remained silent for a while and then he turned to me. 'I have news I do not wish to impart but I must,' he said. 'The servant girl, who I feel sure now has a genuine regret, came to me this morning, for last night in her excitement she had forgotten something. And it is not good news. Before we arrived it seems she had written Cream a brief note by way of reply to his. As we have seen, she is a bright girl, who knows her letters, which is presumably why he thought she might be useful. In one way she had little to say for thank heaven she had never set eyes on you. But it seems, Doyle, she had heard your name.'

I felt a sudden stab of dread. 'How could she have?'

'Because she asked her fellow staff. The stable boy told her he had heard it.'

This was the last thing we had wanted. 'So have the police made any connection?' I asked.

'It is not the police I am worried about,' Bell replied. 'They would make nothing of it at all unless we pointed it out to them, but the stable boy told her he had heard it from a Mr John Herne who knew you had been staying with a local naturalist called Middleton. Of course, once given this information, Cream would see at once how you escaped the police and the arrest he hoped for. Middleton had harboured you, which is why we are going to visit the address you gave me for him before we catch our train.'

At once I shared all the Doctor's apprehension. In other circumstances I would have delighted in visiting Middleton with Bell, but I felt a heavy heart as we took the same roads I had travelled with Herne some days earlier. Within half an hour we were at the little house on the lane that had proved my salvation. We got down and walked to the door. How I longed to see that small figure peer out at us but there was no answer to our knock. After a time, we moved back in the direction of the cab, but before we could get in, a local farmer's cart came past and stopped.

The driver was small and cherubic, though a little wary. I asked if he knew where we could find Mr Middleton and he seemed surprised. 'Did you not hear of the accident, sir? A terrible thing indeed, for a man as careful and skilled as he, but that river is dangerous, I always said so.'

It turned out Middleton had gone out early one morning only three days ago for his shooting, as the whole neighbourhood knew he did, and his body was found the next day, floating in the deepest part of the river. It was thought he had fallen, for there was a gash on his head and he was still in his heavy boots, which would have weighed him down. The community, including the police, inevitably concluded there was no foul play. 'For who would want to hurt him?' said the farmer. 'He had not a penny on him and he was as gentle as a lamb.'

# THE MYSTERIOUS CONVALESCENCE

I was silent for a long time, as the cab continued on our journey to Salisbury, and Bell was tactful. There was no denying I had experienced a premonition of such an event and naturally I felt a direct responsibility. It was as if when I arrived at Middleton's home, seeking comfort, I had been little more than an angel of death. How I cursed fate that my name should have been repeated at all! Had John Herne merely said there was a gentleman in the cab, the naturalist would have been spared, his wife's life unblighted.

'It is not your fault, Doyle, whatever you may think.' The Doctor's voice interrupted my thoughts. 'He must have returned here without visiting the Quarter Moon to establish Middleton's identity and habits, which were well known. You cannot be held responsible for his actions.'

Despite his words, the death of Middleton had a profound effect on me. I had not yet even attempted to return the money he had given me. Obviously I must ensure the debt was repaid to his wife, but this thought hardly helped my mood. Were she to discover the truth, she would surely throw the money back in my face, for in its way the transaction had ensured the destruction of all her happiness.

After some discussion, the Doctor agreed we would send her a slightly larger sum of money, taken from the funds he had set aside for our mission, explaining that it was to repay her late husband for a great act of kindness. Later, once Cream was gone, we would visit her to try to honour Middleton's memory. However, he was quite adamant that we could not, at this juncture, allow the news to distract us from our quest.

Even so, I was distracted. We reached London quite uneventfully, and were soon ensconced in the Doctor's usual railway hotel, but increasingly I found myself apprehensive about the coming reunion with the Morlands. I still felt enormous relief that the family, who had given me such comfort, were unharmed and I longed to see Sally again. But these feelings were entirely overwhelmed by the knowledge of the risks she would face, quite unknowingly, if she had any further dealings with me. In view of what had happened in Wiltshire, it was already a small miracle that Cream, who had befriended the family more than a year earlier and whom they knew as Tim, had not harmed them.

To my surprise, when I raised the matter, Bell entirely agreed with me. 'I have been giving consideration to these latest developments,' he said ruminatively as we stood in his old room that night before going down to dinner. 'They have led me to conclude we cannot in all conscience involve the Morlands any further in a public way. Already he certainly knows they are hospitable and that they enjoyed your company. In itself, given the extra risk, that was not enough to interest him when he had you, and they never got in the way of his plans as Middleton did. But I am sure now that, if he had observed the affection you felt for them, their fate would have been sealed. I conclude, therefore, he never did. It is fortunate there was such a long lull in his dealings with them. And on that last night, from what you tell me, he was in the drawing room while Sally greeted you so warmly in the hall. It is a mercy and we must do nothing to alter it in any way.'

'But surely we should warn them?' I said. 'That is the least I owe.'

'Yet it might be to seal their fate,' said Bell. 'Listen to me,' he continued, for I was about to interrupt in protest. 'You may terrify them with your story but you cannot arrange police protection for them. There is not even a sufficient case against Cream to make his arrest certain, Meanwhile, the very fear you induce in them would alert Cream at once if he returned and make it certain they would die. Without it they stand more chance, for as long as he does not suspect you are intimate with them, why should he bother?'

His logic was brutal but of course I saw the reasoning even as I hated it.

'But my God,' I said, 'it is cynical to allow them to know nothing.'

'It may be, but I scarcely care if it offers tham a better chance.' With that he made his way to the door and we came out of the room into a corridor that was long and, as the Doctor made sure, empty. 'However,' he continued, 'I believe a very short meeting in their house is perfectly safe. I suggest we telegraph Sally Morland in the most plain and ordinary way, informing her you will be there to collect your things tomorrow. You must stay no longer than a few minutes.'

In normal circumstances a meeting with Sally Morland would have lightened my heart, but now I did not look forward to it with any pleasure. Was it not possible that Cream was waiting for just such an eventuality? It would not be hard for him to have the house watched. After what had happened with Middleton, nothing at all was certain.

The Doctor thought this unlikely. 'There are limits to even his resources. He cannot know our decisions before we make them ourselves, nor can he be there indefinitely.' With that he closed the subject. But his words did not offer much comfort and the following afternoon I found myself looking around rather warily as I knocked on the door of that little house in Esher Street.

It was one of those grey cloudy London days which constantly threaten rain and I could see no one at all in the street. I suppose this should have been reassuring but it only added to my own sense of foreboding.

The maid opened the door and smiled to see me and then Sally Morland herself came out of the small sitting room where we had so often talked as she sat with her children. She wore a plain blue dress and her hair was a little longer but her smile was as wide and childlike as ever and she would have run to embrace me. This was something she had never done before, but it was the last thing I wanted before an open door and, rather to their surprise, I only nodded with a smile and turned to make myself busy, closing the door before I was ushered into the drawing room.

Sally's manner changed now. She detected at once something had altered in me, yet her passionate nature was not easily deterred.

'Are you well, Arthur?' she said. 'We were so worried.'

It was strange to be back in that room. I eyed the armchair where I had endured those last moments of consciousness and also the rocking chair, where Cream had sat, which was now placed inno-cently by the window. I was very conscious of that large window on to the street, knowing that anyone could be observing us, and I kept my distance from Sally, something that she noticed.

'I have recovered, I am glad to say.' I adopted as cheerful a tone as I could, though it was still guarded.

She watched me a little uncertainly but still warmly. 'We were so relieved when we heard from Dr Bell but he said he would explain it all. What was it?'

'Ah, the Doctor could not be here unfortunately,' I replied. 'It seems I had a severe nervous infection, which caused a temporary inflammation of the blood vessels but it is utterly gone now.'

This was the best I could do, and to be truthful my heart was not in it. No doubt the Doctor would have produced something less ridiculous but Sally never doubted me for a moment, only now a new anxiety came into her eyes.

'Is there any concern you are still infectious? Is that why you stand so far away?'

The question was so artless and natural it almost broke my heart. I longed to go close to her as a friend would, and pour out my feeling but I was still so conscious of that window. The whole length of it lay between us. Indeed we faced each other as if it were an invisible barrier.

'No there is no danger of that at all, I assure you. But I suppose I am still not quite my old self. I will not trouble you long.'

I could see a little relief in her eyes but it was quickly buried as she took in the fact that I would not be staying any longer. 'I gather the practice were able to manage?' I added.

'Oh yes,' she said. 'Dr Baird understood the position and they managed. Fortunately things were quiet and now Dr Small has returned from Egypt. They all ask kindly of you and would be happy to see you. But,' I could see she was returning to another of the many questions that had no doubt haunted her, 'what of Tim?' We have had only one telegram from him since he left here that night.'

'Well,' I said, having prepared for this, 'I myself only saw him briefly at the beginning of my convalescence so I know no more than you. And now I must collect my things. I am sure you are busy too.'

Even in the midst of my anxiety, this was needlessly harsh. I have written that there was never any impropriety in my friendship with Sally, something that is perfectly true. But we were close and good friends and I for one had often wondered if, in another life, we would have been more. But now I was no longer behaving as a friend and, of course, she could not understand why.

'Well I am not so busy,' she said with dignity, 'for as you see the children are with my sister but come and I will take you to your things.'

We mounted the stairs and I entered my old bedroom which was clean and anonymous with my packed case standing by the door. Here, for some reason, the curtains were slightly drawn, enough to ensure our invisibility.

I moved to my case. Sally was at the door, looking at me a little strangely, for she was no doubt thoroughly confused. I knew in that moment I could not maintain this charade, which, thanks probably to my own inability to play it correctly, was having a worse effect than anything I had intended. What if 'Tim' appeared and she told him I was utterly changed and my feelings towards her and her family had inexplicably cooled. In such a case he would guess the truth at once.

Checking again that the window offered no view from the street, I moved towards her and gave her one of my old smiles. She smiled back but I could see she was still at a loss.

'Sally,' I said, 'I cannot stay long, that is true, but I have to trust someone and you of all people have earnt that trust. What I tell you now is going to be very hard to understand but I swear to you I am not mad, and it is vital you follow it to the letter.'

Because we had once been close, she accepted this immediately. 'I do not for one moment think you are mad *now*,' she said, 'though downstairs I was troubled, for you were so unlike yourself. Arthur, please tell me the truth.'

'I cannot,' I said. 'But this is what you must do and all I tell you now is the absolute truth even if I cannot reveal all of it. When anyone asks, you tell them that I came back and was just as usual, though you might voice your irritation that I was too busy to stay longer and see your family. When asked about me, talk of me as a pleasant man who was a good lodger but not with any great affection. In fact, you should complain that my illness was inconvenient to you, for you were unsure whether you could re-let the room.'

She considered this and it baffled her. 'It is no great matter to do as you say but am I not to ask why?'

'There are so many things that are my own problems. I wish to be sure you are not involved in them.'

This made it clearer to her. 'And tell me, is this connected to what you told me once, that you had a friend who suffered a crime?'

108

This was unerring, pure brilliant instinct. I had almost forgotten but Sally had once seen me greatly affected by a picture in Madame Tussaud's, a picture which referred to an unknown poisoner I felt sure was Cream.

'Yes there is a distant connection,' I said. 'But you must mention that to absolutely nobody, not even your own family.'

'I never would,' she said simply. And I felt a surge of relief, for I knew it was true and I could cast aside the horrible idea of her telling 'Tim' such a thing. If she ever did, he would know in an instant I had been close and her fate would certainly be sealed.

I took a pace forward. 'I am only sorry to ask you to participate in this small deception, and that it will be some time before I can return, and perhaps release you from it.'

'That is nothing, I will do what you say,' she said, clearly distracted by another thought. 'But what of Tim?'

This was harder but I dissembled as well as I could. 'I fear he had to arrange to take me right out of London at some inconvenience to himself because of the infection.' I could see some doubt in her mind and struggled to add some conviction. 'I believe his visit to this country was brief and my illness interrupted it. So you have not heard from him recently?'

'Nothing,' she said.

'But that is always the way with him, is it not?' I said quickly. 'I am sure there were periods before when you heard nothing.'

'Yes it is true,' she said. 'Long periods.'

'Then I suspect it is his way,' I replied. 'As a matter of fact, the Doctor wished to be in touch with him to discuss my illness, and asked if he could borrow any letters you have. I would also be interested to see his cable. '

'Why yes of course, I can give them to you directly. There are not many, but he was always, as you say, a poor correspondent.' And here she paused, for of course she was no fool. 'Arthur, he is what he seems?'

'Oh he is quite as nomadic and engaging as he seems,' I said, somehow managing to smile, 'though he can be feckless. I had not seen him for some time and was astonished to find him here. I will be interested to read his letters too. But I warn you he is anything but discreet, so with him, above all – please I mean this, if you see him – talk of me as we agreed.'

I think she understood then. I do not mean for a moment she had any sense that 'Tim' was as I knew him to be, but she had some awareness she should be careful of what she revealed to him as she went off to find the letters. Of course I am sure she knew much was being concealed from her even if she could not understand its nature. But this, I had to agree with the Doctor, was in the end far better than telling her the truth and thereby ensuring she would be terrified out of her wits if 'Tim' ever returned. Such terror offered no real protection against him, indeed he would enjoy it. And once observed, it would probably compel him to kill them. Whereas if they remained mere bystanders, and he had no inkling of my affection for them, it seemed likely he would not bother with them again. And, if by some chance he did, then their ignorance might well be the only thing that would save them.

Sally soon returned with the letters. I thanked her and added, 'Because we have had to discuss some painful things, I have not said the most important. Despite our little arrangement about what should be said in public, you of all people must surely know the times I spent in this house with you and your family were among the happiest of my life. I will always treasure them.'

She waited and looked at me, her eyes brimmed with feeling. 'Yes I think I did know that, Arthur. And it gave me great pride. I only hope you will return to see us, the children especially.' There was a sudden loud knocking on the door from downstairs which made me jump. At once I moved nervously from the room and along the landing to where I could see the front door. Sally had followed, uneasily aware of my agitation. We both stared down but it was only to see the children and Sally's sister tumbling into the house as the maid closed the door behind them. Sally saw my relief at once. 'Go to them,' I said. 'I will see myself out and God bless you.'

'God bless you, Arthur, a safe return.'

A little smile, that smile I loved, and then she was gone. I slipped the letters into the bag and waited till they were all in the drawing room and then went down the stairs, which rang with laughter as the children greeted their mother. I looked around as I left the house, glad I was leaving it with that laughter ringing in my ears rather than the silence of terror. But also regretful that once again out of necessity I was leaving a happy place because I brought only fear and threat to those in it.

I deliberately froze my expression into a mask of indifference before I opened the door, hoping that any onlooker would think of me as an unimportant lodger who was not even bid farewell. But, as I reflected miserably, was not this description close enough to the truth? Unimportant except in a propensity to bring darkness and danger to such places of tranquillity. Outside, the street mocked me with its emptiness.

# The Memory of the Clerk

For the rest of the day I made some attempt to sort out my affairs, writing letters to the practice, explaining and apologising for my absence, though I knew Sally had ensured there were no problems in that direction. I had already heard from the doctor who was covering for me in Southsea that he was happy to carry on for a further few weeks. Some time later Bell returned to the hotel in an excellent mood.

'It was not a day without its uses, Doyle. The worst news is that the post-office box in Charing Cross to which she wrote was closed earlier today, in other words shortly after the letter from the girl arrived. Clearly it was his only reason to keep it open.'

He must have seen my face fall. 'No, do not despair yet. This is as close as we have ever been since Edinburgh. Moreover, I have been observing the place closely and one of the clerks is of a thoroughly garrulous disposition. There is a period shortly after eleven in the morning when he is alone at the counter and I suggest we visit him tomorrow. Now tell me of your visit to Sally Morland.'

Later, I sensed all the old energy of the Doctor as we pored over the material I had collected. The letters from 'Tim' to the family were brief enough, if friendly, speaking warmly of forthcoming visits to the Morlands or of ones he had just enjoyed, with some teasing references, which I found chilling, to the children. But they did help us to establish a proper chronology of our opponent's movements. Cream had first met the Morlands over a year before in September 1882, when he was presumably preparing the ground. We thought it likely this was his first return to our country since he left Edinburgh and that, while he was enjoying himself in London, he had inspected likely practices which might need a locum with a view to luring me there. It was around then, too, he must have written to Sir Henry Carlisle.

Once he had noticed the large riverside practice, he could easily have found some pretext to introduce himself and was informed of Dr Small's visit to Egypt the following year. No doubt he mentioned he might know of a locum and was subsequently introduced to the Morlands. The rest could easily be achieved. After this some months are missing, though we suspected from the evidence of the police artist's drawing I had seen at Madame Tussaud's he had probably attempted to poison a girl in London on the eleventh of November. It seemed likely he had left the capital shortly after this interrupted encounter, possibly travelling to Europe or Edinburgh, but he returned in time to visit the Morlands with presents around Christmas time. Then in January a note showed he was re-embarking for America. He would have stayed there most of the year (as was indicated by other letters we had in our possession written from Chicago to Hanbury, the seaman who was now dead) and the next letter to the Morlands was dated only a few weeks earlier. Here 'Tim' tells them he hoped to make a surprise visit sometime around Christmas and Bell felt sure this was when he had re-entered the country.

'So,' said Bell, 'we can now be confident of his whole plan.'

'Yes,' I said with a certain frustration, for I could not see how any of this helped us now. 'But why not just come to Southsea and murder me?'

'That should be entirely obvious, Doyle,' said Bell, giving me a somewhat sharp look as he took out the last and most recent item, a telegram. 'He wanted you on his ground, not yours. Here he could poison you with impunity, and watch you suffer as you realised you had been duped and delivered into his hands. In Southsea such a thing would have been far more difficult to achieve. He might possibly have prevailed against you in a direct struggle but it is hardly the kind of risk he enjoys or seeks.'

I had to acknowledge the truth of this. But Bell had already forgotten his rebuke. He was staring down at the telegram with far more interest than he had manifested in the letters. After a long time he tossed it over to me.

The telegram was from Salisbury, which is what might have been expected since it was dated on one of the days Cream had been with me in the cottage.

GOOD NEWS. DOYLE OUT OF ANY DANGER AND CONVALESCING FROM HIS ILLNESS BY THE SEA BUT MAY TAKE SOME TIME TIM

'It is odd, is it not, Doyle?' said the Doctor, his eyes closed.

'I suppose it is odd he bothered to write,' I said. 'He had no need, for what further use were they to him?'

'None I certainly hope, but his effort to communicate is in itself not so remarkable. If they had heard nothing they would certainly have raised an alarm in due course. I doubt in truth he had much to fear from that, but as we have seen the man does not take utterly unnecessary risks.'

'But what else is there here?' I said. 'It is just a lot of obvious lies.'

'But sometimes,' said the Doctor, a lie can be suggestive. Why "by the sea"? Salisbury is not by the sea. Why indeed say anything about the place at all?'

'To make it sound more convincing,' I said with a little impatience. 'People often convalesce in sea air.'

'Indeed they do but the question remains, why did he choose it?' he persisted.

'It was to distract attention from Salisbury,' I said, rather surprised he had not considered this.

'But there is no need. The town is a long way from that cottage and hardly a clue in itself. You could have been dead and he far away long before anyone ventured to make such connections if they ever did.' He began to get out his case, which contained the lenses and other equipment he used to examine letters. 'No, I am sure "by the sea" was the first thing that came into his head and I wonder if that might not help us, for these things are often the most revealing. Now I would like to make what I can of these with my tools, I will see you in the morning.'

About ten o'clock the next day, which was dull but not cold, we set out for Charing Cross and were soon outside the post office in question. It seemed obvious to me it had been chosen carefully. There was another much larger post office by the station but this was a smaller affair at the end of a nondescript thoroughfare called Adam Street. The place was staffed by two or three people at best and Bell had no need to point out the clerk, whom he had described as garrulous, for the man's voice was audible from well down the street, expressing his diabolical outrage that a light single brougham he had seen in a carter's yard that morning was being sold for as much as seventy-five guineas.

Since it was still twenty minutes before the hour, Bell was in no mood to hurry, so we changed direction and took a turn down the Strand, gazing into the shops, which were now bright with Christmas fare, not least the 'Chocolate in Spain' shop I had sometimes frequented. Later we returned and, as a nearby clock struck the hour, Bell entered the place while I lingered by the doorway, reading a dull notice about the use of adhesive stamps.

The clerk, now alone, proved to be a florid gentleman with whiskers who smiled broadly at the sight of us for it was obviously a torment to him not to hear the sound of his own voice. At once he launched into a torrential discourse on the weather before Bell interrupted him to make an enquiry about Dr Mere's post-office box, emphasising he was extremely anxious to contact its former owner.

'Why, sir,' said the clerk grandly, 'that is impossible, not only are there rules of confidence in such matters but I would have no record of a closed box, even though it was shut down only yesterday.'

'And did he come in person to close it and collect his letters?'

'I have told you,' intoned the man ponderously, 'I cannot comment on what must be considered private . . .'

The Doctor ignored this. 'Of course.' He spoke in his most mellow and avuncular tone. 'It would be quite improper to intrude on any confidential matters but I am Professor Joseph Bell of Edinburgh University and the gentleman happens to be a very old friend whom I am anxious to contact while I am here from Edinburgh. I am sure he would have no objection to your answering a few civil questions.' And there was a chink of coins as he opened his purse and produced a small sum.

Bell had judged his appeal to both cupidity and snobbery well. The clerk's eyes fairly gleamed at the amount and he smiled broadly. 'Well,' he said, 'I am sure there can be no harm in replying to a gentleman's honest queries.' Then he must have recalled my presence for I heard Bell comment, 'That gentleman is with me and also a friend, indeed we are old colleagues.'

'Ah,' came the relieved reply. 'Well, as I was saying, there can be no harm. No he did not come in person, we had instructions some time ago with a forwarding address, telling us when one more letter arrived to forward it and close the box.'

'I see,' said Bell, rather disappointed. 'Who forwarded it yesterday? Was it you?' The man nodded and Bell's manner became more hopeful. 'And did you happen to note the address on it?'

'Now there,' said the man, sadly, 'you place me in a difficulty. It is not that I am unwilling, sir, to tell you. But during a day we have many many letters to forward and return. Why, I have already written six addresses this morning. I would never remember one in particular.'

'And you did not see the man?'

'Not to my knowledge, sir. No.'

I sensed the Doctor's impatience. 'Yet this was only yesterday and you cannot have many people using such a service here. I assume he would have left a sum of money to pay for stamps, the calculation would therefore be yours. Is there nothing you remember? Was the address, for example, in London or abroad?'

'Not abroad, sir,' the clerk mused, obviously enjoying the attention. 'No it was out of London, I am sure of that, for I recall wondering when it would reach him and adding to the postage. Yes, you are right, sir, now it comes back. It was by the sea, I think.'

I sensed Bell's excitement. 'So it was somewhere you recognised?' Bell pressed.

'Ah now, sir, the truth is I hardly knew the name of the place. But I think it began, yes I am sure the word "South" . . . That was the first part.'

'Southampton?' said Bell, and my heart raced. Was he returning to America or seeking me out?

'Why no, sir. I would have remembered that. I have a sister there.' The man laughed at the small coincidence. I knew his slowness must be infuriating the Doctor but you would never have known it, for he laughed too. Southsea was also quickly ruled out, eliminating the possibility Cream was searching for me there. 'No,' the clerk went on, 'the thing is I didn't know the name well though I had heard of it, so I doubt I will recall it unprompted other than the South. But I rather think, sir, it was the east coast. I cannot say why, I have never been there, but I do recall thinking that it was a little odd to have south such and such on the east coast and not on the south. We get to think about names and their whys and wherefores of that kind here. Why only the other day I had to address a parcel and it struck me how many streets in London have a "gate" somewhere in their name.'

'You are right there.' The Doctor's voice was still merry but there was a hint of command in it. He was clearly not prepared to let this man ramble any further off the subject, which he would do at the slightest opportunity. 'So you are sure it is "South" and the east coast?'

'Yes,' said the man, and I looked up to see he was beaming with pride at his feat of memory. 'I can be fairly certain of it, certainly the South and I think, sir, yes I am almost equally sure it was in the east not the south or the west. And that it was on the coast of England. I hope it is of some help to you, sir. We always try to oblige. Why the other day a man was here having posted his letters to all the wrong places and we had to try and get them back, the place was quite a muddle but we got them, sir, we got them. Those I can remember, some of them.'

Bell quickly interrupted with other questions about the address, whether it was an inn or a private house, but the man remembered no more and, with some difficulty, as further stories were proffered, Bell thanked him and managed to beat his retreat.

He was, however, not remotely dispirited as we walked out into the street. 'We have come away with rather more than I expected,' he said once we were out of earshot. 'I am glad it is not Southampton and America.'

I was less sanguine. 'But there must be many towns with a South in their name and he is not the most reliable of witnesses.'

'Certainly not the most reticent, but on the whole I believe he was fastidious enough about his facts to be reliable. This afternoon I will consult a gazetteer and with any luck we will narrow our choice considerably.'

To my surprise that night the Doctor was late for our appointed dinner in the hotel dining room, but I did not think he would wish me to wait and sat down to my chop, wondering where he could be. As I ate, I reflected that the day's developments were surely a good deal more dismal than the Doctor admitted. Half a place name is not a very positive way in which to begin a manhunt.

I had almost finished my meat when I became aware of a commotion at the door of the dining room. There were some raised voices and a few waiters rushed over and then a tall figure strode out of the scrum in my direction. As people scattered in his path, I could see it was the Doctor but he was wearing a jacket several sizes two big and a tie slung round his collar like a piece of string. Such clothes would have made any other man look like a music-hall clown but the Doctor's eagle-like features and bright eyes created an overall effect that was sinister rather than comic.

However, he smiled heartily as he sat down and summoned the bemused waiter. 'I am afraid, Doyle, I was so caught up in various matters I quite forgot to put on a jacket, but as you see I have now borrowed one from a friendly porter so they were forced to admit me.' And he broke off to order what he saw on my plate and a quart of beer. 'Yes,' he continued. 'I quite neglected to eat and drink, but I must do so now for we are leaving tomorrow and the east coast it is too.'

'So did you trace the name that begins South?'

'Oh yes,' he said. 'Our talkative friend was quite right on that. What he told me was extremely useful, indeed I went back late this afternoon and the clerk confirmed my location. I will explain all that in due course. It is trifling enough and I believe our man has now moved a few miles down the coast but certainly he is nowhere that will take him back to America.' The Doctor's beer was brought to him in a foaming tankard.

'And now, Doyle,' he said solemnly after he had taken a long draught, 'are you an admirer of ghost stories?'

'I do not see the relevance.'

'But you will. I have some ghostly reading for you tonight so I suggest you order coffee. You will surely know the horrific legend in question, but you may not know it in its entirety. Nor that now it seems to have come true.' The food had arrived and he cut a large slice of chop. 'Though I would not disguise the fact that the legend has helped me, I regard these new developments as a matter of great concern to us.'

Of course I had seen the Doctor like this before often enough when a case suddenly advances. His mind would trip from one aspect to the next, teasing, questioning, ignoring logical sequences and connections. But since this was not just an ordinary case, I felt it was unfair of him to indulge in such mystification. 'I only wish you would tell me what you are talking about,' I said with some exasperation.

'And I will,' he said, ignoring my tone. 'You must have heard the simpler versions of the tale, it is one of England's oldest. And many a child has been kept awake by the "wylde Decembere hunt" at midnight, with torches through the woods, the desperate struggle by the pool, the curse and the howling man who was driven mad within hours, not to mention all the subsequent deaths.'

A memory was beginning to stir in me.

'Yes, he said, observing this. 'I mean the story of the witch of Dunwich Heath.'

# PART THREE:

# THE LEGEND AND THE VANISHING

# THE WYLDE HUNT AT DUNWICH

Later, in my room, as I read the book he had given me, I reflected that Bell had somewhat exaggerated the fame of the Dunwich legend. England has many ghost stories, while Scotland and Wales may well have even more. Most, like the witch of Dunwich, are located in distant corners of the kingdom, and can hardly compare in popularity with the ghosts of the Tower of London or Berkeley Square.

Yet the violent witch hunt across Dunwich Heath all those years ago has been widely related, partly because of the vividness of its setting and also the violence of its conclusion. Dunwich itself feeds such legends, situated as it is on the windy easternmost tip of England, where the sea has made spectacular inroads. I first read of the 'wylde hunt' and its aftermath in my schooldays, but then it is true I took a great interest in such weird stories and I have encountered many who never heard of it.

The plain circumstances are easily told, though why the Doctor should have seized on it now must come later. One freezing December night in 1690, a ferocious chase took place in the woods and marshes around the Suffolk town of Dunwich, a place already haunted by the all-conquering sea, which had buried so much of it and given rise to the story of 'the city under the sea'. The chase climaxed on the heath directly to the south of the place. Many of the pursuers were on horseback carrying torches and they were hunting Mary Goddard, a woman who had long been under suspicion of witchcraft. The woman was no pauper, indeed she was relatively wealthy, but she was an outsider who had a reputation for great ferocity and it was claimed she had bitten off the finger of a nearby farmer who left the town rather than confront her again.

The main charges against her remain unspecified but some versions of the story talk of a rune and of the fact she had drawn strange figures on a paper she had passed to others, which brought them harm. By December of 1690 such accusations had become widespread and some weeks before Christmas a deputation went to Mary Goddard's house. There are many excellent sources who chronicle what happened next. Mary Goddard was described as a *mad divell in a poysonous rage* who refused to be taken away. When they persisted, she fled on foot into the dense woodland behind the town that borders the heath. She must have run with great speed and skill because in all the descriptions by witnesses it is reported that, for hours, no trace of her was seen.

Indeed the search would probably have been abandoned except that one of the riders, a young man called George Crome who had wandered away from the others, was found unconscious with a deep gash on his forehead. Subsequently he died. Of course the wound could easily have been accidental, for the wood was so thick that riding in it at all was bound to be hazardous. But fear drove the men to fury, the search continued and soon one of those at the flank caught a glimpse of a shadow moving through the thickest part of the trees where the horses could hardly penetrate. It was Mary Goddard who had been drinking from a spring which evidently only she knew, another source of grievance. And now the hunt became more vengeful. Matthew Snell, one of the great chroniclers of these events, writes:

*The riders were all in a great rage, and the whole wood rung with the utterance of oaths. Two ran their mounts so fast they were unseated, with bones broken. And much of screaming was hear'd now and the other mounts circl'd round and men ran into the thickets. And then at last a cry went up for they had seen the wytch flee out on to the heath.*

Now, again, for a time she was lost to them, but at last they caught sight of her beside an old quarry pool of standing water, known then as Farler's Pool after an old and worthy cavalier who had used the pool while hiding in the wood from Cromwell's men forty years before. She was standing on the edge of the water, her face shining with hatred, daring the men to come forward. According to the record, the men were frightened and nobody wished to take up her challenge.

*And there was,* Matthew Snell wrote, *something so direful in her countenance, that it made them fearful and perplex'd. Nor was she herself trembling but her face was shining whyte. Indeed she was more firm of purpose than at any time.*

It even seemed she might have got away, for it was later discovered she was carrying enough gold to make her welcome elsewhere. But in answer to an appeal from the magistrate, who I had noticed even when I read this as a child did not venture towards her himself, William Bowker, a wool trader, stepped forward and went to her. Bowker said he would not draw his sword on her but she must come with him back to the assizes.

There is some confusion about what happened as he approached her. Some say she fixed him with a look, others that she had some small sharp instrument. What all agree is that she made a movement with her fingers as if she was anointing him upon his forehead. Bowker flinched and then fell back, evidently hurt. Seeing this, three or four men came forward at once, and the witch turned and cursed them all. She rejoiced in the death of Crome in the wood and told them, according to Snell, *that she would herself return so all would knowe what it is to drown. And all the rest would slide into the sea.* Then she ran into the dark water, which was in places quite deep and perhaps the weight of her gold dragged her down but she vanished from sight.

Bowker was not among the men who returned to the town that night. Realising he was not of their number, they called for him throughout the wood but heard nothing. Later a great howling was heard and a figure was seen by a passing carter. Bowker was all but naked in the moonlight and screaming in a way that made it clear his mind had given way. Next day they searched and, though the witch's body was recovered, no sign of Bowker was ever found. It was assumed that either he had gone over the cliff and been swept away by the sea or he had drowned himself in the deepest recesses of the pool.

That was the substance of the legend of Dunwich Heath and there was little more in the *Suffolk Companion* Bell had purchased at a bookstall near our hotel than I recalled from the more sensational version of the story I read as a schoolboy. Here, as before, the story ends with the warning that there have been further (usually unspecified) sightings of the poor howling figure of William Bowker over the years and that such sightings always portend a death. The book also points out how Dunwich continues to crumble into the sea. And how the bells of its vanished churches can be heard tolling through the waves on a stormy night. By now the last church on the cliff and most of its graves were gone. This could be put down to the curse, but of course the process was already well under way when Mary Goddard uttered it.

It was, I reflected after putting down the book, a good enough yarn as such things go, but what possible relevance it might have to our quest I was at a loss to see. Indeed, though I had once relished all the thrilling aspects of the tale, now that I was older I found it more troubling. For in many respects the narrative seemed little more than a graphic illustration of men exercising their taste for cruelty. The Dunwich affair, it is true, had some peculiarly vivid witnesses but it was still characterised by the savagery of the mob. And reading it again now I found myself wondering if the only truly courageous person in the whole saga was not Mary Goddard herself, especially if she had been the victim of malicious gossip. Though

William Bowker, who at the end had tried to behave honourably, also seemed to deserve some credit.

Fortunately, Bell had not left me to ponder the thing on its own or I would probably have gone and banged on his door in frustration even though he had specifically asked me not to disturb him. He had also provided an article in that morning's paper to be read after I had reacquainted myself with the legend. And I turned to that now.

I am sorry to say it only increased my irritation. The reader may wonder at this. Had not the Doctor so often directed my attention to various fanciful pieces of data and then proved them relevant? Of course I reminded myself of that now. But it is one thing to recall such a fact in theory and quite another to recall it amidst all the thwarted hopes and delays and problems of an investigation. Also it must be remembered there *were* occasions where Bell had been wrong, including one I have alluded to. Since I felt the consequences of that particular mistake every day, perhaps it may be considered understandable that I frequently questioned his more bizarre assertions.

Moreover, the news article he had given me tonight was not, as I had expected, a report of some major crime. It was, in fact, a humorous item, concerning a disappearance which was widely regarded as a hoax. Indeed I seemed to recall seeing some mention of it in a newspaper earlier in the week and not even bothering to read the rest.

*A Gentleman's Prank?* the article was headed. It was brief, it was given no due prominence and the tone was whimsical throughout. It seemed that a London man called Oliver Jefford, who had something of a reputation as a rake and a joker, and who was the son of the late distinguished lawyer Sir Thomas Jefford, had recently inherited some property in Dunwich, including a house near to the witch's pool, traditionally known as The Glebe. Jefford had long held authorial ambitions, which were unfulfilled, and he had recently turned his attention to the legend, announcing that he had little belief in the witch and defied her curse but hoped she might help him advance his cause as an author. This was taken to be the precursor of some trick, for Jefford was notorious for such things. When last seen, the man had been in a state of some intoxication in the Ship public house in Dunwich but he sobered up and set off for his dwelling. Next day, the first of December, a local farmer searching for a lost pig glimpsed him walking the woodland path to his house with two others whom he did not properly see.

The following morning, some bloody marks were found in his house, blood that the local farmer and others were certain belonged to a slaughtered animal. There was no sign of Jefford and the place was otherwise empty, for one of the man's many eccentricities was that he liked to live without staff, cutting the figure of the Bohemian artist.

A few newspapers, the article said, had fallen for this feeble attempt at sensation which was surely designed to advance Jefford's career as a writer. But most had not. The general conclusion advanced by many, including friends who were thought to know his intentions, was that he had returned to the lights of London. And the authorities were unconvinced there was anything to be investigated.

I tossed the thing aside, for it was obvious I needed some more education on the matter before I could make up my mind about any of it and lay down to sleep. I found myself thinking not of these new events or of Jefford but of Dunwich itself. I had never been there but the idea of a town crumbling into the sea from eroding cliffs often haunted me. Had not Poe himself commemorated in it in his 'City in the Sea'.

> No rays from holy heaven come down
> On the long night-time of that town
> But light from out the lurid sea
> Streams up the turrets silently

Suddenly I tensed as I lay there, for the words had reminded me of something. What was it Cream had said? It was while he was lecturing me, taunting me with questions about himself. He wanted to know if I thought he was mad and then had launched into a tirade about England's corruption. I saw his face leaning over me, his eyes sparkling, his mouth taut. I struggled to recall the exact words. 'Your country here is rotten, it is eroding before your eyes, eaten by the sea. *Why there are places literally collapsing into the water. A fine symbol of the corruption of England's soul.*'

I had no idea whether the Doctor had taken this into account. But I for one was absolutely sure it could not be coincidence. Cream must have been thinking of Dunwich. It was the only place that truly fitted the description. In that moment all my scepticism vanished. I did not sleep well, I was imagining that last church on the cliff with its graveyard slowly crumbling grave by grave, as all the bones and decayed flesh scattered into the North Sea. And I seemed to hear Cream's soft voice singing a strange discordant song which echoed the destruction.

# The Disappearance of Oliver Jefford

Later, when we had seated ourselves in the corner of the Great Eastern railway compartment bound for Ipswich, the Doctor apologised for giving me such a small and uninteresting newspaper clipping about the disappearance. 'The more sensational stories have rather better information to offer even if they are interweaved with nonsense,' he said as he arranged his coat comfortably over his knees. 'That is generally the case but I wished to go through them again myself. You must read them in a moment, but first I will tell you what happned to me yesterday.'

He leant forward to itemise his research. 'It did not take me long to establish that there are fifty-five English place names prefixed by the word South. However, as you would expect, few are on the east coast. The only ones that suggest themselves are South Shields in Northumberland, Southleigh in Lincolnshire, South Walsham in Norfolk, Southwold in Suffolk and Southend in Essex, not a large group and some of them are little more than hamlets without an inn. Of course the clerk might have been mistaken that the place is on the coast at all and, if that was the case, our task became nearly impossible. But I recalled our quarry's telegram to the Morlands and those odd words about your fictitious convalescence 'by the sea'. There was, as you and

I agreed, no reason for the lie to take this form and I concluded it must have been the first thing that came into his head. Therefore it is certainly possible he was already thinking about a town by the sea.'

'On the whole,' he went on, 'I therefore tended to believe the clerk, who from his conversation seems a man of particular, if limited, observational skills. Moreover, the place had to be more than a hamlet for the man said he had heard of it, even if he did not know it well. That, I think, narrows it down to South Shields, Southwold and Southend. Already I could have gone back there and asked him, but then I recalled Cream's words to you about coastal erosion. The most spectacular coastal erosion in England is just along the shore at Dunwich and my inclination for Southwold and Dunwich was now becoming very strong. Then yesterday afternoon I suddenly recalled reading of the disappearance of Jefford in that town. At once I went out and bought all the newspapers and some of them, as you will see, were of great interest. Amidst much nonsense, which was to be expected, I discovered facts that immediately convinced me there must be a connection. I returned to my clerk and mentioned Southend. He shook his head. I then plumped for Southwold and he recalled it at once. It was the place. And even better, he was able to supply an inn. He is sure it was the Harbour Inn, for that turns out to be the reason he felt confident the town was on the coast.'

This was excellent news and now I settled down to look at the newspaper articles which had excited him. The case was certainly a bizarre one and the best article of all came, as he had said, from the lowliest source – a crimesheet called the *Penny Illustrated Police News*. At the top was a rendering of the old legend of the witch with graphic pictures of the wild chase and its aftermath. The article followed.

# DISAPPEARANCE OF JEFFORD HEIR

## Bloody Lettering in House

## The Mystery of the Witch of Dunwich Heath

*Has an ancient curse claimed a modern victim? Many strange circumstances surround the disappearance of Oliver Jefford from a house in Dunwich, not far from the celebrated witch's pool, and further news is anxiously awaited.*

*The legend of Dunwich Heath is a famous one. No evening of ghostly tales around the fireside at Christmas would be complete without a recounting of the 'wylde hunt' at Dunwich Heath on a frosty winter's night in 1690. And the witch's awful words that 'all would know what it is to drown'.*

*But now a modern sceptic may have fallen foul of the ancient curse. Oliver Jefford is a name not unknown to the sporting public after his success with the horse Wandering Minstrel at Newmarket some years ago. A single gentleman of means with many acquaintances, Mr Jefford has often occasioned comment for his colourful lifestyle, whether in the fashionable clubs of Pall Mall or the more out-of-the-way-places of the capital. Perhaps known best of all for his extravagant wagers, it was recently reported he bet a gentleman of the colonies he could walk across the river at low tide and nearly drowned in the attempt till his friend managed to drag him out and revive him.*

*Recently he inherited some property in the town of Dunwich, which added to his already considerable fortune, including a lonely house known as The Glebe not far from the celebrated witch's pool of the legend.*

*Mr Jefford announced at once he would use it as a retreat to write some verses, for though as yet unpublished he has often talked of writing poetry. Seven days ago he was seen at the Ship Inn in the town of Dunwich, making light of the story of the witch. Several witnesses attest that, as the night wore on, Mr Jefford became more and more vehement, protesting loudly that he wished only to make the witch's acquaintance and that he defied her curse, inviting her to come to his house and mete out revenge by taking his gold. He also indicated he had made a discovery that would disprove the thing once and for all, for, through his inheritance, he had come into possession of the celebrated witch's rune, which is supposed to bring death on all who hold it. It must be added that some of his language was regarded as intemperate and even blasphemous by those present. Many of the citizens of Dunwich have respect for the legend and do not like to hear it taken lightly, especially on the eve of the anniversary of the hunt itself which is 1 December.*

*There was already much talk in the town that only a few hours earlier as darkness fell a forester going through Dunwich wood had heard a great wailing and caught sight of a naked figure screaming and moving in the trees. Several villagers believe this was a sighting of the howling man of the legend, which always presages a death.*

*Whatever the truth of this sighting, it is certain that late that night Jefford returned to his house on foot alone. Next day, which was the first of the month, he was seen by a local farmer on the path to his house with two figures. The farmer recognised Jefford walking beside a tall good-looking stranger of commanding appearance but did not catch a sight of the third.*

*Next day, the same farmer, who was his nearest neighbour, had occasion to visit the house in the course of searching for a lost pig.*

*Having knocked on the door and receiving no reply, he entered but thought the house to be empty. He called out and came to the main room where he found a quantity of blood on the floor, some of it formed into letters. There was no mistaking these letters, indeed when last reported they were still observable as first found.*

*witch*
*here*

*Poor Jefford in his last hours seemed to be trying to relate that the witch had returned. But, after an extensive search revealed nothing else at the property and no sign of Mr Jefford, others have scoffed at the message on the floor, declaring it is obviously a prank for Jefford's own amusement. They claim he will be found soon enough enjoying his new-found glory, and ridiculing the curse, in the fashionable haunts of Mayfair. Certainly the farmer believes the blood is only that of his lost pig and wishes to take action against Jefford for his act of slaughter. But as yet any sign of the missing pig or of the man has not been discovered. Until Oliver Jefford reappears to set the record right, it must be prudent to keep an open mind. The powers of darkness are not a matter for jest, and never will be.*

I put the paper down and the Doctor could see at once its effect on me. The other accounts had some details of interest, but only the somewhat scurrilous columns of the *Penny Illustrated Police News* revealed the true nature of Jefford's character. The man was obviously a rake, an *habitué* of London's lowlife and therefore exactly the type Cream would be likely to encounter in the course of his own pursuits. Moreover, it appeared he was rich, while we also knew Cream had been frustrated in his attempts to find money in that cottage and was eagerly seeking it. There was the 'tall good-looking stranger of commanding appearance' and even that most telling aside about the wager and 'a gentleman of the colonies'.

'Of course, Doyle,' said the Doctor in reply as I picked out the detail, 'in itself that could have been nothing at all. There are plenty of gentlemen from the colonies who enjoy a bet. But, taken together with everything else, as well as our enemy's established movements, his own words and the description of the figure in Jefford's company, I do not believe this could be coincidence. The scent of him is too strong.'

We journeyed to Ipswich where we spent the night and then across country to Droxford before we joined a coach for Southwold, by which time it was late the next afternoon. I had never been to this part of England and, as our vehicle picked its way along the little roads in these last hours of daylight, the view was exquisite. I

am aware some aestheticians like Ruskin have pronounced that a
flat land holds no mystery. But as the wind got up and sent great
clouds scurrying over that majestic panorama of fields and ditches
and standing water, I reflected I had rarely seen anything so
mysterious. With little sign of habitations or people, the sky and
the landscape held sway and the lines of dykes and field borders
seemed to recede away almost into infinity, as the unknown
beckoned from behind every ditch and tree. Of course there was
nothing here of the corruption of the city but it still seemed to me
an extraordinarily fitting landscape for our enemy, being both bleak
and yet suggestive.

The Doctor's voice broke into these reveries. 'We must be on our
guard from the moment we arrive, Doyle. You will remember what
happened at the Quarter Moon. I have no intention of telling the
landlord anything beyond the fact we are enjoying a leisurely
excursion and looking out for some seaside property.'

'And if he is there when we arrive? Perhaps waiting for us?'

By now, we were in Southwold itself and passing low buildings
we came to the harbour where fishing boats bobbed frantically, for
a storm was threatening. 'I have to consider that as well as
everything else,' said the Doctor, looking out at the rain that was
starting to fall. 'You may not know I make a regular visit to
Glendoick in Perthshire every year for the shooting. It is something
I have done since I was nineteen and I am a tolerable marksman.
Of course I would prefer to see him tried but, if the thing was in
the balance, I have a firearm.'

Though Bell seemed quite serious I had to smile at this, for the
idea of the Doctor entering the Harbour Inn at Southwold and
shooting one of its guests in cold blood was incongruous. But in one
way I felt reassured to hear it. The quest for Cream was entering a
new stage. If only this time, I thought as the coach finally came to
rest, he could be delivered into our hands.

The inn proved to be a very modest establishment indeed, for
there could not have been more than two or three guest bedrooms

at most and we quickly established, rather to our disappointment, that the others were unoccupied. I suggested we should sound out the landlord at once but, rather to my surprise, the Doctor merely replied that the man did not look to be of a helpful disposition and he had urgent matters to pursue elsewhere in the town.

The landlord was indeed a small and somewhat furtive man called Burn, who showed little interest in us. Later we discovered he was a former fisherman who had lost his boat and had only undertaken the job so he could chat with the fishermen who congregated in the bar several evenings a week.

Few boats were out that night so there was a great throng of people in the bar when Bell reappeared and we descended from our rooms. They looked at us without much interest and returned to their talk as a maid showed us politely to the snug, a small room with a fire and a serving hatch which opened on to the main bar.

Here we were brought plates of halibut and egg and some tankards of beer, both of which were very welcome. Bell ate thoughtfully, surveying the bar and its occupants who were discussing the previous day's catch. I understood his caution but was becoming increasingly frustrated by the fact he was yet to strike up a conversation with any of the people here, where our enemy had been. Of course it was comfortable enough by the fire and the fish was wonderfully fresh, but it hardly helped our cause. I was on the point of saying as much, when suddenly the outside door flew open, and a boy of about fifteen stepped in out of the street carrying a small packet.

He looked around and, as soon as he saw Burn behind the bar, he went over to him at once.

'Mr Burn, I have an urgent packet for Dr Mere who is here. Please take me to him.'

## The Figure on the Cliff

I put down my fork with a start. This was an extraordinary piece of luck. Burn came over to the boy at once. 'Another?' he said. 'Why, I had a letter for him here from London a day ago. Who gave you this?'

'Mr Andrews, the blacksmith. A stranger gave it him with a couple of coins.'

'Well he ain't here. I'll take it though,' said Burn sourly, dismissing the boy as he turned to his customers. 'Can you credit the man?' he said. 'This Dr Mere,' he scrutinised the address, 'yes that's his name. Comes here for one night more than a week ago, moves on. And now I have not only this but another letter for him. I know he was making for Dunwich for he enquired after the coach. And why, may I ask, did he not have his precious post directed to the inn there? But then Hamish who works at the Ship came in here last Saturday and he claimed he never heard of him. Well I suppose I must send it on there, if I find anyone who can take it for me, but I am damned if I will pay anyone to do it.'

At this, the Doctor was on his feet. 'Pardon me, Mr Burn,' he said, walking forward into the bar. 'I could not help hearing what you said just now. And it so happens my companion and I are headed for the inn at Dunwich tomorrow.'

The publican stared at him. I was beginning to apprehend that out host was a bad-tempered individual and I strongly suspect, had it not been for the Doctor's commanding presence, Burn might have replied by asking what the blazes he was doing listening to conversations that were none of his business. But then, for all he knew, the guest before him could have been a judge or a retired admiral. And so, as I watched, Burn's expression moved from aggression to thoughtfulness and then prudence.

'Well now,' he said, 'that is quite a reasonable offer, that is. Not that it is of any importance, sir, but I suppose if you are headed that way.'

'I would be delighted,' said the Doctor, holding out his hand. 'It seems to me you have been ill used. And I will tell the man so if I do run into him, not that from what you say it seems very likely. Allow me to offer what should have been invested by the gentleman and I will exact it from him if I see him.'

With that he placed a couple of coins in the hand of the landlord, who gave a sly smile. Clearly money was one key to his heart. 'Well that is more than fair, sir. More than fair.' He was obviously well pleased with himself and handed over the packet. Then he went to a drawer in a recess behind the bar for the other letter. 'I certainly hope you do find him, and he reimburses you. If he should return here, I will redirect him to the Ship of course.'

Bell now had an excuse to make enquiries about Dr Mere, but he learned little more. Later, therefore, in my room, I was extremely anxious to see what the package contained and I was irritated when he utterly refused to open it. 'We take them on to the Ship in good faith,' he said. 'I wish to see no mark upon them.'

'But, Doctor,' I said, 'there may be vital information here. I grant you the forwarded letter is from the maid at the Quarter Moon but the other feels like a book.'

'You are almost right,' said Bell. 'In fact, it is a *Bradshaws Guide*. Indeed, I took it from your luggage.' I stared at him.

'My dear Doyle,' said the Doctor, 'you are no fool but sometimes your lack of concentration amazes me. It seemed obvious to me as soon as we arrived here what would be the fastest method to employ. So, while you were preparing for dinner, I put on my stoutest coat and advanced into the rain. I found a blacksmith two streets away and gave him the money with a parcel, asking him to get a boy to deliver it here. Then we took up our station. And at least we need waste no further time, for I am quite sure he will never return to pick up these trifles. Tomorrow, much as I expected, we make our acquaintance with the town of Dunwich.' Shortly after this he bid me good night and left the room.

We set out early the next morning, once Bell had telegraphed to the Ship to say we were coming. The weather had cleared a little and in some ways it would have been better to make the journey by boat for, though Dunwich was only about five miles south along the coast, the terrain was interrupted, not merely by the river Blythe, but by innumerable marshes. Indeed, the whole coast around here was a treacherous swathe of water and marsh, forcing us to ride inland and then come back to Dunwich via the huge forest that lay behind it.

The journey was arduous yet in its own way magnificent, affording spectacular views of the marshland, covered in many places by a beautiful ground mist, which was a ghostly pale grey in the early sunshine. Finally the road plunged into the forest, which in places looked to be thick and impassable. Emerging from it we came to more marshland and finally to Dunwich, which was altogether different from the place we had just quitted. Southwold had every appearance of being a respectable seaside town with a fishing industry and a town hall. Dunwich, or what remained of it after the depredations of the sea, was not only tiny by comparison but a much more unusual and forbidding community. There was a single main street where most of the houses faced the marsh and beyond it a track led to a broad shingle beach. Moving past the town were the treacherous cliffs, more woods and finally the heath.

The inn, whose official name was The Barn Arms, but was known to all as the Ship, was plain but comfortable and, because we had started early, we were there in time for lunch. But I could see Bell had no intention of taking any, indeed from the moment we arrived in Dunwich he seemed energised. Almost at once he established from the polite maid who showed us our rooms that the inn had not recently played host to any American traveller, and certainly not to a Dr Mere. There had been a few English gentlemen of the press, interested by the Jefford disappearance, but they had now departed and none of them matched our man in any obvious particular.

Other than that, she told us, the place had been very quiet, as it usually was at this time of year. Bell did take the trouble a few minutes later to check this information with the landlord, a solemn grey-haired man called Brooks who ran the place with great civility. But he was equally certain that nobody of that description or name had been here.

You might have thought such news would make the Doctor despondent. In fact it was as if he had anticipated it. Within a few minutes he had checked the visitors' book, to absolutely no avail, and was studying a map of the vicinity. At such times, more than anything he reminded me of a hound who has the scent of his quarry, though of course it was a scent unique only to him. He was galvanised, not merely by the atmosphere of this strange place, but by the knowledge that we had successfully traced Cream this far. In such circumstances, he no longer expected clues to be delivered to him, he knew he had to go out and find them.

I had a room right at the top of the inn and the Doctor urged me to change so we could do some walking. I followed his advice, and was emerging from my room, when I became aware of a large figure striding down the corridor towards me, singing in a deep baritone voice:

> There is a green hill far away,
> Outside a city wall,
> Where the dear Lord was crucified,
> Who died to save us all.

As the man stepped out of the shadows I could see he was big and in his forties, with a large head and an even larger growth of black beard. He had a stout stick and at his side was a big obedient retriever dog with sandy-coloured long hair who stared at me thoughtfully while his master broke off his song.

'Good afternoon,' he said. 'There is no use in your being here. You might as well pack your bags and return to where you came from. It is fine today and you should have an easy journey back. Perhaps I can be of service by arranging the coach?'

'Perhaps you could be of greater service by telling me who you are,' I said, looking him straight in the eye.

'Dr James Bulweather,' he said. 'And we have no need of journalists prying here. It is a matter for the citizens and perhaps the police but certainly not for the press.'

'That may well be the case,' I replied, 'but since I am not a representative of the press it is hardly my concern.'

He peered at me. 'Then what of your companion? I am told you have one.'

'His companion stands directly behind you, Dr Bulweather,' said a voice. Bell had climbed the stairs and stood there, leaning on his silver-topped cane as Bulweather turned. 'I am Dr Bell of Edinburgh University,' the Doctor continued. 'What can I do for you?'

Bulweather stood absolutely silent for a while. 'Why, a good deal, sir, a very good deal,' he said in changed tones. 'I confess I am astonished to see you.'

Now he turned back to me. 'And therefore I owe you, sir, an apology. I had heard two gentlemen were arriving and I made the mistake of assuming you were both jackals of the press. It is all we seem to get here now, in view of what has happened, though I am glad to say the interest has waned somewhat. But then the police are hardly better.' He stuck out a hand. 'So I shake hands with your colleague first, Dr Bell, for I came very close to insulting him.'

We shook hands vigorously and I felt the strength of the man, his hands were huge in size. I told him my name, which clearly meant nothing. Then he turned to the Doctor. 'And I take it as an honour to shake your hand now, sir. You see I am Dr Bulweather, the practitioner here and, though I never had the good fortune to be taught by you, for I studied medicine in Manchester, I have better occasion to know of all you do than most people. For you once assisted a poor cousin of mine in solving a crime, a Mrs Anne Pettigrew.'

'Ah,' said the Doctor with interest. 'I understand now, yes. Not a major affair but it had some difficult aspects. It was an Edinburgh robbery, Doyle, odd because almost nothing important was taken, which of course was not only its most puzzling aspect but in the end its solution. We are pleased to meet you, Dr Bulweather.'

'It is a wonderful thing for me,' he said eagerly. 'I was at my wit's end with this business and now you of all people walk into it. Why, it is a cause for celebration. You must both have dinner with me tonight. I will be able to give you a tour of the place and introduce you to anyone you wish. I would consider it an honour.'

'That would suit me admirably,' said the Doctor. 'I want to spend what is left of the day on the ground and then we will come on to you.'

Bulweather offered to accompany us some of the way, for he had a patient to see. And so it was that, a few minutes later, we were tramping beside him along a hillside leading to the cliffs and woodland and heath. The man had enormous vigour and took the path in great strides, his dog by his heel. I became aware he took risks too, for once or twice he was very near to the cliff's edge as he pointed out some of the local landmarks including his own house.

'It is not so grand a place, but my housekeeper is a good cook and we can talk over this business. Let us meet tonight. And I can promise you the freshest oysters and sea trout after your labours. I wish you luck with your mission.'

Then he left us, for he had patients to see at a cottage nearby as the Doctor and I continued up the path, which led into a tunnel of

trees. But before he disappeared inland with his dog by his side
Bulweather called after us to be careful. 'You will see why, but it is
worth seeing,' he shouted, and then he was gone.

After that, the Doctor and I plunged into the trees, with Bell in
the lead, occasionally slashing at the vegetation in our way with his
cane. After a little time as the trees began to thin we became aware
of the noise of surf far below to one side and of a great expanse of
sea beyond it.

Directly ahead of us now were the broken arches and tower of a
ruined church, two or at most three ivy-covered arches tottering at
a mad angle, the others already over the cliff. As I ventured to my
left to look at the drop, trying not to go too near the edge, I could
see the churning foam far below and what I took to be stone and
rubble that had recently fallen.

Around us were several graves. Yet it was obvious these graves
had once been here in large numbers, and one headstone close to
the edge was slanted and cracking and would surely crash into the
sea at the next landslide. There was about the whole spectacle a
sense of terrible impermanence, it spoke of the frailty of human
flesh and of the vulnerability of the world we inhabit and the
message was constantly underscored by the great crash of the tide
below.

The Doctor and I glanced at each other, for both of us recognised
this was a spot in which Cream would find the utmost inspiration.
Little wonder he had come here, the place would be like a beacon
to him. So much so that I almost expected him to step out from
among the broken gravestones.

Then I turned to the sea, for it was uncanny to think that where
I looked, under the waves of that ocean, lay the remains of a bold
seafaring port with its harbours and inns and dwellings. I thought
again of Poe's frightening poem and wondered if he referred to this
place. As I turned back, with the Doctor still staring out over the
cliff, I saw a shadow amongst the tilting gravestones. The shadow
moved and became a figure and it spoke my name.

For just a moment I was sure it was him. This was so much his setting, and who else knew my name? But as the figure walked forward, I saw I was wrong.

Before me was a tall man certainly but his hair was fair and he had a round face with penetrating blue eyes. He was smiling at us and he had a slight limp which made his head bob up and down as he walked. Bell had turned by now and he addressed him as well. 'You will be Dr Bell?' he said, and though it seemed unlikely in this spot, his accent betrayed the fact he was from London. 'And I gather from Dr Bulweather, whom I met on the path just now, that you are interested in this business of ours here.'

'I am,' said Bell. 'And may I ask your interest?'

It was a strange setting for such a conversation and we started to walk away from the noise of the surf to the path leading inland by which this man had come.

'My name, sir,' he said, 'is Derry Langton, Inspector Langton. I am in charge of the investigation here, which is hardly a boast since so far barely anyone will admit there is one.'

'I see,' said Bell with interest. We were back in the trees now, on a broad path leading up and west. 'Then I would be grateful to hear your views, for I intend to look at the Jefford house this afternoon. You are from Scotland Yard?'

Langton's smile vanished. 'I was at the Yard until a little over two years ago. Then I moved down here. You could say I retired, for I have had little to do until this business occurred. Of course, there is a local constable in the village but I was asked to look into it. Since it is not regarded as a serious crime, they have sent nobody from the Yard. But Dr Bulweather told me of your interest in the field and I'm prepared to show you the house, make of it what you can.'

'So what do you think, Inspector,' said the Doctor, surveying this man with interest as we walked. 'Is it a prank as the papers have indicated?'

'Why no, I take no view on that,' said Langton, perspiring a little as he walked. 'I am a newcomer here and bound to be a little critical but it is certainly a diversion. And there are entertaining aspects to the case, I grant you. The "howling man" that people claim to have seen. I tell you, sir, I would love to catch a glimpse of him.'

'Yet those who do show no signs of amusement,' Bell observed.

'If they are speaking the truth,' said Langton. 'If they are making it all up, of course, they will still claim to be scared out of their wits. It is part of the tradition.'

'Then you are not a believer in the legend?' I asked.

'No, I cannot say I am,' said Langton. 'There are tales, of course, we had them in the East End, but this seems to me too much of a pantomime. I am happy to take it seriously when there are serious matters to consider and as yet I am not sure there are.'

We had emerged from the shelter of the wood now and there were fields in front of us and then another huge swathe of trees, which marked the start of Dunwich forest. To our left the land sloped upwards into heath and we turned in this direction.

'So you are not treating it as a crime?' said the Doctor.

'What?' said Langton, his head bobbing furiously as we proceeded. 'Why of course I am, I take my work extremely seriously, if nothing else. For where would I be if it turns out more than it seems and I have done nothing. No, I have made all the investigations I can.'

As we walked, the terrain began to change and the wind got up. It was more exposed here as the fields gave way to heathland with outgrowths of gorse and dead grass. The forest was now only a hundred yards to our right and soon I saw we were approaching a large pool, with two great stones beside it. I stared down at the black and stagnant water, which looked to be quite deep, and then back at the forest with its trees swaying in the wind. In this wild place it was easy to picture the flickering torches reflected by the water with Mary Goddard standing on the far edge of this pool, so furious and defiant, her pursuers frozen with fear, until poor William Bowker stepped forward and became for ever the howling ghost.

It was certainly a memorable spot and Bell took a great interest in it. He circled the pool twice, making a minute study of the water's edge and all the vegetation around it. There is nothing in there, gentlemen,' Langton said. 'It is deep but we have dragged it and Jefford was not to be found.'

'Then what of the cliffs?' said Bell.

'Well now, they are used to seeing human remains at the bottom but I am quite sure we would have found a fresh one. The tide can be fierce but it was not so last week and there would be some trace.'

The far side of the pool was irregular with a curious loop of an edge, forming an inlet almost in the shape of an inverted V. It was noticeable there had been some disturbance of the ground here, as if someone had dug a hole and filled it in. Bell examined this.

'How recent are these marks?' he asked Langton, looking up.

'Yes, we noticed them when we searched,' said Langton. 'That was the first time. Nobody we asked had seen them before but there is nothing to indicate what they are, for nothing is buried there. We dug up the earth again to make sure.'

When Bell was satisfied he had seen everything, Langton led us away from the pool towards the forest. Soon, just before we reached the more dense woodland, he pointed out a track; at the end of it, stood an ancient red-gabled house, which was the property Jefford had inherited. Some sun was now filtering through the clouds and its rays caught the upper windows. I suppose the building must have dated from the early 1600s and it was surrounded by the remains of an orchard. But the fruit trees had not prospered in the shadow of the great wood, for they were gnarled and stunted, giving the whole prospect a very grim air. The house itself was in good repair and had some of the comforts of a modern dwelling but nothing could compensate for this sombre outlook.

'The place is very old, though it has been refurbished as you see,' said Langton as we approached the door and he put the key in the lock. 'They say The Glebe was a cleric's house in Elizabethan times, though the church it served is long gone. In recent years it belonged to Jefford's uncle, a lawyer hereabouts, but he had another dwelling in Saxmundham so he only used it on occasions. Jefford inherited it in the summer and had some work done but he spent most of his time in London. Even when he came down here he was often the worse for drink and stayed at the Ship so, as you will see, it has lacked company.'

We could observe what he meant as soon as he unlocked the door. It was not that the interior was bleak, for the place was quite substantial, and had some appurtenances of luxury. The sparse furniture was good quality, the floors were of polished wood and stone. And there were hangings of some curious Eastern design. But despite all this it seemed unwelcoming and there was about it a sense of desolation.

We walked through the wood-panelled outer hall where on one side a corridor led to a kitchen. On the other there was a staircase and the entrance to a larger room. Bell had a cursory look at the kitchen but it was bare and unrevealing. Rejoining us, he explored the desultory furniture and then the panelling, noticing at once one of the panels in the outer room was unlike the others, in fact it was a very discreet cupboard. Opening it, he found an extensive selection of brandies but nothing else.

Ignoring the stairs, we walked on into the larger room. This had little furniture and the flagstone floor was covered in a dark stain which spread almost all around the centre and in one place up to the wall. There was only a gloomy light from the windows, making the place somewhat dull, and, as I stared down, it was easy to understand the press's scepticism. For one thing the sheer size of the bloodstain was unnerving, for another now that it had dried, its dark colour looked less like blood than paint.

Low down on the far wall, just as we had been informed, the dark red had somehow been daubed in ugly yet distinct letters. Bell moved forward in an instant to stare at these and to make a record of them.

They were much as the newspaper had indicated, though the shape and texture was erratic.

I could distinctly make out the word *witch*. And then less easily the word *here*.

But there was another mark after the the two words, a half-formed letter it seemed.

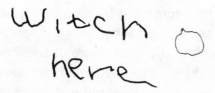

This letter was different from all the others in that it was unevenly drawn and oddly spaced. It was probably an O but a very hurried one or incomplete. Bell paid the greatest attention to this and to all the marks on the floor. In particular he paused a long time over two small and indistinct shallow imprints on the edge of the stain.

Then he circled the room again, staring at the letters and making a note of them in his book, but always he returned to the edge nearest the writing. Here the stain was different from the rest, for it was less smooth and its perimeter formed a series of V shapes.

As for the rest of the room, though once perhaps grand, for an engraved chair rail circled the wall, there was almost nothing in it. The walls were of plaster, a rarely used fireplace jutted out from the east wall. To the left of this a window gave on to that dank orchard which was another reason the illumination was so poor.

'And you have not touched anything?' asked Bell.

'Other than taking a sample of the blood, which proved inconclusive,' Langton replied.

'Yes, that is often the case,' said the Doctor quickly. 'Where was the sample taken from?'

The policeman pointed close to where he stood. 'From here. There is no proof it is human and as you know a pig has gone missing. A big one too, so it could easily have had this much blood. Jefford had no pet incidentally.'

The Doctor spent a long time studying the blood but at last he concluded his examination and moved into the corridor beyond the room. There was little trace of staining here, but it was dark and oppressive with narrow walls and a smell of damp. I have known many hateful corridors in my life. One led to my father's room in George Square in Edinburgh. Another was in a place called Abbey Mill, where a man had been trampled to death. By comparison, the corridor in The Glebe held no associations other than the mysterious bloodstain in the room, which gave on to it. And yet its atmosphere was horrible. There was a slight chill as you entered and somehow, partly no doubt because it was so narrow, the light hardly seemed to penetrate it. The plaster exuded a smell of damp and, though I made some pretence of observation, I found myself hurrying through the darkness as quickly as I could, almost as though the space were some dangerous railway tunnel.

Not that there was much to see in the next room. It seemed to be little used and was currently housing some surplus furniture including a small and uncomfortable-looking couch that lay against the wall.

Langton did not follow us and the policeman was still leaning on the wall of the larger room when we returned to it.

Now, once again, Bell addressed himself to the bloodstain, particularly its edge. After a few minutes, he looked up. 'And you are sure nobody has attempted to clean this?' he asked.

'Nobody has been here,' said Langton. 'I have visited once with a constable and once with some gentlemen of the press.'

'And yet,' said the Doctor, 'it is clear someone attempted to wipe this away, while it was still fresh.'

I could see exactly what he meant. The shapes at the edge of the stained area close to the fireplace were exactly what you would expect if someone had begun to scrub the floor with a cloth.

'So you think someone was trying to conceal it?' said Langton.

'Possibly,' said Bell. 'The work is quite meticulous, yet what would be the point of cleaning a small amount? They could never hope to remove it all and have not even attempted to do so.'

He had moved to another part of the floor that seemed clear of the blood. 'And see there are traces here too. The cleaner was more successful in this area.'

At last he walked away and looked out of the window. 'Tell me, Inspector Langton, you said you had made your investigations. Can you describe them?'

'Of course, Dr Bell. Firstly I looked everywhere outside the house for traces but found nothing. Next we went all round this house, we tapped walls, made absolutely sure there was no place of concealment but found only that brandy cupboard. Now, Jefford had last been seen on the first of the month, in the last hours of daylight. This was discovered on the second. It seemed to me, therefore, if a crime had been committed, it could only be on the night of the first of December, which of course is the anniversary of the hunt. I made enquiries throughout the village to ascertain if anything unusual had occurred or been seen. It seemed likely the crime was committed by a stranger but I also wanted to know where people had been on that night. It is a small parish so the task was not so hard.'

'Admirable,' said Bell. 'And what did you find?'

'Well,' said Langton, 'it was a bad night so most were indoors. However, those who were out could not easily conceal the fact, for their servants would know.'

'And were any out?' I asked.

'A few were,' said Langton. 'But I could easily establish where most of those were, the Ship as often as not. There is a widow here called Mrs Marner who was an actress in London, and moved here some years ago. She was at home but her maid was not there and would hardly say where she was. A young man, I must guess, and I cannot see it is more than that, for the girl is a timid thing.'

He hesitated, then went on. 'But there was another person who, well, I would just say his story did not satisfy me entirely. However, I may be wrong and, of course, we do not even know a crime was committed.'

'And who was that?' said the Doctor.

'You have met him,' said Langton, looking at Bell directly with a crooked kind of smile. 'In fact he introduced us, so to speak. He walks everywhere hereabouts and people worry he will fall off that cliff, for the wind can sometimes take you unawares.'

'Dr Bulweather?' Bell was interested. 'Was he not with a patient?'

'No doubt you can ask him yourself, sir, it is indeed what he says,' said Langton. 'I repeat, since there is no crime I can hardly point a finger. There is talk too of colourful associations in his past and that he has a mistress, but it may just be wagging tongues.' And it was clear, we would get no more from him.

Naturally we studied every interior in the rest of the house, but there was little more here to interest us. A comfortable bed in an upstairs room had evidently been used quite recently but otherwise, just as Langton said, the place seemed devoid of life.

Once we had satisfied ourselves of that, Bell's first wish was to talk to Colin Harding, the groundsman who had found the blood and also caught sight of Jefford and others the previous day. Harding, it seemed, was in the employ of a nearby estate owned by a local landowner called Sir Walter Monk, but since today was market day there was no prospect of finding him there.

We bid goodbye to Langton who now had other duties to fulfil, but promised to give us any further help we needed and took the most direct route, a woodland path that led away to the road. From here, it was a pleasant mile's walk back down to the village, which was bathed in a scarlet and gold sunset.

As we admired the view before us, the Doctor asked what I made of the room and the bloodstain.

'If it is Jefford's blood,' I answered, 'I can only suppose someone lifted the body and carried it out though what they did with it is open to speculation.'

'And yet,' ruminated Bell, 'there are no marks. It would have taken two men to carry him and surely there would have been traces. The imprints would be deep and Langton is no fool. Also, though it is fantastic to say it, there are distinct signs he moved himself.'

'What?' I said. 'How could he have moved?'

'Oh that is not in doubt,' said Bell. 'Though much else is in darkness. I made out the distinct imprint of a knee and the tip of a toe. He was crawling.'

About two hours later, having changed our clothes, we turned into
Dr Bulweather's drive under a bright winter moon. The Doctor had
told me nothing more, in fact he had said little since, and as so
often his answer to my question had only provoked in me a dozen
more urgent questions.

Bulweather himself greeted us at the door, his dog bounding
happily behind him. 'Ah come in, gentlemen. We dine alone but I
have some company for you to meet beforehand.' He pointed the
way through his brightly lit hall as a bustling middle-aged
housekeeper appeared in the doorway. 'It is all right, Mrs Harvey,
I will show Dr Bell and Dr Doyle in myself. You need not wait on
them.'

She greeted us and retired as we entered a large drawing room
with a huge wood fire. A dapper and well-groomed man with a
fleshy upper lip turned from the fire and was introduced as Angus
Hare, the other medical partner in the practice. I expressed my
astonishment that so small a place could support two doctors.

'We have our quiet times,' said Bulweather, 'but then we cover
quite a bit of ground. We do not restrict ourselves merely to the
village here.'

'And,' said Hare with a sardonic smile, 'we have a captive

audience. Other than the asylum back at Westleton Heath, which is a very different kind of speciality and one the people here do not trust at all, there is not a doctor for miles so although James does not like to indulge in it we can always vary our charges accordingly.'

'No,' said Dr Bulweather, 'we are not always in accord on that. But then there is no law that two doctors have to organise things exactly the same way.'

'Especially when they differ in circumstances,' said Hare without obvious rancour. 'Perhaps I would have greater scruples about what I charge if I were buttressed by family money. But I was left very little and must make my way however I can.'

'Now, Dr Bell,' said Bulweather, evidently not wishing to pursue this subject, 'I want to hear all about your work in Edinburgh. We are set in our ways here and no doubt you have much to tell us.'

The conversation moved on to Scottish medicine and the doctors plied Bell with questions. Hare was clever, I could see that, but he seemed altogether less interested in Bell's techniques than in his scale of charges. It was a relief when the door opened and Mrs Harvey showed in another guest and neighbour, a woman in early middle-age with very sweet fine features and dark exquisitely coiffured hair who was introduced as Mrs Leonora Marner.

It turned out she was the widow Langton had mentioned who had once been quite a successful performer in musical theatre in London, specifically the earliest productions of Richard D'Oyly Carte at the Royalty. But I found her manner utterly removed from anything I might have expected, indeed if Bell and I had been playing our games of deduction I would have put her down as the beloved wife of the local vicar. She spoke very quietly, and thought long and hard before she answered even the most ordinary of questions. But there was an enjoyment about her, a humour in her eyes, which was highly sympathetic and perhaps accounted for some of her former success. The others were courteous but it was left to me to talk with her and, since I decided she was of a somewhat nervous disposition, I did not enter into the Jefford matter but merely said Bell and I had been in London and were visiting the village in connection with some medical business. She told me she had been here for two years and had come to enjoy the isolation.

'I was worried,' she said, 'I would miss the bustle of London but I do not. After my husband died I found all I wanted was nature, the ability to play – for I have my piano – and a little comfort. So it has been a blessing, though I still miss him.' This was stated with simple conviction and I learnt in due course her husband was a senior officer who had died of a fever while serving his country overseas.

Later, when we were joined in general conversation with the others, she described something of Edinburgh, which she had visited as a child, and Angus Hare indulged at length in his own memories of the city, which held, I am afraid, little interest to me as they were mainly rhapsodies about the fine carriages his relatives owned and the splendour of his long-lost ancestral home. And then the guests departed to their own houses for their own meals and we sat down to dine with Bulweather.

'You must excuse me for showing you off,' said he, as his housekeeper served us plates of what proved to be the most wonderful soup of local fish in his long dining room. 'I knew Angus would welcome the chance to meet you and I felt Mrs Marner would benefit from a break in her solitude. She seems to me to live too lonely a life.'

'Yes,' said Bell, taking up the subject. 'She spends most of her time playing music on her piano, sometimes as much as four hours a day. She also reads a great deal and walks out most afternoons around two o'clock. Her young maid from London has served her well over the years but, though she is skilled and attentive, the girl is given to fits of absent-mindedness which concern her employer.'

Dr Bulweather's bushy eyebrows positively soared in astonishment. 'You have the better of me, sir. Did you meet with her earlier today?'

His question was a good one. I knew Bell had not overheard my conversation with Mrs Marner and later he had scarcely exchanged one sentence with the woman as Hare droned on about Edinburgh.

'Oh no,' said Bell as he took a last mouthful of soup. 'As Doyle will testify, I never set eyes on her before.'

Bulweather himself smiled now. 'Ah, so you are adopting your famous method. But how?'

'If you would think,' said Bell, 'I am sure you will deduce it. I have had occasion to study pianist's hands before in a case in Edinburgh and there was another celebrated affair in Bournemouth when a pianist strangled his wife. Mrs Marner's hands told me at once here was a pianist who practises regularly. As you would imagine, the skin becomes hardened exactly to the degree in which practice is applied. The reading? Well she carries glasses for reading and studied your books with interest, while she must by definition read a great deal of music, though I suspect much else. Fortunately she walked the short distance here, allowing me to see her outdoor shoes, which were of great interest. Their condition tells me she walks very regularly and they had been rained on recently, so she was out at two for it was the only rain we saw today and indicates her constitutional is taken after lunch. As to her maid, did you not notice the exquisite French plait in Mrs Marner's hair at the back? Such a thing could only have been done by young hands and would certainly be impossible to do oneself. Yet it is sophisticated and speaks to me of London. It also suggests an intimacy over some period though, from the state of the shoes which were only partly wiped, the girl is also given to fits of absent-mindedness, or I would have seen no traces of wet at all.'

Bulweather looked very impressed. 'And yet,' I intervened, 'there is surely a flaw in some of your logic. You deduced she was out in the rain but it might have been some urgent errand that compelled her. Why do you say it was the time of her regular walk?'

'I did not exclude that,' said Bell. 'It was certainly conceivable. But for any errand of the more mundane kind she would undoubtedly use her maid rather than get wet. And a social engagement hardly fits with what we have already heard of her solitary habits. Even if she did go out on a visit, she would surely have used an umbrella. No, she was caught in the rain and on balance, therefore, I feel it is safe to assume she takes her constitutional after lunch.'

'And you are right,' said Bulweather, 'right in every particular. It is a remarkable thing. Her maid is called Ellie and I think has always been with her since London. A shy girl who is sometimes a little too furtive for my liking.'

With this we addressed ourselves to some superb roast mutton. As we ate, Bulweather talked of Dunwich and his affection for the place. 'It has its own ways, and as unique a history as any place in this island. But there is an interesting enough collection of people here. In the winter it is wild, but I think all of us share a great love of its beauty and its legends.'

'And, tell me,' asked Bell as we finished our meal, 'are the legends taken seriously?'

'Yes,' said Bulweather. 'When I came here many years ago I was surprised how seriously. They are part of the fabric of the place and you cannot help respecting them. I have no idea if Mary Goddard was hunted in the way the story relates, but there is no doubt she existed and was once quite a powerful figure in these parts. Then the witch fever came, just as it did in so many other places along the coastline, and the people around here still talk guardedly of it and of witchcraft. We have mentioned Mrs Marner's maid, Ellie Barnes. That girl, for example, believes it, for she told me she would never dabble herself but is frightened of others who do.'

Bulweather now offered to show us his medical rooms and Bell gladly assented, though I was myself wondering why he was delaying any discussion of the Jefford case. 'Tell me,' said Bell as we got up, 'is that Mrs Bulweather?' The picture he was referring to showed a pretty fair-haired woman seated in the very room where we had been entertained before dinner.

Bulweather nodded. 'I lost her six years ago, just before Easter. Septicaemia. That used to hang in the room where it was painted but I placed it here, knowing I would see her and think of her at every meal where she used to sit opposite me. Though it is hardly necessary, for I think of her most of the time in any case.'

The Doctor nodded. 'It is nine for me and November. Peritonitis.'

Neither man continued the conversation but you could see it changed things a little for them. Bell looked at the country practitioner with a certain affinity as he led us to his consulting room.

It was an impressive place. His instruments were up-to-date, and his collection of medical books was extensive, including, I noted, a large number of works on nervous disorders. Bell showed his approval at once and Bulweather seemed pleased. 'When I came here from the city,' he told us, 'I expected it to be quiet and peaceful with diseases of an unspectacular kind. I could hardly have been more wrong. I begin to think, gentlemen, we should set up a new branch of our studies and call it Fen Medicine. For at first, before I came here, I was in the Fens. And though this is a little distance I found it much the same. There are many different kinds of ailments, some that I never saw in town. You may be amazed to hear it but the deprivation I have found is in some places far worse than anything you will see in the East End.'

Bell listened with interest. 'Then the isolation has its own peculiar effects.'

'Yes, indeed,' said Bulweather. 'And in places there is terrible sanitation, and ground poisons. Diphtheria is one thing I have come to dread, especially in the children. Now look here. This is unique and of my own devising.' And he pulled out a curious glass contraption and wiped off a little dust. 'If you suck on this pipette at one end you can remove the thick grey membrane that forms on the back of the throat or else—'

'Or else they choke,' cried Bell, seizing it with great excitement.

'I have done much the same, but you must be careful – swallow it yourself and your chances of infection are very high, as I can tell you from bitter experience.'

'Fortunately I have managed to avoid that,' said Bulweather, 'but I have had narrow escapes.'

'Well. I was not so lucky but it was more than twenty years ago,' said Bell. 'And I recovered. But I am astounded to learn of such things here.'

The conversation continued in this vein and I could tell Bell was impressed and I suppose this triggered his own doubts. For, as we left the surgery, he raised the Jefford matter at last.

'So you take this Jefford business seriously from all you were saying?' he asked.

'I do,' said Bulweather as we flopped into chairs in his large room, declining the offer of brandy. He poured himself a large measure and studied it ruminatively. 'I hope it is nothing, I hope it is Harding's pig, but I fear it may be what it seems.'

'Did you know Jefford?' asked the Doctor.

'Slightly,' said our host. 'Some time ago I had occasion to discourse with him in the inn where you stay. He struck me as vain and rash but not as a man likely to bother with a prank of this sort, which is why I take it seriously.'

'You have not seen him since?'

'I have not.'

'You have been to The Glebe, his house?'

'Never.'

'Did you witness anything on the night of the first?' said Bell quietly.

Bulweather hesitated. 'I was out but I saw nothing.'

'And where were you?' said Bell.

'Ah yes,' said our host. 'It was a patient, a child at Westleton. He had an inflammation of the kind I have described. I had not seen one for a while.'

'Ah, the pipette,' said Bell.

'Yes I used it to no ill effect. I was there for more than an hour. Then I returned. He is well now.'

'And who brought the message to you?' Bell asked.

'The child's father. He came here around eight.' Bulweather replied, taking a drink of his brandy. 'My housekeeper was away seeing her sister that night so I answered the door myself.'

'I see, but perhaps the father saw something on the road. If you give me the name, would you allow me to question him?'

It was a tactful way of verifying the alibi. 'Well to be truthful,' said Bulweather, not raising his eyes, 'the people are a little close. They asked me not to say what had happened. The condition is passed and, as a doctor, I must obey their wish for confidentiality, so I cannot help you.'

There was silence, punctuated only by a crackle from the log fire. 'But I assure you,' he went on, 'the father saw nothing unusual. So he cannot be of any help.'

'That is indeed a pity,' said Bell, who now fell to talking about other things including our host's retriever, which we were informed was very rare in these parts so he was greatly proud of it. It seemed Bulweather would be showing it off to some friends in Ipswich the following day and would not be back till early the next morning but he hoped to see us soon.

Later, trudging back under that moon, with the salt of the sea in my nostrils, I felt a little forlorn. We could have done with an ally in this strange town and I would have wished to like and admire our host. But it was obvious to me now, whatever the truth of the matter, Bulweather could not be trusted. Despite many attractive traits, his odd refusal to be forthcoming was highly suspicious. Perhaps, even his pretence of grief was some calculated act. Regrettably, just as Langton had told us, Dr Bulweather was not all he seemed.

## The Pale Monk

There was no need for the Doctor and I to discuss our doubts about Bulweather, for we both knew they were shared, but next morning I felt despondent as I stared from my window over the marshes. It was a fine cold day and a lonely black-backed gull was flapping his way seawards. Perhaps Cream had been here, the evidence suggested as much, but what was there to prove he was present now? He could easily be in London or on the high seas or anywhere, possibly all the richer for Jefford's money and laughing heartily at the thought of us.

I said as much to the Doctor in the inn's small dining room as we ate our breakfast. Bell had insisted we eat well, for he did not wish to concern himself with food for the rest of the day. There were rashers of thick bacon before me, besides two poached eggs, potato pancakes and local mushrooms. But I was hardly hungry.

'After all,' I said, 'we have no proof. He could be anywhere.'

The Doctor continued eating for a moment. 'In London,' he said at last, 'when we were hunting down Hanbury, you had certain feelings of his presence, feelings I will admit I derided. Tell me, do you not feel him here? For I do.'

This was unexpected. The Doctor was rarely given to admitting to instinct before reason. 'I do not know. But we have no proof he is still here whatever you may feel.'

He smiled at this as he laid down his fork and knife. 'Then our roles are reversed. Good. That could be useful for both of us.' I was about to interject but he went on. 'No, I am not being entirely illogical. You see, as an investigator I am presented here with a puzzle and what I strongly suspect is a crime. You will recall I was mistaken once in Edinburgh about animal blood, believing it was human. It is impossible to be sure but I do not think I am mistaken here. If we were to accept the newspapers' view that this is a prank, surely by now Jefford would have come forward? It is hardly the publicity-seeker's way to allow the sensation to fade away before revealing himself. So I stick with the assumption there has been violence, though I can make no assessment as yet even as to the victim. And, moreover, we have clear indications of Cream's involvement, not least the description of the man seen with Jefford shortly before he died. We also have evidence that Cream was after money and that Jefford had money.'

'But he may have taken it and left,' I protested, 'and be laughing at us from far away.'

'Laughing even more heartily, Doyle, if we do not reach a successful conclusion here. What you say is possible certainly, but it is equally true we can only move forward at all by unravelling the mystery at hand and exposing any misdeed. Not only is that our duty, but I am glad to say I have a little more than mere instinct to tell me matters are not as simple as you are speculating. We have not, after all, found Jefford with his brains blown out and the empty sacks of gold by his side. There is much more here, not least the mysterious third companion, which tells me we must pursue it as urgently as we can.'

About an hour later we had walked up the hill and could see Greyfriars House, Sir Walter Monk's large and comfortable farm, which lay in considerable grounds about half a mile north-east of Jefford's. I call it a farm because people often referred to it as such, but really it was more of a small manor house with a pillared portico and a grey paling of split oaks in a grass clearing.

Langton had sent word to Sir Walter that we would be calling and a grave manservant admitted us to a large hallway, which went right up to the roof with a long gallery above. The hangings were heavy and the atmosphere was hushed. Bell stated our business at once and it seemed we were indeed expected as he led us through a door and corridor and then stopped before another door which was closed.

'Sir Walter has asked,' said the manservant in sepulchral tones, 'that your conversation is conducted in as quiet and polite a fashion as possible. He has a minor hearing condition which makes loud sound intolerable to him.'

The Doctor nodded and the door was opened on to a dark but extremely warm room, almost as warm as a hothouse in summer. There was only a little light streaming into the place from the half-open shutters but it was luxuriously furnished and, as the manservant retreated, we walked forward across a thick carpet. There was a sofa and a chair but the room was L-shaped and we could see nobody until we advanced.

And then we came to the main area of the room and before us was a vast polished dining table in front of a huge flickering fire. There was a pale shape at the end of this table and I saw a white hand with a pen in it and realised that the shape was a man, who stared at us. He was pallid and somewhat enfeebled, with thick beautifully groomed silver hair, indeed he looked more like my idea of a neurotic French marquis than an English landowner. Bell was as surprised as I was.

'Sir Walter,' he said by way of introduction, and the man put out a restraining hand, though we had not forgotten the manservant's injunction. 'We are sorry to intrude. I am Dr Bell and this is my colleague, Dr Doyle. We are here because we wish to interview your groundsman, Colin Harding.'

Sir Walter nodded and now spoke. The voice though certainly

languid was not as feeble as I had expected. 'Ah yes, Langton informed me you are interested in the Jefford business, it is a tiresome affair. But of course you may interview Harding. Have you a view on the matter, sir?'

'Not as yet,' said Bell.

'That is wise,' said Monk. I saw now the pen in his hand was for sketching and I tried to see what he drew. It looked from here like a face, but I could not make out the details. Bell had taken this in too and was staring at the table beside him, as Monk continued in his languid way studying us both carefully with beady eyes. 'I myself, as you will observe since you are both doctors, live on the sufferance of the almighty. I endure what you might call a certain morbid acuteness of the senses. No doubt you would call it other magical names in your medical books, though to me all of them are like witch's runes themselves.'

'Do you think the witch's rune in the tale is real?' said Bell. 'Do you think Jefford found it as he claimed?'

'Oh, Jefford was a fool,' said Monk. Then he stopped and corrected himself. 'Or should I say "is" a fool, for I know no more than you if he is still alive. I believe, though, Harding was a help to Jefford when he arrived here. He did him some service – I have no idea what. I rather think Jefford may have taken advantage of that help and frightened the man with his stories. All I know is Harding claimed he may have seen a rune. No doubt if he did it was some party trick.'

'But what do you understand by a rune, Sir Walter?' said Bell with interest.

'Oh, it is something they talk of hereabouts. If you are in possession of it within a specified time, usually a month, you will die.'

'Did Jefford tell you of finding the rune?' asked the Doctor.

'No, I barely knew him,' said Monk.

'Tell me, do you live here alone, Sir Walter?'

'Apart from my servants,' came the reply. 'Of course, much of the time I am in London where I have a tolerable house and many friends. I could not stand the country life too long at one time.'

I am sure Bell wanted to ask more but Monk tugged at a ribbon, which was carefully placed to snake under the carpet and arrive just at his chair. Somewhere outside, a bell quietly tolled. 'Now you must go about your business and I must go about mine. My man-servant will show you out.' And indeed the manservant was there almost before we could reply. He had evidently been given instructions to stand by.

'Sir Walter's physical condition is the least interesting thing about him,' commented Bell with irritation as we walked the short distance to the outhouse where Harding would be found. 'It is ninety-five per cent affectation and five per cent dissipation. Yet in other respects he is certainly worthy of our attention. Here is a man with London connections as well as a large house to service, and, for all his protestations, he was not alone in that room before we entered. There was another exit and someone had been there sitting at that table with him. Fortunately its surface is highly polished and I saw the clear imprint of a glass at the place opposite him where he could not possibly reach.'

Having been intrigued by Harding's employer, we had high hopes for the interview ahead, but in the event it proved far from satisfactory.

We found Harding, a leathery-skinned, clean-shaven man of very broad build in a nearby outhouse sharpening an axe at a lathe. Evidently he knew we were coming, for he grunted acknowledgement at Bell's introduction, but still glared at us and declared he had told all he knew to the police. When pressed, he went over it again. He said Jefford was a gentleman who had treated him well enough. Harding had given Jefford a little help now and then, for he had no servants and Sir Walter permitted it. But he had never seen any company in his house. He had, however, seen Jefford and two other figures in the twilight of early evening on the first of December. They had not seen him for he was in the woods searching for the sow that had left its pen. He overheard nothing, for the men walked in silence while one of the figures was masked by the trees, Jefford being the nearest. When pressed on the other figure he had seen, he would only agree he was tall and good looking, that he had a considerable quantity of thick dark hair and that he had never set eyes on him before or since.

'How would you describe him apart from that?' Bell persisted.

'A gentleman,' said Harding reluctantly. 'Well dressed, no, heavy but I think he'd have run well in a race. There was a strength about him.'

Bell nodded, for that sounded like our man, but he could get little more. He went on to confirm Harding had happened to pass the cottage the next day and knocked on the door, wishing to ask Jefford if he had seen his pig. He got no answer and, after entering and finding the bloodstain, had gone to raise the alarm.

'But I have no more to say of it, sir. I have told all I know more than once and if ye will be kind, there is work for me to do.'

'Of course,' said Bell, 'but I have one more question. A simple one. Have you seen the rune?'

The man scowled. 'And who would be saying that?' Bell would not answer. 'For anyone who does is a liar. I ha' no wish to talk of such things.'

'But you believe in them?' the Doctor urged.

'I cannot say,' he answered fiercely, his eyes glittering. 'They are nowt to do with me. I keep awa' frae all of that and pay no regard to what the rest say. Now if you please, I must get on.'

And so the interview ended. Here was our principal witness and little more could be extracted from him than we had seen in the newspapers. It was clear Bell had found it frustrating and, almost as if to vent this frustration, he returned to the area around Jefford's house where we spent long and what seemed to me fruitless hours, searching the ground. 'Obstructive, yes,' said Bell afterwards, interrupting his silence to answer my question about Harding as we walked back through the woods in the direction of the town, 'but frightened too. Now why?'

There was a sudden noise from the trees beside us. A rush of movement and a fluttering. We whirled round and could see a figure. It had just grasped something in his hand. It came closer and we saw it was a boy and, in his hands was a live bird, which he held tightly. He was about twelve and there was a brightness in his eyes as he clasped his hands fiercely shut. He did not seem to notice us.

'Tommy,' came a shout from behind. 'Tommy, where have you gone to?' A man was coming along the road, dressed in smart country walking clothes. 'Where is my wee Tommy?' He saw us and smiled. 'Good afternoon, gentlemen. Have you seen a boy?' And then he caught sight of him and smiled broadly. The boy had squeezed his hands shut and the fluttering was still. He looked down at what he held with pleasure.

'Ah there is my boy, it is my son Tommy. What mischief are you doing there, Tommy?' he asked, beaming with pride. He had a very fleshy face and a florid complexion. 'I fear I am guilty of failing to introduce myself,' he said as he turned to us. 'My name is Edward Norman, I am the local solicitor and this is my oldest boy, Tommy.'

We told him who we were and he nodded vigorously, ringing his hands. 'Yes, I heard from Inspector Langton you were here, helping us with our mystery. Well, it is only small as befits a small community like ours. Now let us see what poor dear Tommy has got for us. Show, Tommy.'

The boy gave a little smile, which I thought lacked warmth, and opened his hands to reveal what he was carrying. It was a thrush but it was no longer alive. He had rung its neck and the head flopped at a horrid angle. Yet his father's beam never faltered.

'Ah, Tommy, you are a very clever boy. He has a wonderful collection of dead birds, don't you, Tommy? Well, this is splendid. You must come and dine with us, gentlemen. Nella would be only too pleased to see you. Oh and I told Inspector Langton today after hearing of your visit that we made a small discovery of our own last night. Tommy here has a little story. He saw a figure that evening in which everyone is so interested by the pool, did you not, Tommy?'

The boy nodded, though he looked troubled. The father wrung his hands again beaming. 'Ah yes, he gets everywhere and on that night he had gone up there in search of birds. Is that not so, Tommy? You saw a man.'

'Did you see his face?' said Bell without ceremony.

The boy shook his head. 'Just that he was looking at the ground, is that right?' His father smiled anxiously. 'He was staring at the ground by the pool but then Tommy came away and was not seen. Of course, it may be nothing at all. He would not know the man again.'

The boy shook his head to show us this without question.

'Are you sure it was only one man?' said Bell with interest.

'He said there was another figure in the shadows, but I think it *was* just shadows, was it not, Tommy? Well, we must go back but you will come and dine. It would be a fine thing for us and for Nella and for Tommy.' He wrung his hands again. Then he raised his hat, took the little boy with his grisly relic by the hand, and was gone.

I have no idea what the Doctor made of this strange duo. He was lost in thought afterwards and clearly not in any mood for conversation. As soon as we had reached the inn, he went to his room without a word.

This left me with little to do. I wondered whether to go and seek out Langton but doubted the Doctor would favour such an action and it was already getting dark. So I decided to read what I could about the history of this strange place and picked up a tome in the inn's private sitting room, which was set aside for guests. This was not nearly so comfortable a space as its equivalent at the Quarter Moon. Indeed it was little more than a fireplace with three armchairs, but that concerned me not at all as I settled down to what was certainly an extraordinary story.

In 1200 the town of Dunwich had been one of medieval England's wealthiest ports, with thriving fishing and wool industries. The chroniclers accorded it fifty-two churches, chapels and hospitals, a King's palace, a Bishop's Seat and, of course, a busy harbour with numerous wharves and quays. None of this has survived. The battle with the sea began in the middle of the thirteenth century, when various storms breached the harbour and its walls. Soon after this, the lower town was taken, inaugurating a pattern of moral and physical decline. There seemed almost to be a tradition of dark happenings in Dunwich at Christmas time for it was during the Christmas of 1327 that one of the worst storms raged and literally hundreds of houses were submerged. The town's battle against the hungry sea was both courageous and haunting, as was the notion of what now lay under the sea beside it. I was astonished to think of all these churches and dwellings and towers at the bottom of the ocean, a veritable Atlantis right on the edge of England. And of course the most famous of all Dunwich legends, more famous even than her witch, was the notion that on a stormy night you could hear the sound of the old town's bells ringing out under the ocean.

A sound made me look up and I was startled to find I was not alone. A smartly dressed young woman had entered the room in a state of slight agitation. 'Oh I am sorry,' she said, 'I did not wish to disturb you.'

'Not at all,' I said quickly. 'This room is for all the guests. My reading is finished, in any case. I must join my friend.'

'No please,' she said, and then stopped as if a little uncertain. She wore a red trim jacket which complemented her fair hair but her face was sad. 'There is no need to leave. I know some people do not feel it is right for a single woman to travel and visit an inn on her own, but sometimes it is essential . . .' She broke off. 'I am sorry if I ramble. I must introduce myself. I am Charlotte Jefford.' She could tell at once by my expression the name meant something to me. 'Oh yes,' she said. 'I see you have guessed my mission. I have come today hoping against hope I will find some trace of my poor brother.'

At that point the maid arrived with some tea she must have ordered and, after further introductions, we sat down. I was not quite sure how much to reveal of our own mission and therefore merely told her that I was here with another medical colleague on some private business but that this man had taken an interest in the Jefford case and talked to the police and she might find it very useful to meet him. At this, her eyes fairly lit up and she gave a smile that would have melted most hearts.

'That would be very kind.' She drank some tea and seemed to be making her mind up about something. 'I am not pretending, Dr Doyle, that my brother was a very nice man.' She broke off. 'And here I say "was", when I hope he may yet be alive. But some people tell me I should assume the worst and so I must say again that while he was in some ways not a very good man, he certainly does not deserve a fate such as this. He could be foolish, he could be vain, he could be impetuous and even thoughtless. But I swear he was not wicked.' Her eyes were wide with emotion. 'And I must know the truth. For I think of it a thousand times an hour and I tell you there is nothing in the world worse than this uncertainty, this never knowing what the future will hold. Nothing could be worse, I swear it.'

We talked in this vein for some time. I suppose a year or so earlier I would have accepted her appeal for sympathy without the slightest question. But it so happened there had been a matter in Southsea in which I was to some extent deceived by just this kind of charitable appeal and I was also aware of how uncertain we were of our ground in this whole affair. Therefore, I tried hard to see if I could detect anything artful about Charlotte Jefford but I could not. There was nothing to suggest she was anything other than a worried and loving sister. After a time, the Doctor entered the room, looking for me, and I introduced them.

Rather to my surprise, he showed only a degree of interest. Of course, he was civil and he scrutinised her appearance as he ascertained when she had last seen Jefford (something I had conspicuously failed to do). Evidently she had not encountered her brother since the funeral of their uncle some months earlier and knew little of his London acquaintances, so it seemed unlikely she would have anything valuable to convey about his recent companions. After this the Doctor expressed his hopes that her brother would be found safely, and offered to send her news as soon as he had any to send. I thought this was an odd thing to say to someone who had just arrived but she thanked him gratefully enough and then we left her.

## THE HOWLING MAN

It turned out that Langton had arranged for us to make an early-evening visit to Balneil, the forester who claimed to have seen the spectre of the howling man in the woods. He lived close by and within a short time we were sitting comfortably in the man's parlour.

I suppose I had expected some boastful drunkard or else a rambling nervous type who would jump at the slightest shadow. Balneil was nothing of the kind. He was a burly robust man with a down-to-earth manner and a quiet smile. 'I know how foolish it sounds, sirs, I am aware of that but I saw what I saw and I know what I saw.'

'Then will you tell us as simply as you can?'

'Of course, sir. I had been doing some coppicing on the last day of November quite near to the pool. I used to tend a spot for Lord Coates called Broomgreen Covert which is near Halesworth before I moved here, so I am not one of those who takes much notice of the superstitions, but I love it for all that, and Sir Henry has been kind enough to make use of my skills. That night we talk of there was a moon and I took advantage of it to work on a little. Then I gathered up my things to walk the track back here.'

Bell nodded with great interest. 'I understand, please proceed.'

'I know it well,' continued the man, 'and there was nothing

different about it that night, which was fine. Of course it is a ghostly kind of place if you are that way of thinking, but I don't see ghosts, I see trees. And I was studying the trees and thinking how it might be good to extend the path a little. And that was when I heard it.'

'Heard what exactly?'

'Well, sir, as I've said, I never took no notice of such things. But I don't ever want to hear the noise again. It went through your head, a great wailing, almost like an animal. And it came from off the track.'

'What did you do?' said Bell.

'Well, I stopped at once, and it came again. And I'll admit I was a little afraid but I reasoned it might be someone who was in trouble, so I turned off the path in that direction. I went a little way and suddenly, about thirty yards away through the trees, I see something pale. I got a bit closer and I lost it and then suddenly that's when I saw it properly, there in a space between two oaks. Only a pale shape at first but then you could see it was human. Pale skin, and it was crawling. It was horrible, sir, the way it crawled. And then I saw the head, a big head, and, while I watched, it howled. Like a madman it howled. But then it was back in the shadows.'

'And what did you do?' Bell asked gently.

'I stopped where I was. But then I thought I must try and go after it. So I walked a little but saw nothing. And then the sound came again, that awful sound, but far away now. I could hear nothing near me. So I turned and came back as fast as I could.'

Balneil's face was alive with the memory and it was impossible for me to believe he could be dissembling. How many men, I wondered, who boast of their disbelief in phantoms, would have acted as courageously as he did? Certainly the Doctor was impressed. 'Thank you,' he said. 'That is very clear to me. Tell me, you say the noise was far away when you heard it after you had seen it. How far?'

'Half a mile, at least. And no living man could have covered the distance in the time, I would swear it.'

'No,' said Bell. 'Well, whatever it was you saw, Mr Balneil, you are very brave. I congratulate you.'

Outside, the wind was getting up and the weather was changing for the worse. As we walked back through the darkness to the inn, I longed to ask the Doctor what he made of this strange story. Could Balneil be guilty, not perhaps of dishonesty but of self-delusion or embellishment? Moonlight can play tricks on the mind and I once knew a woman in Edinburgh whose chain-rattling ghost proved only to be a wind-blown curtain in a room with a noisy water cistern. But Bell was still in no mood for conversation. His replies to my questions were monosyllabic at best so I knew not to persist and not so long after a silent dinner of various cold meats, which compared rather meagrely with our feast of the previous evening, he retired to his room, bidding me an early goodnight.

It was not yet very late and I returned to the sitting room and my book. Once again, I became immersed in the heroic struggle of those men of Dunwich against the sea. I learned of the apocalyptic final storms of 1740, when the water broke all boundaries and began to run rampant through the streets of the town. Outside, as a suitable accompaniment, the weather was becoming fierce. The wind howled in the chimney and rain battered the glass as I read of hundreds drowned on one single night in the great battle to secure the last sea wall. Then suddenly the door opened and the inn-keeper, Brooks, stood there, a look of concern on his face.

'I am sorry to bother you, Dr Doyle, but I am a little worried.'

I got to my feet at once. 'Is the Doctor all right?'

'Oh, Dr Bell, why of course. I imagine he is asleep. No, it is Miss Jefford, sir. I knew you took tea with her earlier. And she went off some hours ago to look at her brother's house. But she had no key so she cannot shelter there. She said she merely wished to walk up to it and back.'

'Good heavens,' I said. 'And she is still out?'

'Yes, she has not returned. I would go after her myself, but I do not like to leave when there is no other help here. I am trying to arrange the village cab to go up there but they think it is away in Saxmundham.'

I interrupted him at once. 'No of course, I will try to find her. I know the path.' And I ran upstairs to get my coat.

Within a few minutes I was in the elements, making my way hastily along the road to where the path forked off through the trees to the pool and Jefford's house. It was now the foulest of nights and I bent forward against the rain and wind, wishing the landlord had informed me of this development earlier. I had decided not to disturb Bell but, even so, I would have been grateful for some company. Fortunately, there was little real navigation to be done and the landlord had provided me with a lantern but, of course, the journey seemed much longer in such conditions than it had in the daylight. I did not see a soul and, despite my heavy coat, I felt as if I were soaked by the time I reached the turning off the road.

I was deliberately not thinking about all the stories I had heard of this place and the enemies who might lurk here. This was just about feasible on the high road but it was far harder when I turned into those trees. In the road the lamp had given out a solid beam, here its light merely flickered and dispersed amongst a myriad trees, creating ghastly shadows. I had hoped the forest track would afford some protection from the elements, but the wind howled around me with a vengeance and the rain was still intense.

Eventually, after what seemed like hours, I could make out the shape of the Jefford house ahead of me. It was then I heard the sound. At first I thought it was an animal, perhaps a rabbit caught in a trap a little way off. But the cry rose ferociously in volume, a great howl that made my ears ring. There was something utterly uncanny about that noise – a quality neither human nor animal, yet ferocious. Until, quite as suddenly as it had begun, it stopped.

Despite the loudness, I had a distinct impression whatever had made the cry was a little way off. But it seemed I was wrong, for now I could hear it thrashing through the trees to my right. Whatever it was, it moved in a circle and seemed to be breaking branches as it went.

I forced myself to enter the wood in the direction of this sound. A branch snapped and I moved cautiously towards it, hoping I could be as brave as Balneil. But foolishly I failed to see a dead tree stump, my foot caught it and I stumbled, only just keeping hold of my lamp.

There was no time to straighten up. Suddenly the noise changed direction and came straight at me. And then the thing was upon me, its breath rasping out, its body hitting me so hard I was almost winded. But even as I caught hold of it, I knew at once my mistake. For below me was a face, the terrified face of Charlotte Jefford.

# THE FIGURE AT THE CROSSROADS

'Thank God you are here,' she burst out. 'Oh, thank God you had the light. For I have seen the howling thing. It was crawling. It crawls through the wood.'

I managed to calm her a little, though I have no idea what words I used. She was exhausted and somewhat cut by branches, but after a time she was able to walk with me to the road. Considering her condition and the weather, I did not think it fair to ask more of her than that and would have sought shelter at the nearest cottage while I arranged for transport. But by great good fortune the village cab had returned and Brooks had sent the driver along the road to look for us. I have never been so glad to see a country cab in my life and together the driver and I managed to get Miss Jefford into it.

The landlord stood in the doorway of the inn, relieved to see us, and within a short time Dr Bulweather had come to offer what help he could. He confirmed my own diagnosis that Miss Jefford was suffering only from shock and exhaustion, besides some minor cuts, and counselled that some restorative and a night's rest would probably be all that was needed. Naturally, he was curious about the circumstances, but I merely explained to both him and the landlord that she had got lost in the woods and become frightened.

I had already told Miss Jefford as we travelled back in the cab that, both for her own sake and in order not to cause undue alarm, it would probably be better for her not to say any more about what she had seen until the morning, a plan she accepted at once. Yet it was during this conversation that, for the first time, some doubt entered into my mind about her story.

Perhaps this was dishonourable, since I had heard the noise too, but, beyond that single howl, I had seen nothing and heard nothing except her. Naturally therefore, following the usual precepts of the Doctor, I was beginning to wonder if it were possible, even remotely, that she could have made that noise. But when we were back at the inn, some of these doubts disappeared. She was certainly far too pale and troubled to be acting.

Soon she was asleep and I went to bed myself after drinking a brandy, courtesy of the grateful Brooks, who could see perfectly well I was exhausted myself. Even so, I awoke early and sent a maid to ascertain that Miss Jefford was all right. She returned to inform me the lady was sleeping peacefully and I went to meet the Doctor for breakfast.

Bell already had a version of the previous night's events from the landlord and, when I had established that we were not overheard, I told him the true facts. He questioned me in detail of course, most specifically about the exact location where I had encountered her. 'A pity you did not see more, I wish you had gone out earlier,' he observed when I was finished.

I felt a little stung and was on the point of saying this was an easy enough remark to make, sitting at a well-stocked breakfast table in a warm inn room. 'But I am very glad you asked her to keep it to herself,' he added, perhaps feeling he had been a little harsh. 'That much was vital if we are to come to any understanding.' And it was the nearest he came to praise.

Miss Jefford was indeed much better when she awoke but agreed to spend the day quietly in her room, where Bell interviewed her in, I will admit, a highly sensitive and sympathetic manner. It appeared that she had gone up to the house well before the storm started while it was still light. Langton would have gone with her but he had been called away to some dispute between two farm labourers so she walked out on her own.

However, after a delay, she had misjudged the distance, and reached the place far later than intended. Bell asked her with great politeness, which I knew perfectly well concealed a certain impatience, what she had intended to do there, given that she could not even go in.

'I just wanted to go to his house, Dr Bell. It is foolish, I suppose, but I must hope to find some trace of him.' She went on to describe how, upon reaching the house, she had sensed that someone was inside. She was sure she could hear sounds but had peered in and seen nothing. Then, with the light fading, she thought she heard movement in the woods at the back of the house. Bravely, she walked a little way in, comforting herself with the thought that, once she had seen what it was, she could make a direct line back to the track and then the road.

The noise, however, receded a little and she followed it. Eventually it stopped and then came another noise, the noise I had heard, only repeated. This frightened her so much she started to run away, but it was dark now and she had no idea where she was going. What was worse, at some point the noise seemed even nearer and then she caught sight of the figure, which sounded very like Balneil's description. It was crawling and naked, though Miss Jefford described its head as huge and ferocious.

After this, she panicked and ran around in the wood and the darkness with no idea at all of where she was. Soon she was completely lost and despaired of finding safety until finally she stumbled into me.

The Doctor extracted all this carefully and considerately before leaving her with the hope that once she had rested she would be fully recovered from her ordeal. 'I would ask only one thing of you, Miss Jefford. Please do not venture upon such an expedition on

your own again whatever the circumstances, is that understood?'
She agreed but she had one last question.

'What I saw,' she said, 'it is what the forester saw before they
found my brother's blood. And is it not said in the legend of this
place that always it signifies a death?'

'There are many legends here,' said Bell. 'Some no doubt
true, some invented, some also the product of coincidence and
overworked imagination. I would ask you now to think of the
present, for that is what must concern us.' And the interview was
closed.

Later that morning we visited Mrs Marner and the door of her
elegant home was answered by Ellie, the maid, a small dark
woman with pixie-like pointed features who seemed somewhat
nervous of us, looking away when Bell tried to engage her in
conversation.

Mrs Marner stood in her comfortable drawing room beside a large
globe, something Bell commented on as she welcomed us.

'Oh yes,' she said, 'I have some affection for geography. When I
was a performer we would play in other countries, most notably on
the continent, and I like to look at this and remember the cities
and the people.'

We sat down in front of a fire where Ellie brought us tea, but the
maid would not look at us, and she was chided gently by Mrs
Marner for her rudeness.

'Ellie, you must not look away. These are friends of mine.' She
bobbed at this and gave a little smile but, even so, she could hardly
get out of the room quickly enough.

'She has been acting strangely lately,' said Mrs Marner in her soft
tentative voice. 'I do not know why, but I believe the Jefford
business has put her out of sorts. Ah, this is Lady, the other
member of our family. In fact, she belongs to Ellie.'

A large well-groomed black cat with some small ginger stripes
had slunk into the room and came quickly to Mrs Marner, who
fondly stroked her arched back. But when her hand went a little

higher, Lady flinched and moved away. 'Like her mistress, she is not quite herself,' Mrs Marner added.

'Tell me, Mrs Marner,' said Bell now that the subject had been introduced, 'did you ever encounter Oliver Jefford?'

'I walk a good deal in the afternoon after my practice,' she said, sipping her tea. 'On occasions I walk up to the heath and I met him in the road. That is all.'

'Alone?' asked Bell quickly.

'Alone both times, I believe. We merely bid each other good day, I doubt he even knew my name.'

This was disappointing. 'And you were here at home on the first night of December?' asked Bell.

'I was,' she said, 'but . . .'

'Yes?' Bell waited.

'But Ellie was not, she went out.'

'Do you know where?' Bell asked.

'She did not tell me the next day but I would not be surprised if . . . it were to see Colin Harding.'

'The groundsman who found the blood?' Bell's eyes were on hers.

'Yes, Sir Walter's groundsman. I believe they have seen each other from time to time.'

'You mean they are courting?'

'There is not much scope for courting here, Dr Bell, and I do not like to pry into Ellie's affairs. They are her own and she has served me well. I know she has taken tea with Harding in the servants' kitchen of Monk's house. I also know she has been upset by this business. She is very superstitious.'

'A believer in witchcraft?' Bell asked.

'Oh, she has many queer fancies. I had hopes Colin Harding would put them out of her head. He is a practical man and I talk to him occasionally, only now he seems preoccupied. Oh, but Ellie did tell me one thing.'

'Yes?' said Bell.

'I know she passed Dr Bulweather that night. She said he had his scarf on and his hat pulled down as if he did not wish to be recognised. And no dog. But it so happened she saw him first and stood out of his view and watched him and she is sure it was him.'

'Did she say where this was?' Bell was not bothering to hide his interest.

'At the crossroads above the town, but she did not see which way he went, for she did not follow him but hurried home.'

Bell's next question seemed to me a *non sequitur*. 'Tell me, Mrs Marner,' he said, 'have you ever had occasion to play or perform locally?'

'Locally, good heavens no, Dr Bell. I retired completely when I married and there is no theatre of repute for miles.'

'So where is the nearest theatre?' said the Doctor, watching her carefully.

'There is a low music hall at Lowestoft, I believe. But I was not a music-hall artist, Dr Bell.'

'Of course, I merely wished to be sure.'

After this the conversation returned to other things, and soon Bell pointedly insisted that Mrs Marner would wish to be proceeding to her music room so we were shown out.

In the hall, Dr Bell explained to Ellie we were investigating certain matters with regard to the mystery of Mr Jefford's disappearance and wished to know if she had seen anything while she was out on the night he disappeared.

The girl looked quite frightened and blushed but would only shake her head.

'And can you not say where you were, Ellie?' said Bell with as much kindness as possible.

Ellie merely stammered. 'I would rather not say, sir. I was just out walking.'

Bell did not press her and we left. Outside, the weather seemed to be following the same pattern as before. The mist on the marshes had dispersed and clouds were looming over the horizon.

'We must talk again with Harding and this time rather more forcefully,' said Bell grimly. 'I would also like a word with Dr Bulweather. That crossroads could have taken our friend up to the pool and to Jefford's house but there are other directions too.'

The rain had started again and we were already a little damp by the time we came close to the inn. But the Doctor had no intention of lingering there. After we had collected the necessary clothing, he insisted on going back up to Jefford's house and the pool in order to talk to Harding and re-examine the ground. 'Whatever was seen up there last night, it must have left traces,' he said, 'and so must Charlotte Jefford.'

We made our way quickly along the road and turned down the woodland track. The rain was still light and the wind whipped up the trees in a manner that reminded me unpleasantly of the previous evening. Not long before we reached the house, our attention was distracted by the sight of figures in the woods. They were a good way off, but well clad for the weather, and there seemed to be some excitement, for voices were calling, so the Doctor decided we should investigate further.

Coming nearer, I had a sense of emergency. There was shouting and someone was sent racing off in the general direction of the village. As we approached, we recognised Langton.

'Thank heaven you have come,' he said. 'I will need all the help I can.'

'But why?' said Bell and then stopped, for the company had parted and we saw what was below them. Colin Harding lay there in the grey light and drizzle. His corpse faced the sky in the centre of the clearing and his arms were outstretched, his eyes open, his mouth wide.

There was not a mark upon him that I could see but he looked like a man who had lain down and invited the devil into his flesh, an invitation that, in the last moments of his life, had been accepted to agonising effect.

# The Unfathomable Death

The Doctor was at the side of the corpse at once.

'He was only discovered an hour ago,' said Langton. 'I have just sent a word for Dr Bulweather to come. Dr Hare is away till tomorrow.'

Bell did not reply, he was too intent on examining the body, which, as I have indicated, betrayed no obvious marks other than mud. He stared long and hard at the face, putting his head right next to it, then he looked at the hands and the position.

Getting up, he turned to Langton, his tone urgent. 'I think we must get him down to the village at once, he has been dead for several hours and it is imperative an autopsy is performed without delay. But first, may I ask if you could clear all of these people right away from the site, we must examine it and I am already concerned vital evidence may have been lost.'

'Very well, Doctor.' Though Langton looked slightly doubtful. 'I know from Bulweather you have great experience of these things but, of course, Harding may have simply had some kind of seizure.'

The Doctor made no reply, he was already studying the ground immediately around the body as Langton told the other men they should go back to their work but stand by to carry the corpse down. The village constable, a tall and dependable man he introduced to us as John Wallace, would meanwhile obtain the necessary stretcher for this task.

I followed Bell as he picked his way across the site, using his silver-topped cane to move vegetation. But even I could see the task was almost hopeless. The ground had been damp, it had rained intermittently if lightly over the past hour and all that now remained were tracts of mud, marked out by the boots of the other men. Bell moved around these in despair and then walked to the perimeter of the clearing. This area was slightly less trampled but even here there were muddy trails.

After a time Dr Bulweather appeared, looking extremely concerned. And, once he had stared at the corpse, Bell walked a little way off with him and the two men were engaged in urgent if inaudible consultation. I could see Bulweather nodding in agreement and Bell asking question after question at some length. Occasionally Bulweather shook his head but mostly he seemed to agree. Bell looked so pleased by his agreement that I found myself wondering what on earth they could be discussing. At last the dialogue concluded and Bell went over to where Langton was standing with the stretcher.

'Inspector Langton,' Bell said, 'an autopsy will be critical for us as will the speed with which it is concluded. Your doctor here has only limited experience, I understand, but he will vouch for my considerable expertise as a surgeon and pathologist. I therefore suggest that I undertake it myself with his assistance. Otherwise there could be delays which would be folly in the circumstances.'

Langton looked a little astonished. 'Undertake it where, Dr Bell? In the inn?'

But the Doctor had no interest in jests at this point. 'Bulweather has an outhouse he has used for occasional surgery,' he answered. 'It should be sufficient, and we are lucky in that he seems to have a good set of surgical tools inherited from his uncle who was a surgeon, as well as some chemistry equipment. He has itemised these and I believe it will be enough. We may perhaps lack all that might be desirable but I am satisfied.'

'I would have to contact my superiors before—' Langton began.

'Absolutely,' Bell said, interrupting him. 'And if they can get a pathologist here before tomorrow I will be happy to offer my assistance. But I suggest they telegraph to Inspector Miller of Scotland Yard who will, I believe, testify as to my fitness for the matter in hand.'

Langton was happy with this and now arrangements were made for the body to be removed. They decided to carry it back down to the town by the most direct route rather than make a detour to the road.

Upon hearing this, Bell pointed across one particularly noticeable muddy line where the men had already tramped. 'May I ask, Inspector,' he said urgently, 'if those carrying the body use this as their mark for entering and leaving the clearing and do not depart from it? My suspicion is that any evidence here has been obliterated already but it is always possible something may be found and I do not wish to see any further devastation.'

'Are you so clear, then, this is not a natural death?' said Langton.

'I make no assumptions about anything,' said Bell, 'but I believe it is a duty to leave the site of any death untouched until we are more precise about its circumstances. I am afraid that has not been followed here, something we must all certainly regret.'

I do not know if Langton took this to heart but he was certainly punctilious in carrying out the Doctor's instructions. Within a few minutes, the pallbearers approached the body along the exact line Bell had indicated. They needed several of them, for the body was big and it was quite a struggle to lift. The rain was heavier now, adding to the melancholy spectacle as they finally bore it aloft and then began to march away down the hill towards the town.

After a further brief conference with Bell, Bulweather came over to me. 'I am sorry, Dr Doyle, not to have greeted you before but Dr

Bell hardly allowed me time to breathe and I cannot complain of it, for this is a terrible business. We are lucky to have you both here. My only regret for your sake is you have seen our little community in such bad circumstances. I will bid you farewell, through I know you will be at my house shortly for we all have a long working day ahead. At the very least I can endeavour to see that Mrs Harvey keeps us well fortified during our labours.' And he walked off after the others.

The rain was now pouring down and I am quite sure it put paid to any last hopes the Doctor may have had of extracting evidence from that clearing. Even so, he persisted, inspecting the muddy tracks and the vegetation around it for what seemed like hours. Much of his time was spent pacing lightly around the perimeter of the place, scanning the ground. I thought it wise to keep my distance for I had no wish to add to the disturbance, though after a damp hour, during which I was sure he had seen nothing, I was half-minded to turn back to the village, given that I was no use to anyone here. The Doctor was paying particular attention to a stick he had picked up, balancing it in his hand as if it were a string of pearls rather than a stray piece of wood that bore no markings of any kind.

I could hardly help reflecting that whatever else had killed Colin Harding, if indeed he had been unlawfully killed, it was certainly not a stick. But soon he discarded it and came over to me, indicating he was ready to leave.

By the time we reached town and turned into Bulweather's house, the body had already been placed in a tiled outhouse which had once been a dairy. It lay on a slab where the milk had originally been left to cool, and where more recently Bulweather had conducted minor surgery. Since the day was so overcast, lamps had been brought in and they cast a flickering glow over the body.

After looking round, Bell fell to examining Bulweather's tools, which were I thought remarkably comprehensive in the circumstances, including a variety of knives, saws and even rib shears. It seemed his uncle, who had occasionally undertaken post-mortem work, prided himself on this equipment.

Langton had, however, expressly forbidden any work to commence until he had authorisation and there was no telling when that might be. The Doctor visibly fretted at the delay and insisted on making a preliminary examination. I stood beside him for this informal procedure, at which Bulweather's presence was not required, and could see that the only marks on Harding were a few light and fairly harmless bruises on the arms. We also found a bruise beneath the hair on the head, which was recent and Bell paid considerable attention to it.

'Is it enough?' I asked, for I knew that was what he was debating.

'I cannot see it,' he said at last. 'Yes, it might be enough to cause concussion and in some rare and unlucky cases death might follow. But if this is what killed him and it was a deliberate blow, then "manslaughter" is a better term than "murder". No cold-blooded murderer would risk leaving the outcome uncertain in such a way.'

After that, he examined the rest of the body meticulously, but there was nothing else that I could see. Most of his time was spent on the mouth, where he found a little frothy sputum inside the upper lip.

Once finished, we went through to Bulweather who confirmed there was as yet no reply to Langton's telegrams and we might yet wait many hours. The Doctor hardly concealed his irritation, pointing out there could not be much more than thee or four hours left of daylight. Bulweather reassured him more lamps could be brought if needed and so, for the moment, we retired to the inn.

In retrospect it would have been far better if Bell had proceeded to other business while we waited. But he did not wish to risk losing any time and was, in any case, distracted by the task ahead. Following a late and fretful lunch, I ascertained that Charlotte Jefford was now more or less recovered and was reading in her room but nobody had had the heart to tell her of the death that had occurred. I asked the Doctor if I should take it upon myself to do so and he answered rather curtly she might as well hear it from me as from a maid or some other gossip.

Miss Jefford was sitting comfortably enough in an armchair beside the fire that had been made up in her room and greeted me kindly. Her fair hair was loose and curled prettily around her face but her eyes were still troubled.

I had decided to make as little of the matter as possible and I merely told her in passing there had been some bad news involving Sir Walter Monk's groundsman. Miss Jefford seemed determined not to give way to undue alarm and, once she understood he was dead, merely asked if we had any idea of the circumstances. I replied it could well be a heart attack or some such condition and we would know more shortly. She seemed satisfied and I left her, pleased that neither of us had referred to the events of the previous evening. Perhaps, though, I was guilty of a slight deceit, for she may well have supposed from my words that Harding had died in his bed. I certainly had no intention of alluding to the fact he had been found close enough to where she saw the apparition, or to our mutual knowledge that the ghost was supposed to be a harbinger of death. Indeed, given the ripple of alarm Harding's death had already caused in the inn, I thanked God we had kept Charlotte Jefford's experience secret.

As Bell had feared, it was already evening before Langton came to us with the news that the post-mortem could proceed. True to his word, Bulweather had installed more lamps in the outhouse but, though he has positioned them as best as he could, the illumination they gave was somewhat ghastly. Flickering shadows were everywhere and, as the Doctor and Bulweather stood before the corpse, they cast huge and blackly grotesque outlines on the tiled walls. But the Doctor showed no sign of being distracted and began his work as if he had been in the Edinburgh mortuary, leaving me to make a record of all he did.

After a further examination of the body's exterior, with particular concentration on the mouth, nose and ears, he took the leading knife and made a deep Y-shaped incision, extending from the arms to the bottom of the sternum and then down to the lower abdomen. As the structures of the neck and chest cavity were exposed to view, Bell examined them in situ, before he took the shears and began cutting through the rib cage.

I have seen many autopsies but this must certainly have been one of the strangest. Outside the rain was blowing hard against the building's roof and I vividly recall the hawk-like shadow of the Doctor's features on the tiles as his face bore down on the organs of the corpse. But there was only limited time for such romance, for I was also busily recording each procedure in the book I had been given for the purpose. To this end the Doctor offered an intermittent commentary of what he was doing while he did it, interjected with occasional grunts as he utilised his tools.

There were times too when I sensed a slight quickening of interest as when he found a small amount of foam in the trachea. After the thoracic cavity was opened, he was silent for a moment and then asked me to note the paleness and the distention of the lungs.

A few moments later, I noticed Bulweather catch the Doctor's eye and there was bafflement and alarm on the country doctor's face. Then they continued as before.

The work itself took many hours, for Bell was always thorough in such things and it was not so far away from dawn before he called a halt to the proceedings and returned the organs, some of which had been dissected, with tissue removed, to the body. Finally, he sewed up the incisions and the corpse of Colin Harding was almost whole again.

Meanwhile, I had cleaned down the surface and the floor with the buckets of water my host had provided and at last we repaired to the drawing room. The housekeeper was not to be seen but she had left beer and various cold meats and bread and cheese, which we ate hungrily. The Doctor was obviously famished after his exertions, but I was aware Bulweather was uneasy, evidently anxious to talk of Bell's conclusions yet reluctant to raise the matter himself. Outside the weather had eased a little, with no rain now although the wind still howled.

Finally Bell drank a glass of the beer Mrs Harvey had left and sat down, staring into the fire.

'It is impossible,' Bulweather muttered now, staring at him, unable to leave what concerned him any longer.

'It is, however, certain,' said Bell.

'It is miles from that spot to anywhere it could have happened.' Bulweather flopped back in his chair, exhausted. 'Look at the weight of the man. Five men had trouble getting him down here on a police stretcher. They will all remember the witch's words.'

'Yes, that was my calculation from the map,' Bell said. 'You are sure there is none?'

'Some damp earth maybe. Otherwise nothing. And there was no earth in him.'

I had been so busily recording impressions and data that my medical brain was all but switched off and I was only now starting to grasp the implications when we were interrupted by Langton, who showed himself in without ceremony, anxious only to hear the results of the night's work. Outside there were streaks of light in a dull sky while the wind had dropped further as dawn approached.

'Well, gentlemen,' said Langton, 'what is your story? Was it a seizure?'

'It was not,' said Bell, who still sat in the chair, his eyes fixed on the fire. 'There was water in his swollen lungs, foam in the trachea, sputum in the mouth. The symptoms are unmistakable. The man suffered death by drowning.'

# THE CHAMBER OF DOLLS

Langton stared at Bell with utter incredulity. 'Are you sure?' he said. 'There is no mistake? Perhaps it was the rain, for he was there for some hours.'

'No rain could possibly produce the effects we have observed,' said Bell, still not moving. 'Let me repeat: the man died by drowning, he was immersed in water.'

Langton turned to our host who had got to his feet and was by the table. 'I am afraid it is true,' said Bulweather.

'Well, you are saying he drowned.' Langton paced towards the window. 'Even though I cannot fathom it, at least it may have been an accident not a murder as we might have feared.'

And now Bell did raise his eyes from the fire, his face very solemn. 'An accident?' he said. 'Usually accidents have causes. I am afraid that term is utterly irrelevant when at present we can deduce no way in which it could have occurred at all.'

The conversation continued as all of us tried to imagine how such a thing could happen. Was he sure there was no water near? But Bulweather who was, among other things, a keen local historian, produced a hydrographic map which proved the point. Even as the crow flies it was a mile and a half from the spot where the body lay through thick trees and over rough ground to the witch's pool, which was the nearest standing water or river.

'Is it possible,' Langton asked, 'the body was dragged?'

'It took five men to carry him down here,' said Bulweather. 'How could it be dragged? Perhaps if it were slung over a horse.'

'I considered that,' said the Doctor, who had got up from the fire and was studying the map with enormous interest. 'But even though the clearing itself was disrupted I believe a horse would leave distinctive marks well beyond it. We must look again but I could see none whatsoever.'

'And no horse goes through these woods now,' muttered Langton. 'It is too dangerous.'

By now it was fully light and Langton left to make arrangements for the body to be moved and telegraph his superiors with these confounding developments. Bell admitted he was anxious to get back to the wood. But first, since Mrs Harvey was busy in the kitchen, he was persuaded to take breakfast and we were soon in the dining room consuming toast, eggs and some very welcome coffee.

The Doctor ate in silence, and Bulweather and I talked only sporadically. I complimented him on his housekeeper's skills as a cook and he acknowledged he had been extremely fortunate to find her shortly after his wife died.

The remark seemed to trigger some memory of Bell's, for I saw him look up. He thanked his host for the generous meal, putting down his knife and fork and pushing his plate to one side. Then he went on casually: 'Dr Bulweather, I have been thinking again about that pipette you improvised with cases of childhood infection at the back of the throat. The one you used on the child on the night we mentioned before. Remarkable we both had the same idea for helping the patients, is it not?'

'Ah yes, the pipette, it is a useful invention. I am glad to think I followed in your footsteps, Dr Bell.' But I could see our host was a little surprised the Doctor would return to so trivial a matter at such a juncture.

'I would like to inspect it again if you have no objection. I want to see if we use the same method.'

'Why of course, I will get it,' he replied, getting up hastily.

The Doctor did not look at me, though I certainly wondered why he was bothering to relive memories of old treatments at such a time. After a few moments, Bulweather was back with it.

'Incidentally,' said Bell to our host, 'did you know you were observed out walking to your patient that night?'

Bulweather came over to Bell with the pipette, which gleamed in a way it had not before. 'I did not know, sir. Who saw me?'

'It is of no consequence,' said Bell. 'But which road were you taking?'

'I was going towards Westleton Heath,' he answered.

Bell nodded and took the pipette, turning it over in his hand. 'Ah yes,' said Bell smiling, 'it has been recently cleaned, has it not?'

'Possibly,' came the reply.

'For I could not help noticing when I picked it up before that, though you had wiped some away, it still had a layer of dust. There was no way it could have been used for months, certainly it had not been used in the past few days.'

Bulweather stared at him. 'Ah, yes, now you remind me, I did have another in my bag which I utilised that night. But it was old and I thew it away.'

'That is most convenient,' said Bell. 'So you still maintain you saw this child?'

I have written that Bulweather was a big man. I am sure he was also strong and he towered over Bell now, looking almost menacing, his mouth taut in an expression of suppressed rage or perhaps pain. But then he controlled himself and returned to his seat. He placed his hands on the table. 'Gentlemen, you may believe as much or as little as you like. I will say no more about it.'

Shortly after this, we left. It was hardly a pleasant way to leave a house where only hours earlier all three of us had been working as a team. But, given the man's reticence and lies, it seemed clear to me that he must have some involvement, if not in Harding's death, at least in the murky events that surrounded Jefford's disappearance.

And so, fortified by the hospitality of a man we could not trust, we climbed the road leading south out of the town and finally plunged into the woods ahead.

I will admit as we made our way through the wet trees after a night without sleep, I felt low in energy and spirit. But Bell pushed in front of me with all the vitality of a man who is anxious to move ahead with his plans. Of course, I knew this quality of old, it reappeared whenever he had a chance to do the work he loved, no matter how desperate the circumstances. The Doctor was more likely to flag when nothing presented itself than in the field.

Once we had reached the spot where Harding's body was found, he made a cursory examination of the clearing but concentrated most of his energy on the woods around it. Indeed, he embarked on a series of concentric circles that took him further and further away from the spot itself but no doubt gave him a good idea of the terrain by which it was approached.

It seemed foolish for me to trail after him so I stayed closer to the clearing itself, but because I knew that had already been well covered, I concentrated my attention on the woodland. It had been raining much of the night and I half hoped to see large puddles of water which might provide an answer to the riddle of Harding's death. But there was nothing like that, the rain had merely soaked in and the wettest thing I could see was a slightly sodden ditch, but even here no water had collected.

Langton appeared after a time and we talked in a desultory fashion. When I explained that the Doctor was searching the wood, he shook his head. 'Well if he is searching for water, he is wasting his time, he will find none.'

As if in answer to his words, the Doctor appeared and I saw that once again he was carrying a stick, though I still could not see why these pieces of wood were of any interest to him. 'Tell me,

Inspector Langton, how far is it from here to Sir Walter Monk's farmhouse?'

'Directly through the trees? More than a mile,' replied Langton.

'Then I would like you to obtain his permission to search it,' said Bell.

'But why?' said Langton. 'It would be just as hard to bring a drowned man from there as from the witch's pool.'

However, Bell insisted and, within half an hour, we were standing in Sir Walter Monk's hall, waiting for Langton to conclude his interview with Sir Walter. I could hear raised voices but ultimately Langton appeared, somewhat flushed.

'You may proceed, gentlemen, and I hope you know what you are about.'

The Doctor expressed his thanks and almost at once we had embarked on an exploration of the house, starting upstairs as some astonished servants scurried out of our way.

It was, as I had anticipated, an extremely luxurious establishment. The bedrooms had rich embroidered hangings, thick carpets and tapestries, though I could take in few details because the Doctor's inspection was anything but thorough. Indeed he positively raced from room to room. Coming to a small anti-chamber I was amazed to see that, despite its position in the middle of the country, the house had some of the most modern plumbing arrangements I had encountered, with hinged water closets and two fine bathtubs with piped water. Since a man could surely drown in this, I assumed it was what Bell wanted to see and called him through, but the Doctor showed not the slightest interest, turning away and moving on through the rooms.

We saw nine bedrooms, including what was obviously Sir Walter's, and then made a whirlwind tour of the servant quarters before going downstairs. Bell showed little interest in the reception rooms and soon we were back in the hall where Langton was waiting.

'Did you see what you required, Dr Bell?' he asked.

'I did,' said Bell and we were soon admitted to the drawing room, where the desiccated figure of Sir Walter was wrapped in a dressing gown before the fire. He looked extremely irritated.

'Well, Dr Bell,' he said, 'perhaps you would have the kindness to explain why on earth you are trampling through my home, frightening my livestock and the servants.'

I noticed the way his animals (of which incidentally we had seen nothing) were placed before his servants in importance.

'Sir Walter,' said Bell, 'your visitors have departed, I see.'

'I do not understand the connection.'

'You had guests when we were last here. I wished to ascertain exactly who they were.'

Now Monk looked positively furious. 'What possible business could it be of yours who is in this house?'

But the Doctor was not even faintly ruffled by his tone. Indeed, he stepped forward boldly until he was very close to Sir Walter, who did not like this at all and shrank back in his seat. It was clear no one ever behaved to him in this way.

'You may or may not be aware,' said Bell in a voice so quiet that he might have been in church, 'that a man died not far from here yesterday. There are several questions regarding his death that have to be answered urgently and the authorities entrusted me to carry out his autopsy and provide answers. I cannot yet ascertain who is to blame but I have the most intense interest in everyone who is staying in this parish, not least its visitors, and most particularly visitors who conceal themselves from me as yours did. Any such person may have something to hide, and this gives me every right to ask such questions, therefore I say again *who* was staying here?'

This tone, which I knew well, for Bell often lowered his voice when at his angriest, had its effect. Sir Walter was pale as he turned to Inspector Langton. 'I will talk to the Doctor but in private,' he said. And we both retreated to the hall.

Bell emerged a few minutes later. His expression was unreadable and he merely thanked Inspector Langton for his help. 'Sir Walter was most accommodating. Now I think I should return to town, the site will yield no more for the moment.'

Of course I was anxious to know what had transpired between the Doctor and Sir Walter but I had little chance to discover it on the way back. Bell and Langton walked ahead of me and I heard Bell ask him a question and receive an answer that appeared to take the form of some directions. Then he was silent.

His silence continued at the inn, where we ate a hasty meal. Eventually the landlord came through to inform us that Charlotte Jefford had emerged from her room that morning, apparently fully recovered from her ordeal. In fact, she had been invited out to lunch with Mrs Marner, with whom she had struck up an acquaintance. Brooks was, however, suitably sombre about events and went on, 'We understand poor Harding died of a heart attack, what a sad business.'

Bell merely agreed how unfortunate the matter was and Brooks left us. I had rather supposed we might now get some rest but there was to be no such opportunity, for the Doctor informed me we had another visit to make. He had business in a place about two miles inland known as Westleton Heath.

Outside as we trudged out of the town, not turning up towards the forest or the pool but keeping going along the road in a westerly direction, I asked what business it was.

'Oh, I wish,' the Doctor said, 'to visit an asylum.'

The weather was fairer, indeed it was now quite a pleasant evening, and the sun was beginning to set over the marshland that bordered the road as a little flock of redshank circled over our heads. But even so, I quailed at the prospect. My experience of asylums is intimately connected with my father, who entered one while I was at university and was still, at the time of which I write, an inmate.

I visited him all too rarely. It was hard enough to bear the condition to which he had been reduced, but there was also something utterly degrading about these monstrous castles of incarceration.

Naturally enough, therefore, my thoughts were gloomy as we walked past another great belt of forestland and eventually, after a mile and a half, turned up an isolated track. By this time it was dark and, before us, Bell pointed with his cane at a large grey hulk of a building with narrow leaded windows.

I knew at once this must be the place, for it was exactly as I had feared: a grim, gothic monstrosity in a godforsaken landscape, miles from the lights and amenities of any community. How I hated such institutions and wished they would all be swallowed up into the earth, their inmates allowed to roam free. My father's condition, though cyclical, had certainly never been remotely improved by his confinement.

Inside this place, no doubt, I would find the dark hallways, the misery, perhaps even chains and padded cells, certainly bullying orderlies. The prospect was so uninviting I was on the point of asking Bell to enter the institution alone and report on anything he found that was useful. For my part, I doubted it would be much.

But my thoughts were interrupted by the Doctor. 'I believe you may find this of interest to you,' he said. No doubt he was thinking of my father, and at the time the observation struck me as tactless beyond belief. I had already derived quite enough 'interest' from visiting such places to last me a lifetime. But there was now no question of offering some excuse. His remark made me determined to proceed.

And so we walked up to the great door, which opened before we had any chance to make ourselves known. I expected some fierce orderly to question our business but instead here was a smiling, suited man, wearing spectacles and carrying a book.

'Ah,' he said, in a cultured voice, 'I saw you gentlemen from the window. Dr Bell? Dr Doyle? I am Roger Cornelius. I received your telegram and you are welcome. I am delighted for you to see what you will.'

He led us into a carpeted hallway which was about as far removed from what I expected as it could be. It was well furnished and snugly warm. Two nurses went past smiling politely, both women rather than the male orderlies I generally expected in such places.

We moved on past a number of rooms, which I could see through the doorways were comfortable. One contained of all things a harp and a prettily ornamented table. A woman was sitting there in a shawl, sketching.

'These are very pleasant quarters for your staff,' I said. 'Are the inmates upstairs?'

Cornelius smiled. 'Why, you have already seen two of them. Several have their own sitting rooms.'

I was astonished. 'But there are no locks?'

'Oh, we rarely if ever need them,' he said, leading us up a flight of stairs and into a book-lined room. 'You see I am a follower of the precepts of the late Dr James Connolly. And also more recently Henry Maudsley. We believe in the moral system of non-restraint, rather than coercion and cruelty.'

'It is remarkable,' I said, glad now I had persevered in entering this place and silently apologising to Bell for misjudging him. Of course I had heard something of the approach and had occasionally encountered enlightened doctors who talked of the subject, but I had never dreamt it could achieve this kind of transformation. 'You have no locked doors at all?' I said in wonder.

'We have them but as I say we rarely need them,' said Dr Cornelius, whose manner was a little pedantic but not unpleasant. 'As you know, most of our asylums are in the grip of the idea that insanity is the end product of an incurable degenerative disease carried in the victim's inherited biology and therefore can never be cured. Fortunately, some of us disagree. We are not always successful but we are always humane and believe above all else in the dignity of the patient. Now here is an inspirational book. I recommend it.' And he handed me a copy of *Body and Mind* by Henry Maudsley.

Bell had been taking in his surroundings and was looking with enormous interest at other books and papers, especially drawings and architectural designs that the asylum keeper appeared to have made himself. Cornelius seemed pleased.

'Yes, Dr Bell, I am also an admirer of John Connolly's *The Construction and Government of Lunatic Asylums*, though we do not follow Bentham's idea of the all-seeing eye here or the panopticon. It would take a considerable sum to refurbish the place in that way but it might well be worth while, as I often say to those who are disposed to help us.'

'Ah now,' said Bell, 'that is precisely what I wished to ask you, what of the funding?'

'Yes indeed, Dr Bell, that is the question. Our patients are not coerced, they are not forced here, but we have to charge a good sum to keep the place up. This does not mean, however, all of those we treat are rich. Fortunately, there are still philanthropists in this world and some have donated considerable sums. Even from as far away as London.'

'And talking of the wealthy, can I ask,' said Bell, watching him closely, 'if you ever encountered Oliver Jefford?'

'Never,' said Dr Cornelius. 'He had nothing to do with us and I am not sure I regret the loss. No doubt if he had come here, he would have done so in the spirit of the eighteenth-century gentlemen who used to visit Bedlam for their own amusement.'

'Dr Cornelius,' said Bell after he had made sure Cornelius had encountered no strangers recently, 'we have no wish to keep you from your work. Tell me, would you have any objection if we went around a little to see this on our own?'

'Not at all. Mr Edmunds is our night manager and he knows you are coming so address any questions to him. You will find his office at the end of the main corridor.'

My admiration for Westleton House, as it was called, only increased as we saw more of it and I understood now why Bell thought I might find it interesting. Not that I mean to give the impression the place was without suffering. A patient with a nervous disorder is still ill and some of those here were distracted or unhappy and under special supervision, but there was a level of comfort which was in total contrast to anything I had seen before, while the staff seemed kind and efficient.

My assumption was that Bell had come here to see if any of the patients might possibly resemble the crazed man seen by Balneil and Miss Jefford. If so, as we moved from room to room in the company of Mr Edmunds, an elderly man with white whiskers, he seemed destined for disappointment. None of the inmates resembled that vision of torment in any way. Indeed those that were here seemed almost to be selected for their lack of any truly disturbing symptoms. Perhaps, I thought, Dr Cornelius was right in believing that the majority of lunatics needed no compulsion, but I found myself wondering how such a place would have coped with the few who did.

Bell certainly showed no disappointment, not even when he asked if any inmates had gone missing in the last few weeks and was answered with an emphatic negative. In general, his conversation was admiring and affable and it was only when we were almost done with our inspection that he turned to Edmunds and I sensed something in his manner. 'Mr Edmunds,' he said, 'do you recall the night when Jefford disappeared? It was a Friday, first of December, the night Dr Bulweather was here.'

'Why yes, sir,' said the elderly man, nodding. 'I remember. Dr Bulweather always likes to . . .'

And then Edmunds stopped, realising what he had said. He looked worried and stammered a little. 'But it is not right I should . . . he does not like people to know.'

'You must not fear,' said Bell. 'I am involved in an investigation and any matters that do not relate to the crime will be kept quite confidential.'

The old man nodded. 'I see. Well then you must come and see

her. She is one of the few you have not seen. In fact, we tend not to display her to visitors.'

And he led us away from the kitchen and down another corridor. A nurse came past smiling at us and then Edmunds showed us into a small comfortable room where a pretty fair-haired woman sat on a chair beside a cot, upon which were dozens and dozens of dolls. All had pretty white faces and dresses. It would have been a little girl's dream.

Indeed, the woman seemed almost doll-like herself. She was, I judged, about thirty years old, in her arms was yet another doll and she was humming softly as she cradled it back and forth. She looked at us and stopped for a moment but barely seemed to take much notice and then started her humming again. Her mind, I could see, was gone, her expression quite vacant.

'Hello, Claire,' said Edmunds and turned to us. 'That is Claire.'

'His wife?' I said, for there was certainly a strong resemblance to the picture in Bulweather's house

Edmunds shook his head. 'Oh no, his wife is dead. No this is Claire Warren, his wife's poor sister. He has given a great deal of money to ensure she is properly looked after, though it seems Dr Cornelius feels there is no prospect of her getting better.'

'What is the story?' said Bell quietly, and I could see he was moved by what we saw here.

Edmunds spoke in a low voice. 'It seems she was in Southwold and a man from London got her in the family way so she fled to the city. For some time she lost touch with her family after she fell on hard times. Dr Bulweather's wife suffered a great deal of sadness, for they had been close and I am told her last wish was that he would find her sister and help her. This took time and when he found her it was discovered she was living as a common prostitute and that she had had another child taken for adoption. A man had used her badly and there is even talk she fell under a horse and her head was trampled. But when she came here she was as you see now, though never a harsh word for anyone. Always calm and, we hope, happy. But not really with us, as you see. He has done all he can for her.'

'And why,' said a voice from behind, 'did you have to know?' Both Bell and I turned. Bulweather was standing in the doorway, his face pale with anger.

# The Whispering Hate

Edmunds looked terrified. 'I am sorry, sir. They—'

'No. It is all right, Joseph,' said Bulweather. 'These gentlemen have found out my secret on their own, it is not of your doing. You may go on now.'

Edmunds took his leave gratefully. Bulweather was angry but said nothing for a moment and I saw his anger visibly soften as he looked at the woman who still sat so placidly in the chair, rocking. You could see the affection in his eyes. When he spoke again, his voice was quiet.

'You know what you wanted to know. I only ask you do not tell a soul here, for it is very personal. I wanted to carry out my wife's wish and I did, though what she would have felt when she came upon Claire I do not know. But I have had to keep the matter private, not merely for my wife's sake but for my professional reputation. People here are extremely narrow-minded, especially when it comes to madness.'

The Doctor nodded and within a short time we withdrew. Dr Cornelius awaited in his study, intrigued to hear our impressions. Upon discovering we knew of Claire Warren and had met Dr Bulweather, he was happy to talk of the matter, indeed he had her file in front of him and Bell was most interested in it. 'I update it because Bulweather insisted her behaviour was recorded,' Cornelius said. 'He has tried for years to find some way of improving her mental state, it is a tragic case. Of course we have honoured his wish to keep the matter confidential, for the country people might well shun a practitioner associated with madness and scandal. But then it was a promise he made to his wife and he has carried it out to the letter. She suffered grievously after her sister's decline. And I cannot tell you how generous he has been to our establishment.'

Bulweather arrived shortly after this, looking no longer angry but resigned. He talked for a little to Cornelius about the arrangements of Claire Warren's room and then he offered to accompany us back. 'For my dog is at home and if I am with you, nobody need suspect I have been here,' he said. 'I am ashamed, gentlemen, to show you how I must submit to local prejudice. But it is a plain fact that once I was branded as a carer of lunatics, many would refuse to consult me.' And so we set off.

How different was the walk back to Dunwich that evening from the journey that had taken us here. Then I had been reflecting moodily on my father's affliction. Now I was ashamed of such sterile self-pity, which was of little use to anyone. I had discovered there were places that truly cared for the mentally afflicted. And I also felt a new respect for Bulweather, as I am sure did Bell.

He assured the country practitioner we would respect his confidence and he was evidently pleased. 'Thank you,' he said as he strode out vigorously, 'and I am most curious to learn how you made your discovery, Dr Bell.'

'Well,' said Bell, 'it was not so difficult. In your own living room your partner Dr Hare made a somewhat scathing allusion to Westleton House, indicating the prejudice that exists against it and against lunacy in general. This immediately alerted me to the fact it was something you might not wish to advertise. Yet your bookshelf contained a very high proportion of recent titles concerning nervous disorders. I also knew, as a matter of fact, both from Mrs

Marner's maid and yourself, that you appeared to be travelling in the direction of Westleton on the night you visited your fictitious patient. It seemed to me, therefore, a serious hypothesis that you were concealing an association with the asylum. Moreover, you are right, there is loose gossip about you, which caused me to reflect how much more necessary concealment might be if the association with it was personal rather than professional. Naturally, therefore, I did not question Cornelius who would have kept your secret, but the night manager seemed an ideal opportunity.'

'Well I am glad you are friend rather than foe, Dr Bell. And I am extremely grateful you will breathe not a word of this. I care nothing if people suspect I have a mistress, as long as I protect my wife's family name.'

I asked him if there was any hope.

'There is always hope,' he said. 'But it is terrible to observe a person trapped by their own mind, to see it failing them, a kind of living death. And I do not deny she reminds me also of Mary.' And he lapsed into silence.

The name was common enough but it struck a chord in me. For Mary was my mother's name and I was acutely aware how much she had suffered, as our whole family had suffered, from my father's disease of the mind. The connection released a flood of painful memories. I thought of the early years when our whole family had dreaded the screams from my father's room. Of how, while a student, I had once opened the door to it and saw him crawling and sobbing by his fireplace. Of his tiny cell in one of the asylums with a bare table and chair and nothing else at all. Not that I had visited him for well over a year. Perhaps I might even seek advice from Bulweather. I was quite sure he would be sympathetic.

Before we parted, Bell asked if the country practitioner would keep an eye open for any household in the vicinity that might be harbouring a man from London. 'I am convinced that one of those responsible is being sheltered here by someone,' Bell told him. And we said goodnight.

Back at the inn, as we waited in the parlour for our dinner, Bell and I were approached by the worried landlord. Was it true, he asked us, that Harding may have been the victim of foul play? Rumours were beginning to fly and many were now talking openly of the legend and of witchcraft. 'People are already very nervous hereabouts, sir,' he said anxiously if politely. 'There are all kinds of things in the air, that the witch's curse is starting to come true. Some of them are even saying she has followers among us now, women.'

'I understand,' said Bell, 'but you must stamp on such nonsense at once. We are not yet even at liberty to say for certain if there is foul play, so there is no place for such talk.' Brooks seemed to take some consolation from that and now he remembered that two packages Bell had been expecting had finally arrived.

He returned with them and Bell opened the first. It contained recent copies of the *Lowestoft Advertiser*, which the Doctor scanned with interest. I picked one up but could see absolutely nothing worthy of our attention.

After we had eaten, I left him in the dining room and wandered through to the public bar, for I felt it was worth hearing any of the gossip that was rife. Of course, Bell and I had both tried on previous evenings to elicit intelligence from this source, always without success. Nobody would even acknowledge having seen Jefford drinking here, and we felt sure this was an evasion. I purchased a tankard of beer and sat down to drink it by the window. There was a group of men, fishermen I guessed, in the corner by the fireplace, their heads close together talking in such undertones I could not overhear them. But closer to me were two others I had seen before. One was a blacksmith called Laing, a startlingly good-looking man in his way, the other a horse handler named Hepton with sand-coloured hair.

These two were usually friendly enough when we encountered them before, though they told us little, but now they gave me a dark look and lowered their voices. I tried to engage them, no doubt clumsily, with talk of the weather and the state of the sea but they remained taciturn. So finally – driven by their sullenness – I raised the thing straight out.

'I know you have some misfortunes here,' I said, 'but surely you do not ascribe it to a woman who has been dead for nearly two hundred years?'

At this, the two of them turned and looked right at me. 'As to that,' said Laing, 'perhaps we do and perhaps we don't. But Colin Harding was a good man, however he did die, and there are all kinds of stories. And one thing is for sure, without any disrespect to you, sir, we have all been worse off since the strangers came here, especially the women. That Ellie from London who fairly turned poor Colin's head with all her airs and graces. Then Jefford and now his sister. None of it has brought us any good. We don't want such people here. And there's some here say if any more happens they will act rather than watch the whole place be dragged down.'

Before I could reply, the landlord entered to whisper that Charlotte Jefford was requesting an interview with me. Meanwhile the two men had returned to their whispered conversation.

Miss Jefford was standing in the inn's little sitting room, looking composed but pale. For the first time I noticed how very frail her figure was, almost like that of a boy.

She turned and smiled and thanked me for coming. 'I am greatly in need of your advice, Dr Doyle,' she added. 'You see I do not quite know what to do. I am no nearer understanding what has happened to my brother. I have been to the house and found little there. Now Mr Harding is dead and you may know that rumours have begun to circulate that the death is unnatural.'

I told her nobody could yet be sure of that.

'Even so, a message was left for me saying I am suspected of doing mischief, that I make spells and must leave here.'

I looked baffled and she smiled. 'Oh I travel with some herbal remedies. I took them out after my fright and left them on my table. No doubt one of the maids saw them in my room and thinks they are the stuff of witchcraft. It is hard to imagine in these times but it is the only explanation I can think of.'

'Have you the letter? I want to see it.'

'No, I burnt it at once. I do not wish to be intimidated in this way and I am afraid I am not the only one. Mrs Marner's maid has also, it seems, been cast as the victim. Now she is frightened to go out.'

'Yes,' I said with urgency, 'and your letter may well have come from one of the men I have just been taking to in the public bar or someone they know. The Doctor will be interested in it and I think we should talk to him.'

The Doctor, who was still sitting reading his newspapers, got up at once when I brought Miss Jefford into the otherwise empty dining room, though I do not think I was mistaken in sensing a slight irritation at this interruption.

He listened to her story with courtesy but seemed more interested in the persecution of Mrs Marner's maid, indeed most of his questions were about Ellie. He asked about her mood and was told she was a little sullen, because Mrs Marner had instructed her to stay in the house for the moment, not wishing her to be pestered. This seemed to satisfy Bell and he told Miss Jefford we would visit Mrs Marner the following day.

'And now, Dr Bell,' said Miss Jefford earnestly, 'you must advise me what is my best course. Am I to take this note seriously?'

'I cannot be sure of that,' he said thoughtfully. 'I wish you had kept it for me to see, and I ask that any others you do keep. But on balance I doubt it is serious.'

This naturally pleased her. 'So I should ignore it?'

'On the contrary,' he spoke firmly, almost coldly. 'I advise you to leave here at once, preferably tomorrow morning early.'

His words were unhesitating and it was as if she had been slapped in the face. 'But I have done nothing wrong,' she protested. 'I want to discover what has happened to my brother. Why should I fly from here like a coward?'

'I never suggested you had done anything wrong, Miss Jefford,' said the Doctor more pacifically. 'But you asked my best advice and I offered it. The note may not be serious, but the legend is a different matter. I am in no position to be sure of my facts yet and so I err on the side of caution.'

'But it is to give way to superstition of the most primitive kind,' she cried, her cheeks positively burning. 'I am not yet so weak as to do that. But I am grateful for your opinion.' And she got up to leave.

Bell returned to his newspaper and although I remained silent I was angry. By now it seemed obvious to me Charlotte Jefford was a woman of considerable spirit. Many of her sex, and indeed of my own, would have left after the night in the woods. Yet here she was, vigorously, if somewhat tearfully, protesting her rights to a stranger. In this respect she could not but help raise memories of another indomitable female spirit in Edinburgh.

The thought of Elsbeth only stirred my feelings further. There was nothing personal in my wish to protect Charlotte Jefford. But I felt she was essentially a good woman who was owed our sympathy and support. The Doctor had not exactly been ill-mannered, he was too polished a performer for that, but there was still great insensitivity in his words. Here was a woman, almost certainly bereaved of a brother, showing huge courage and he offered her little except a cold dismissal.

After a time, as I sat there, I could bear it no longer. The Doctor was now intent on the amusements section of the *Lowestoft Advertiser*. 'I am sure there is much in the newspaper that is of interest, Doctor, but I do not think it gives you any excuse to dismiss the feelings of someone who has come to you for help.'

'I do not follow,' he said flatly, not even looking up. It was, as I well knew, very difficult to provoke the Doctor.

'We both know she may well be bereaved and her brother dead. She is frightened and has endured a great ordeal and now it seems she is being threatened by one or more ignorant and superstitious persecutors. Yet all you can do you is pronounce that she should act on their prejudice at once.'

He spoke lightly as he often did when we disagreed. 'That is really nothing to do with it, Doyle. If she leaves she would prove her innocence. And also ensure her safety.'

And to my fury he went back to his reading. Of course he had stoked my anger even more. And I said something I had never said before.

'Her safety! It hardly helped another persecuted woman's safety when you counselled her to leave Edinburgh.'

And with bitterness in my heart I turned my back on him and left the room.

# THE COMPANY OF WITCHES

It was a cruel remark and, though I was still irritated with the Doctor, I regretted it almost as soon as I was back in my room. Bell had not failed many times and it was only by chance that I had paid so dearly for his greatest failure.

Despite my anger, I wondered if I would have said such a thing – or indeed if he would have reacted quite as coldly to Miss Jefford – if we had not both been up without sleep for the best part of forty-eight hours.

I was on the point of going to bed when there was a tap on my door. I opened it and Bell was there. He did not smile but nor did he show any anger. He merely looked at me and I stepped back to let him in, closing the door.

He walked to the window and then turned.

'I will endeavour to explain, for we both lack sleep and perhaps I did not do so very well.' That was, I knew, in its way an apology from the Doctor and I nodded, though still not completely relenting.

He turned away, closing his eyes, as if feeling his way back into the case, or rather his conception of the case, for my benefit. 'Look at it,' he said, and there was for the first time in many hours, some passion in his voice, 'in its entirety. Of course we are trying to avoid panic but I can tell you I am as certain as I have ever been that Harding was brutally murdered. The precise nature of how this was achieved is, as yet, a mystery but I already entertain suspicions about the mechanism and the motive. I would direct you also, however, to the spectacular nature of the deed and the sensation it was designed to cause. Only he would invent such a thing to create as much bafflement and fear as he possibly could. Nobody else would imagine it, nobody else is capable of executing it.'

The Doctor had opened his eyes now and turned back to me. 'But I do not for a minute imagine he is here alone. Even our enemy could not concoct such a thing from some hideout in the woods. And it is not his style anyway. Which means, Doyle, one of these people, any of them, is harbouring him. And we must necessarily be particularly suspicious of those with London connections. I have not yet established if and how that applies to Edward Norman or Hare, but it most certainly applies to Sir Walter (who claims that his mysterious guest was a mistress from the capital), Mrs Marner, her maid Ellie Barnes, Langton and, yes I am afraid, Charlotte Jefford. Therefore, if she left here, it would be doubly fortunate for her and for us.'

There was nothing more to say and we agreed to disagree. Of course I could see some cold logic in his position but it seemed, if anything, overly logical, and made little allowance for character and probability.

Next day, after a good night's sleep, Bell and I ate our breakfast without any reference to the discussion of the night before. Inspector Langton entered the dining room, anxious to know whether we had discovered anything further about the mystery. He seemed a little disappointed when Bell merely replied that he had sent an urgent telegram to Lowestoft and would journey there that afternoon while this morning he wished Langton to show us Harding's accommodation and revisit the house with the bloodstain.

Outside, it was blustery but fair and, though the marsh lay

between us and the sea, I could hear the sound of breakers on the
wind. Harding went on ahead but, as we walked up the road away
from the inn, there were two figures before us, pointing out over
the marsh at a flock of seabirds. The figures turned and I recognised the florid if youthful features of Edward Norman, who
smiled, though his son Tommy only stared at us with hostility.
'How lucky I am to catch you, for I wish you to lunch with us today,'
Norman said, wringing his hands in his characteristically unctuous
gesture. 'Nella has commanded it and Nella will not be gainsaid.'

Though no doubt kindly meant, I cannot say that I relished such
a prospect, but it fitted our plans and the invitation was accepted
before we went on our way. Evidently this family was not greatly
disturbed by the news of Harding's death.

Harding had, it turned out, lived alone in a small cottage on the
Monk estate. It was a bleak situation and little more than one
room, for he took his meals with the servants in the main house. A
small bed lay in the window with some clothes and a few letters and
personal things.

Bell went through all of these with extreme care but Langton
showed impatience for he had already looked at them. 'There is
something from his sister, we have written to her ourselves, and
some cuttings from newspapers about forestry, woodcraft and
livestock. You will find nothing of interest there, Dr Bell.'

Bell, however, studied them at great length, lingering over some
passages. After that, he commenced a very thorough search of the
house. It was while he was reaching under the bed that he pulled
something out. I moved forward hopefully, but once again all he
had was some broken sticks, little more than pieces of firewood.
Bell frowned at them but finally cast them aside.

After that, we made our way back to Jefford's house. I must
confess I felt a chill the moment I saw that hideous orchard with
the bent, stunted trees. The temperature seemed to drop as soon
as you came anywhere near the place.

And the chill was just as evident as Langton unlocked the door and we entered. I have often had to make do without servants, but if ever a house cried out for someone to tend its fires and its beds and give the place some heart it was The Glebe. Soon we stood again in that grim empty room with the stain. Bell made his way to the far corner of the room where he turned his back to the wall and stood facing the stain. He stayed like that for a very long time. Once he closed his eyes and then he opened them again as if wanting to get a fresh view of the place and that stain, which, although somewhat dark and theatrical, was beginning to trouble me far more than bright crimson would have done.

Then he moved around the room, taking great interest in the chimney. 'You will find nothing there, sir,' said Langton. 'I paid special attention to the fireplace naturally. It is quite empty and solid brick. No apertures, no spaces, nowhere to hide.'

'Yes, I think I would agree with you, Inspector,' replied Bell. 'It seems to hold no secrets.'

'Which leaves only plaster and flagstones,' said Langton.

But Bell, who had continued his circumnavigation of the room, had stopped and was studying something on the skirting, quite close to the door. He bent down and took it up. From what I could see it was a tiny human hair, very fair.

After studying it closely, the Doctor put it carefully away. Then he announced that he wished to go through every personal object in the place. As I have already stated there were not many: some novels, some fairly opulent clothes; no personal papers or letters, for it seems Jefford had not used the place in this way or, if he had, they were destroyed.

Langton had already protested there was nothing of interest, even the clothes had been searched, but Bell insisted on going through every garment. They were all empty but it seemed a side pocket on one of the jackets had been overlooked, for it contained a folded and half-torn piece of paper. Naturally all of us had hopes it was a letter but to our irritation it turned out there was no writing on it at all. One side was blank and on the other was a rather feeble drawing of a plant or a flower, something like a six-leaf clover. We stared at it for a moment but could make nothing of it.

Bell was still musing over the illustration as we said goodbye to Langton, for the Doctor had now decided he wished to interview Mrs Marner's maid.

'From everything I have heard about Jefford, he scarcely seems the kind of man to indulge in nature sketches,' he said to me as we walked to the Marner house. 'It is a most odd find.'

The interview with Ellie Barnes proved to be very frustrating. Mrs Marner, her usual graceful self, acknowledged how oddly the girl was behaving as she led us through to a small anti-chamber where Ellie waited. 'She does not seem nearly as upset as I feared by Colin Harding's death. But she is distracted and stares out of the window.' With that she handed us the one-word note Ellie had received the previous day. Bell looked at it carefully before we entered.

The envelope had been delivered by hand. The message, like the girl's name on the envelope, was scrawled in big ugly capitals.

WITCH

As we opened the door, Ellie was sitting at a little stool where she evidently did her mending, her little pixie's head cast down. 'Now, Ellie,' said Mrs Marner, 'Dr Bell and Dr Doyle are here to see us, and you must answer whatever they wish.'

Ellie nodded but did not look up and Mrs Marner withdrew. The Doctor began his questioning very softly and kindly. He emphasised she was in no trouble, that he understood some stupid people had accused her of mischief, that she would be protected and had no need to go out, for he understood all provisions could be delivered. But he was especially keen to know about all her dealings with Mr Harding.

At first she said almost nothing. No matter how it was phrased and how many times he asked, we were learning very little: that she had been friends with Colin Harding, that she had sometimes seen him, that she might have seen him on the night of the first. It was hard to extract anything definite. She was not even prepared to admit she was frightened, though that certainly seemed to be the case.

During the interview her cat came out of its basket and jumped up on her knee and her hand stroked its head but it flinched slightly and suddenly she seemed to recall our presence and pushed it away.

Given all of this, I expected Bell to allay her fears by firmly denouncing these stupid superstitions. After all, he had already counselled Langton to come down hard on any wild talk. But to my amazement, instead he appeared to take them entirely seriously.

'You must tell me,' he said, 'if Mr Harding practised witchcraft. Did he have power?'

She shook her head violently. I was bemused by this line but he persisted.

'He had found a rune, is that not so?'

She trembled at this. 'No, I never said.'

'You must tell me,' said the Doctor.

She said nothing. He pressed again. 'I take these things very seriously. What did he fear?'

'That he would be drowned,' she said at last.

'And was it because of magic?' he persisted.

'I cannot say.' She shook her head violently.

'But he did find something, did he not, and it frightened him?' She nodded. 'A spell?' said Bell. 'Did you see it? What did it look like?'

'Letters and shapes.'

'Where is it now?'

She shook her head, evidently not knowing. 'He feared it meant he would be drowned. Did it, sir?' She looked up at him pitifully.

'Only in his mind,' said Bell, at last returning a little sanity to the conversation. 'But was there more than this, Ellie?'

She paused and then she nodded. 'Are you sure Mr Harding is dead?'

Bell's eyes narrowed. 'I can be utterly sure. Why?'

She smiled and it was an unnerving smile. 'Because, sir, I have every reason to think he may yet live.'

# The Solicitor's Children

Bell tried not to react. Indeed he paused and then asked why she might think this.

'Once, sir,' she said, 'you admit to the power there are so many things. For if such a power could drown him by magic, then might it not . . .?' Bell nodded for her to continue. 'Might it not,' she repeated, 'bring him back?'

'Do you know a spell to do it, Ellie?' he said.

'They talk of it in books,' she said. 'That is what I know.'

'I fear he will not be back, Ellie,' said Bell. 'At least not in this world.'

This was effectively the end of the interview, for we could get little more. Bell told Ellie she must try not to worry and put these things out of her head for, once the solution was known, nobody would think her guilty of anything. But he did stress one point. 'I do not think you should leave this house. Not for the moment. Do you understand that?' She nodded.

Later, Mrs Marner offered us tea, which we declined, but we did share some words with her and again I was surprised to hear Bell ask her about witchcraft. She smiled gravely in her pretty way. 'Oh we are a very superstitious profession, Dr Bell. I rule nothing of that kind out.' Fortunately it seemed, she had a sister arriving soon to help with things, a woman who had been many times before and was well liked in the village. This, we thought, would take some of the pressure off this little household. But before we left, the Doctor repeated the same instruction to her as he had to Ellie, namely that on no account should her maid leave the house. Not for any reason.

We returned to the inn before our luncheon engagement with the Normans, and Bell was extremely irritated to find there was no reply to his telegram. 'I must go to Lowestoft later in any case,' he told me as we walked to the Norman house.

It was a squat ivy-covered building where a tall maid opened the door. Almost at once we were greeted by Edward Norman, who came out of the dining room wringing his hands. 'Ah you are welcome,' he said. 'Nella, they are here. It is Arthur and Joseph.' And soon we were shaking hands with a woman with short grey hair, who asked us to come through to dine.

It might have been thought from our host's free use of Christian names that the meal would be an informal affair. In fact, it was the opposite. The place was not grand but the service and atmosphere were exceptionally formal and very slow. Tommy, whose fondness for dead birds we had already witnessed, had two much younger sisters, Jenny and Dora, and all three sat at the table as correctly as if they had been wax dummies. Even so, their parents chided them quietly yet repeatedly for entirely imaginary transgressions as when Jenny's elbow almost touched a plate or a mouthful of Tommy's was chewed too slowly.

The result was one of the most excruciating meals I have ever eaten, indeed it was less tolerable than many I have consumed under circumstances of great discomfort or even danger. While our hosts addressed us in apparently cordial tones, asking us about ourselves and commenting on their own good fortune, the whole place had about it a sense of the ultimate frustration. Norman himself kept parading the virtues of his children in an incessant catalogue, which was clearly agony for the children themselves. We learnt of Tommy's skill at observation, of Jenny's sewing. Of Dora's talent for baking pies. 'I am a little worried about Tommy's chest though,' said Norman. 'He is so often in wet places and he wheezes, do you not, Tommy? Yet you will not go to Dr Bulweather. Though I suspect you will give in when we threaten the stick. Or we get Inspector Langton to put you in his cell. You do not like him coming, do you? It is a wonder these days children will do anything at all. Dora does what she is told, do you not?' Dora beamed.

And so the meal continued in this endless way. After a time, I longed to see one of the children pick a plate up and smash it against the wall or cry out in rage. At last, Bell was able to turn the conversation to London, for I was sure we were there to see if Norman had any connections to interest us. 'Ah yes,' said our host, 'I visit the great capital regularly, for my late father had some property there. I would often meet with Jefford, which is why I do not take the matter as seriously as some, for I am used to his pranks and games.'

Of course I could see the Doctor's interest quicken. And when at last the meal had ended and the children had gone to play (though I could not even begin to imagine what form of 'play' was permitted in this oppressive place), Bell sat down in the overheated drawing room with Norman and returned to the subject.

I am sure the Doctor had calculated there were two issues at stake. The first was the possibility Norman himself had some involvement, for his contacts with London and Jefford meant he must now be added to the list of suspects. I myself found no great difficulty in seeing the father of this horrific household being implicated in some way. But there was another issue entirely. Assuming his innocence, was it not possible he could shed light on Jefford's London companions? Perhaps he had even met Cream himself.

At first, the questioning seemed to go promisingly. Norman talked with amusement of Jefford's endless gambling and his capacity to offer wagers of the most outrageous kind. But when pressed for details of these activities or his other acquaintances, the man's manner became irritatingly coy and superior. 'Ah no,' he smirked, 'you will not lure me there, these are gentlemen's confidences, Dr Bell. When gentlemen go out to play, they have their own rules and their own little secrets. I cannot possibly betray such things, but you are a man of the world and I am sure you can imagine some of the more interesting activities of gentlemen at their leisure.'

This tone was as unexpected as it was infuriating, all the more so in the light of the oppressive atmosphere of his house which we had been enduring for the past two hours. In the event, Bell did not press the matter but pretended an interest in the local architecture so he could investigate the rest of the house.

'What a household,' Bell said to me with open disgust as we made our way back along the road.

'Could you not have demanded he answer your questions?' I asked, for I would love to have seen the man's monstrous complacency pricked. 'Even Sir Walter did so in the end.'

'I was tempted to try, Doyle, but Norman is a solicitor who would no doubt make great play of his rights and of the fact we cannot yet prove any crime has been committed. At least I am sure if Cream were ever in that house, he is not there now. We will come back to Mr Norman.'

As we walked towards the inn, where already we could see the cab that would take Bell to Lowestoft, I noticed that inspite of our lunch the Doctor was in better spirits than he had been all day. 'I believe,' he said, 'Mrs Marner's maid has a solution to this, if she would but tell us, and perhaps we will have another attempt later. The Norman household too holds great points of interest, especially the father's treatment of his children. I hope to be back not too long after dark, Doyle, and would ask only that you field any messages that arrive. But I am glad to tell you we are making progress.' And he moved off to confer with the driver.

I had decided to walk out that afternoon, wanting the air and the isolation. For reasons of my own, I am not fond of beaches but I forced myself to explore a little of the Dunwich shingle and it was good to feel the wind on my face and smell the salt in the breeze. Because it was a blustery day, the waves were huge and white clouds scudded across the blue sky. After a time, I turned around from the sea and came back to the little path which led up to the cliffs.

Soon I had climbed through the trees to that extraordinary spot where the ruined church stood on the very edge of the cliff. Here again were the cracked and mossy gravestones, those closest to the edge at a perilous angle as the wind moaned in the trees behind me. But I took some care not to go too near the drop.

After a time, I plunged on, trying as far as possible to keep to the cliff and not walk inland. Often it was hard but there was a path of a kind and I pressed on with the booming surf below on my left. I suppose it was foolish weather to have chosen for such an excursion, for a freak gust might have taken me over the edge, but the view was extraordinary. Stretched out below on my left was the rough sea and pounding waves, around me the blowing grass, above a turbulent blue and grey sky.

Suddenly there was a great cry from in front of me. I had not noticed the figure, for it was far ahead, at a point where the path curved away to take account of a further landslide, but it had seen me and was waving.

Moving quickly on, I recognised the solid outline of Dr Bulweather, his dog not far behind. However, much of his attention was centred on something below. Indeed he was standing in the teeth of the gale, which sent his black coat fluttering behind him like a bat and I was amazed the hat was still on that great head.

He turned as I came closer. 'I am very glad to see you,' he shouted into the wind, smiling. 'I believe I have solved one of the mysteries, though only the smallest.'

He pointed with his stick directly below him. Soon I was beside him, and I will admit it was a fearful place to stand. If any more of the cliff gave way while we were in this spot there would be no hope for either of us. And the wind only had to go up a notch to sweep us over. I kept my balance on the back foot as I struggled to see what he had found.

At first I could make out nothing except the swooping seagulls and roaring waves. But then I steadied myself and leant forward. Following the line of his stick, I observed that ninety or so yards beneath and across from us was a rocky outcrop. A dark shape lay upon it. At first I could not be sure what this was. Then I made out the leg and a large head and ears. At once my mind raced back to Jefford's room and that great stain of blood. So now it seemed the sceptics' hopes of an innocent explanation for all that blood were utterly dashed.

For lying below me, perfectly intact though long dead, was a huge pig.

## The Snow on the Beach

I was shouting my confirmation of the sight when the wind
suddenly whipped up and we lurched forward. Bulweather clapped
a hand on my shoulder and, for a second, the weight of it might
have caused me to lose my balance altogether but he got a firm hold
and yanked me back and away from the edge, throwing his own
weight backwards too.

'My apologies,' he said as we took a few more paces for additional
safety until we reached his waiting dog. 'I did not mean to
manhandle you but I know the treacheries of this cliff in the wind
as well as anyone and it was my fault for putting you at risk. Did you
see it?'

'Yes, it is the lost pig,' I said, my heart still racing, for I knew how
close we had come to calamity.

'It must be.' He nodded. 'And we almost suffered the same fate.
Well at least we can tell Dr Bell we have eliminated one theory
about the blood in Jefford's house.'

Together we walked back along the cliff, though we had learnt
our lesson and kept well away from the edge. Naturally we talked
of the case, and Bulweather said he was obeying Bell's injunction
to look for any guest or stranger in the houses he visited. It so
happened he had been called out to the house of Inspector

Langton whose leg was giving him trouble. 'It was a wound he contracted in a fall in London and he is never quite free of it. There was somebody else in the house and he saw I was aware of it. He told me he had a friend from London staying a while, an old colleague.'

We had almost reached Dunwich now and, before we went down the path, we both took one last look at the majestic view. It was becoming colder and Bulweather pointed up with his stick to where a great ridge of white cloud had gathered to the east over the North Sea. 'We are in for some weather,' he said. 'Well, that is the nature of the place.'

Of course, he insisted I return to his house for some refreshment. And soon we were by his fireside with hot tea and scones and had fallen to talking about medicine and my early experiences as a doctor. I can still see his eager face as he sat forward in his armchair, munching a buttered scone. He was intrigued to hear about my many initial difficulties in practice in Southsea, for he obviously loved nothing more than to talk about such things.

'So was medicine always your vocation?' he asked.

I hesitated and then I decided for once in my life I would be honest on this question, for – despite his own sadness – this man had ultimately been honest with us.

'No it was not, in fact it was not even my idea,' I said.

'So it was your father's?' he replied. 'That is not so unusual.'

'No,' I said doggedly. 'It was not my father's. My father has suffered from a long illness. It was a friend of the family who suggested it.'

I had never quite admitted this to anyone before. I had, of course, confided to Elsbeth about my father's illness and done so in detail but I had not thought it necessary to tell her I owed my medical career to a man who was not even part of my family and whose influence over my mother I had come to distrust.

Bulweather, however, showed little surprise. 'Well,' said cheerfully, 'we all come to medicine in a variety of ways, what matters is that we arrive there. And it is good you have. I am sorry, though, to hear of your father's malady. There is nothing harder in the world than facing up to the illness of those we love. We have that in common.'

I wondered whether to tell him now we had more in common even than that, for my father's malady was a nervous condition quite as crippling to the pursuit of a normal life as that which afflicted his wife's sister. But I decided I would wait to talk of this another time. And we moved on to discuss more positive things.

The discussion in front of that comfortable fire proved so absorbing I suddenly realised with a start I must be getting back to the inn, for I had promised the Doctor I would be on hand. Bulweather urged me to bring Bell back to dine that night for he had Angus Hare and Sir Walter as guests, but I told him I could not be sure of the Doctor's plans and must therefore decline.

Outside it was already starting to get dark and had become very cold. When I reached the inn, the landlord handed me an envelope marked urgent. It was for Bell but I tore it open.

> Please come at once. Ellie has gone.
> Leonora Marner

Fortunately, Bell arrived just as I was setting off, stepping down from his cab and smiling as he saw me. At once I thrust the note into his hand, explaining it had just arrived. He took one look at it and his smile vanished.

It was not yet dark, but the whole village seemed quite deserted and a few flakes of snow were starting to fall. As we made our way along the street and came to Leonora Marner's house I told Bell of our discovery of the missing pig. And also the intelligence about Langton's guest. But what might have interested him a day earlier now seemed minor, for all his attention was on the note in his hand. Mrs Marner came to the door almost at once, wrapped in an elegant shawl, looking extremely concerned.

'Oh but I hope she is all right,' she said as she led us through into the main room where the cat was in the corner, staring at us as we entered. 'Her cat is back here at least, that gives me hope.'

'Would you please tell us,' said Bell, 'when you found Ellie was gone?' His tone was gentle but I could see great concern in his eyes.

'Certainly,' she answered. 'I went out for my walk as usual at around two. I left her here. As a matter of fact, she was in this room, for she does her sewing here sometimes after lunch. I took quite a long walk up the hill and then I called on Miss Charlotte Jefford in the inn. I find her a sweet person and we have become fast friends. She too is bothered by these accusations.'

'And you returned here when?' said Bell.

'It was after four. The house was entirely empty, Ellie's sewing had been put away. The cat was back a little later.'

'Had she taken anything?' Bell's eyes flitted around the room.

'She wears her coat and boots, no personal things have gone.'

I saw a flicker of anxiety cross Bell's face. 'Tell me, Mrs Marner,' he said, 'how exactly had Ellie been acting today since we were here? How was her manner?'

'She was still a little nervous but I thought she seemed slightly more at ease except—' She broke off.

'Yes?' the Doctor pressed.

Well, she would pace about a little. She would walk to the window and stare out then return to her chair. I wondered if she was frightened some ill-wisher was outside but there was nobody about.'

Bell turned to the window, which had a view of the street. 'Do you mind if I look around your house, Mrs Marner? It may be important.'

Her permission was granted and Bell wasted no time. He went straight to the waste-paper basket and looked into it. He found nothing and went out to the hall. There he bent down before another waste receptacle and seemed to see something, a ball of paper.

He took it out and unwrapped it. In his hand was an envelope with handwriting upon it. One word only: Ellie.

The envelope was empty but Bell seemed very excited. 'Mrs Marner,' he said, 'this may be very important. You have mentioned that Ellie walked out with Colin Harding. Have you any idea where?'

'Well, I believe she went to the servants' quarters at Greyfriars House.'

'But anywhere else? I must urge you to think.'

She considered. 'Why, I recall they sometimes walked along the beach.'

Bell turned to the door at once. 'You will stay here, Mrs Marner, in case she reappears.'

In the street it was now bitterly cold and tiny flakes of snow were falling in the last of the light. They were not thick but seemed to add to our growing sense of apprehension. We made our way as quickly as possible down the little path and then turned out on to the beach. There was not a soul to be seen as the wind blew the snowflakes in our faces.

Bell scanned the narrow belt of shingle, swinging his silver-topped cane. On these pebbles it was hard to see anything but he detected what he thought were some imprints and we moved off.

Once the shingle gave way to sand, it became far easier, for here the footprints were quite clear. The feet were small but it was notable that no marks returned in the other direction.

We plunged on along the sand, jumping the black groynes leading down to the water, and I remember the grimness of the Doctor's face in the light from the sea. The beach at Dunwich extends for miles to the north and very soon there is no sign of human habitation, not a human creature, just the sea on your right and the marshland on your left, but still the footprints stretched out before us. Indeed there was something quite horrible about the way they led on and on into such desolation.

Soon, we were running. I even called Ellie's name but there was no response, not even the sound of a gull on that endless beach as the snow fell.

And then all of a sudden Bell stopped short, for he had seen, before I had, that the footprints veered off up the beach towards the marsh. We raced up the sand and had soon reached a watery waste where of course all obvious marks stopped. Was there hope I wondered. Had she somehow crossed this expanse and turned back towards the town? I was about to voice it when Bell gave a cry and pointed.

A grey shape lay on a reedy bank, not twenty yards away. It was bunched up oddly. A trench of shallow water ran between us and the place but we waded across this with ease.

Ellie Barnes was on the bank but she was not destined to tell us or anyone else what had led her there. She lay on her back, arms beside her, the snowflakes landing and melting on her open eyes. Her mouth was one great gaping bloody wound. And her tongue, neatly excised, lay beside her hand.

# Part Four:
# The Rune and the Deaths

# The Writing in the Water

As Ellie Barnes was carried off the sands by a sombre, torchlit procession, I tried desperately to suppress a torrent of memories. For Elsbeth's body had been found on a beach.

Bell himself was ashen grey, talking grimly to Langton, before he returned with me to resume his search of the site. There was no question that the business was now serious and it was likely, the Inspector thought, that a Scotland Yard man would join us some time the following day. As to the post-mortem, since foul play was certain, Bell would have to concede the body to the official pathologist in Lowestoft, though he had already established there was little to see other than the savage wound which had so obviously caused death.

'But what possessed her to come out here in the first place?' said Langton. 'She knew nobody else beside Mrs Marner and Colin Harding who was dead.'

'That may be so,' said Bell as we approached the site. 'Yet something did possess her. She came here, I am persuaded, because of her belief in it. If we could but find the letter that summoned her, yet it was not on her person. We can only suppose her murderer removed it.'

Once back at the spot in the marsh, the Doctor paid particular attention to the water around the bank where Ellie had been found. He had borrowed some waders and now stood knee-deep in freezing water as two men on the bank close by illuminated his way with lanterns.

Even in that cold miserable place, it was an unforgettable sight. The two shadowy figures with stick lanterns bent forward to send their beams of light down on this eagle-featured figure crouching above the water like some human heron, while the tiny snowflakes fell all around.

I imagine Bell was calculating whether the letter could have been in Ellie's hand and dropped into the water as she was struck down. This was why he concentrated on a spot near to the corpse's right hand and then worked his way on and round, constantly trawling his own hand in the depths for, despite the lanterns, he could see very little of the bottom.

It was so cold, the Doctor had to withdraw the hand frequently but, despite my protests, he would not let me join him. 'If it is there other feet may stamp on it and destroy it completely. It is better you leave this to me,' he replied, for all the world as if he were discussing some map he had laid out before the fire in his study rather than the waters of a muddy marsh at midnight on the easternmost tip of England.

He had come about halfway round the bank when his expression changed and he plunged his other hand in the water as well. There was a long delay and I could only guess how cold his fingers were becoming, but very slowly he drew out a sodden and folded piece of paper. There was clearly writing on it of a kind and once he had seen this he placed it carefully in a small dry bag he had brought for possible evidence. I could see his fingers were blue and I insisted he stopped now and let the men continue or waited till morning. After a time, he agreed.

Since Mrs Marner was being consoled by her sister, and Dr Bulweather had kindly gone to see they were all right, Bell and I returned to the inn to examine the paper. He unpacked it with enormous care in his room, remarking how fortunate we were that it had remained intact.

What Bell had pulled out of the marsh was a handwritten letter, although much of the writing was illegible where the ink had bled and faded. Indeed there were only about forty character we could decipher.

– –l– –

I –m  – – t– – – – –  t– –  sp – – –  h– –  w– – – – –

Yo–  m– – –  – –t – –  fr – – – – – – – –

– –me  – –  – – –  – – –ch  – –  – – –  sp– –  wh– – –  –e

us– –  – –  me– –

Yo–  m– – –  – – – –g  – – –  ru– –  – – – –  y– –

– –l– –

The Doctor showed real satisfaction. 'We are very lucky,' he said, 'because the best line with pairs of letters comes in the middle, no doubt because the water was held off slightly by the fold in the paper. Indeed, it confirms what I suspected.'

But after a few moments, as he stared, his face fell. 'So she had it,' he said, 'making me a fool for not pressing harder. I could have saved her life.' He did not, however, elucidate. Instead a copy was made and he handed it to me to see what I could do. I still have it beside me now.

'So, Doyle,' he said after I had puzzled over this for a time, 'what can you deduce?'

'Certainly some words are easy enough,' I agreed. 'The second is "am", the fourth "the", the eighth "you". The last line must begin "you" and end with it too. I suppose I could do better with more time but what I cannot understand is why the thing begins and ends with the same word. For the first must surely be the address "Ellie" and yet so it seems is the last. Is she writing letters to herself?'

He moved over from the fire he had asked to be made up in his room where he was thawing his hands and took it up again at once. 'Ah,' he said, 'well that is not very likely but to be fair I am coming to it with assumptions which you lack. You see,' he said, leaning forward again to pore over it, 'there are two principal ways of approaching a simple task such as this, which has none of the complexities of a cipher. The one most favoured is to rely on the commonest of words and phraseology which is exactly what you have done with your deductions. For example, that after the greeting the first two words are "I am". That is indeed hardly a deduction at all in the sense there is nothing else in the world they could be. Assuming the writer is literate, no other letter in the English alphabet could be inserted here and fit.

'However,' he continued, 'I believe we can assume literacy, given the general care of the characters. Therefore you moved swiftly to identify obvious words but you could have taken it far further. Let us look for example at the ten commonest verbs in English which are, in order: *be, have, do, say, make, go, take, come, see, and get.*

'Now, can we see any of those here? Indeed we can at the start of line three there is an obvious "Come". And considering two other lines have "You" with a capital, I think we can say definitively this is a letter largely of instruction, apart from the first line which is information about its writer.

'Now,' he went on, 'it would be possible to apply the rules I have just outlined and solve it but it would take a few minutes. I had a far easier way than that, for I already knew something of this letter before I found it. It was obvious from all Ellie Barnes had told us that someone was manipulating her feelings in some way. Colin Harding was a strong possibility with all his talk of runes, but after he was found dead, I still received that distinct impression. This, rather than any fear of the superstitious townsfolk, was why I insisted she stayed inside the house. But then today Mrs Marner told us how Ellie kept watching the window. She was clearly waiting either for someone or more likely some communication. You saw me find the envelope in which it arrived and now we have the communication itself.

'Therefore, at once I start to look for words that I associate with the girl and what is clearly preoccupying her, making the task no more difficult than the clues in a crossword puzzle. Immediately it seemed very likely the noun after "the" (which you identified in the first line) is "spell". And on the second line, surely "frightened" is unmistakable as the fifth word, not only because I associate it strongly with her but also because only a tiny number of words in the language have ten letters beginning fr and the others, "frequented" for example, cannot be intelligible here.

'Also in the last line, that "ru" surely must be "rune" following on from "spell". Again, there would seem to be a definite article ahead of it and the only alternatives are "rule" or "ruin", neither likely.

'Now let us look at it again with these words in place.'

– –|– –

I am – –t– – – – – the spell h– – w– – – – –

You m– – – – –t – – frightened

Come – – – – – – – –ch – – – – – sp– – wh– – – –e

us– – – – me– –

You m– – – – – –g the rune – – – – you

– –|– –

'At once,' said Bell, 'most of it becomes clear. "You must not be frightened." That is absolutely obvious for the second line now we have come so far. But why should she be frightened? Well, that must be what follows. She is being summoned somewhere, the "come" tells us as much, but of course we know very well where she *was* summoned. To the beach. And there it is at once in the spaces and the "ch" of "beach".

'The second part of the line might be considered more difficult but we can assume now it is instructing her exactly where to come, for the beach is miles long. The "wh" therefore give us "where" instantly. For the word following there are only five possibilities for two letters ending in "e", namely "be", "he", "me", "we" or "ye". Well, given the letter's familiarity surely "we" seems the more likely candidate and should be tried first. So now we have: "Come to the beach – – – – – sp– – where we us– – – – me– –"

'Clearly a child would fill in the gaps,' said Bell. ' "Come to the beach to the spot where we used to meet."

'And now the last line. Again an instruction. "You m– – – – – – –g the rune – – – – you."

'See?' said Bell. 'Once again, having filled in a little more, the rest is a small child's puzzle. What do you read?'

' "You must bring the rune with you," ' I said, 'So she had the thing then, whatever it is.'

Bell nodded gloomily. 'I very much fear so. Therefore, now we return to the first line, a line of information. I would add one simple word to what we already know. The only possibility after "spell"; is "has", or "had", the former being more immediate and likely.

' "I am – –t– – – – – the spell has w– – – – –." It is a fraction harder than the others, but need not detain us long. The writer is clearly stating that the spell has done something. What could a spell do? I suggest "worked".

'The third word must therefore reflect that. How has this spell worked? On its own there are a few difficulties, I admit. Not so many words are that long with a "t" as third letter. Even so, I accept you might prefer to consult the dictionary to be sure, but then we have no need for that, for there is other evidence to help us.

'You stated your confusion that the letter begins and ends with the same name, but there you fail to consider the possibility of pure coincidence. There are other names besides Ellie that have an "L" as a third letter. You have only to consider who we know for a fact she met before at the beach, and whose instructions she would be likely to obey.'

'Colin?' I said. 'But he is dead.'

'Yes,' cried Bell, 'but do you not recall her voicing her belief that the power would bring him back? She believed in magic, Doyle, and necromancy is a branch of magic. Now go back to the line again. It must be a verb and one describing something that has happened to him.'

'My God, it tells her he has *returned.*'

'Precisely.' He put it down.

I spoke quietly, all the excitement of discovery quelled by the thought of it. 'But that is horrible. The idea of the girl lured along the beach by the idea a lover had returned from death. And someone waiting there. Surely she would have some doubts.'

'I suspect it is more than likely,' said Bell sombrely. 'She was not a fool, but someone had worked the thing in her mind over a period. And we must check this writing against Harding's.'

There was a long pause. 'Someone? You think it is him?'

'It has his flavour,' said the Doctor.

# The Roots of Fear

Next morning it was obvious to me Bell had not slept much better than I. But he still ate breakfast, though I had little stomach for it.

'He has what he sought, whatever it may be,' I said. 'If that is the case, will he not now be far away?'

'Yes,' said Bell. 'I have considered the same possibility and if you are right it is a gross failure on my part. I am coming to understand several aspects of this case, some of which are mere dressing. But I never dreamt Harding had given Ellie Barnes the rune. It must have been in the house with her and it explains her fear. Yet until we know more we must not give up hope. Indeed,' he thought for a moment, 'the nature of the business makes me inclined to think there are still grounds for hope.' This did not give me great reassurance but I said nothing.

Langton, too, was not in the best of moods when he joined us after breakfast. There was some delay in getting any help to him from Scotland Yard and meanwhile word of Ellie Barnes's death was spreading rapidly throughout Dunwich and its surroundings.

'Of course we have not divulged details but the rumours are racing,' he said grimly, as we sat in the small sitting room. 'That she died a witch's death at the hands of her familiar, or was punished by the victim of her spells. There is real fear here now.'

'Which is precisely what is intended,' said Bell. 'It was done for effect.'

'So you do not suppose this was done out of some fear of witchcraft?' asked Langton.

'Certainly not,' said Bell. 'This was not caused by fear, it was done to create it. And if we are not very careful it may succeed. Now I urgently need a sample of Harding's handwriting. I am sure Sir Walter Monk will have some, for Harding was his employee.'

Langton agreed, allowing Bell to keep the letter in the meantime. 'For until they send someone, I will be glad of your help.'

'Thank you, Inspector,' said Bell. He leant back in his chair, looking at Langton. 'Now I do not wish to show ingratitude but I suppose I must ask you about Stoneleigh Street.'

I have never seen a man's jaw drop quite so far and so fast. Langton went pale too and stared back at Bell with quiet anger. 'Well, did you know before or have you been enquiring?'

'I thought I recalled your name,' said Bell brightly. 'And a day ago I refreshed my memory with the help of some newspaper cuttings and other material which Inspector Miller kindly sent. I thought it was time to bring it out into the open.'

'Why?' Langton asked fiercely. 'For if you enquired you will be aware no charges were ever brought against me.'

'Indeed,' said Bell, 'but it was thought prudent for you to leave the Yard and London.'

'And so I did, but it has no bearing on anything now,' Langton asserted.

'You were accused of breaking up a gambling den after receiving bribes from some of the men who were its customers and had large debts. Once the place was closed, they were clear of these debts, is that correct?' Bell said.

Langton sighed. 'Yes, and there was not a word of truth in any of it. The place was cheating everyone who crossed the threshold and that rumour was their way of paying me back for exposing it,' Langton said.

'I understand that was the conclusion, but I raise it for one reason: one of those who benefited was Oliver Jefford.'

Langton looked at him, somewhat sheepishly. 'You are a resourceful man, Doctor.'

'Which means you knew him before he ever arrived here and you did not even tell us as much?'

'I admit I had met him, yes. I admit also I did not want to have it all gone over again. But he was hardly a friend, we knew of each other, that's all.' Langton lowered his eyes under Bell's fierce glare.

'And did you see him when he was here?' Bell asked.

'I passed him here once or twice when I was about my business. We conversed a little but I never went into his house, I never sat down with him.'

'And you did not meet his companions here?' The Doctor was still staring fiercely.

'Of course not, that would have been something to report. I did not.' Langton clenched his fist. It was obvious he disliked these questions.

'But you knew his friends and associates in London?' the Doctor pressed.

'Not at all. Apart from that business we were hardly in the same circle. And if you are curious about his Stoneleigh associates, it is a matter of record.'

'Yes,' Bell sighed. 'I have consulted that record. It is, I will admit, inconsistent. But I understand, too, you have had a guest from London in your home.'

'You are the devil himself,' said Langton, his head bobbing. 'I am free to do so if I wish. It was only a cousin of mine who is a clerk and wanted some rest. He is gone now.'

'Yes, I am aware. And we can move on but we may return to the business in London one day and I wished to bring it into the open merely because you had not spoken of it before, which made me somewhat suspicious.'

'It was perhaps foolish of me to think I could evade it with you,

Doctor. I hope we can now return to being allies, for there is no question we have a murder to solve.'

'That is my hope too,' said the Doctor, getting to his feet. The conversation was closed.

For the rest of the morning, rather to my surprise, Bell was not out on the scene but busying himself with telegrams and, of all things, an interview with Norman's son Tommy, so I went in search of Charlotte Jefford. I was not surprised to learn she was with Mrs Marner so, not wishing to intrude, decided to have another look at the ground.

Outside it was still bitterly cold but the snow had not lain and the sky was clear. I was turning down to the beach when I encountered Angus Hare, Bulweather's partner, who hailed me and came over to talk.

'Dr Doyle,' he said, 'this is a dreadful business about Miss Marner's maid. I am spending my time today consoling people. You know Edward Norman is in quite a state about the whole thing. He says Bell has been intimidating his son. Who could possibly be behind all this?'

I was not so surprised to hear of Edward Norman's state, especially when I recalled how he had constantly denied the seriousness of these events and talked of 'little' mysteries. He was exactly the type of man who refuses to acknowledge unpleasant truths and then panics when they become inescapable.

'Dr Bell has experience of such matters, as your partner will tell you,' I said as calmly as I could. 'I have hopes he will come to an answer.'

'Well, I for my part have hopes it is soon,' he said. 'For it seems to me this place has not benefited from any of its new visitors in recent weeks. I will bid you good morning.' And in this rather hostile manner he went on his way.

It was not a very auspicious start to my investigations and indeed the day went on as it had begun. I paced the beach but found no one and saw nothing. I trudged back up to Harding's little hut, now occupied by another labourer, but again there was nothing at all to see. I began to feel like a fool and would have gone in to visit Bulweather, except it seemed much more likely than not he would be out. And so I returned to be told Bell was asking for me in his room.

I found him there, staring down at something on his table. 'Where have you been?' he said. 'This was sent over and I find it most interesting.'

Before him on his table was the original note and a letter Harding had written in connection with some purchase on behalf of the estate. Bell had his magnifying glass out and was studying them eagerly.

'You see,' he said, allowing me to look. 'It is not exactly the same writing, how could it be? But it is a good copy. Someone went to the trouble of making a fair facsimile of Harding's hand. He is good on the "e" and the "m" yet see how the "g" gives him away.'

Even without the aid of the enlargement, I could see exactly what he meant. There were good copies of many of the letters but the "g" was entirely different, smaller and without a loop. And, as Bell showed me, the "h" too was deficient. I knew that Cream had the ability to do this, for experience had shown us he was adept at disguising and varying his handwriting if he wished it.

So I supposed it was progress, but already two and probably three people were dead and I was beginning to feel we were being laughed at. Was he watching us, stumbling around in search of him? My mood was not improved when the Doctor announced he had once again to travel to Lowestoft today and that he wished me to accompany him.

'But where is he?' I cried. 'Even if he is still here, he seems to be able to act with impunity, while we move around the periphery of things.'

Bell put the letter away, showing no offence whatsoever at my outburst. 'Yes, we are having to clear the way to him. He has put a number of obstacles in our path, some clever, some foolish, but we must not be distracted, we must be methodical. My belief is he remains here, for I am sure the rune is connected to something here. So we continue our work.'

'If only,' I objected, 'it was more rewading. You send telegrams and talk to a child who strangles birds. While I walk empty beaches. And what if it is nothing to do with him at all? After all, we still have no direct proof other than a possible sighting and some coincidences.'

'More than one, Doyle. It would seem our positions are still reversed. Do you not feel him here?'

I did not reply. The truth was these deeds did bear his stamp, but I found it hard to endure the fact he still seemed to be ahead of us in all of it. And to know also that others in this place could be harbouring him.

'And as for the child who strangles birds,' said Bell. 'You may be interested to learn it was the most eventful meeting I have had. I learnt more that was truly important about the case from him than anyone else I have met.'

# The Rune

Although the weather was no longer freezing, the journey to Lowestoft was long and arduous and I felt a certain impatience to be leaving the scene of these crimes for another place entirely, no matter how much it helped the Doctor's enquiries.

Nor was he very forthcoming about these enquiries or why he wished me to accompany him. In the event, he called at several fairly humble addresses in the town while I waited with the cab and seemed to come out frustrated from each one until the last, where he stayed longest and appeared satisfied with whatever business he had conducted.

Then we visited a library and also (more satisfactorily for the Doctor, it seemed) a large second-hand book shop, where he bought several books and pamphlets, including I noticed some medical texts for which I could conceive no purpose. And then, somewhat to my amazement, we took the cab back. It had been, for me, a completely pointless journey and Bell obviously guessed what I was thinking and apologised. 'I had expected the last interview to be more difficult than it was,' he added, though he did not enlighten me further.

Upon my return after this wild goose chase I was doubly anxious to find Miss Jefford and also call upon Mrs Marner, whom I had not seen since the tragedy. But events were ahead of me. As I came down from my room, Bulweather was at the bottom of the stairs.

'Ah, Doyle,' he said, 'I am very glad to see you. Mrs Marner is outside and wishes to say goodbye. As you would expect, she leaves to stay with her sister. I have comforted her as much as I can and am called out on a visit to Edward Norman who, between ourselves, ranks among the fussiest patients in Suffolk.'

I went out, noticing that the temperature was again dropping, though there was no sign of the previous night's snow. In the road, waiting to join a private coach, was Mrs Marner.

She looked tired and sad-eyed yet she was composed and after the introductions she shook my hand charmingly. 'I will spend Christmas away, Dr Doyle, and I hope to heaven you find the answer to this business, whatever it is. It has all been horrible and I simply cannot bear to think of poor Ellie.' She clutched my arm. 'It would have been quick, would you please at least tell me that?'

I was able to do so because I felt fairly confident it was true, though I did not specify the nature of the speed. Most people had merely been told it was a head-wound and I had no intention of going further.

'If only,' she went on, 'she had not gone out, if only I had stayed to see she did not. But I cannot dwell on that now. And as if all that was not enough, here to be all but driven from our home. I would have gladly had more time but if people are to be like this, what can I do? It is an astonishment to me, especially after all that has happened.'

'Do you feel there is still bitterness here even after last night's tragedy?' I asked. But I was recalling now that Bulweather had said Mrs Marner was leaving 'as you would expect'. Yet I had not necessarily expected it. Certainly there was no mention of this move last night.

'Why, of course I do. Have you not heard, Dr Doyle? My house was attacked, "witch" daubed on the wall, and many of my things lie in ruins. And to do it only hours after Ellie's death. Thank heaven her poor cat was out or they would no doubt have hurt it, because of all this nonsense about it being a familiar. But it has been more out than in and Sir Walter has taken the poor thing, thanks to Dr Bulweather. Let them try to attack Sir Walter Monk's house, that is what I say, I am glad to be gone and I do not know when I will return.'

Here she was on the verge of tears, in her excitement a very changed woman from the discreet widow I had first encountered. But before I bid her farewell, I learnt more of the story from herself and her sister, who had now appeared. Evidently they had left the house earlier that afternoon to walk and visit the small church at the end of the street in order to discuss where Ellie would be buried, for Mrs Marner felt Ellie's parents would approve of such a place.

In the event they had been out for more than an hour and, when they returned, the whole house had been vandalised. It had proved a horrible postscript to a horrible event and there was no question for either one of them of staying there any further.

I was myself incensed at the cruelty of it. Was there such fear and pent-up fury in this place that someone, or perhaps more than one, would do such a thing? If so, I felt deeply ashamed on behalf of my sex for, like the men who hunted the so-called witch across the heath, they were surely the main instigators. Or was this perhaps another act of our enemy, designed like so much else of his doing to promote disharmony and hatred? After I bid Mrs Marner farewell, I watched her cab roll away and the last I saw of this quiet, impressive woman she was sitting bolt upright, head forward, not wishing to cast even a parting glance at the community that appeared to have rejected her.

As I turned back, Bell had just come out of the inn, intending, as I later discovered, to find Inspector Langton. When I told him my news, his shock exceeded even mine.

'What?' He turned in the direction of Mrs Marner's at once. 'And I have missed her, you say. We must go to the house now.'

He looked both worried and exhilarated as we walked. It was now almost completely dark but there was a moon. 'And this occurred earlier in the afternoon, you say?' he said.

'I imagine it was about two that they left the house.' We had arrived at Mrs Marner's, where there was a light inside, and Bell knocked on the door.

It was opened by John Wallace, the village constable, who knew us by now and had no objection to our entering. But he warned us that some women of the village had offered their help to clear it up and were still engaged in the task.

This must naturally have been enormously irritating to Bell, but he was prudent enough to hold his tongue, for what would have been the use of remonstrating either with the constable or with the two kind old women who were charitably engaged in tidying up the drawing room?

In any case, it was not hard to grasp the violence of what had occurred here. One armchair was still upended, the carpets lifted, curtains down, even some crockery appeared to have been smashed. And on the wall by the mantelpiece a piece of coal had evidently been used to smear one word in black ugly letters.

WITCH

Bell stared around at this, and I followed him upstairs, where the damage was similar if somewhat less extensive.

Again a carpet was pulled up and it seemed the bed had been manhandled. Bell spent a long time here before returning downstairs to question the women about what exactly had been disturbed.

He thanked them charitably and we walked back to the hall. 'I was a fool to go to Lowestoft,' he said. 'But I would never have imagined . . . How could I?' We came out of the house as I waited for him to go on. It was much colder now, but the Doctor appeared not to notice as we turned into the road. 'I fear I have sorely underestimated the poor woman's resourcefulness.'

'Whose? Mrs Marner's?' I asked, though I had an inkling of what he meant.

'Ellie's. What vandal would bother to tear up carpets or look under beds? No, our enemy or his ally was searching for the rune. We have to conclude, therefore, Ellie did not bring it to the beach. That much is unmistakable. But why, Doyle? It is extraordinary. She was scared, she was superstitious, she obviously half-believed her love was returned. Why not obey his injunction? There is nobody else she could have given it to. She knew nobody else.'

We were in the village's main street now and a great moon hung low over the marsh, which shimmered in its own mist. 'I agree it is a mystery,' I replied. 'But only now a theoretical one. If she was keeping the rune in that house, he has found it.'

'Perhaps,' said the Doctor lightly as he looked out over the marsh. 'But two things suggest otherwise. Firstly the evidence of the house itself. So extensive a search suggests to me frustration and even irritation rather than success. Secondly, I return to the central question, why did she not take it to the beach?'

'Because she was too frightened to handle it,' I suggested.

'But Harding must have given it to her. She handled it then. No, there is a real question here. The instruction in the letter is emphatic. She was looking out and waiting for it. Yet she disobeys. Why?'

We walked the rest of the way to the inn without further conversation. Bell was thoughtful, saying he wanted to reflect and might see me at dinner. I went to the little private sitting room which was empty and stoked up the fire into a blaze. Then I sat back and tried to find some order in the events that were unfolding.

It was deeply depressing to think that, while I had been sitting uselessly in a cab in Lowestoft, our enemy had been freely ransacking Mrs Marner's house. I could see there was some logic in

Bell's supposition that Cream had been unsuccessful, but still it was only supposition. Perhaps he had found what he wanted. Yet if I had stayed here as I wished, my intention had been to call on Mrs Marner after the events of the day before. Was there not every chance I might have caught him? And even if he had escaped, at least all conjecture would be at an end. We would have found our culprit. And the authorities here would be hunting for an individual rather than a series of ghosts.

Just as I came to this conclusion, the door opened and Charlotte Jefford walked in. She looked far better than when I had last seen her. Her hair, though tied back, was less formal and sparkled in the firelight but her eyes too were brighter and she smiled when she saw me.

'Oh, Dr Doyle, I had been hoping very much to catch you,' she said as she entered.

'You look fully recovered, I am glad to say,' I replied, getting to my feet. And I invited her to sit down.

'Well, I have slept for some hours, and I do feel better,' she said as she sat down opposite me. 'I had a letter from home and it reminded me of other places and other things and, for a time, I did not worry about my troubles here.'

'I am sure,' I said with more certainty than I felt, 'that is an excellent remedy. There are always good things to turn away to from the bad.'

'Yes,' she said. 'It is what I told Leonora. I am glad she has left, although I enjoyed her company. For I think she will be happier with her sister for a little and then can return. But, Dr Doyle, I would like to talk of normal things for once. Tell me of you, how do you live, where is your practice?'

I told her about Southsea. She seemed attentive and interested. She had never been there or to Edinburgh, for she lived in Berkshire with her parents. But we both shared a knowledge of London and also unexpectedly of the Lancashire moors, for as a child she made regular visits to her aunt's country house near

Longridge Fell, which was not far from my boarding school. We talked intensely of the moors and found to our surprise there was one particular spot, a narrow sheep path by a stream studded with furze bushes that each of us had regarded as a refuge.

We were doing our best to forget the trouble around us and must have succeeded for after a time she turned to me and said quietly, 'I have told you of a letter I had from home. Yes it pleased me but it was not just hearing of old places that changed my mood. For you see I had some other good news. It is a secret, though not for very long. And I would like very much to take you into my confidence.'

Of course I told her I would be pleased. 'The truth is,' she went on, 'that someone I hold dear has asked me to marry him.'

It was unexpected. But I was pleased for her and extremely grateful to her suitor at home for his timing. It would surely take her mind away from all that was happening here. So I congratulated her, heartily and genuinely.

Perhaps too, if I am being honest, I felt a slight flicker of envy for this Berkshire gentleman who had found a bride and would surely now find happiness. It was not that I saw myself in his role, but rather that his role inevitably brought memories of my own happiness in Edinburgh and how it was lost.

She was gratified by my words and told me she hoped very soon to make the public announcement. 'And I so much hope Oliver will be there,' she said. 'I am more hopeful now of that than I have been. My mother is absolutely convinced he is still alive. She is a great one for dreams, and she says she dreamt he was at home.'

I thought it wise neither to stamp on such hopes nor to encourage them. And we fell to talking of her plans. She said she would stay another few days but, if there was still no news by Friday, which was the fourteenth, then she would leave. She had not, it turned out, been bothered by further anonymous letters.

Naturally, I invited her to have dinner with myself and Dr Bell, if he appeared, for it seemed the polite thing to do in the circumstances and she looked pleased.

'I admit company would be very welcome,' she replied as we got up. 'But I am not sure I should accept. Your friend is, I know, a very clever man of a particular mind and I should never have become emotional with him as I did before while he was only trying to say what he thought best. Also, now I think of it, I have ordered something to be sent to my room. I have taken to rising very early and walking here. I find the small church very peaceful.'

'But you can change those instructions if you would like to join us,' I said. 'We will go and see if he has come down. He may not even be dining at all, for he often prefers to stay in his room and think.'

But not on this occasion. As we walked out and entered the main area by the stairs, the Doctor appeared at once, looking very distracted. 'Ah, Doyle,' he said. 'I wish to talk to you. I have an idea and it is urgent.'

Then he turned and became aware of Miss Jefford's presence. 'Miss Jefford,' said Bell, 'my apologies, I did not see you. Would you excuse us, I have something very important to talk over with my friend?'

I started to protest that I had already invited her to dine with us but Miss Jefford herself would have none of it. 'I would not dream of disrupting you for the world,' she interrupted me graciously. 'Indeed as I told Dr Doyle, I have ordered something in my room. I hope you have a highly profitable discussion.'

We thanked her but even so I thought it another example of Bell's tactlessness. Could he not at least have been more attentive to her in his demand, no matter how important it was? Meanwhile, Miss Jefford turned to me.

'I am delighted we have talked, Dr Doyle. I hope I see you tomorrow.' And then she was gone.

Looking back at the Doctor, I realised he was very much distracted. His impatience showed itself at once as he moved away from the dining room and back to the sitting room I had just left.

'I am sorry, Doyle,' he said, 'but I repeat I made a terrible mistake going to Lowestoft today. Not that the trip was unsuccessful, it gave me answers to some of the more baffling questions, but you may well ask what good that is when I missed so much here.'

He waved me into a chair. 'Now you will do me a great service. I wish to hear everything that occurred between you and Mrs Marner and her sister. Every word and from the very beginning please. Did they come in here?'

I told him how Dr Bulweather had been here to tell me they were outside. How Mrs Marner was full of emotion and told me she would be spending Christmas away and perhaps not even come back at all if matters were not resolved. I think I repeated almost everything else she told me, though some things might have been omitted. Bell listened with enormous interest, occasionally putting questions but more often staying silent. When I had finished, he sat thinking for a little, the firelight on his face.

'So you say the cat was definitely out when the place was vandalised?' he said slowly, not looking at me.

'Yes, she was very relieved,' I continued, 'ah yes, now I recall she said it would surely have been hurt otherwise, given all the talk it was a witch's "familiar".'

'A familiar,' he repeated slowly. 'Yes, yes of course. Did she say anything else on that subject?'

I struggled to remember anything else, even the smallest detail. 'That in recent days it has apparently been more out than in but—'

Now, quite suddenly, he turned and his eyes were piercing. 'What?'

This scrap hardly seemed worth his reaction. 'I suppose it has taken to wandering away.'

He was on his feet now. 'We must go at once.'

I got up, not sure what he meant. 'To her house?'

'No,' said Bell. 'To Sir Walter Monk.'

I did not relish a walk of more than a mile and a half in the dark to Greyfriars House. But I knew from past experience it was foolish to underestimate him when he showed this kind of excitement. And so, once I had got my coat, I followed him doggedly out of the inn.

I made no attempt to ask him questions as we trudged along in the freezing air. He never answered them when he was in this kind of intense mood, any more than a bloodhound turns aside with the scent of the prey in its nostrils.

It was bitterly cold and we saw not a soul on the road before we turned into the drive, where the lights of Greyfriars House were visible. Bell did not stand on ceremony but knocked boldly at the door, which was soon opened by a manservant.

He was told at once Sir Walter had bidden no visitors. Bell merely replied the matter was official, gave his name and pushed past the man, causing another servant standing in the rear of the hall to run and tell his master. This man returned almost immediately and we were led once again down that carpeted corridor and through a door and finally into the large central chamber.

Four men sat at the well-stocked dining table. Sir Walter had a glass of brandy in his hand and beside him was Dr Angus Hare who nodded at us with a certain coolness. The other men were, as we soon established, local landowners from an adjoining parish.

'My God,' Sir Walter said to Bell, 'you have returned to haunt me. Were you the face we thought we saw at the window? What can I do for you now, sir, if you do not wish to view all my rooms again? Perhaps I should turn out my drawers for your inspection.'

The others laughed at this, rather in the way men laugh at a host who is paying for their brandy of which I could see there was a copious supply.

'No,' said Bell, smiling and friendly, 'I have no idea if there was a face at your window. I merely wish to greet your new cat.'

'My cat, sir! You mean the tabby who Bulweather asked me to take on for that woman Mrs Marner?'

When Bell indicated this was indeed what he meant, Sir Walter got up. 'Well, your behaviour becomes stranger every time you arrive here. As a matter of fact, I think she is by the fire over there, for I keep no dog and we were admiring the brute earlier. She seemed to enjoy the fresh fish my man gave her when she arrived.'

He moved over to a corner by the fire, past an armchair which had blocked our view and there, just as he promised, was Ellie Barnes's cat, who I must say looked none the worse for the death of one mistress and the flight of another. She was bunched up by the fire and stood up on our approach, looking at us without any great interest.

'Now what do you propose to do, sir?' said Monk as we approached, and I could see his pale demeanour was very flushed with drink.

Without answering, Bell bent down and put his hand down to stroke the cat's neck.

It flinched, just as I had seen it do once before, though I had quite forgotten. But clearly the Doctor had not, for now he grabbed the collar, even though the cat tried to shrink away from his hand, and felt under it.

'It is a little tight, is it not, puss?' he said. 'That is why you jerk away when people touch you there, and I recall how your poor mistress Ellie looked so worried when I saw you do so. Ah, what have we here?'

Evidently his hand had found something under the collar. Bell had to work the thing free, for it was effectively trapped and concealed. But at last he pulled out a piece of folded paper.

The cat moved away and the Doctor slowly unfolded the item till he had in his hand a full page. On it was a strange maze of letters, numbers and symbols.

'Gentlemen,' said Bell. 'Here is what I was seeking.'

'But what is it?' said Hare, and it was noticeable that as he spoke Sir Walter stepped back.

'Oh I believe one of its properties is to cause violent death,' said Bell, holding it high. 'It is the witch's rune.'

# The Crawling Visitor

The effect on those present was electrifying. Sir Walter moved back to the table. Evidently when confronted with the thing, it seemed less of a 'party trick' than he thought.

I stared at the page in Bell's hand. It was certainly odd. Many of the symbols I had never seen before, and then came the incomprehensible words and letters:

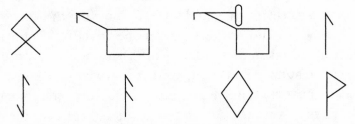

LD KPR UOCVZ BL LWV OYKTT NPBYGTMMEK ZT DIL HW CFE LUM

WRDR LGJEL GNZ VGNAH ZAGNW HVKEKLT KPNZ AH SMDAWPKPRJ

DK PRKS HKWEKXD11V1 ZTJQANWPMM AUJIYIGT GBRVZGQ

UZVQKOTJBNR UDMMBBMB 1X VG UJCCFV 1 1R VQ ZZ TIMJO DAJBN

T VHKMCVWH KWGNWDC LPNBSMEK TJZTG HQ QIIIK FXTPBRSH

'Whatever it is, and I am sure it's nothing,' Sir Walter finally spoke, 'please take it. I do not want it in my house.'

'That is good,' said Bell, 'for I have no intention of leaving it here.'

The other diners were watching this display with amazement. Angus Hare had got to his feet frowning, but Bell had already folded the paper and put it in his pocket.

'So it is a curse?' Sir Walter muttered.

'It has certainly not proved a blessing,' said Bell, 'but you need concern yourself no more with it. I bid you goodnight, gentleman.'

And we turned away to the door.

On the way back to the inn, Bell was excited by this development and generous in his comments. 'As you know, I could not understand why Ellie had not brought this with her to the beach,' he recalled. 'It was baffling, for the injunction in the letter was so forceful. And in other respects she was so pliable, even gullible. What could have possessed her to leave it? Had it been destroyed? Yes that was possible but it would have been done weeks ago, indeed Harding would have done it himself rather than entrust it to her. There had to be some other explanation. And then it was thanks to you, Doyle, for obeying the very oldest of my injunctions and not leaving out the trivia. You mentioned how the cat had taken to wandering off, that it was rarely present, and I recalled at once how we arrived at Mrs Marner's house after Ellie's disappearance and she expressed pleasure, great pleasure, at the cat's recent return. At the time, I thought she meant it had been away a few minutes, now I saw it had probably been away several hours. At once, too, I recalled its odd flinching when stroked in a certain place and how Ellie looked fearfully at us when we noticed this. Then all became clear. *Ellie could not take it because she did not have it.* When she received the note to meet him, she had no way of obtaining the rune because of the nature of her hiding place. The cat was not there. She had hidden the thing in its collar.'

I was interested to hear his reasoning but knew I hardly deserved praise. Indeed, I thought, it might be argued that matters would have moved more swiftly if I had not been there at all. For, in such a circumstance, Mrs Marner would never have left without seeing Bell and then he would have had all he needed from her at once without having to extract it from me.

Back in his room at the inn, Bell cleared the little desk and placed the paper carefully before him in order to begin his work.

I did not enquire further but offered to bring him something to eat. Of course, I expected him to reject the idea and was somewhat surprised when he heartily endorsed it, indeed he asked for two plates of bread and cheese and some assorted meats and two tankards of ale. Yet, when I returned with the food, he ignored it completely as he bent over the table, the light from the lamp shining fiercely on his face, staring at the sheet of strange writing below him.

The pad beside him was now covered in a series of numbers, letters and words. But his pencil had been thrown down and he had turned his attention back to the rune itself.

He did not look up as I stood there. But of course he had heard me enter and, after a while, without turning, he started to talk.

'Yes,' he said, 'the opening lines seem indeed to be runes or runic symbols. These have all kinds of associations with witchcraft, but it is my suspicion the words below them are a code of some kind. There are suggestive aspects, most notably the use of "N". You will recall the methods I used on the Beale ciphers, Doyle, but I fear it will not be susceptible to those. For I believe this is a polyalphabetic cipher, by far the most difficult in my experience.'

Naturally, I asked him to elaborate and he said he would welcome the chance to clarify his procedure for his own benefit as well as mine. 'You will recall,' he said, 'when we discussed ciphers in the context of the puzzle at Abbey Mill that I showed you the basic skills involved. At its most elementary, this consists of comparing the frequency of letters in the text to be deciphered with the commonness of letters in English.

'I can,' he continued, still with the paper before him in his hand, 'cite you one immensely dramatic example from English history. You may recall Mary Queen of Scots was executed in 1587 for plotting against Queen Elizabeth. What is much less well known are the circumstances. It seems that Elizabeth's first minister Walsingham had managed to break the code in which Mary was writing. This historic act of decipherment was done simply by a process of elimination. The code being used, which was, I believe, created by a young man called Babington, was ingenious but fallible. Every letter was substituted for another. But by trial and error, Walsingham established that the "o" of this code alphabet represented "a" and the strangely formed "o" with a tail was our "e". Once you have these important vowels you can always, by a process of elimination, very quickly establish other letters, words begin to take shape and the text falls into place.'

Now he put the paper back on the desk in front of him, as the candle spluttered, sending a shadow flickering over his face as his expression darkened. 'However, with a polyalphabetic cipher, such an approach is, I fear, completely impossible.'

'Does it need a key?' I asked, for I remembered from previous discussions with Bell how a textual key can be used to decrypt a cipher in a variety of ways, sometimes even by taking a whole text and numbering all the words so that if the fiftieth word of the text is 'even', then fifty stands for 'E' but if the hundred and fiftieth word is 'early', then 150 also stands for the same letter.

'In a sense,' said Bell, 'but a polyalphabetic cipher needs only one word or phrase. It employs a system called the Vigenere square, published by the author of that name in a book in 1586. Once you have used the square you do not forget it and I have drawn one out now in case it is of help to us.'

He pulled out a sheet of paper. On it was written a series of alphabets:

```
A  ABCDEFGHIJKLMNOPQRSTUVWXYZ
B  BCDEFGHIJKLMNOPQRSTUVWXYZA
C  CDEFGHIJKLMNOPQRSTUVWXYZAB
D  DEFGHIJKLMNOPQRSTUVWXYZABC
E  EFGHIJKLMNOPQRSTUVWXYZABCD
F  FGHIJKLMNOPQRSTUVWXYZABCDE
G  GHIJKLMNOPQRSTUVWXYZABCDEF
H  HIJKLMNOPQRSTUVWXYZABCDEFG
I  IJKLMNOPQRSTUVWXYZABCDEFGH
J  JKLMNOPQRSTUVWXYZABCDEFGHI
K  KLMNOPQRSTUVWXYZABCDEFGHIJ
L  LMNOPQRSTUVWXYZABCDEFGHIJK
M  MNOPQRSTUVWXYZABCDEFGHIJKL
N  NOPQRSTUVWXYZABCDEFGHIJKLM
O  OPQRSTUVWXYZABCDEFGHIJKLMN
P  PQRSTUVWXYZABCDEFGHIJKLMNO
Q  QRSTUVWXYZABCDEFGHIJKLMNOP
R  RSTUVWXYZABCDEFGHIJKLMNOPQ
S  STUVWXYZABCDEFGHIJKLMNOPQR
T  TUVWXYZABCDEFGHIJKLMNOPQRS
U  UVWXYZABCDEFGHIJKLMNOPQRST
V  VWXYZABCDEFGHIJKLMNOPQRSTU
W  WXYZABCDEFGHIJKLMNOPQRSTUV
X  XYZABCDEFGHIJKLMNOPQRSTUVW
Y  YZABCDEFGHIJKLMNOPQRSTUVWX
Z  ZABCDEFGHIJKLMNOPQRSTUVWXY
```

'In many ways,' said Bell, looking down at the strange mosaic, 'it is a simple system with devilishly complex results. As you see, every letter is given its own alphabet, starting wherever that particular letter is placed in the English alphabet and ending at the same place. I will put it at its absolute simplest.' He looked up and his eye fell on the untouched dinner. 'Supposing you wanted to encode the word "cheese". And the key agreed between the parties is another simple culinary word "bread".'

He took up his pencil. 'Very well, first you write your key at the top of your encipherment and repeat it over and over until the message you are enciphering ends. Our message is very short so we only need to write it twice.

B R E A D B R E A D

Now we put the word we want to encode below it.

B R E A D B R E A D

C H E E S E

'Now we refer to the square. Our master alphabet is at the top, and we wish to translate our word "cheese" into a polyalphabetic cipher using the key word "bread". It is simple: the first "c" is checked against the letter above in the key word which is "b" and therefore we look along the B alphabet in the square and find the corresponding letter for our "c" in "cheese" is "d". For the second using our key word the key letter is "r" so we look along the R alphabet for our "h" in "cheese" and find "y". The process continues exactly like this and we have:

Key word:  B R E A D B

Text word: C H E E S E

Code word: D Y I E V F

'So there is the coded "cheese", Doyle. "D Y I E V F",' said Bell, neatly completing the word. 'And even if we write hundreds of sentences out in this way, without the key of "bread" it is potentially impregnable, for you will notice in the word "cheese" there are no less than three "e"s, all rendered by different letters. There is, therefore, not the slightest point in trying to decipher a polyalphabetic cipher by the usual methods I have shown you. Without the key it is an impossibility.'

'So what hope have we with this?' I asked.

'Ah well,' he said, 'we must find the key. I have hopes. And as I have said there are other very odd features here in the rune at the start which are most interesting. I will work on it further.'

I left him then to obtain some dinner of my own. The inn was deserted that night and after my meal I wondered if I should venture out, but I could think of nothing concrete that would further our investigation. Indeed, as I kicked my heels and stared out at the moon I found myself reflecting how little I had contributed to the case so far. In previous investigations, I had always at least some sense of an indirect involvement in the process of detection. Here I seemed merely to be an observer occasionally repeating to Bell what I had heard. In a case as important as this, one in which I had so huge a stake, it was not pleasant to reflect that it would have made little difference to our current position if I had stayed in London.

I am aware such thoughts did me little credit, for what did it matter in the end so long as we succeeded? But probably I was still suffering from the ordeal I had endured in Wiltshire where I had been so completely humiliated and then failed abjectly in the quest for revenge.

A cheerful booming voice interrupted my reverie. 'Well, you have stirred up Sir Walter and I can hardly think of a more worthwhile occupation. The man has always run his farm as if he were some French nobleman rather than a minor Englishman from a somewhat chequered family.'

Bulweather grinned down at me and I greeted him. 'Yes, Angus just looked in and described to me some of the events at the hall.

How I wish I had seen it unfold. So I thought I would buy you a brandy and congratulate you. It was ingenious.'

We repaired to the snug which was as empty as the bar beyond it and I accepted his kind offer. Naturally I told him that Bell was, at this moment, attempting to make something of the document and described it as well as I could.

Bulweather was most interested in my description of the rune. 'I will be intrigued to hear if Dr Bell can arrive at an understanding of it,' he said when I was finished. It would be truly wonderful if we could put this whole ghastly business behind us.'

The words were spoken with such a heartfelt misery that I suddenly found myself sorry for the man before me. You could see how much Bulweather hated what was happening to his community. So I told him what was true, namely that if anyone could solve the mystery, it would be Bell. And then he recalled he had other news. Evidently there had been some kind of disturbance at the Westleton House asylum. A window was broken and minor damage done, yet none of the patients was missing or put out in any way. The room involved had been empty. 'It is a mystery,' said Bulweather, 'and I expect Bell will want to add it to his list when he is done with the present business.'

After that we talked further about the place, for I was very keen to ask Bulweather if there were other institutions like it. He offered to get Dr Cornelius to make enquiries. 'I have told you how grateful I am to him,' he added. 'Do you have a personal interest in such things?'

I hesitated but at last I told him of my father's condition. He listened with great sympathy but also with genuine interest. When I had finished he paused for a moment and then spoke in a gentler tone.

'Doyle, you have made me a confidence, one with which I greatly sympathise. These things happen, they are not a mark of fate or weakness. They are illnesses. And now I believe I owe you a confidence in return.' He took a drink of his brandy and went on. 'I have not yet, you see, completed my story for reasons you, of all people, will appreciate. What I always intended to tell you and Bell, when given the opportunity, is that the matter of my wife's illness, while true in every detail, is not the whole truth. Yes Mary died of septicaemia. But it arose after she had inflicted a terrible wound on herself. You see she also suffered from a mental disorder.'

I was amazed but also naturally all my sympathies were aroused. I knew only too well what my mother had suffered in such circumstances. 'But was it always thus and was she confined?' I asked.

'Oh no,' he said with passion. 'It happened suddenly as is sometimes the way. And it was never so bad that she had to be in an asylum. There were wonderful periods even towards the end when she was quite herself. When I talked of her anxiety, and of her worry for her sister, that was all true. She did make me promise to do all I could for her. And then the illness arose in a worse form.'

As he revealed the details, it became clear to me what this man must have endured. We talked for some time, and he voiced his firm belief that in some respects an illness of the mind was the same as the illness of any organ. 'In time to come,' he said, 'I feel sure my wife's illness and your father's will not be regarded as a disgrace. People do not wish themselves ill. It is not their fault. It is certainly not fate. It may not even be hereditary. They merely become ill, whether it is an illness of the mind or of the knee bone.'

We talked more of this before he left me. Inspired by all he had said, I made myself a silent promise. I would visit my father within a few weeks and certainly early in the New Year. Then I returned to Bell's room to see how he was progressing.

Before I reached the door it was opened by Bell who looked pleased to see me. 'Ah Doyle, come in, I thought I heard you and I wanted to show you something.'

I entered and noticed with pleasure the Doctor had eaten every scrap of food and also drunk the beer. I was not surprised he was hungry after such an eventful day.

But now he was turning down the lamp so it was very shadowy in the room and opening the curtain. Outside the night was clear and the moonlight shone through the window, making a patch on the carpet, which seemed to satisfy him.

'Very well,' he said. 'I am ready.' And he indicated a chair.

We sat and waited. I did not know what on earth for. Did he expect some spirit to materialise? Nothing happened in that dark room. And why would it? I was about to make some remark. And then I became aware of a slight noise as of furtive movement. I turned. Nothing. It came again.

The noise was louder, and in the shadows beside the bed I began to think I could just make out a shape at floor level. Gradually it became clearer. And then it started to move foward. Slowly it entered a patch of moonlight.

I started at what I saw. It was twisted and ungainly with bare flesh, and a bull-like animal neck. What kind of thing had Bell brought here? As I watched, a sound came from it, low at first like a moan but gradually rising to a scream. And then it was a cacophonous howl.

There was no mistaking the noise. It was what Charlotte Jefford and I had heard in the wood. Yet in this confined space it was not merely frightening but utter agony. I put my hands to my ears. Still the sound persisted, a great shrieking, threatening to drown the entire inn.

I shouted fiercely at Bell, but the Doctor was already jumping to his feet, raising an arm. The noise stopped and, in that instant, the thing withdrew.

All was silent now but he was too late, for we could hear footsteps and soon there was a knocking on the door.

The Doctor went over to it quickly and opened it a crack. A startled man stood there. Behind him, other doors were opening.

'Forgive me,' said Bell to the man, 'there is no alarm at all. Please tell anyone who heard. A friend's dog had to have a thorn removed but the animal is fine now. My great apologies to you.'

He closed the door politely, and I thanked heaven Miss Jefford was a floor away on the other side.

'And now,' said Bell, turning to me and smiling, indicating I should get up, 'I will introduce you to the late Mr William Bowker.'

## THE UNQUIET GRAVE

He went over and raised the lights in the room. Slowly the shape appeared again but it was relaxed now and all its body seemed to have uncoiled. In the full light and without these distortions, I recognised it to my amazement as a man I had glimpsed briefly downstairs as Bulweather and I entered the bar. Seen in ordinary life without his contortions he was certainly striking, with a bare fleshy head that was greatly oversized for his squat body, but he bore almost no resemblance at all to the thing I had just encountered. Indeed even the nakedness was an illusion, for he had merely lowered his skin-coloured shirt below his shoulders.

'But,' added Bell as the man got up and came forward to me, smiling very politely, 'I am sure we should now honour him with his real name, which is Daniel Morton.'

The man nodded gratefully and mopped his brow with a handkerchief. 'I am not, to be truthful, so used to the Daniel, sir,' he said in an accent that was distinctly London. 'Just Danny Morton, that is how I am known. But that, what you saw, is what you were talking of, sir, I take it?'

'It certainly was,' said Bell ruefully. 'Indeed, to be truthful with you, Mr Morton, I was not expecting quite as much.'

'Oh, it was only an indication, sir.' He looked pleased. 'In the halls I used to do it as "The Human Wolf", but I hadn't done it for a while till the two gentlemen saw me in Westons in High Holborn. They knew our lot was coming down here to Lowestoft, which was when they asked me to participate in the wager.'

'I am very grateful to you, Mr Morton,' said Bell. 'But my colleague has not heard your story. Perhaps you would like to explain it to him.'

'Of course, sir.' He turned to me in his likeable way. 'It was confidential, but your friend here was on to it anyway so I see no harm. Like I say, I work in the halls and these two gentlemen see me at Holborn. I think they had heard something of what I do. So they came to me and later they bought me some refreshment and told me of this wager.'

'What wager?' I said.

'Why, as I understand it, they had a friend who said he cared nothing for staying out in the wood and bet them fifty pounds he would stay there till midnight on a dark night and they wanted to give him a scare. So they asked me to do just that. I am known too for having some skills at ventriloquism, sir. I am able to make it seem as if a sound comes from far off. Evidently I did the trick the first time but this gentleman, they say, he never learns and he wants to try it again and I wasn't so keen on that. But they were generous and so I went along with it, even though the weather was perishing. It was a very short time that last occasion. The only thing is, sir, I think I saw a woman and I may have scared her but I could not let my gentlemen down. They understood and said they would square it with her.'

I was aghast. 'So you were in the woods on those nights?'

'I was, sir. I suppose most would think I was a wolf,' he said shyly.

His ignorance staggered me. Bell had made a cache of all the newspapers containing the story and they were laid out in a pile by his bed. I crossed there now, seizing the most sensational of all and pushed it in front of Morton, pointing to the headline:

## HOWLING MAN SEEN

'But did you see this?' I asked.

He glanced at it uneasily and turned to Bell. 'No, sir. What is it, sir?'

Bell had been watching and came over to him. 'Well, it is just a description of how some people heard you, Mr Morton,' said the Doctor kindly. And it was only then I realised that, of course, Morton could not read and was too, I suspected, very short-sighted. 'I think you can go back to your people now,' Bell added. 'They will be waiting and I know you all have to get on to Ipswich.' He took some coins and handed them to him. 'You have been a great help to me and we are agreed if you hear from these gentlemen again you will talk to your manager and he will know what to do.'

'Yes, sir. That is agreed, sir. I am grateful, sir, and much obliged for the refreshment you laid on for my people too.' And with a bow to me, he took up his coat and left the room.

'He cannot read or write,' said Bell quietly. 'He knows nothing of the sensation. I can be certain from his descriptions the gentlemen who employed him in such confidence were Jefford and Cream. He met them both in London, where the thing was first discussed. Later he met Jefford only, around the twenty-eighth of November in Lowestoft, where he was given precise instructions regarding the first appearance. Mr Morton has limited eyesight but he has a very good memory and an excellent sense of direction and of geography. The second unexpected engagement, though in the same spot and of shorter duration, was delivered via an intermediary, the stage manager. I have interviewed this man. He believed the employment offered to Mr Morton was some kind of private performance. As to Mr Morton's transport, it was a cab from Lowestoft, instructed again at second hand. The cab driver set him down for a fixed period of about sixty minutes on the first occasion, much less on the second.'

'So he cannot lead us to them?' I said.

'No, I am persuaded,' said Bell, 'he knows no more than what he told us. He only met Cream once several weeks ago.'

'But he terrified Miss Jefford,' I said bitterly. 'Why? Did her brother wish it?'

'That is very doubtful,' said Bell.

'Then what was the purpose?'

'Certainly to resurrect the legend, also to confuse and distract. It has already wasted my time, as we saw to our cost today. But Mr Morton's second commission was, I believe, rather different. There was another reason for it which gives me hope, though I do not wish to speculate on it further.'

'So that,' I asked, 'was the purpose of your trips to Lowestoft?'

'In part. Though to be fair, it has also yielded other fruit.'

Bell started to rearrange the room, closing the curtain. 'You see, Doyle,' he explained, 'the effect of the howling man was so theatrical and yet I did not think either witness was lying. And that left only two real possibilities. The first that it was some remarkable amateur trick or illusion like our friend Hanbury's lethal box in Rotherhithe. However, the more I studied the description, the less plausible this seemed. Everything about this apparition sounded like a full-blooded performance. And, if so convincing, surely a professional one? Of course that seemed an absurd notion at first, and then my thoughts turned to Mrs Marner's theatrical associations. I could find nothing to implicate her, but unwittingly she led me to the music hall in Lowestoft.

'The more I read in the local newspaper, to your great frustration I recall, the more interesting it became. A troupe from London were performing and fortunately for me the newspaper has an excellent reviewer with a passion for the halls. In the course of his notices, he alluded to Mr Morton's skills as a contortionist and ventriloquist, even recalling his "Human Wolf" of days gone by. My interest naturally became intense, all the more when I established Morton did not go on stage on either of the nights the howling man was seen. But then I arrived at an impasse. You will recall how frustrated I was that day, for just as I felt I had my man, there was no reply to my telegram. Had he flown? Or perhaps all my assumptions were unfounded. It was only when I got to the town that I realised the stupidity of my error. How could there be a reply? It was sent to Mr Morton's lodgings and he was unable to read it.

'Finally I encountered him personally. At first he was guarded but, when I alluded to his "private engagements" and indicated I knew about them, he saw no harm in revealing his odd commission. Earlier today, when you were with me, I also talked to the stage manager. I was a little wary of him, fearing he might be implicated in some way, so I took you with me but in the event he proved perfectly helpful and certainly innocent.'

He had sat down back at his desk now, the paper in front of him. 'However, I fear Mr Morton is only the dressing of the affair and now I must return to its heart. It will be a long night.' Soon he was again engrossed in the rune and I left him.

That night, I slept very deeply and dreamt that I was in a dark well whose water was rising below me. Somehow I managed to wedge myself in a semi-horizontal position to stop myself falling. But it was impossible to climb further and, below me, the level rose remorselessly. I could feel the cold wetness of the water on my legs and elbows, and then my back. Outside and above someone was banging on the side of the well. The noise became louder and I awoke.

It was already dawn. The banging continued, for it was coming from my bedroom door. I got up, pulled on my dressing gown and opened it. Langton stood there, grim-faced. 'I am sorry,' he said. 'You must come at once, Bell is already downstairs.'

It took me only a few moments to dress and descend. Bell, Langton and Angus Hare were standing in the hall of the inn in outdoor clothes

'What is it?' I asked.

Bell came close up to me and I could see the deep concern on his face as he spoke softly. 'Come with us, Doyle. We have been out already, but the site is secure so we returned here to raise you. Langton also had to arrange for certain messages to be sent.'

They moved out of the door. It was early dawn and the frost had gone but a wind was beginning to blow and there were white clouds overhead.

'But why did you not wake me when you went out?' I asked.

'What?' said Bell, obviously greatly preoccupied. 'Oh, I was awake anyway – I have been working all night on the rune and made an early visit to the asylum. I encountered Langton on my return.'

We had no distance to go. I could see at once that the policeman Wallace stood at the end of the street, close to the small church that served the community. The place was not very old, for it had been built in 1830, but it was picturesque, with a small, overgrown graveyard. And a well, which reminded me at once of my dream.

A second uniformed constable from a nearby village stood in the graveyard itself. Beside him something lay on the ground and the gravestone beyond this shape was red, as if covered in paint.

But it was not paint, of course. That was obvious as I drew closer.

And then I saw the object. I was unable to assemble any proper thoughts as I stared at it, but the word Godhead came to me, for there was something saint-like in these features while the wind blasphemously blew the fair hair around the face.

What lay below me at an odd angle on the grass was Charlotte Jefford's head.

# The Line of Reason

The body's torso was, as I soon saw, not so far away, but my view of it had been blocked by the gravestone. In other respects, below the bloody neck it looked absurdly normal.

I moved forward to take all this in, but it seemed my investigative instincts had failed me entirely. For I found I had no appetite at all for lingering at the scene. Logically, I suppose, I could have made some argument to myself that there was little for me to do there, that Bell would miss nothing. But I can scarcely pretend I was feeling logical. The sight of that mutilated body lying by the grave had aroused memories in me even more painful than those triggered by the murder on the beach. I had been moved by Ellie Barnes's death, but I had had no real personal relationship with the victim and she had asked for no help or protection. Charlotte, on the other hand, had come to me, making an appeal as a friend. She had confided in me her secrets, including even the fact she was engaged. Here was her reward.

It was, I felt in my heart, a completely needless death: one which could and should have been prevented by the slightest vigilance on our part.

Naturally, Bell was setting about his usual investigations, studying the atrocity in detail and all the marks around it. But, very unusually in such circumstances, he was also concerned enough about me to come over to where I stood by the wall that divided the churchyard from the countryside beyond.

'It is a desperate development, Doyle. I am closer now but I could not have foreseen this. What was she doing here?'

'She told me she liked to get up early and walk. This was a favourite spot.'

'A crime of opportunity then. The hardest to anticipate.'

I gave him a look then, for the truth was I thought this a contemptible excuse. He had only needed to talk to Charlotte, discover more about her, counsel her as to her safest strategies, establish a reasonable relationship, offer her some protection. He had done none of these things, he had merely issued a peremptory instruction that she should go home, blithely ignoring the fact she was only there because she desperately awaited news of her brother. Following that, he had not talked to her at all. I turned my back on him and left the graveyard.

In one way my behaviour was cowardly, though I am sure I was right to delay telling the Doctor what I thought. I had no intention of betraying the solemnity of Charlotte Jefford's death with an acrimonious and emotional row between us, especially one that would be witnessed by everyone present. But, looking back, it was cowardly not to stay in that place and do what I could, even if that amounted to almost nothing. As it was, I suppose those around me thought I had been given some instruction by the Doctor and was striding away urgently to carry it out. They could have had no idea of the real state of affairs.

I found myself in the street and walked back along the road, turning on to the little path that led to the beach. Of course, nobody was about at this hour. I did not want to walk in the direction where we had found Ellie so, for a time, I headed the other way and trudged along the beach below the great cliffs. Soon I was repelled by the tide but I noticed that, before you came to the ruined church, where the cliff was sheer, there was one spot where the landslide had been gradual and it might be possible to climb from the beach to the woods.

Later, I retraced my steps and took the path from the beach to the cliffs, plunging into the trees at the top.

When I emerged on the part of the path that skirted the cliff, I felt the wind picking up. The surf boomed out below me, for the tide was still very full but I could see a great bank of black clouds forming on the far horizon.

These clouds were much more ominous than any I had seen before here. A real storm was coming, even if it would not be upon us for many hours. I thought of Charlotte's face, the hair blowing around it in the graveyard, and felt almost as if I had killed her myself. Why in heaven had I not counselled her to be careful? I knew the danger well enough and yet last night I had talked to her as if we were friends meeting at some Surrey house party. But, if I could not forgive myself for this lapse, it seemed to me the Doctor was more culpable still. She had sought out his help and he had effectively rebuffed her altogether.

I do not know how long I stayed on that path, but eventually I crossed inland and walked back to the village via the road. By then, the graveyard had evidently been exhaustively searched and the body removed.

I entered the inn, ready to talk to Bell, for I knew my feelings must be expressed sooner or later. In the hall I saw Dr Hare, who was conversing quietly with one of the constables. He turned and nodded when he saw me. 'Yes,' he was saying to the constable, 'if you take the preliminary report, we will await instructions.' And then he turned to me, with a small smile. 'So, Dr Doyle, on which important errand did Bell send you, I would like to know? What a bloodhound the man is!'

I was astonished by his joviality. Had he not been in the churchyard and seen what I had seen? The brutal extinguishing of a life for no reason? But then I recalled Langton telling me Hare had worked with the police in the north before he came here. No doubt he felt experienced in such things. 'Did you reach a conclusion as to the weapon?' I asked, ignoring the question.

'Oh we have the weapon,' he said, 'or rather Langton does. It was behind the grave. A sharp little beast of a knife too.'

'Were there any other indications?' I asked.

'Not that I am aware.' He broke off, for Bell had come down the stairs now, looking somewhat grey and worried.

'Doyle,' he said, 'the post-mortem will not take place till tonight. I want to go back to Harding's house, I fear we may have missed something.' His tone was so matter-of-fact you would never have guessed I had left him at the scene of a crime without explanation, something, in all our time together, I had never done before.

We set off along the road together, quite alone, for Hare had other business and Langton was busily involved in the aftermath of Miss Jefford's death. The storm clouds were not yet overhead but they were massing in the western sky and the trees swayed noisily around us.

I suppose the Doctor's worried appearance should have softened my anger a little but, as is the way with these things. It did not. And yet for some reason, I could not bring myself to say what I was feeling. So the silence continued and the wind blew around us as the only outward expression of this turbulence.

Harding's cottage was now occupied by someone else but a message had been sent to Sir Walter and a key was brought down by one of the servants, who stood by to wait until we were finished.

Bell entered the house, which was hardly changed except that Harding's clothes and personal possessions had been removed and another groundsman's things replaced them. Obviously, Bell had no interest in these at all. Beyond that, the place was bare. The Doctor's examination of this room last time had been very thorough and I could not remotely see how he hoped to find anything more.

But on this occasion he was even more painstaking though to absolutely no effect. He moved out all the furniture and studied all the walls, even laying his hands upon them. He went to the little chest of drawers, removing each drawer one by one and running his hand down the back.

Then he took a chair and began to examine the surfaces that were out of reach of the ground, not that there were many. He searched above the frames of windows and on the top of the shutters. A small shelf aroused his attention but there was nothing on or behind it. I could not think where else he could possibly look.

He stared around him for a time, then he moved the chair over to the door. He climbed on it and ran his hand over the high lintel. His expression changed.

He had grasped something and now he brought it down for closer inspection. From his look of triumph, I thought at first he must have found some weapon. But all Bell had in his hand was a stick of hazel wood with two short branches at the end.

It was, admittedly, a strange thing to find in such a place, but what could it possibly tell us? The Doctor, however, was delighted. He ran his hand over it, examining the way the branch had been cut by some skilled person. Then he quit the place at once and returned the key to the servant.

'Good,' he said. 'Now, Doyle, we must go to Jefford's house.'

I nodded, though it seemed futile, for the place would be locked. But we turned and walked back through the woods till we came to the track. The wind had dropped a little, it was quite still and not very cold, but the clouds still gathered and the air seemed so full it was almost an effort to walk through it.

Eventually Jefford's house stood before us with its barren and stunted fruit trees. There was, of course, nobody about. What, I wondered, did the Doctor propose to do? The place was locked and we could hardly break in.

For a time, the Doctor stood outside the house, studying it carefully. Then he took out a piece of paper and looked at some markings he had made on it. Finally he started to walk around the perimeter.

At last he arrived at the north-western corner and produced a pocket compass. He stood with his back to the house and moved the perimeter of the compass so he had a line running a few degrees off the angle of the house's north-west corner. I saw him look along this line and fix his eye on a landmark – in this case it turned out to be a Scotch pine – that would give him exactly the direction he required. Then he started out towards it and I walked beside him. In one hand he held the compass, in the other the hazel wood branch.

When we reached the pine, he checked the compass and found another tree, albeit a slightly nearer one and set out again, holding precisely the same line.

'This will take a long time,' he said as we walked. 'It may be a mile or more but it is the only way to be sure.'

I know that on other occasions, faced with such mystification, I would probably have maintained a respectful silence. But the thickness of the air, as the clouds built up overhead, contributed to my impatience and I was still obsessively recalling the sight in the graveyard. An overpowering sense of failure, which I first felt on a beach in Edinburgh, had returned to taunt me. It made the complex and abstruse task in which we were now engaged seem utterly pointless, and I felt as if Bell had himself succumbed to this place's obsession with occult lore. What was the use of solving or failing to solve arcane questions, whatever those questions were, when a woman had been cold-bloodedly slaughtered earlier in the day?

No doubt my feeling would have found words but the Doctor found them for me.

'I agree,' he said. 'The death of Charlotte Jefford was an appalling thing.'

By now, we had made three or four stops and were walking in the thick of the woods. He was holding the line tenaciously, though it had become harder to fix an object far away so he was stopping and rechecking the compass on a landmark every forty or fifty yards.

His intuition did not surprise me. I did not even bother to

comment upon it. If he thought to distract me with his 'method', he would be disappointed.

'I think it was avoidable,' I said.

The Doctor was looking straight ahead. 'I agree. Given knowledge.' As he spoke, once again, he stopped, studied the compass and took his line on a holly tree.

'No, even without knowledge, if there had been sufficient concern.'

'Concern is never sufficient, Doyle.' He trudged on. 'If I allowed that to rule my investigations, then I would get nowhere. I have to follow what I follow and that, as here, is the line of reason.'

I nearly laughed out loud at this but not, I am afraid, in any great appreciation. It was more that the setting gave such a ludicrous aspect to his words. With the clouds massing over our heads, it was becoming darker even though we were in the middle of the day. And here was Bell stubbornly trudging through the gathering shadows, along his line of supposed reason, like some short-sighted philosopher studying motion as he is run over by a horse and cab. But it was only funny until you remembered that, somewhere in the village, a dead young woman lay on a slab with her head severed. If the logician, now so intent on marking out this strange line in the forest here, had actually paid any attention to her, she would have still been alive.

So I did not laugh, indeed my tone became harsher. 'But what exactly is the point of reason if you lack the minimum human concern for others? What is the possible gain? Charlotte Jefford came to us for help. The other victims appear to have been caught in some web we do not understand, and had no time for us. Even so, we failed them. But with her it was even worse. She had no connection here, she came to us for guidance and protection before she died. You turned your back on her appeal, indeed you barely talked to her.'

Bell kept going forward. 'That is true, with one reservation: I barely talked to her, *beyond giving her the best advice I could.*'

'I doubt,' I replied, 'it even qualified as advice. She was here because she feared for her brother's life and you told her in peremptory terms she should quit the place at once. You gave her no reason whatsoever for this. Even if it was your intention, why could you not listen to her at length, point out the dangers and then try and persuade her to go.'

'It would probably have been counter-productive,' he said. 'I wanted her to leave.' He had stopped again and was taking yet another line with his compass. 'I did not wish to offer reassurance.'

The answer was more brutal than even I had expected. 'You deliberately denied it,' I said. 'That sounds like a cool kind of cruelty. Especially when your victim now lies dead.'

He set on yet another distant marker and turned to glance at me before tramping on. He was not angry, but his eyes were piercing. 'She is not my victim, laddie, as you perfectly well know. If you encouraged her to stay, she may in part be yours.' His pace did not flag. But I realised my words had, for a wonder, struck something in him, for he continued with some intensity of feeling. 'Indeed more than that, I truly believed, if you really wish to know—' But then he broke off, for his eye had alighted on something, and I would not learn till later what he was about to say.

As it was, I turned to see what Bell was staring at. It seemed to be a perfectly ordinary yew tree right in his line, but he approached it with huge excitement. 'So we are close now,' he said. 'And it is time for me to see if I can apply our own spell.'

With that, rather to my astonishment, he took one last look at the compass, put it in his pocket and grasped the hazel branch by its two smaller ends. Then he held it out at arm's length and began to walk slowly forwards, keeping the branch parallel with the ground. 'I have seen this done before in Glendoick,' said Bell, utterly forgetting our argument, 'and one of the keepers said I was a fair pupil, even though I was only sixteen at the time. Let us hope he was right.'

At first I was lost. Why was he walking forward, holding this wand at arm's length? Was it some further act, connected to the witch? Also, unlike him, I could not so easily forget our differences or the deaths that had caused them.

But as he stopped and walked on, still clutching the two smaller ends of the branch, a recollection began to stir. I had not actually seen the practice performed before but I did have a vague idea of what it might be from books. The dowser, for that was the name I recalled, walks slowly forward with a carefully crafted stick or two metal rods, which quiver when he is above water. And, unlike many other country superstitions, there was, I seemed to remember, good evidence that this was a practical procedure.

Bell turned to look at the line behind him and then proceeded slowly on. He was frowning, uncertain, no doubt desperately trying to recall the process. He was now moving far more slowly than he had been, though still keeping the line and the stick in his outstretched hands parallel to the ground, making only minute paces forward. More than once he glanced anxiously at the sky. And I knew why: for this would hardly be a practical procedure in a deluge. Once the rain started, he would have to give up. But he kept going, his hands lightly clasping the twigs as he stared below him.

Now I sensed the tension in him. Though it was not remotely warm, whatever the oppressiveness of the air, I could see small beads of perspiration on his brow. It was clear he had set enormous store by this quest. If it came to nothing, I sensed he had nowhere else to turn.

Time seemed suspended as he took these tiny paces without the slightest result. Fifteen, twenty minutes went by. Bell was becoming despondent. He looked around and back at the yew tree, now well behind us. 'Nothing,' he said involuntarily, 'nothing.' I had rarely seen him so dejected. His mouth set and I thought for a moment he was going to break the thing in two and cast it down.

Then he remembered his compass and pulled it from his pocket.

He stared at it a moment and his face brightened. 'Ah, we have diverged a degree or two, Doyle, it is easily done. And he took two steps to the right. 'There, that is better. He backed five or six paces, checked the line with the compass and moved forward. Another three or four minutes went past. He studied the compass again but on this occasion it seemed to satisfy him. He moved slowly between two trees. And now he stopped. He had seen something. But also it was as if he felt something. His hand quivered slightly. He took a pace forward and then another, he quivered more. And he looked excited. Just ahead of him there were some bushes but also moss and loose vegetation. Some fir branches were there too, though whether they had fallen or been placed there, it was hard to tell.

Bell was on them now and his hand quivered more. It was a remarkable sight, for his face was illuminated by the prospect of discovery. 'Doyle,' he called urgently, 'can you clear these branches and anything below them?'

I acted swiftly and started to haul the wood aside. At first the task was easy, though I was amazed by the amount of loose vegetation I found here. Once you penetrated it, although the illusion was cunning and the moss was certainly growing, much, like the fir branches, seemed to be here by design. The Doctor put his stick aside to help me and soon we had exposed earth but the earth was notably marshy and damp.

'I fear I should have brought a spade,' said Bell. 'But we must try with our hands, you see how wet it is.'

My first thought was that digging with our hands would be hopeless, for even if there was water here it would be far down. But to my astonishment, the earth came away quite easily. Indeed, like the fir trees, it seemed to be another artifice that had been piled here for a purpose. Soon it was utterly sodden and then, as we clawed away more of it, water was actually starting to seep through from the sides of our excavation.

We dug on a little and then stopped to survey the spring we had uncovered. I remember Bell's suddenly serious look and I am sure, as we stared down, the thought occurred to us both about the same time. Namely that it was now quite large enough to submerge a man's head and shoulders.

# THE SYMBOLS OF MORTALITY

Bell got to his feet and turned to survey where we were. There was, now that we looked ahead rather than at the ground, something familiar about it. I do not think it came as any surprise to find we were on the edge of the clearing where Colin Harding had been discovered.

Soon we were measuring the short distance from where Harding was found to the spring. 'You remember,' said Bell, 'how exercised I was by the way they had stamped all over this place. Harding was easily dragged if the distance was so short, but I knew there had to be a trail. Only it was obliterated long before we got here.'

'Indeed,' I said, 'but it is also true that the murderer might have done that himself. He could make any number of trails to create confusion in the knowledge that the discovery would bring several men here and even the most experienced detective would assume it was their work.'

The Doctor smiled. 'Yes,' he said. 'That is a valid observation, Doyle. He may well not have wanted to leave a unique trail. That would be careless. It is indeed likely he churned it up, and several other paths too, and then the discoverers of the body need only complete the destruction. Thank you.'

I found even now I was pleased he supported my deduction. But I also began to wonder how far this had led us. 'Well at least we can dispel the talk of witchcraft, for we know how Harding was killed,' I said. 'But I fear it is all we have found.'

'Oh no,' said Bell, 'we have found a good deal more than that, I assure you, as you will see later.' And we turned back in the direction of the village.

There was, I reflected as I stared gloomily out of my window at the inn, having changed out of my wet clothes, a hierarchy of murder as of everything else. Ellie Barnes's death, the first that could be clearly and immediately attributed to foul play, had created barely a ripple in the world outside the village. Charlotte Jefford's death, however, was a different matter. The Scotland Yard man originally designated to come here had been recalled and a more senior officer was to replace him. As a result, nobody from that august establishment was likely to arrive for another full day at least, perhaps two. 'Do they suppose,' Bell had said when he heard this, 'that the evidence will wait patiently for their arrival? It is truly a wonder, is it not, any crimes are solved at all.' He then proceeded to point out here was Langton's chance to cover himself in glory, though, whatever his real feeling, Langton was just as scornful about the development as Bell.

More press were about to descend, but the isolation of the place meant we would be spared them a little while longer. News of the crime was only now reaching the larger newspapers. Even the fleetest from the capital would not be here before the following day, though the local press would no doubt descend more quickly. Even so, perhaps because of the impending storm, the street below me was utterly deserted. The black clouds were above us now, enough to create an odd light over the marsh, yet still the storm refused to break.

I do not think I lingered long, staring out of that window, but it is true the events of that day caused me at times to lapse into old memories. For the next thing I recall, a maid was knocking on the door to tell me I was required urgently at The Glebe and the Doctor had already set off.

The wind was very strong indeed by the time I stood again in that ugly orchard before the house. It was bending the trees and whistling around the gabled roof before me. But the rain had not yet started, which was a good thing, for I was sure it would be torrential when it did.

The door was open and the first room I entered was empty but I could hear voices from the larger chamber where the blood was. 'I do not understand,' a voice I recognised as Sir Walter was saying. 'I regard it as a liberty, sir, not the first you have taken. A man in my condition should not even be here.'

I entered and was somewhat astonished by what I saw. Six men faced Bell, who stood with his back to the far wall, two candle lanterns at his feet behind him. It was not yet dark outside, but the place was gloomy enough for the lanterns to pick out Bell's shadow.

Sir Walter Monk was closest to him, his face angry. Bulweather was by the window, watching with interest. Langton was also by the window, looking slightly annoyed.

Edward Norman had retreated to the corner furthest from Bell, wearing an expression I could only describe as peevish terror. Angus Hare was casually stationed in the middle, supercilious and expectant. The biggest surprise was the man closest to me. It was Cornelius from the asylum, who seemed like the good scientist, highly interested if sceptical as he appraised the proceedings.

'I agree. And you are the man who has intimidated my son,' said Edward Norman. 'You terrified the boy.'

'I am not sure it was my doing, Mr Norman,' said Bell. Then he turned to Sir Walter. 'Allow me, if you would be so good, to say why I brought you here and then you can make all the objections you wish. And you, Sir Walter, can rejoin your carriage, which waits I believe on the road.'

'I will give you the courtesy of a few minutes,' said Sir Walter. As he spoke, I noticed his eye kept straying to the bloody writing on the wall, where the words 'witch' and 'here' were so clear. Yet oddly he seemed far more interested by the less indicative part of the message, the odd incomplete O.

'Please proceed,' said Hare, 'I am interested.'

'Why could you not just tell us in the village?' said Norman, his voice rising slightly. 'Why bring us here?'

'For one thing you might not have believed me. For another I may, I hope, have something to show you and I want to see the reactions of everyone in this room. For some of you may be more familiar with all this than you pretend.' There was silence at this and he proceeded.

'This afternoon,' Bell said, 'as two of you know, I discovered how Colin Harding was drowned. A spring, for which I believe there is some historical evidence, was only a few yards from his body. Inspector Langton, perhaps you will confirm this.'

'It is true,' said Langton. 'And it must certainly have been how it was done. Dr Bell gave me instructions and I saw it for myself. Some people here have heard tales of the secret spring and of course it is in the legend.'

'But it has not been seen for generations,' said Sir Walter. 'We assumed if it existed it was dry.'

'Well it is not,' said Langton. 'And if he were taken unawares or knocked over the head, close to the spot, for there was a blow to his scalp, one man could have done it. Two, of course, would have an easier job. What I don't understand, sir, is how you found it?'

'Something,' said Dr Bell, 'you will shortly discover, but first let me say a word about Colin Harding. It has always seemed to me there was a matter of significance to be deduced from Harding's association with Oliver Jefford. You, Sir Walter, told me you thought Jefford had played upon Harding's nerves in some way. I believe you may be right, for it appears Harding was a deeply superstitious man. I found broken hazel sticks in his house, and finally the working rod he had concealed carefully from others.

'That showed me he had kept secret one of his own skills,

namely the art of dowsing, no doubt fearing it would be taken for witchcraft. He must have thought it was a kind of magic, and who can mock him for that when science has yet to explain the phenomenon? Now what else did we know of Harding? We knew there was talk that Jefford had given him a rune, a rune evidently connected to this house, and it had frightened him. Harding then entrusted it to his friend Ellie Barnes who hid it for him.'

Bell paced a little as he mused on the question. There was not a sound in the room, other than the great rush of the wind in the trees outside. 'Why, you may ask,' Bell continued, 'did Jefford wish to pass on this so-called rune? Was he frightened it would kill him as in the legend? Or was he afraid someone else would get hold of it and Harding picked up on this fear? It is now clear to me it was the latter. For I believe, I am sorry I will correct that, I *know*, the rune does have power.'

'We are surely not going to endure a lecture on occult magic from someone who is reputed to be a reasonable scientist,' said Dr Hare, his lips curling contemptuously.

'I will come to its power in a moment,' said Bell without bothering to look at him. 'But why did Jefford choose Harding for the rune? It is true he found Harding credulous, but there must have been more to it than that, for he was, as I have said, entrusting him with something of value. Harding had done Jefford some special service, I was told, and I thought of this a great deal. What could it be? It was hard to imagine a bond between two such apparently dissimilar men. Surely it *must* be connected to Harding's secret skill, which I deduced some time ago from the literature in his house and the broken hazel rod was dowsing. It seemed, therefore, Harding had identified a water source for Jefford. And then there suddenly occurred Harding's miraculous death by water. This was the key.'

Bell had the attention of the room. Every eye was focused on his face, grey in the miserable light from that window. 'And at that point, thanks to some luck and some skill,' he went on, 'I succeeded in one objective. I obtained possession of this, the rune.'

He had kept it out of sight and now he held it aloft, waving it so that some of the letters and symbols were visible. Of course there was a small sensation in the room. Several people audibly gasped. Edward Norman clapped a hand to his mouth.

'Now,' said Bell, 'what is this thing? A magic spell, a curse, a charm? Certainly it contains ancient runic symbols. And at first I assumed these would be impenetrable. Until I began to study the symbols more closely.

'Let us look at the first.'

I could just make out a diamond shape with continuing lines at the bottom. The Doctor pointed to it as he spoke: 'I had a vague idea what it meant, but as it happened I purchased a book on witchcraft before I came here and it has been enormously useful, for it also contains a chapter on ancient runic symbols. We must first recall that, above all else, and whatever powerful superstitions have been attached to them, runic symbols are a language. And it turns out this first rune is one of the earliest, a Germanic rune standing for ownership. It is considered as the rune of ancestry and of the home and therefore of possessions in general. Considering the connection to this house, it seemed therefore wholly appropriate as the announcing rune of a document that had come into Jefford's possession with his inheritance and might well be connected to that very inheritance.

'I therefore moved eagerly to the next rune.' He pointed to it.

'And here was a brick wall, for I had never seen anything like it. I was sure it was not a runic symbol from any of the known sources and there was certainly nothing like it in my book. The next, an embellishment of the one before, seemed equally baffling,'

'And yet, though they meant nothing, I could not help noticing the symbol of the key on the end of the line where an arrow had appeared in the second rune. This struck me, for I was in need of a key and now these two runes taken together were pointing to one.

'I turned to the next rune along.

'And at once I felt great excitement for if I was not mistaken here was the runic symbol for water. Surely then this was telling me that water was the key, and possibly a secret source of water as I already suspected. And not just a key to the tragic events of Harding's death but possibly another kind of key entirely, a key to the secret code of this rune.' The Doctor's tone was passionate. It was easy to imagine his excitement the previous night as he set about his decipherment. 'I moved,' he said, 'on to the next in the line.'

'This quite specifically stands for a yew tree. But it also means transformation. For me this signified that a yew tree must point to the key, which in natural terms was more than possible. But with the next . . .

'I was in difficulties again.' The Doctor's shrewd face was picked out now largely by lamplight as he talked.

'I did not recognise it but when I consulted the book I found it a not uncommon runic symbol, standing it seems for God or mouth or blessing. It was the second reading that interested me most, for the idea of a mouth could indicate the mouth of a spring.

'The sixth I knew at once, for it is one of the most common of all runes.'

'This is Ing for fertility or God. But fertility seemed the appropriate reading here, for it supported in a general sense the notion of a spring. So finally I arrived at the last and eighth rune of the line which is . . .'

'And here was surely the conclusion of the runic message, for I knew quite well this stands for happiness. So now if we look back, it is not difficult to read the progression.' The Doctor turned away to the window a moment. He frowned as if he might have caught a glimpse of something in the orchard trees but clearly could make nothing out and after a time he faced us again. 'Consider then all of them taken in order. The line starts with a possession bequeathed by ancestors. There follow two unknown runes which nevertheless point to something which seems to be a key. The key leads us directly to water and this water stands beside a yew tree. After the yew tree is a mouth, which could well be the mouth of the spring with an additional association of blessing. And finally comes happiness.

'All of this then seemed fairly clear, if only I could but understand the second and third runes. I examined them over a considerable time last night and at last decided they were not so difficult to read at all. The square could stand for a house, indeed it is exactly the way a child draws a house. If so, it would logically be this place in which we are standing, not only because all the associations point to The Glebe but because it is here we have been told the rune was found.

'The diagonal line on the second and third rune was in each case, I discovered to my great excitement, meticulously drawn, showing a forty-eight-degree angle, diverging three degrees from what must be cartographically the north-western corner of this house. Now there was no indication of how far this line might extend but it did not take me long to realise that if you lengthened it far enough you would be in the vicinity of the clearing where we found Harding. And so it was, using a compass glass, I was led to that yew tree and finally to the spot itself. There I discovered the spring, but I believe I may also have found much more.'

The Doctor put down his paper. It was now so dark in the room it was fortunate he had the lanterns, though one of them looked to be badly trimmed and was flickering, adding to the bizarre lighting effects.

The wind had reached its full strength now and rain had started to splatter on the windows.

'And so,' he said, 'it is time to test that belief.'

Nobody moved. There was no sound other than the wind and the rain. The Doctor ignored the flickering lantern and took the good one in his right hand. The shadows were now becoming truly fantastic, a great crooked one of Bell played on the wall as he advanced to the side of the room.

He moved to the recess beside the empty fireplace and stood at the edge of it, though there was absolutely nothing there that I could see.

For a time, the Doctor waited. 'I think I would ask you to keep your distance, gentlemen,' he said. Then he moved forward, placing the lantern down on the floor in the corner.

The light from the other lantern being increasingly feeble, it was much harder to see anything in detail now. I could make out the Doctor was standing bolt upright, and then he seemed to kneel. I strained to hear but the tempest was so loud that sound offered no clue to his movements. I was aware of the stillness of the other men behind and beside me. To an outsider it would have looked as if we were participating in some strange spiritual ceremony, a black mass perhaps, with Bell as its leader.

Now he was crouched down and turning backwards in a contorted movement and I heard a great gasp from Bulweather. For, impossible as it seems, the figure before us was disappearing into darkness. Soon I could see nothing of him and suddenly the lamp too had vanished, leaving only an empty space.

We all moved forward, of course, despite his interdiction, and Bulweather had now picked up the other lantern. While dim, it was better than nothing. He held it aloft where we had last seen the Doctor to no avail. There was nothing at all here. Just the plaster and the engraved chair rail and the flagstones. In the corner his silver-topped cane lay where he had left it. Naturally we tapped and banged, pressing on the engraved rail and the skirting board and other places too, looking for a secret entrance of some sort but without the slightest result. Bell had been swallowed up by the house.

# THE NIGHT OF THE STORM

After some minutes of fruitless searching, I turned and stared at the faces around me. The lamp was at shoulder height and I could make out most of them, but if anyone in that room knew the secret of this place and was in some way prepared for what had just happened, they showed little sign of it.

Each man looked startled and baffled, though also certainly intrigued. After a time, some decided to look elsewhere in the house in case Bell was in a passage that came out upstairs or next door. Other intrepid souls thought to go outside into the storm and examine the wall from the outside, something was certainly seemed logical but I suspected would yield nothing. That left only Hare who moved to study the fireplace beside the alcove, where the wind howled with a particular fierceness and I joined him there. But the Doctor had been nowhere near it when he disappeared and the brickwork seemed utterly impregnable.

Eventually Hare left me to examine the other rooms and I walked over to the smaller window to peer out at the storm. Suddenly I was assailed by a foul foetid odour, like putrefying beef.

Turning around, I saw Bell crouching on the floor close to where he had disappeared, looking pale and nauseous. I ran over to him at once but he said nothing, simply raising the lantern for me to see.

There was a perfect rectangular space in the plaster, in itself this seemed miraculous, and below it the beam picked out steps. They were covered in dried blood and at first I could see no further. But Bell raised the lantern a little and I glimpsed something of what lay below the steps. It was among the most grotesque sights I have ever seen. The space was small, with some kind of ancient bench and stone table. Slumped forward in the table was a figure whose skin was starting to give way to flesh and even in places to bone, putrefaction having set in quickly because I suppose the area was so ill-ventilated.

For the same reason, this figure was not alone. Everywhere were insects, with gossamer webs so thick and plentiful that in some places it was impossible to see anything at all because of them. The dark cloud of cobweb shrouded every surface in the place, untouched, it seemed, for years. Jefford must have disturbed this teeming life when he slumped forward to die, for they were all about him. In his hair, in his neck, even in his eyes. Most of the builders of the webs were no doubt long dead, but their modern counterparts were visible enough, and very large. A great beast of a black spider worked its way along the side of the table by Jefford's skeletal hand as I watched.

I was having to cover my mouth against the stench of the place but now I made out something else. A strong box lay on the table and had recently been opened, presumably by Bell. It was obvious that a huge quantity of money lay within it, but this was not some ancient trove. Jefford must have decided to put this room to work as a useful and secret bank vault.

There was something so horrible about the whole spectacle that I almost forgot about the others. But Bell had not. He was already up and out and calling for Langton. Bulweather appeared and took one look at our faces, before he too caught a glimpse of what was below.

'I think you should keep the others away, at least for the moment,' said Bell to him. 'It is not something they need to see at close quarters and I want to make sure at all costs the place is not disturbed.'

Bulweather nodded and went to summon Inspector Langton, one of the brave souls who had decided to face the storm in order to examine from outside the wall into which Bell had disappeared. There would have been little enough to see out there, for the room lay directly under that dank forgotten orchard. Little wonder its trees had failed to flourish.

'He was tortured, Doyle,' said Bell when we were alone. 'One of his ears is mutilated and worse. Cream, perhaps aided by others, was trying to obtain the whereabouts of the money. I am sure it was his sole purpose in befriending Jefford. But Jefford guarded his secret. Even when tortured, he still would not tell. Then when he was alone he managed to crawl down there, wiping away traces on the floor that would lead them to the place. Now we can understand why the writer of that letter to Ellie wanted the rune so badly, for he knew the key word that would have enabled him to read it. Indeed I thank heaven for her wandering cat. If Cream had got his hands on that paper, he could have taken the money and left. As it is, we have thwarted him just as long as we can move this out of here securely.'

Inspector Langton appeared now, dripping wet from outside, but he stared when he saw the opening. Bell allowed him a quick look and I could see the impression it made. 'It is him?' he asked.

'It is Jefford,' said Bell. 'And he was murdered. Now, Inspector Langton, I want you to send Sir Walter's carriage to alert your two constables to join us with their own transport. There is a considerable amount of money here and it must be secured at once. Indeed, I think you should make emergency arrangements for the bank in Southwold to receive it. Jefford escaped from his assailant only to die where you see him and his attacker had no interest whatsoever in witchcraft beyond its ability to scare people. What he wanted is still there.'

'But who was he and how did he know of the fortune?' Langton was still staring.

'I suspect Jefford was fool enough to boast about his fortune,' said Bell, 'and I will come to the other. My first objective is to get this to a bank vault, for I will not feel confident we have frustrated his intention until it is there.'

Langton nodded. 'I will send the carriage. I can ready it in a few minutes.' He got up and walked off.

Bell stood aside now and the trap opening fell into place behind him. At last the air was a little more breathable. But before he closed it I had got a good look at the mechanism, and it was only now I began to take account of the ingenuity with which the thing was concealed. The top and bottom of the trap were respectively masked by the engraved dado rail about two or three feet off the ground and by the skirting board. The trap itself was oak framed, plastered and muffled, as I subsequently learnt, with horse hair and cement. The four heavy hinges were controlled by metal rods that utilised spiral screws and springs to open a space just big enough for a man to crawl through with ease.

The Doctor had followed my eye. 'Yes it is ingenious is it not, Doyle? And it is up to us to defend it now.'

'I take it,' I said, 'the key to the cipher was a word connected to your find this afternoon.'

'Yes,' Bell nodded. 'It was "spring". And it allowed me to read the whole thing.'

Before taking out the paper, the Doctor turned around to make sure the room was empty. 'It is fairly unique, in my experience, Doyle,' he said as he unfolded it. 'A runic instruction to search for a cipher's key based on a real, if hidden, geographical feature. Whoever made up this was a clever man. But let me read it for you.'

And he showed me his workings, three lines of writing, covering several sheets of paper.

'As I showed you,' said Bell, 'once I had arrived at the key I had only to write "spring" across the top and put the letters below and translate them and at last some sense was made.

```
S   P   R   I   N   G   S   P   R   I   N   G   S   P   R   I   N   G
T   O   T   H   E   O   W   N   E   R   O   F   T   H   E   G   L   E
L   D   K   P   R   U   O   C   V   Z   B   L   L   W   V   O   Y   K

S   P   R   I   N   G   S   P   R   I   N   G   S   P   R   I   N   G
B   E   W   H   O   S   O   E   V   E   R   E   H   E   M   A   Y   B
T   T   N   P   B   Y   G   T   M   M   E   K   Z   T   D   I   L   H

S   P   R   I   N   G   S   P   R   I   N   G   S   P   R   I   N   G
E   N   O   W   Y   O   U   H   A   V   E   F   O   U   N   D   T   H
W   C   F   E   L   U   M   W   R   D   R   L   G   J   E   L   G   N

S   P   R   I   N   G   S   P   R   I   N   G   S   P   R   I   N   G
E   K   E   Y   T   H   I   S   I   S   T   H   E   S   E   C   R   E
W   Z   V   G   G   N   A   H   Z   A   G   N   W   H   V   K   E   K

S   P   R   I   N   G   S   P   R   I   N   G   S   P   R   I   N   G
T   E   T   H   A   T   I   S   B   E   Q   U   E   A   T   H   E   D
L   T   K   P   N   Z   A   H   S   M   D   A   W   P   K   P   R   J

S   P   R   I   N   G   S   P   R   I   N   G   S   P   R   I   N   G
T   O   T   H   E   E   A   S   T   O   R   E   F   O   R   R   I   C
L   D   K   P   R   K   S   H   K   W   E   K   X   D   I   I   V   I

S   P   R   I   N   G   S   P   R   I   N   G   S   P   R   I   N   G
H   E   S   I   N   H   E   A   V   E   N   O   R   T   H   A   T   N
Z   T   J   Q   A   N   W   P   M   M   A   U   J   I   Y   I   G   T

S   P   R   I   N   G   S   P   R   I   N   G   S   P   R   I   N   G
O   M   A   N   M   A   Y   F   I   N   D   E   W   E   S   T   A   L
G   B   R   V   Z   G   Q   U   Z   V   Q   K   O   T   J   B   N   R

S   P   R   I   N   G   S   P   R   I   N   G   S   P   R   I   N   G
C   O   V   E   O   V   U   M   I   X   I   A   C   U   L   U   S   V
U   D   M   M   B   B   M   B   1   X   V   G   U   J   C   C   F   V

S   P   R   I   N   G   S   P   R   I   N   G   S   P   R   I   N   G
I   I   A   N   D   T   H   E   R   E   W   I   L   L   S   T   A   N
1   1   R   V   Q   Z   Z   T   I   M   J   O   D   A   J   B   N   T

S   P   R   I   N   G   S   P   R   I   N   G   S   P   R   I   N   G
D   S   T   E   P   P   E   S   T   O   T   H   E   O   L   D   C   H
V   H   K   M   C   V   W   H   K   W   G   N   W   D   C   L   P   N
```

*301*

| S | P | R | I | N | G | S | P | R | I | N | G | S | P | R | I | N | G |
|---|---|---|---|---|---|---|---|---|---|---|---|---|---|---|---|---|---|
| *A* | *M* | *B* | *E* | *R* | *E* | *B* | *U* | *I* | *L* | *T* | *B* | *Y* | *B* | *R* | *A* | *V* | *E* |
| S | B | S | M | E | K | T | J | Z | T | G | H | Q | Q | I | I | I | K |

| S | P | R | I | N | G | S | P |
|---|---|---|---|---|---|---|---|
| *N* | *I* | *C* | *H* | *O* | *L* | *A* | *S* |
| F | X | T | P | B | R | S | H |

I stared at his working and then at the words that had emerged from it.

> To the owner of the Glebe whosoever he may be
> Now you have found the key
> This is the secrete
> That is bequeathed to thee
> A store for riches in heaven
> Or that no man may finde
> West alcove ovum 1X, iaculus V11
> And there will stand steppes
> To the old chambere
> Built by brave Nicholas

'I feel sure,' Bell's tone was respectful as he walked over to the ornamental egg-and-dart chair rail, 'this must refer to Nicholas Owen, the famous Catholic who, in the sixteenth century, built places of concealment and worship for others. The man was surely one of the greatest of Englishmen whatever your faith. He was a kind of genius, a cripple who always worked alone at night after taking mass. In 1606 he was tortured in the Tower of London for days on end and still he never betrayed a single person or hiding place.'

'And he compiled the cipher?' I asked.

'Oh no, that dates from later. Subsequent owners must have used this more as a bank vault than a spiritual place, as the message suggests. No doubt Jefford loved the romance of it but spoke of it much too freely, even if he did not betray the details. Now,' he said, 'can you read the code within the code?'

'This is the west alcove,' I said, 'and "ovum", that is part of the egg-and-dart engraving on the rail, is it not? The ninth egg?'

'Yes,' said Bell, 'the Roman numerals were a major problem to me until I realised what they were: the ninth egg from the fireplace and the seventh dart together. There is the genius of the thing. You could press every surface here and still not find it. They must be pressed simultaneously to release the spring. And even when pressed, it does not swing open, you have to push on the plaster below.'

He bent down and placed one hand on the smooth 'O' of the egg and the other on the tip of the seventh dart some feet along.

There was only a faint click but I thought I detected a slight movement at my feet. Sure enough when I put my hand firmly on the plaster it began to tilt back and upwards. But Bell pushed it higher then let go and it swung back shut. Once again you could not tell it was there. 'We will keep it closed for the moment,' the Doctor said. 'Since nobody else knows the secret of the mechanism, it is safer.'

Langton entered the room after a few moments to say the carriage had left and eventually we were rejoined by the others, Sir Walter showing some irritation at the loss of his transportation. 'If necessary,' he said to Langton, 'I will seek your surety, for a bill. This is not a wholesome place for me to be. As it is, I feel like I am half-dead.' But it was striking to me how much better he looked, his supposedly delicate senses apparently restored by the excitement of murder. By now, everyone there knew Jefford had been found dead in macabre circumstances and Bell informed them the secret passage was closed and would not be reopened until the constables were here with a police vehicle.

After this it was only a question of waiting but it was an odd kind of hiatus, punctuated by a burst of thunder from outside where the storm had now begun in earnest. Bell added to the effect by pacing the room urgently, lantern in hand, like some latter-day Diogenes searching for truth. As his light flickered over the other faces, Norman stared out the window as if expecting someone, and I began to wonder if he saw someone out there in the shadows. Bell may have felt the same thing, for he came up beside the man, who seemed a good deal calmer now. In fact, he had smiled when the Doctor confirmed the death, though whether out of bravado or cynicism I could not tell.

'If someone murdered him for the money,' Norman spoke slowly to Bell, 'surely that person or persons will be somewhere near now. They may be here or outside.'

'Yes, it is possible,' said Bell quietly. 'We will all be vigilant.'

'How was it, then,' said Hare, 'that his murderers did not seize the money?'

'I am interested you use the plural, Dr Hare?' said Bell.

Hare looked irritated. 'The murderer of Harding would have to be strong if he dragged his body from the spring to the clearing.'

'Yes,' said Bell, 'I have reason to believe he is strong.'

'So you say he acted alone?' said Hare.

'I did not say that,' said Bell. 'I merely said he was strong and did not necessarily need assistance.'

'Even so, Jefford must have escaped down there,' said Bulweather. 'How did he do it?'

'I wonder,' said Bell, 'if you have any ideas on that, Sir Walter? I suspect there is something in this room you found of great interest, for I saw you looking at it when we arrived.'

Monk, who had been relatively quiet since his outburst about the carriage, looked at Bell. 'Very well. A landowner knows most of his own geography. The letter on that wall after the words, it is not a letter at all.'

'Yes,' said Bell. 'I agree'. And he took his lantern over to the bloody words, which were still plainly visible on the wall beside the recess, pointing at them with his silver-topped cane. 'Some of it is, I think, missing, partly so we would not know the full message. And partly to raise fears and feed superstition.'

Witch here O

'So what is the O it if it is not a letter?' said Hare.

'It is a representation of a landmark,' said Bell, 'though I will admit I only recognised it as such the second time I saw it.'

'What landmark?' asked Bulweather. And then he stopped and stared at it again. 'Oh,' he said, 'I begin to see.'

'I wish someone would enlighten me,' said Cornelius, who had been quieter than any of them.

'The pool,' said Monk. 'I know the shape. See the gully at the top.'

'You are right,' said Bell. 'It is the witch's pool. And the irregularity at the top is where that mysterious digging took place on the south-western corner. This, as you know, was witnessed by Mr Norman's son, who saw one or possibly even two men there. This writing, gentlemen, was not, as has been asserted, Jefford's announcement that the witch had returned. It was his successful attempt to stop their torture by pretending to give away the location where the money was concealed. The full text was "witch's pool here". And an arrow would have pointed to the marked spot. No doubt his persecutor or persecutors told him they would return and kill him if he misled them. They could be confident he was not strong enough to leave this place. But they had no idea he could crawl beyond their reach.'

'My God,' said Bulweather.

And in the silence that followed, as the rain beat upon the window, I am sure all of us imagined the man crawling across the floor of the room, knowing that his place of escape would itself mean death.

'Yes,' said Bell, at last looking around at the others. 'The torture must have been vile, if down there could seem a haven from it. I accept Jefford brought much of this upon himself. He had found dangerous company. But his last act was as brave as anything he ever did in his life. It was a miserable death, but at least Jefford had the satisfaction of knowing he had beaten them. They would not steal his money and he would suffer no more torture or indignity. He had protected his estate for his heirs, though I fear poor Charlotte Jefford will not be one of them.'

There was a sudden noise from the other room. We all froze as a figure towered in the doorway. It was Wallace. Behind him was the second constable. Bell was pleased to see them and Langton thanked them too, whispering a few words as they took up their position beside him.

'Now,' Bell said, 'Doyle, myself, Langton and these gentlemen will secure what must be removed from below here. I would ask you, Dr Bulweather, to oblige me by seeing everybody else back to their homes. It has been a long night and Jefford's remains can be dealt with tomorrow. I am sure this vault will never be a secret again and perhaps it is as well.'

Bulweather agreed readily enough with this plan, but Sir Walter

Monk did not move. For a man who had been complaining so much about being invited to attend, he was showing a remarkable reluctance to leave. 'I take your point, Dr Bell,' he protested, 'but there are surely several remaining questions. I will not trouble you to explain all your discoveries like the code but it would seem a very vicious murderer was responsible for this, aided or unaided. Who and where is he?'

Bell paused. All looked at him. His face was starting to look tired but it had lost none of its fierce intensity. The constables had taken up a position by the wall with the trap behind them. The other men stood largely by the opposite wall. And now, still holding the light in his hand, Bell walked slowly towards them. 'I could give you a name but it would mean nothing,' he said, close by them now, studying their faces, the shadows from the lamp making him look rather like some Satanic general inspecting his troops. 'And, Sir Walter, if that name or his description did mean something to any of you, then I am convinced you certainly would not tell me. You are perfectly right in your suspicion that there is more work to do.'

Monk shugged. 'Very well, but it seems a poor sort of conclusion.' And he turned for the door.

At this, the group started to make their way out. But then Bell appeared to recall something. 'On reflection,' he called after Bulweather, 'give everyone some brandy before you go and perhaps I should take one extra man to help. Dr Cornelius, would you be so kind?'

I could only suppose that, since he needed someone as reliable as Bulweather to escort the men back, Dr Bell had chosen Cornelius as the next best alternative. But it was still an odd choice. The asylum keeper was a bookish, frail sort of man and had looked very anxious more than once in the course of the night. Now he seemed a little startled and not entirely pleased as Bulweather led the others away.

Bell suggested I show them out so I followed after a little and stood watching in the next room as Bulweather doled out the brandies, which were gratefully received by the men. 'Tell Dr Bell,' said Bulweather quietly to me as he downed his own tot, 'after the refreshment I will make sure each man goes home and nowhere else.'

I thanked him and watched as he led the group out. Norman went first, flushed with the brandy. 'It seems poor dear Tommy was a great aid to Dr Bell,' he said to me. 'He is a marvellous boy but I hope this is the last of the matter.' After him came Angus Hare who merely gave me a small sneering smile. And then Sir Walter, who looked a good deal more robust than he had before, as if to prove my conjecture that the discovery of death had given him energy for life. 'Men are beasts, are they not?' he said to me. 'It is something I have long known. I hope some sanity may descend upon our community when you and Bell have left.' And with that the door closed and they were gone.

I returned to the room with the trap where the Doctor was informing the police and Cornelius of his plans. His intention on this occasion was that I would descend into that grisly place and retrieve anything of value that could be found. He had already investigated closely enough to be sure there was little more than the box. But even so he asked me to have one more glance at the place's floor before coming back with the money.

'I do not believe,' said Bell, 'this house holds any more secrets, but nobody is yet in custody and I intend to take every precaution. I want absolutely no risk of disruption or interruption while Doyle is down in that room.'

Therefore Langton and Bell were to wait by the open trap door, the two constables would guard the front door, Cornelius would be stationed in the passage to the adjoining room.

The others took up their positions and once again Bell released the springs. This time he pushed the trap firmly open and held the light as I climbed in. The stench was so foul I had to take a handkerchief and tie it around my nose and face, though I could see nothing but darkness below as I wriggled through the gap and my feet found the stone.

Then I grasped the lantern and turned. From above I had not realised the full extent of the place or of its cobwebs. The ugly emaciated body was slumped in the centre of a great sea of them.

Descending the steps slowly, I tried not to dwell on the gruesome sight or on the dried blood at my feet, but I could hardly help noticing how skeletal Jefford's body had already become. And I could see, just as Bell said, that part of an ear was missing where someone had cut him. As I looked down, it seemed horrible to reflect that this place had once been designed by a good man as a sanctuary for prayer.

Finally I reached the bottom, but I was finding it hard to breathe and I was aware of things touching my leg, cobwebs and insects. Even so I had to inspect the floor before I could grasp the box and go. The smell had now become so disgusting I was near to retching but I bit on my handkerchief to keep control and forced myself to examine all that was before me. The bench and table held, so far as I could see, only the slumped figure and the strong box. The stones below me were filthy and infested but there was nothing I could observe of value.

I straightened up and moved forward to the box, trying to ignore the figure. Yet as I reached out, I found my elbow was touching the corpse's outstretched hand, now almost bone, and one of its fingers was missing.

This nearly caused me to drop the light. As it was, I could not bring myself to put it on the table where it would have starkly illuminated Jefford's head but placed it on the first step of the stairs where its rays were more muted.

Then I turned my attention to the box. It was, as I have said, already open and contained a great mass of gold sovereigns and notes. There was certainly a small fortune here, quite enough to allow Cream to luxuriate in cruelty and greed for years to come. Jefford had been brave enough to deny him and I rejoiced to think of my enemy's fury as he found he had been cheated. But Bell was right that our task would not be complete until we had removed the treasure to a bank.

I closed the box and turned the key in the lock. It was quite heavy to pick up but I thought I could manage to carry it with one hand and keep hold of the light in my other.

Hoisting the box up, I found I was able to bear its weight. And so I turned back to the steps and the lantern. Facing the stone staircase and looking up, I saw to my surprise the Doctor's face was no longer peering down at me. There was only the space where the plaster had opened beneath the dado rail.

In that moment there came a great shout from above. I heard the sudden sound of smashing glass. Almost at once it was followed by Bell crying out.

I took an urgent step forward, calling his name. But I had forgotten about the lamp. My foot connected with it and it went over so that it was instantly extinguished. The only meagre light left to me now came from the room above but not for long. In that same moment, the trap above me closed and I was alone in utter darkness.

# PART FIVE:

# THE REUNION IN THE TEMPEST

# THE VIGIL

For a terrifying few seconds as I stood there in the dark with only that horrible smell in my nostrils, I suddenly felt that I was back again in the cottage with Cream.

Perhaps the thought helped because it made me remember that somehow I had managed when I was drugged and weak. Now I had my faculties at least.

There was no point in trying to reclaim the lantern. Not only was it extinguished, it was somewhere on that infested floor behind me. At least I was on the first step of the stone staircase and, if I moved slowly up, surely I must come to the trap. Turning back would be the worst option.

Slowly I felt the next step with my foot and then the next, keeping hold of the box in both hands now. How many steps were there? I thought I had counted nine. I took the third and then the fourth. Gradually I became more acclimatised to the darkness and, though I could see nothing, l started to sense the height of each step.

Soon I was nearly at the top. Did I dare to put the box down on a step? What if I then moved involuntarily and dislodged it as I had dislodged the lantern, allowing it to fall down the step? The notion of my going back down into the darkness to scrabble on that floor for money and coins was too horrible to contemplate.

I was well aware I had no idea how Bell had opened the entrance from the inside. But I reasoned it must be quite simple and straightforward. There could be no point in concealment from within the hiding place. I took the last step and felt my head brush against the closed trap.

Keeping one arm firmly round the box, I groped with the other. The surface was smooth on this side and I could find no handle or aperture of any kind. At the top, I felt something long and spindly and gave it a tug, but nothing happened and I realised this must be one of the rods built on spiral screws and springs that allowed the mechanism to work but it could not be operated from here.

My arm carrying the box was beginning to hurt badly. I did not know how much longer I could hold the thing but I still hesitated to put it down.

I tried feeling the bottom of the trap, where it opened under the guise of the skirting, but again it was smooth, as was the step. My hand went back up and suddenly I did find something pliable and small, it was a loop of rope, nailed there presumably for exactly the purpose I needed. This had evidently been preferred to a handle.

But I needed to be careful, for I did not want the trap to unbalance me as it opened. Consequently I went back two steps. Then I pulled.

At first nothing. Then, almost magically, the mechanism engaged and it came open an inch. I pulled some more and it tilted up completely, only just missing me, so that I could see into the room.

It was dark of course for I had taken the better lantern. And there was only one thing in my corridor of vision. It was a prone body.

I was so startled by the sight I almost dropped the box.

Fortunately I kept a firm grip. Suddenly legs came into view, a figure crouched down. To my huge relief, it was Bell, though he looked concerned.

'Doyle? You have the box? Then come out at once. It is a risk we must take.'

I needed no further encouragement and soon had the box down on the floor by the skirting board and was clambering out beside it as Langton came through from the corridor.

'I can see nobody outside,' he told Bell. 'But the branch has made a fine mess of the window. You think it was an accident, Bell?' The prone figure, I now realised, was Cornelius, who was conscious but pale.

'I am a little sceptical,' said Bell as he turned to help me. 'A branch came down, Doyle, and shattered the window of the room beyond the corridor. Cornelius also claims he saw a figure. He fainted and, though he is otherwise unharmed, I told him to lie down for a few minutes. Meanwhile I closed the trap as a precaution.'

'So you think it was him?' Is he out there?' I said, looking around.

'Perhaps,' said Bell. 'Of course it may be nothing more than the storm, and the trees casting shadows.'

The idea of Cream lurking in the trees, no doubt observing us, was not a pleasant one. Bell now went back to assist Cornelius and within a few minutes was able to help him to his feet. Cornelius was soon talking again, apologising for his fright. But he was sure he had seen a figure, a face peering out of the darkness.

Bell discussed this with Langton now and a plan of action was formed. Two police cabs had been procured. Wallace, Bell and I would travel with the money in the first. Langton, Cornelius and the other constable would take the other.

The rain was still torrential and the prospect of a walk through the woodland path, possibly shadowed by our enemy, was daunting, but I was heartened to turn my back on The Glebe. And as we closed the door, despite our discovery of Jefford's final act of bravery, I heartily hoped I would never set my eyes on the place again.

We must have looked a bizarre party as we struggled through the wind and rain to the road. Bell and I took the lead, then Langton, Cornelius and the two constables. The wind was howling all around us in erratic gusts, forcing us to lean into it as it came against us and other times to resist its great push from behind. The rain whipped in our faces, also dripping in streams from the trees above.

Of course, I kept imagining what would happen if Cream and perhaps others came at us murderously from out of the wood. But we were five and all his instincts must surely be against that kind of martial conflict. He always made his way on his own terms and would be more likely to create some kind of extraordinary diversion, though there was never a way of knowing what it would be. Certainly, I reflected, if we were to come across a body in that wood or an injured labourer or hear cries for help I would have urged the others not to alter pace or direction by even a hair's breadth. And I suspect Bell would have done the same. As it was, the Doctor strode before me, holding on to that box with a grim determination, intent only on cheating Cream of his prize. Twice, great flashes of lightning illuminated his hawk-like profile and I feared branches would come down on us, with or without human aid, but he never flinched.

At last we were by the cabs and climbed into them. Wallace, the taciturn constable, sat upright opposite us, and for the first time it occurred to me to wonder if we had trusted him too much. But then, as our cab emerged from the trees at last and turned into the road leading to the village and then to Southwold, I reflected this was the true curse Cream had brought on this place, the curse of suspicion and distrust. It had led me to suppose that almost anyone could be Cream's accomplice and now I was suspecting the village constable. Such evil fantasy could only be vanquished when Cream himself was away from here, preferably in the condemned cell that we hoped awaited him.

The weather improved little yet we made the journey to Southwold without further event or hindrance. Most of it took place in silence, with Bell keeping both hands firmly on Jefford's box, placed squarely on his knee. As we turned into the main street, I was startled to see lights and people. I had taken no thought to look at my watch but, after all that had happened, I had it in my head we must have reached the early hours of the morning. In fact, since this was of course the time of year when darkness came early, it was only shortly after eight o'clock.

This had one great advantage for Bell. The police were in time to obtain the good offices of the town's bank who had agreed, no doubt with great alacrity considering the sum involved, to take formal custody of the money and secure it in their vault until Jefford's posthumous affairs were in order. Bell never let go of that box until he was in the bowels of the bank itself, flanked by several officials, who counted it solemnly and at his demand wrote out a note taking full responsibility for the amount from this time.

The Doctor's spirits lifted a little as we left the building, and it was agreed Cornelius would accompany us on the return journey. 'Yes,' he said, 'for I wish to get back as soon as possible, Dr Bell, if you have no further need of me. I am hopeful there will not be any repeat of yesterday's unfortunate incident.'

The Doctor, who was on the point of moving towards the cab, stopped at this. 'To what do you refer, Doctor?'

'Oh, did you not hear? There was some break-in to an empty room at the asylum. Nothing seems to have been stolen.'

I have rarely seen the Doctor's expression change so quickly. 'What? But why was I not told?'

'In fact, I did tell Bulweather to mention it to you or Doyle,' said Cornelius, frowning somewhat prudishly.

Bell turned to me at once. 'I am sorry,' I said. 'I was informed of it late last night and because of all today's events I had forgotten.'

He nodded. 'A great pity, Doyle, that you neglected to inform me of something of such significance.' I was amazed, but he spoke without the slightest irony. 'It explains almost everything that was puzzling us.' And he strode off towards the waiting cab.

# The Message from the Cliff

I could not see what he meant and felt a mixture of emotions as we rode out of the town and back into the dark, windy countryside. It was true we had frustrated our man's intentions and that, following the Doctor's dazzling display, Inspector Langton accepted Bell was probably right about his various conjectures, including the identity of the criminal who had been named to him and Cornelius in private. But what use could that be to us when he continued to hide in the monstrous shadows of this place?

My thoughts were interrupted when the Doctor took a piece of paper from his pocket and, after looking at it a little, turned to Cornelius.

'Dr Cornelius,' he said, 'I am grateful to you for accompanying us on such a foul night. And I am glad no extra man was, in the event, needed to protect our cargo. But I had another reason for asking you, which is all the more important in view of what I have just heard. Can you tell me what this is?'

I could see he had in his hand the drawing of a plant or a flower rather like a four-leaf clover with six leaves we had found amongst Jefford's things. Its effect on Dr Cornelius was, however, unexpected. He went rather pale and shook his head. 'No, I cannot say.'

Bell stared at him coldly. 'I would urge you to look at it again. It is, after all, an extraordinary thing not to recognise something that you drew yourself.'

Cornelius's head slumped. 'It is the panopticon,' Bell went on, 'the all-seeing eye of Jeremy Bentham's, is it not? A model for the design of an asylum where very few staff can keep a watching eye over a great many patients. I did not recognise it at first but then it came to me and I returned to your office to make sure. You had made several copies and you gave them to those like Oliver Jefford whom you thought might be rich enough to help you with such schemes.'

Cornelius raised his eyes, but he looked terrified. 'I did nothing wrong,' he said.

'We will see,' said Bell. 'You have lied about this, you have lied about Jefford, whom you did know. What else did you lie about? Were you hoping to see some of that money we have just deposited for your precious asylum?'

Cornelius was shaking now, the fear in his eyes was intense. 'No,' his voice was raised almost hysterically. 'I would never have dreamt of entertaining such schemes. But they told me nothing of their plans. They were just gentlemen.'

'Who?' said Bell. 'You must tell us everything.'

'Jefford came to see me with another man, Doctor. But his name was not Cream, I swear it. It was Dr Mere.'

The description that followed was close enough. 'They both talked of their interest in such work and how they might wish to offer a generous endowment. Jefford asked about my plans and I gave him the sketch. But he did not seem as interested as Dr Mere, who returned later without Jefford.'

'And what did he wish from you, this other man?' said Bell.

'He wanted a place to stay on occasions and in confidence while he made his visit and did some ornithology. It was something I was happy to accommodate. We had room, he paid me amply, asking for privacy. He came and went as he pleased, there was an exit he could use from the basement. I did not often see him. Nor did others.'

'And he is still here?' I said urgently.

Cornelius shook his head violently. 'No. Some days ago I terminated the arrangement. I had already asked him to quit the place, for I was worried, in the light of the crimes, that his presence might be considered unorthodox.'

'When did you last see him?' Bell said coldly.

'Some days ago,' said Cornelius. 'He came to my study and talked. He made some comments about our female inmates that I found deeply distasteful. By then I had decided he had no intention of making an endowment and I asked if we could terminate our arrangement. He said little and therefore—'

'The day before yesterday you changed the locks,' interrupted Bell. 'He would have broken in to retrieve his things and probably have another night. Perhaps he was even there last night?'

'No, no,' said Cornelius, still shaking his head like a man in the grip of a nightmare. 'He was not, we put on a bolt and chain. The room was checked.'

'Did anyone else see him?' said Bell.

'No. It was a basement room. A little-used entrance, nobody needed to see him.'

Naturally, we pressed him for every word of Cream's, but there was nothing I considered to be of much value. He had never, he said, seen Jefford again, so if Cornelius told the truth he could not be the third man seen in the woods.

I found myself accepting his story, though it was infuriating to me that this feeble man, for now I certainly regarded him as feeble, had harboured the creature we sought without once seeming to realise the consequences of his actions. And why? Because he hoped his institution would gain from the arrangement. Cupidity may not, I reflected, always be a matter of individual greed. It can also be a greed on behalf of your ideas or your ambition. That money Dr Cornelius wanted might indeed have benefited others but the wish for it was still an evil wish born of personal vanity and it had evil consequences.

'You will listen to me now,' Bell was saying to Cornelius, his voice menacingly soft. 'You have given serious aid to a common criminal. If you had been more honest with us before when I asked you of strangers, lives might well have been saved. As it is, you have blood on your hands.'

Cornelius was almost sobbing now. 'But I had no idea, I had no evidence against him.'

'That is no excuse for telling lies when you are aware there is a serious investigation. However, I see no reason to waste Langton's time with you. You can consider your own conscience. We will come back now and search the rooms, indeed I want to examine the whole basement. If anything else occurs to you, or you have any hint of this man again, you will send urgent word to me at the inn, is that understood?'

Cornelius nodded, his breath coming in little gasps. I stared at him now without much pity, indeed the only emotions I felt were irritation and contempt. Instead of a monstrous collaborator for Cream we had found, of all things, a feeble, cowardly and personally ambitious philanthropist.

And there was worse to come. For, after reaching the asylum, we soon discovered that this place, even while it represented the most tangible proof yet of our enemy's presence, offered nothing whatsoever in the way of clues. Of course we saw the room Cream had used. It was, as Cornelius had indicated, now bolted and quite empty. There was an easily used direct exit to the grounds. I was reminded at once of Cream's rooms in Edinburgh, which Bell and I frantically invaded so many years ago just before he flew the country. There we had found nothing except traces in the dust. Here were the same vague indications that a man had been present but that was all. I could detect nothing and, though he made an exhaustive search, I felt sure the Doctor was equally frustrated.

We were glad to quit ourselves of Cornelius after the Doctor had again warned him to report any new information as a matter of urgency and, in the cab back to Dunwich, Bell looked pale and disappointed.

'It is the way with him, is it not?' he said fiercely to me as we bumped back over those roads into the woodland. 'He engages several strands: the asylum, the howling man, the rune, the notion of witchcraft, the impossible drowning, the dead man returned and more. But it is only a web, Doyle, like those in that secret room, and you can easily lose yourself in its strands. What have I always said? That the final and most dangerous stage of a Greek labyrinth is a single straight line! I felt I was clever to expose his howling man, for example. In fact, I could have let it go entirely and would have been better served if I had. Desperate time was wasted, no doubt what he intended. It was a strand that circled back on itself.'

'Has he gone then?' I knew the question was in both our minds.

He frowned. 'We should, no we *must* recall that we have detected his intention and frustrated it. I believe he was in that house many times trying to find its secret. Certainly the howling man was hired the second time to be sure nobody came near because a search was being made, yet still he could not find the secret of the place. He nearly had the cat before us, recall the face at the window, and was checked. To that extent, at least, we have beaten him.'

'But he has killed several times, innocent people. And he is still free,' I protested.

Bell did not answer. I am not even sure he heard. Returning to his thoughts, he turned to stare out the window at the dark swaying trees.

There was little news to greet us at the inn other than a telegram from Scotland Yard, left by Langton for our perusal, announcing that their man would be arriving by noon of the following day. This naturally aroused Bell's scorn. 'I am surprised they act with such speed. Surely it would be sufficient to have someone here by early next year.'

Langton also left word that Charlotte Jefford's mother was so distraught at the news of her daughter's death that her other sisters had gathered at the family home in Berkshire to comfort her. He had sent them news that Jefford's body was found but there was no prospect of any of the family arriving imminently.

Upon reading this, Bell suggested that I should compose a letter to Charlotte Jefford's mother. 'I imagine the family would greatly benefit from a sympathetic account of developments here, Doyle,' he observed as he finally put aside Langton's message. 'Jefford's bravery at the end and the saving of the fortune might offer a grain of comfort where it will be sorely needed.'

I was, I will admit, a little surprised to find the Doctor's thoughts turning to the plight of the bereaved, far away in another county. It was not that he was a cold or unkind man, and he would certainly have offered comfort to Mrs Jefford if she had been present. But in the midst of a case as fraught as this one he was usually far too single-minded to be distracted by such matters. In that sense, I took it to be a bad sign. Could it mean he was convinced that Cream had left the scene and that the matter was finished? This did not, as I looked at him, seem to be so. His senses were fully engaged, for he was staring around the inn with intense interest and I saw none of the lassitude that occasionally came upon him after an investigation.

In any case, I had already decided to write to Mrs Jefford, for I was the only one who had talked at length with her daughter, and it could not be put off. So, after a maid had brought me some beer and ham and bread, I sat for an hour or more in my room, deep in composition. As the wind and rain beat on the window, I poured out my thoughts. First, I introduced myself and explained briefly how we had been helping the police to solve the mystery. Then I talked of her daughter Charlotte's intrepid character, how she had been so anxious to hear of her brother that she had stayed on. Assuming her family must have known something of her impending engagement, I also very much wished to communicate through Mrs Jefford my profound sympathies to her suitor who faced such terrible loss. I wanted him to know her sheer delight and excitement in the news of her engagement, which she had been gracious enough to confide in me, and I was aware I must now be the only person who had witnessed her unalloyed delight at the prospect. I even took it upon myself to describe Charlotte as I saw her that last evening when she was so happy, reasoning that any mother would prefer to think of her daughter's last hours in this way. Of course, I also spent a lot of time describing how heroically Jefford had behaved at the end and how his fortune had essentially been rescued, largely through his own courageous effort.

By the time I finished it was well past eleven, though there was no sign of any change in the weather. I left the letter in my room and went down to procure an envelope and make sure there had been no developments. The landlord was still obligingly up but before I could broach any subject he handed me a folded message with my name neatly inscribed on the front.

I knew that careful hand at once, it was from the Doctor.

'Has he gone to his room?' I asked, feeling a tiny alarm.

'Why no,' said the sombre Brooks, 'he went out some time ago. A message came from Inspector Langton, I believe. Apparently it said something had been found along the cliff, close to the ruined church.'

'What? But why was I not told?' I exclaimed and then remembered myself, for it was hardly Brooks' place to hunt me out when the Doctor knew quite well where I was. 'But of course,' I added, 'it is not your fault, Mr Brooks. I am grateful to you. How long ago did he leave?'

'Oh some hours, sir. The strange thing is Constable Wallace came in here half an hour ago and he thought the inspector was back at his home. Well, I am sure Dr Bell will return soon.'

I nodded dumbly and left, tearing the letter open as I dashed upstairs for my coat. The Doctor's fine flowing hand was unmistakable.

*My Dear Doyle,*

*You must not be annoyed that I have decided to pursue the latest step, in what has been a very treacherous case, alone. I had anticipated there would be a development of this kind and indeed it was the reason I suggested that you undertake your letter to Mrs Jefford. This is one occasion on which I am quite sure there is no point in both of us enduring risks where one of us alone would be sufficient.*

*Miss Jefford's death this morning did, as you saw, catch me unawares. I had hoped that severity would be my best tactic in persuading the young lady to leave, and only now fully understand the nature of my miscalculation. It is greatly to your credit, Doyle, that you preferred kindness but for your own peace of mind I have to convey to you that, while desirable in themselves, care and kindness would have made no difference to the outcome. If I had been more astute, I would have instructed Langton to order her to leave, for in retrospect I am satisfied that nothing else could have saved her, except perhaps a constant guard which she would never have accepted.*

*I would like to put on record that I am modestly pleased to have thwarted Cream's plan to obtain a great fortune, for I believe by restricting his opportunities we can only save lives. I dare to hope there is even a chance my present endeavour will free us of him for good, though, given the topography, it could well be at a cost that I know will give some anguish to my nearest, Doyle, and to you.*

*In such circumstance, I would only ask you to reflect that I could think of no higher reward for my application to the study of this craft than the removal of Dr Cream, and his vile notion of the future, from our land and our time for ever.*

*Very sincerely yours*
*Joseph Bell*

I stared down at this cryptic message with deep unease. Everything in it concerned me greatly, not least the reference to 'topography', which could only be a reference to those wild cliffs and surely the spot by the ruined church. But there was little pretence here of some message from Langton, which seemed to be a flimsy deception. Was it possible the Doctor had deliberately allowed himself to be lured into a trap of our enemy's, a trap he had evidently anticipated? His aim, a desperate one, would surely be to get Cream over the cliff.

And what was his weapon? His cane certainly, for he could wield it very effectively, and perhaps his firearm? In my hurry, I nearly abandoned my coat but I was now beside my room and must get it and leave at once.

As I opened the door, the figure was leaning back, legs crossed, in the chair by the desk at the window, observing me. Cream held something in his hand. And he was crying.

# The Ballad in the Room

I stood there, forcing myself to keep as calm as possible and weighing up the position.

He looked a little different, his hair was shorter and it made him look younger, still with that sheen of energy I remembered so well. He was good looking enough to have made a career on the stage or music hall, and I was reluctantly reminded of that as I watched those tears fall in the candlelight with the wind howling outside.

The crying became him, of course, the head held upright, the eyes wide open and sad. It was the noble melancholy of Byron and of 'Childe Harold', of the tragedian rather than the afflicted. But beneath his delicate features, I sensed a tiredness. I could not see his clothes for he wore a dark full-length coat but it was by no means dry, so he had been outside in much of this weather.

'You are probably thinking, Doyle,' he said softly, and I saw he was reading my letter to Mrs Jefford, 'that I cry because I have failed or out of remorse for my misdeeds.'

'On the contrary,' I replied, 'I have no view on anything you do.' I was aware now of the smell of something in the room, a chemical smell. And oddly I saw he had stripped some of the clothes from the bed.

Of course I could have run out, but what would be the point? No help was at hand and he would have disappeared either through the door or the window long before I returned with it. The candelabra on the table a few feet in front of me was heavy, with five lighted candles. If I could reach it before him, and wield it effectively, there might be a chance. In a flash, I thought of bringing the heel of it down on his skull.

'Come, come,' he said and turned to me a little, smiling, more his old self again now. And I was sure I could see him take in the candle holder, calculating quickly any other potential weapons I might have, eyeing my condition. For his part, seeing him full on, he looked as fit and sleek as a panther, his build a little thinner but robust. How much his animal good looks repelled me now. I quailed to think of the university days when I had drunk and laughed in his company.

'You must do better than that,' he continued. 'No, my crying has nothing to do with such things, though I was touched by your kind expression here of sympathy to myself.' He waved the letter.

'What?' I said.

'You extend your utmost sympathy to Charlotte's suitor who faces such terrible loss. You want him to hear of the sheer delight and excitement you saw in her when she spoke to you of her engagement. That is kind, Doyle. I am flattered. She is lost to me now. It is another thing we have in common.'

I stared at him. 'Oh yes,' he went on, 'I met her through Jefford. Even he did not know of our romance, for I swore her to secrecy. We would meet each other in all kinds of places and here I pretended I was secretly searching for her brother. It was very sweet. But then it became a burden. So I conjured a rhyme.

' "First I proposed
Then I disposed." '

Of course, I should have seen it at once, Charlotte Jefford was so flushed and secretive that night, with all the animation of someone who had met with a lover. Little wonder she stayed on and was sometimes mysteriously absent. She thought she had a secret ally and protector. How could she know her brother's charming friend was in truth the one man who had tortured and killed him?

Bell must have guessed as much after her death too, for it was referred to obliquely in his note. But where was Bell?

Cream tossed the letter aside. 'But as I say, that is not why I weep. It is another death which concerns me. Someone I greatly admired,' he went on. Again his eyes filled with tears. And I dreaded to hear the name that would come forth.

My stomach started to tighten into a knot. 'Who?' I said, hating to give him the satisfaction of the question.

'You must remember,' he said incongruously. And he sprang up in one great movement.

I recoiled slightly but he had moved in the opposite direction from the candelabra into the space by the wall. This gave me a better chance of seizing the implement, but he was out of immediate striking distance and now he began to sing in a sweet voice.

> Jesse James was a man
> Who killed many a man.
> He robbed the Glendale train.

The song had a pretty tune but I felt as if he were trying to drive me mad. His feet moved a little, as if in a minute dance. When I knocked Cream unconscious with the candelabra I would, I was thinking, try to set him alight. Or perhaps I would bring the holder down on his head repeatedly until there was not the slightest chance of his ever getting up.

'I told you of Jesse James so often,' he said. 'I have been travelling a great deal and only heard of his death recently in a newspaper. It is a case for mourning. He is the only one to understand the glory of the killing that began in our civil war. Rapid-firing pistols were uncommon before in our country, Doyle. Now the war has brought them to millions; Jesse killed for glory.

And would to God he were alive today to make a righteous butchery of more.'

I was still measuring the distance and considering if I could take a pace forward. I did not care about his 'man of destiny', I wanted only to reach that candelabra and bring it down as hard as possible on his head.

'You do not listen because you suppose I am a lone voice,' he said with a smile. 'But these words about "righteous butchery" are not mine. They were written by his greatest obituarist in one of my country's newspapers. Already Jesse James is the legend. And not just for our nation. For the future.'

Of course I had heard him talk like this before. At Edinburgh he had revelled in tales of robbery, slaughter and violently clashing causes in the new world. But the idea that murder itself should be considered heroic (for what was killing in the course of robbery but murder?) and written of in the way he described seemed to me beyond belief. I utterly refused to believe it was a future or to dignify his words with a reply.

'Ah,' he said, 'but I bore you and you may wish to look at what is behind you there. I would like it to be something I give you at Christmas.'

I did not know if this was some trick. I certainly did not wish to take my eyes off him. But he laughed and pointed. 'No, it is all right, I assure you I will not pounce. Take a glance. I know you will find it of interest. See, I walk a pace back.'

He did. I turned my head a fraction.

A long object was lying there on the floor by the wall.

It was Bell's silver-topped cane.

Slightly dulled from rain and vegetation but unmistakable, just as I had seen with him earlier. I turned back, trying to hold my expression.

Cream laughed then, his old laugh. 'So, Doyle, if you would not grieve with me over Jesse, I am sure we can still join in grieving for another death.' I reacted, of course. I could not stop myself.

'Oh yes,' he continued. 'Let me tell you something else Jesse James wrote. "A man who is a damned enough fool to refuse to open a safe or vault ought to die. If he resists or refuses to unlock, he gets killed." Those are the published words of a fine man and I honour them. Jefford prevented me first, but today it was Bell. He stopped me from opening the Jefford vault by his meddling. But he paid the price. He came to the cliffs even though I am sure he knew the message was false. And of course he came with some heroic notion he could send me over, either alone or in his arms. I was not such a fool, it is not my way to be involved in a cumbersome wrestling match.

'Therefore, I had a small blade and when he sprang, I went low and stabbed his lower leg so he had no balance.' His face was visibly shining now with excited pleasure at the memory as he came forward a step. 'I held the firm ground, he teetered and I used my head to butt him and he went over. Right to the bottom. He screamed too, Doyle. He is gone.'

## THE DEATH OF THE DOCTOR

The words were horrific. I wanted to disbelieve them: surely this must be one of his tricks? Yet in my heart I knew with sickening certainty, not least from Cream's sheer triumph, the words were true. Bell himself had certainly perceived the danger. And I had never known Cream to lie about death. When he claimed a kill, he had always killed, as I recalled to my great cost.

So he had won. But it was intolerable that this man should stand here before me now, gloating, and I braced myself.

He must have seen this in my eyes, for he sprang first. He had taken a step while he was talking and he was lithe and judged his move well.

We both reached the table together but he had the heavy candelabra before me and thrust it right into my face, forcing me to back away to the wall.

'I wish,' he said, 'to burn you alive and make you a martyr for all your noble causes. Another detective martyr.'

The flames were agonising on my face so I could only try to get my head away and back. Cream's head was not far away now, madly illuminated by the candles, which were singeing my hair and eyebrows. I sank lower on the wall but he only increased the pressure and the pain. No doubt he could have hit down but the candles might have spluttered and he truly did want to burn me.

I was blinded now, the pain was horrible and I knew I would catch fire but my hand, pressed uselessly back against the floor, came up against a long smooth object. It was Bell's cane. I gripped it like a drowning man gripping rope. Swinging it would be impossible, but I knew the cane well and my hand was quite near the top. With one movement I jabbed the cane forward at my attacker with all my strength. Of course I struck in the direction of the pain and the cane knocked one of the candles half in his face so that he recoiled a few inches, alleviating my own agony.

I jabbed harder then, finding his head and forcing him back, removing the flames from my face entirely. I just had time to stagger up before he came at me again but I had the cane now and moved along the wall away from him into the corner, preparing to swing it.

To my amazement he did not follow, but went to the door, which was still ajar, and closed it. Then he bent down and touched the candles to the carpet.

I was moving towards him, welcoming the chance to make a proper assault, but suddenly a great wall of fire sprang up before me. I had to step back, and beyond the shooting flames I could see him laughing. He turned and picked up some object, pouring liquid from it on to the rising flames and throwing the bedclothes I had seen on to them too. Now I knew what the chemical smell was, it was kerosene from the lamp by the window and the wall of fire was becoming denser. 'Oh yes,' he cried, 'I had to work quickly while you were downstairs.' I cowered back and saw Cream's pleasure, he was exultant, almost dancing. 'A martyr must have a pyre, Doyle. Like a witch.'

I had only a short time before I was consumed. And in that moment I thought of the Doctor. He had attempted to give his life to get Cream out of the world. He had failed. Now was I going to die without even the attempt?

Forced back into the corner of the room where the fire had not yet reached, there was only a chair and the coat I had slung over it when I returned from The Glebe. I seized it, got my arms half in the sleeves but only half so the shoulder and collar covered my head and most of my face. I thanked God in a silent prayer that it was still wet and lunged forward.

The pain was excruciating. My legs felt as if they were being raked by red-hot wires but I knew only speed would save me. And then the pain was less, for I must have been through the worst of it. At once Cream was on me, for I felt a sideways blow from the lamp.

He would have been better to desist. For I took a step back and the coat came off my head so I could see him. Now I had a chance to attempt the second part of my plan, which was inspired only by the thought of Bell's fate. Cream was holding the kerosene lamp high, preparing to make a lethal blow but I was ahead of him, for I moved aside, grabbing his arm as it came down and pulled him towards the ring of flames.

He was caught off-balance and in any case this was the last thing he expected. I got the other arm round him now and pulled with every once of strength. I hated to feel his body so close to me, I loathed the touch of him. But I had only one wish and that was to fulfil the mission in which the Doctor had failed. Cream was probably stronger than me but he was unprepared and I was driven by pain, hatred and desperation. And so we toppled down together on the edge of the widening flames.

It was agony and I felt the searing pain for my head was no longer protected. But nor was Cream, who cursed. And, even through my own pain, I relished that sound. My arms were still clamped round him, that was the only thought left to me now even as my senses blurred. Then suddenly he gasped and I was unable to hold on any longer, for my hand on his coat was burning and as I withdrew I got my head up and saw what was happening: his coat, unlike mine, was going up in flames. He had spilt kerosene on it in his recklessness while he was spraying and now it was burning faster than anything else.

His head was already further in the blaze than mine and I could see the skin under his nose almost seeming to liquefy, mottling his face, just as he had intended the candles to disfigure me. Meanwhile, my coat was singeing but still offered protection and my face and hair, though agony, were not yet alight.

I felt joy at that moment. I had never succeeded in landing as much as a blow on him previously and here I saw ultimate pain. It was a new sensation to me, he was mortal and his face burnt.

I could not breathe now, so instinct drove me back and I found almost to my surprise I was out of the worst flames. My body was still agony but I was able to breathe and I pushed myself further along.

I could see the door and crawled on through the smoke, remembering my crawling in the cottage, then humiliated, now avenged. Finally I reached the door, aware that though I had burns I was not burning now. And I managed to pull myself up to my feet.

Looking back, I could not see much but I could make out a shape writhing in the smoke and flames. I took the key and pulled the door open, closing it and turning the key in the lock. It was a death sentence, I knew, and I felt a thrill as I did so.

As yet there was no alarm and I knew one would not come soon enough to save him. And then I heard the scream from inside, though not quite from the direction I expected. I relished that scream. I felt it was owed to all the victims, to the Doctor, and particularly to the women he had killed. For other murderers I had often felt different things: contempt, mercy, sadness, even sympathy. But never for him. He was beyond such emotions.

As the sound faded, I moved quickly along the corridor to the staircase. The scream had alerted people on the landing below as had a smell of smoke and I heard the shout of fire.

I came out of the inn without being seen and the rain and the wind were more welcome than any cooling balm. I suppose I must have looked a strange sight. My heavy coat had great burnt patches on it, my hair was singed, my face flushed and in places sore, but at least the coat had survived intact and now it covered the places below the knee where my trouser leg was burnt through. I was very grateful for the coat, it was certainly the only reason my burns were of a lesser kind.

But my moment of exultation passed now as I thought of Bell. Once again I reviewed Cream's words about the struggle on the cliff, searching for some chink. But I knew there was none. Cream would have had no pleasure in lying to me about such a thing even to achieve a temporary amusement. It was not his way. Bell had given everything and yet saw no satisfaction of victory, only humiliation, and my heart became heavier again as I moved quickly down the street.

The tempest had barely abated, for I heard thunder and the rain sheeted in my face as I walked with occasional lightning to guide the way. Again I turned down the track to the sea and then mounted the coastal path into the trees. I knew the spot where I must look, though it was a dreadful place to visit on such a night.

Finally, I came out into that great space where the noisy surf crashed far below and in front of me lay the broken arch and the graves, tottering at a mad angle. It was a miracle the storm had not dislodged them, though of course it was far from over. And it was a fool who would stand close to the cliff in such conditions, let alone engage in a struggle, but if the Doctor had taken the risk, so must I.

I did not dare to walk to the edge in that wind, so I got down on all fours and crawled through the sodden grass towards it. In a lull I shouted the Doctor's name aloud and it seemed to echo along the cliff before the wind drowned the call, but of course there was no reply.

Finally, I was at the edge and held tight to a stray lump of masonry beside me, though I knew quite well it would not help me if the ground gave way as I peered over.

At first I could see little, but there was more light here from the sea. I could make out waves, though the tide was not now full, and stones and rocks. But nothing else.

Suddenly there was a great flash of lightning which illuminated all starkly: the sand, the stones, the cliff. And in that moment I saw him. I saw his broken lifeless body stretched out far below me, twisted by the impact, covered in blood. And I wept.

# The Sound in the Passage

I did not and could not attempt to get down to him from here. There were some rocky outcrops below me but a climb of any kind would have been a horrific undertaking. I ran back along the path, for I knew I had seen a spot where the subsidence was so gradual you could climb down to the beach.

I remembered roughly where it was and turned off the path through the trees until, by good luck, I found it almost at once. It was not a pleasant scramble in such weather but nor was it particularly dangerous as long as you avoided breaking an ankle on the slippery descent. Soon I was on the beach and I ran the relatively short distance back along it to the spot below the ruined church where I had seen Bell.

I came round the head of the cliff and soon I thought I was at the spot, yet without the lightning I could see no sign of him. Had he been buried by some stone from above? For this was directly under the most dangerous part of the cliff and fallen masonry was all around us.

I turned to the left and realised at once my mistake. For there was the outline of his shape, I could see the blood on his face and the twisted ungainly posture. I came beside him, hating to see the lifeless form and bent down to look at his body.

It was as I had seen. Limbs twisted by the impact, copious blood on the face. I turned away, partly because I could not bear what was below me, but also to take off my coat to place it over his lifeless form.

The voice behind me was frail but distinct. 'You will forgive me, Doyle, for not greeting you more cheerfully but I had no wish to encounter anyone else in my present state.'

I whirled in amazement. This lifeless thing was suddenly straightening itself, the limbs uncurling, the head rising a little way. He was hurt, certainly, but by no means dead or even unconscious.

'Doctor?' I cried out.

'The deception, I fear, is only partial,' he said. 'You see I had no wish to meet anyone less friendly in this condition. You have sustained burns, I see?'

I ignored this in my anxiety to know. 'But how could you fall to here and live? It is impossible.' I was helping him now to sit up and it was amazing to me how vividly he had mimicked the twisted limbs, though his other injuries were, I feared, all too real.

'Of course and I did not. But I did fall badly and I hurt myself as you see. Fortunately, I made some preparation before I ventured out here tonight, Doyle. Given Cream's taste, it seemed to me a likely spot for an encounter so I had undertaken a close examination of the cliff, which is not as sheer as it seems. Look and you will see a ledge a quarter of the way down. I calculated I could push him further out but land there myself. I failed in the first, as you know, but just succeeded in the second. Not that it is an experience I recommend. You have to know how to fall and I have injured my shoulder, cracked a rib, and broken a bone in my foot, not to mention much lost blood.'

'Do you think you can walk?' I said, for I wanted above all to get clear of this spot.

'Of course,' he said, 'but I would be glad of your shoulder.'

He staggered to his feet and with my help he was able to limp along the beach. I did not want Bell to tire himself with more explanation and I could guess much of the rest. Cream had won, certainly, but not as clearly and dramatically as he supposed. The Doctor had prepared the nature of the struggle with care and, if Cream had not produced the knife, I have no doubt Bell might even have succeeded. As it was, he fell, but very much on his own terms. His scream was carefully managed to stop his enemy investigating further.

But the rest was the worst, as he told me later. He had waited out of sight, for he was so weak Cream could easily have finished the business if he had known. At last, confident his enemy had gone, his only course was to climb down, for there was no way on earth he could get back up. It would have been a hellish climb in any circumstances but, considering his weakness and his wounds, this was, as he said, as rash an undertaking as he had ever attempted. The wind howled around him, the sea pounded below. Twice he lost his footing and nearly fell. Once a lump of masonry hurtled close by but somehow the rest held. At the end he was so weak he did fall, but by then it was only a matter of feet to the sand.

For a time he had no energy to move and he later heard a voice calling. Dreading Cream had come back to make sure of his work, and feeling he would want concrete proof, Bell feigned the death posture, employing some of the skills he had been shown by the contortionist Morton. Later he was trying to drag himself away from the spot when he heard my running steps. Having no chance of winning any encounter, and nowhere for concealment, he took up the same position, albeit in a different, if similar, place. And here I found him.

Much of this detail I learnt later, including the fact that Bell had decided his pistol would be too risky in such weather. Now I was simply overjoyed to guide him back along the beach and to tell him he need have no fear Cream would be greeting us on our return. The Doctor was too weak for much talk himself, but he was insatiable to listen and wanted to know all that had transpired, not

least the source of my own injuries. I managed to give him the
salient details as we hobbled along, now strangely oblivious even of
our wounds and the wild weather in our great joy at being reunited.

I was concerned to obtain treatment for the Doctor and
Bulweather's house seemed the obvious refuge. I know how hard
that walk was for my wounded companion and more than once I
urged him to stop and allow me to run and get help, but he was
adamant we must proceed. 'I have no wish to sit on this beach any
further tonight, Doyle. My foot is hurting so much anyway rest will
hardly help.'

I did not bother to point out the uncharacteristic illogicality of
this statement, for I was merely glad to hear his spirit. At last we
were at the village and making our way to Bulweather's door.
Looking along the road, I could see there was still considerable
disturbance at the Ship but the fire was clearly quenched and it was
amazing to me the place was not razed to the ground.

Bulweather was still up and delighted to see us, indeed he
looked somewhat ecstatic when he saw me and I learnt why soon
enough. His dog seemed equally pleased and pranced around,
enjoying the social festivities. It turned out Bulweather had been
out on a case and had only recently returned to call at the inn,
where he had examined the remains of the fire and feared I was
lost. Evidently the place had been saved by its tiled roof, which had
collapsed on to the floor of my quarters, letting in the torrential
rain and also sealing off much of the blaze from what was below.

Now, while we were making ourselves comfortable, Bulweather
insisted on walking back to the inn to set Langton's mind at rest
about our safety and inform him Bell would make a full report in
the morning. He also obtained some of Bell's clothes, which were
sorley needed, though of course he had no hope of obtaining mine.

Later he talked cheerfully to us as he stoked his fire, which was
soon roaring. And, after bringing in some pastries and steaming
punch, which his housekeeper had been preparing that afternoon
for a Christmas festivity, he proceeded to a full examination of Bell

as the two of them compared notes on his various injuries.

'You are far fitter than you have any right to be,' he said at the end of it, after dressing his head wounds with great care. 'If the rib is trussed it should give you no trouble, though I would urge you to keep the weight off your right foot for some weeks as far as possible. I am anxious to hear of your adventures, if you are minded to tell me, while I apply something to Doyle's burns.'

The ointment he applied to me was wonderfully cooling and with Bell's agreement I now took it upon myself to enlighten him of the latest developments.

Naturally he listened with great interest. 'Well,' he declared at the end, 'it would seem, gentlemen, that your case is all but over, for I have some information which may interest you. No man could have escaped from that blaze, but more than that Langton told me this evening that burnt human remains were found in Doyle's room. Nobody is missing. We can therefore be certain your man did not survive.' He turned back to warm his hands at the fire.

Joseph Bell and I looked at each other then and raised our glasses in silence. I closed my eyes and said a prayer for Elsbeth. Bell was looking at me when I opened them.

It had already been agreed we would stay with Bulweather that night. And shortly afterwards he showed us to comfortable rooms and beds. I lay awake in mine, listening to that incessant rain and marvelling at the events of the day, some so awful and yet at the end so positive. We had finally avenged the dead and come to a successful resolution of our unending problem. I felt angry, though, at the fate of Charlotte, yet another of his dupes. If only tonight's events had happened the previous day, she would have lived. Yet at least the thing was over and there would be no more like her, no more women killed for his own amusement.

I slept and then much later I awoke. There were sounds in the passage outside my room, someone walking or rather shuffling. Could it be Bell? The odd footsteps came to my door and passed, then came back. They stopped.

Suddenly the door swung open violently. I saw the outline of a distorted figure, its head tilted oddly up as if it were smelling the room. Then it darted forward.

And it was in that instant I knew it for Cream, but not the Cream I remembered. No sneer, no scorn, no lofty good looks. His body was crushed and disfigured by deep burns, the skin black, the shoulders hunched in pain, the hands like red claws. And he was right over me before I could move, his taloned fingers ready to tear out my eyes.

I felt the blinding pain as they descended. And then, gasping for breath, I came awake in the bed. It was a dream, of course, a horrible dream, and it took me a little while in the darkness to confirm I was in Bulweather's spare bedroom and to convince myself that the blessed events of the previous night were real. They had happened, all but this apparition conjured out of my darkest memories of the blaze had been true. He was dead.

Yet now I heard again what had triggered the nightmare. There *were* footsteps outside, not, admittedly, the shuffling footsteps of my dream but slow purposeful steps, the steps, indeed, of someone who wishes to be silent. They moved past my door and were gone. I lay awake but there was no recurrence. Perhaps Bulweather or the Doctor had been sleepless.

Eventually, after more time had passed, I slept again and this time I slept peacefully. Hours later, when I awoke, the room was full of sunlight. The storm had passed away and, casting aside the memory of my dream, I thrilled to the thought of our victory.

Bulweather's housekeeper, Mrs Harvey, was cooking breakfast and the smell of it made me hungry even as I was dressing in the borrowed clothes my host had laid out to replace my own tattered remnants. Of course he had little that would fit me, but somehow he had produced a reasonable pair of trousers and various other garments, so I put them on and walked through to find the Doctor and Bulweather already seated. I was delighted to see Bell was eating heartily and the two medical men were engaged in an avid discussion about post-diphtheric paralysis. I sat down to attack the great plate of mushrooms, eggs and bacon with equal enthusiasm, reflecting as I listened to them that I had rarely seen Bell enjoy so great a rapport with another doctor as he did with Bulweather.

After we had finished, we went to the country practitioner's great fireside with our coffee. 'I was shocked to hear of it,' exclaimed Bulweather, for he and Bell had now turned to discussing Cornelius's connivance. 'I can only suppose the man acted out of weakness rather than serious dishonesty, for I am sure he is no criminal.'

'I tend to agree,' said the Doctor, drinking reflectively. Though still obviously in some pain, his eyes were now bright again and his voice was already taking on a firmer hue. He was also paying great attention to Bulweather's retriever, patting it expressively and looking down at it. 'And I am very grateful for your sound advice and your great hospitality to us while we have been here, Bulweather. So there is only one outstanding question left to us: namely, was anyone else, besides Cream, involved in the quest for Jefford's money?'

'And what do you think?' said Bulweather, interested.

'I will admit I keep returning to that night,' said Bell. 'The night of the first of December. You remember, three people were seen: Jefford, Cream and another. Cornelius utterly denies it was him.' He put down his coffee and leant back, crossing his legs. 'Still, perhaps we will never be sure. Tell me, how is your wife's sister?'

Bulweather's eyes brightened. 'I have hoped there is a change. Only slight. But in a case so tragic, that would be a miracle.' He looked at Bell and went on. 'I am not sure if Doyle has told you, Dr Bell, but I have no shame about it. My wife died of septicaemia. But she also suffered from a milder form of her sister's affliction.'

'Indeed,' said Bell, 'thank you for your candour. No he did not.'

'I did not want it to be a secret from you,' said Bulweather graciously.

'But I would be very interested to hear,' said Bell, 'the precise mode of your wife's nervous illness.'

'Of course,' said Bulweather, 'though I do not pretend the subject is pleasant to me. Her illness was delusional.'

'And its precise nature?' asked Bell gently.

Bulweather sighed. 'I am afraid even between friends that is too painful . . .' His voice trailed off.

'Then I will tell you,' said Bell. 'She supposed, did she not, you were having a relationship with her own sister? And indeed what is even stranger, thanks to an acquisitive innkeeper in Southwold called Burn, I have met several friends of your wife's sister who, though they appear quite sane, actually *share* this delusion. They think you had an obsessive regard for your wife's sister years before she became ill. That you were her first and most lasting seducer, long before she destroyed herself in London; that your wife's sister's baby was, in fact, your baby. And that in the end all of this destroyed your wife.'

I put my cup down with a clatter. Bulweather took a breath. 'But I have told you of the local gossip,' he said with enormous patience and dignity.

'Indeed you have,' said Bell. 'And I took it into account, not least because I owe you much gratitude. But this is gossip of a very persuasive kind. One of them actually saw you come and go regularly at your wife's sister's lodgings on your own. But if this were all, Doctor, I can assure you I would never have dreamt of bringing it up.' He paused; I waited. 'Unfortunately it is not all.'

## THE LAST VICTIM

'Then perhaps you will explain what is left,' said Bulweather quietly.

'First a triviality,' said Bell. 'You are proud of the uniqueness of your dog in these parts and I have no reason to challenge you. Jefford had no dog; Cream, from my studies, dislikes the animals. But I have matched a long-coated dog hair I found in The Glebe some days ago to your dog exactly, even though you claimed never to have been in the house.

'Secondly when, in The Glebe, I asked you to give the men brandy, you went to a cupboard that is fairly well concealed and got it out without a thought. Strange, indeed, if you had never been there before. Third my investigations have satisfied me that though the asylum provided an excellent second alibi on the night of Jefford's death, you were, in fact, there only a relatively short time. Fourth and much more serious, despite all the beatings administered by his dreadful father, little Tommy Norman will not, on any account, come to you as a doctor. Why? Because of something he was very frightened to tell me. At last, yesterday, he did and, though he is afraid to tell anyone else, it seems you were the man he saw most clearly by the witch's pool on the night Jefford died.'

Bulweather's expression changed now. He was pale and sat lower in his chair. The Doctor had not, however, finished. 'All of this I knew,' he said, 'and considered almost conclusive. Then last night I took the liberty of walking around a little in this house, for my wounds were aching. There was not a great deal in your desk but enough. It is clear you travel to London regularly, though you do not advertise it. There are credit notes which I assume to be associated with card games. Several mention Jefford. And it seems you have debts. I suggest you met Jefford in London. That, having little liking for the man, but knowing of his concealed riches, you connived with Cream, whom you also met there, to share it between you. I am sure you both assumed Jefford would lead you to it. Then you would divide it.'

The door opened and Mrs Harvey was there, offering us more coffee. Bulweather indicated we were adequately provided and she withdrew. His face was ashen now.

Bell's tone became a little gentler. 'Cream may well have led you on, I accept that. I know you were indeed in Ipswich when Harding died and with Doyle when Ellie was killed on the beach. It has therefore occurred to me you may have sickened of the thing after that horrible bloody night at The Glebe and took no part in any of the rest. Cream would certainly have let you abandon the hunt, for you were of no further use to him and could hardly incriminate him without incriminating yourself. But you undoubtedly helped to kill Oliver Jefford.'

I looked at Bulweather but drew little confidence from his expression. How, I thought, could this man have colluded with Cream? In every way he was so different.

Bulweather saw the question in my look. He patted his dog and got up now, stretching his great height before the fireplace. He looked different in one way, less certain, and yet it was clear he wanted to justify himself.

'He called himself Dr Mere when I met him in London.' He spoke slowly. 'I could see at once he was a formidable man. I will admit I admired him. He was clever. I have rarely met anyone so clever. And there were times in London beyond . . . well beyond the horizons I had known before.'

Now he turned to me. 'What I have said to you, Doyle, about the mentally afflicted was no lie. I believe it. I was deeply in love with my wife's sister Claire. That is true, it is not proper, but it is a fact. While my wife was alive, I kept it at one remove. Claire went to London after our baby was adopted. She fell into evil ways. Once my wife was dead, I was able to seek Claire out. I honoured my wife's memory and my love. And have I not served that love even now? I brought Claire back here, I paid for her comfort, all for love. Is that not one thing I can be proud of? There is much I am not proud of in my life but I have no regrets about Claire.'

'Will you tell us about that night with Jefford?' said Bell.

Bulweather's expression changed. 'Jefford was just a little fop,' said Bulweather. 'I had no regard for him at all. And we felt taking his money was hardly a sinful act. But he was stubborn, far more than we had expected. Cream came here, encouraging Jefford to play tricks and get up a lot of ghostly rumours. He was waiting only to get his hands on the money. On that night at The Glebe at first it was just a drunken game. We wanted to see his vault or, as he called it, the "witch's vault". Jefford refused. This kind of jesting about his "vault" had been going on for days. But now suddenly it changed. Cream lost patience and used a knife and Jefford was on the floor and there was blood. Yes I would have robbed the man, I do not deny it. But I had no stomach for any of this. I turned away, but Cream went on with the torture. He cut him on his ear, on his foot, on his face. Jefford was screaming. And I did nothing. I just kept silent, hoping he would die. Finally, he told us what we wanted to know, or so we thought.'

Bulweather was no longer looking at us but at the fire. 'He seemed so badly hurt I would never have dreamt he could even move, except for his hands, which drew that message. We believed it was the true place. Cream thought we should go and dig and come back and torture him more if he had lied. But when we returned, he was gone.'

Bulweather turned back to face us. 'Cream went into a fury. He cursed and hit the walls. After a time, I told him I wanted no more of this. He cursed more and said I was a damned coward and a fool. But, in truth, he barely cared. In fact, he was probably glad to have it all to himself. He knew there was a map somewhere with a code, and intended to get his hands on it and solve the riddle. Already he suspected Harding, for he knew Jefford had talked to the man. After that, I never saw him again.'

I said nothing. In the end. I had trusted this man and liked him, even loved him a little. It was sickening to me to find he was an accomplice of Cream.

There was a long silence in the room.

Bell broke it. 'And how,' he said, 'how would you like me to proceed? Do you wish me to call Langton? I am prepared to report the good you have done us as well as the bad, but these are matters that can hardly be overlooked.'

Again there was silence. Bulweather went to his great dog and patted it so that its tail wagged furiously.

'I think I must admit I have appetites that would not meet with universal approval,' he said at last, and he looked very old and grey now. 'But I could not spend my life in prison and it is true to say I love this community. I will therefore ask a favour. If you agree not to mention what has been said here, I will not trouble you or anyone else further. You will tell my housekeeper that word came of an urgent case. I am known, you will recall, as an intrepid cliff-walker.'

I saw Bell sizing this up. Then he nodded. Bulweather gave his dog one last pat. 'You will go to my sister,' he whispered. 'She will come,' and then he got up and turned to me.

'I am glad of our conversations, Doyle,' he said. 'Let me just say that all I said to you I meant. I believe that to be true, in spite of my own weaknesses.' Then he turned away and he was gone.

After he had left the room, neither of us spoke for a very long time. Finally, Mrs Harvey came and offered us more coffee, which we accepted. Since she looked a little troubled, the Doctor told her of how her employer had been called away on a case and we would stay till mid-morning and then take our leave. At this she brightened. 'Oh he is always so busy,' she said with a smile in her Irish brogue. 'But I will keep something warm for his return.' And she left us.

We sat on in that room, in a strange silence, knowing we would not be disturbed. The past twenty-four hours had been so momentous for both of us we just wanted quiet and thought before the fire.

Eventually Bell did offer his view of Bulweather. 'It is my belief,' said the Doctor, 'he was not always a bad man. But it seems from all I can discover he was already in secret a considerable lecher. Cream would have found him perfect material.'

About eleven, Bell suggested I should take one of the coats hanging up in the hall and walk the coastal path while he would hobble to the inn and talk to Langton. For Bulweather's sake, we would keep our side of the agreement and mention nothing of what we had learnt in this room.

Outside it was bright if still bitterly cold. I had little appetite for making the excursion to the cliffs again, even in such glorious weather. But in the event there was no need. On the beach, a fisherman and his family came running to tell me how a man had been found lying at the bottom of the cliff. He had fallen a good way and was dead. The wife recognised Bulweather and said it was widely known he would take great risks on his walks.

Bell was standing outside the Ship on my return and I told him the news. There was real emotion in his face as he reflected on it. 'It was his choice,' he said finally. 'Pray God he is the last of the victims.'

We turned back to the Ship, which was, thanks to the protection of the slates and the fact that my room was on a projecting wing, still intact. My things were, of course, irrecoverable but it was no great loss, for there was nothing of great monetary or personal value, indeed they were all purchases I had made in Edinburgh.

The Doctor had already talked at length with Langton who soon reappeared to tell us a cab was on its way. He was as yet unaware of Bulweather's death but rueful at the imminent arrival of the Scotland Yard man who, he was sure, would claim all the discoveries as his own. The detective seemed more than happy when Bell promised he would write a detailed account, offering a glowing report of the local police's conduct of the investigation.

Later, as the cab came out of the trees for the last time and turned on to the Ipswich road, Bell told me his final piece of news.

'From what I can gather, Doyle,' he said, 'there was nothing very much found in your room. Of course, the damage was very extensive, they are still going through it.'

I stared at him. 'But surely,' I said, 'Bulweather mentioned they had found human remains.'

'I know,' said the Doctor, turning to survey the road ahead. 'And we can hardly question him now about what he meant. There were all sorts of rumours last night. Perhaps he misunderstood them. They did find traces of a coat. It was badly burnt.'

'His coat,' I said. And I thought of that scream at the end. But I also thought of how the Doctor had screamed and deceived Cream. And the scream had not come from where I expected. 'I know the coat was alight. But is it conceivable he got out of it and through the window?'

Bell turned to me. 'Listen to me now – and I think you will agree I am nothing if not rational – there is no point in adding imagined doubts to a clear victory. You saw him burn. Even if he somehow survived and it is hard, if not impossible, to imagine, he must be mortally changed, perhaps half-dead. I am not, as you know, Doyle, a rash man. But I am prepared to wager we will hear nothing more.'

As I looked out on the fields in the midday sunshine with the great ditches receding into the infinity of sky, I prayed he was correct. My thoughts turned to the resumption of my practice in Southsea and to the prospect of being an ordinary doctor again. I consoled myself with the thought that, where Bell had been prepared to wager in the past, he was invariably right. Later we turned to speak of other things.

And Bell certainly seemed to be proved right. His wager held through the following year's strange case involving a governess and the nightly ritual of the 'Dead Time', which I disguised years later in milder form as *The Copper Beeches*. It held through many other new developments in my life, indeed throughout all the investigations and changes which punctuated the 1880s. It was not until the spring of 1891, with the receipt of a fateful phonograph cylinder from America, that our hopes of final closure were shattered.

# Epilogue

*5.05 p.m., Friday, 21 October 1898, Hindhead.*

It is done. I spent this morning in London and then returned to finish my narrative. Now I close the second box and replace it on the low shelf at the back of my study beside the others containing materials relating to the cases. At last there is a proper record of our first encounter with him.

I have broken the strict vow of secrecy I offered Bell. But with reason. A little over three weeks ago, I received the first in a series of mysterious and anonymous parcels. The first contained a cryptic clue. The second a scarf I recognised. Years before it had belonged to Elsbeth who died on that beach near Edinburgh.

The third arrived two days ago but I do not understand the meaning of its contents. They appear to be nail clippings from fingers and foot. The postmark was Crewe. Of course anonymous, but indicating to me that somehow he is alive and is moving slowly towards me. The consequences, when he arrives, are unknowable but also unthinkable.

I am in one of the most difficult times of my life. My wife Louise's condition continues very bad. Indeed, now I must go to her again. But I feel I have to complete this work before he makes it impossible for me to do so. Whatever happens to me, there will be then some record of the cases, those that concern him and the others.

I put the next box out, containing the matter of the 'Dead Time'. God willing, I can return to it in the morning.